TIME TESTED

TIME TESTED

Sam Morris

Three Firs Publishing

Dedication

Much of the editing, formatting and other busy work with this novel was performed during the long days of the COVID-19 pandemic in 2020. As I worked, I often thought of the brave men and women who are on the true front lines of this tragic situation. Their efforts in treating and caring for the sick and dying, even risking their own lives in the process, are not to be forgotten. God bless them.

"Trusting is hard. Knowing who to trust, even harder."

Maria V. Snyder, "Poison Study"

PART I

CHAPTER 1   Oct 12, Friday

It wasn't a loud noise or a bright light or even a rough shake of his shoulder that edged him toward consciousness. Rather, it was the foul stench of rotting meat and body odor that caused Brock Sinclair's face to contort into a tight grimace. In quick succession his other senses began rebooting as his body's survival mechanisms engaged.

From his supine position on a sagging surface that offered far less support than any sofa he'd ever crashed on, Brock slowly opened his eyes. A dingy, gray ceiling high above with an intricate, block pattern came into focus punctuated by a dusty, cobweb-laden chandelier that loomed overhead.

The headache, dry mouth and slight nausea that Brock sensed were familiar hangover symptoms, but he could remember drinking only a beer, maybe two, at Wally's place. And this was definitely *not* Wally's apartment.

Brock turned his head slowly toward a pitiful moaning on his left until a sharp pain behind his ear halted the movement. He slowly raised his left hand to examine the area of concern but stopped when a stinging pain in his forearm revealed a blood-stained cloth tied just below the elbow. Still, he inspected his head and found a noticeable lump but no evidence of bleeding.

He pushed himself up on an elbow in the crude bed, sensing its coarse sheets on his bare skin. A long, narrow room with more than a dozen, evenly-spaced, beds lined an outer wall with its four tall windows above. In the low level of natural light Brock could see that the bed to his immediate left was empty but in the next one a man with a ragged beard moved his legs constantly under a stained sheet. He was the source of the moaning.

Brock's attention returned to the room, its layout and its few furnishings. It appeared he was one of several patients in a hospital ward of centuries past, the room like from a drawing he remembered in his high school American History textbook. A woman in a long, drab dress scurried about at the far end of the room but didn't seem to notice his movements. He started to call to her but stopped, unsure, deciding instead to lie back down and close his eyes, hoping the illusion would be gone when he reopened them.

Memories prior to waking up were clear only to a point. He had been at Wally's apartment where they smoked some weed before leaving for a reason he couldn't remember. Then his memory just stopped; it was a complete blank beyond that point.

Brock tried to focus. The hallucination was something he had never experienced though he had been thoroughly stoned dozens of times. Anxiety was building with panic not far behind. Whatever this…this illusion was, he was *not* enjoying it.

A man approached from the room's doorway. With no scrubs he didn't look like hospital staff but his baggy, gray shirt with no collar under a vest and shapeless brown pants were consistent with the room's historic theme. The guy, maybe in his twenties with a short ponytail, strode to the foot of Brock's bed. "At last you awaken," he said in an odd British accent. "I am physicians intern Isaac Jamison. Who might you be?"

Brock's tongue was thick in his mouth. "I'm..." He swallowed. "Brock Sinclair." He cleared his throat. "What the hell is this place?"

"Well, Brock Sinclair. This is Pennsylvania Hospital. But I must ask how it is that you come to be here? The night staff observed your presence in this bed, adjacent to the wall, sometime in the early morning hours. But no record of your admittance has been discovered."

Even more confused, Brock said, "Pennsylvania Hospital? Is this in Huntsville?"

The intern frowned. "I know not of Huntsville. We are at 8th and Pine." The intern hailed one of the women at the other end of the room. "Nurse, bring tea for this patient."

"No, just some cold water," Brock interrupted. "I don't want any tea."

The intern shook his head. "I strongly suggest you avoid drinking the water. A bout of the flux would only add to your discomfort."

Brock didn't understand the reference to "flux" but tea was better than nothing to relieve the taste of roadkill in his mouth.

The young nurse, in a grayish-brown, floor-length dress, appeared with a crude mug of liquid. Brock sat up with the intern's help and took a sip. The tea was only warm and weak but sweet. He drained the mug and handed it back. "Thanks," he said. The nurse, also in her twenties, was not very attractive with her hair tied up and no makeup. Oddly, she smelled like flowers but with notes of sweaty socks.

Lying back as the nurse moved away, Brock's energy increased slightly. "Look, man, this whole ancient hospital thing is not cool! I *am* hallucinating all this, right?" He looked around his bed then back at the intern. "So, what happened to my clothes? And my phone!?"

"Do not rile yourself for Dr. Rush will be round presently to do his examination. He is well-known for his knowledge of head trauma." The intern paused. "You speak of visions. What can you say of them?"

Brock struggled to calm himself. "All I know is that I was with my buddy in Huntsville. Then I wake up in this hospital of horrors." He gestured to indicate the historic ward.

The intern straightened and took in a quick breath. "Pennsylvania Hospital is the finest medical facility in Philadelphia and arguably the best of any in the colonies. Your insult is quite offensive."

Brock softened his tone. "Okay! Okay! Don't get your panties in a bunch."

"I beg your pardon!"

"Never mind." Suddenly, Brock frowned. "Did you say 'Philadelphia'?"

"Of course." The intern returned to his clinical approach. "Perhaps you can enlighten me concerning your unknown presence here."

"*Unknown presence*? I don't even know where the hell I am much less how I got here." Brock ran his fingers through his blond razor-cut.

The intern pursed his lips. "It does appear that Dr. Rush's requisite blood-letting this morning has been beneficial since you are now awake and speaking. Yet you are apparently quite confused as your statements would suggest."

Brock raised his left arm, his wide eyes staring at the blood-stained cloth around it. "You drained blood from my arm?" He struggled to a sitting position.

With a dismissive nod the intern said, "Dr. Rush ordered no more than one pint. The procedure is quite routine."

Brock continued to stare at his bandaged arm, his breathing rapid. Suddenly, he felt faint and fell back on the bed.

The intern was unmoved and continued his questions. "I know not of the Huntsville of which you speak. Is that a village near Philadelphia?"

"Look, ah...Isaac. I have to be—"

At that instant the man two beds away screamed, "Me leg! Me leg's gone!" He was sitting up in his bed, thrashing wildly. Suddenly, he swung his leg and a stump over the side of the bed toward Brock and tried to stand up. Instead, he collapsed onto the floor, screaming in pain.

The intern rushed to the man on the floor and with the help of a nurse was able to get him back onto his bed. The guy continued screaming and crying even louder. It took both of the staff members to hold him down as his bandaged stump turned bright red.

Brock felt nauseous and turned to face the other direction as the screaming continued.

CHAPTER 2   Oct 12, Friday

For what seemed like forever the intern, the nurse and another man worked with the amputee trying to calm him. Gradually, his screams subsided after they spooned some liquid into his mouth.

With the amputee calmer, Isaac disappeared for several minutes then returned directly to Brock. His shirt was wet at the neck and under his arms and there was blood on his sleeves.

"How's that guy doing?" Brock said, nodding toward the other bed but not looking in that direction.

"His prognosis is guarded at best. He struck his ankle with an axe this past week and unfortunately, gangrene forced the surgeon to take his leg. All we can do now is comfort the poor soul." The intern looked up, closed his eyes for an instant before looking back at Brock. "And pray."

The intern composed himself. "Mr. Sinclair, I believe you said you felt you were hallucinating. Why might you feel thusly?" He stood with his arms crossed, occasionally glancing at the softly moaning amputee in the nearby bed.

"Call me 'Brock', will you? 'Mr. Sinclair' is my dad."

Isaac nodded. "And where might your father be?"

Brock considered asking about contacting his father then dismissed the thought. "I don't know, probably at work. What time is it anyway?"

Isaac fished a dented pocket watch from his vest and released the cover. "The time is half past four." He snapped the watch closed and returned it to his pocket.

"And what day is it?"

"Why today is Friday, the twelfth of October," Isaac replied without hesitation.

Brock frowned while he searched his memory. "Friday? Are you sure? It was Monday when I went to see my friend! Where have I been for the last four days?" The panic that had subsided returned with a vengeance. He suddenly remembered he had scored tickets to the Houston Texans game on Sunday the 14th not that it mattered now.

Brock took a deep breath, his memory returning. "Okay, look Isaac. On Monday a friend and I drank some beer and smoked a little weed. Everything was normal at that point. But I got really down bitching about my dad. So, to salvage the buzz, Wally brought out some new bud he had scored but hadn't tried. He said it was supposed to be awesome. We took a couple of hits off his vaporizer and got really high. I felt a little nauseous then better in the fresh air when we left to get some food. I seem to remember stumbling. After that everything is a blank."

Isaac had frowned during Brock's comments. "Why would you and your friend smoke weeds?"

He frowned at the intern. "Why are you making this so difficult? Marijuana, Isaac. We smoked marijuana. Okay?"

Isaac shook his head. "I know not of this substance."

Brock took another deep breath and continued, his hands shaking. "You need to understand that I'm really confused right now. You say this is Philadelphia. I was in Texas when I blacked out. How do you explain that? And to top it off nothing about this place is normal. This room, these beds, your clothes! Nothing!" Brock's voice quivered. "It's really freaking me out."

Isaac stood quietly for a moment with his thumbs in his vest pockets. At last he said, "Brock, your statements continue to confound. You spoke of a Huntsville and now of a Texas. I know of neither. Perhaps Dr. Rush can make sense of your ramblings."

"Screw it," Brock said under his breath. "I'm getting out of here." He threw back the covers and swung his legs toward the side, but realized that he was naked. He flipped the covers back. "Get me my clothes! I'm leaving."

"I'm afraid we do not have your garments." Isaac stepped to the side of the bed. "As I indicated, you were found in this bed as you are. Regardless, Dr. Rush should examine you before you leave. You are his patient."

Brock lay quiet for a few seconds, fists clenched. "Okay, where is this Dr. Rush? Maybe I can get some straight answers from him."

"He should be here straight away. His rounds started at four in another ward."

As if on cue, a clean-shaven man with a receding hairline appeared through the doorway. He wore a long coat open in front with some kind of scarf wrapped around his neck. He stopped at one of the other beds and walked to its side.

"Dr. Rush will be here soon," Isaac said nodding in the doctor's direction. The intern's demeanor and tone suggested allegiance to the physician. But Brock also sensed something else, maybe distrust.

Perhaps five minutes later the doctor arrived at the amputee's bed, the patient thrashing about slowly in a stupor. The doctor raised the now-bloody sheet then motioned to one of the nurses trailing him. "Before he awakens fully, change the dressing." The doctor's tone hardened. "And replace these sheets." The nurse nodded and raced toward the other end of the room.

Dr. Rush, middle-aged and slim, did not smile as he approached Brock's bed. "I see you are awake, young man. How are you feeling?"

Brock glanced at Isaac then back at the doctor before speaking. "My head hurts and my arm is sore as hell where you or somebody sliced it open." He narrowed his eyes at the doctor.

"He must be improving to express such impertinence," Dr. Rush said, glancing at the intern. He then moved to the side of the bed and raised Brock's head off the pillow and probed behind his ear.

"Ouch! Damn it! That hurts." Brock jerked his head away from the doctor.

"The knot remains but it's no larger," Dr. Rush said

"Doctor, this fellow claims his name is Brock Sinclair," Isaac said. "He also claims he is having visions."

Dr. Rush's eyes brightened as he looked down at his patient. "Young man, are you seeing angels or demons?" He opened his coat and held his arms akimbo, a crooked smile on his face as he stared at Brock.

Brock raised himself on an elbow and spoke in a slow, forced, civil tone. "Look, Doc. I don't know what this place is. But I know I rode my Harley to the Sam Houston campus to visit a friend." He then restated what he had told Isaac. "The only explanation I can come up with is that I'm hallucinating."

Dr. Rush turned to the intern and frowned.

Isaac shrugged. "He shared essentially the same statements with me soon after he awoke. Doctor, are you familiar with the Huntsville of which he speaks?"

The doctor shook his head. "Perhaps he is delirious from the blow to his skull." Dr. Rush turned back to Brock. "That strike on your head could be the source of your confusion. Additional rest may resolve your symptoms. Can you tell me how you received such a blow?"

Brock shook his head slightly and grimaced. "Like I told Isaac here, I don't remember anything after my friend and I left his apartment."

The doctor nodded but made no response. Turning to the intern he said, "A night's rest is indicated. If the patient will take some food, it may speed his recovery. I'll be round on the morrow." With a smirk he added, "He may need additional treatment."

"Yes, Doctor," Isaac said. As Dr. Rush moved away, Isaac turned to Brock. "Perhaps some soup and bread will improve your symptoms. I'll have it brought directly."

Hearing the doctor suggest that the head injury might be what was causing him to imagine the historic hospital was oddly comforting to Brock. Maybe that was the explanation. He resigned himself to eat something and sleep through the night. Maybe the antique hospital would be gone in the morning.

Moments later the same young nurse that had delivered his tea arrived with his food. She propped him up in bed with additional pillows and held a bowl of soup so she could feed him. The soup was bland but hot, the bread very hard, probably stale. Yet the food felt good in his empty stomach.

"How long have you been a nurse?" Brock asked, trying to shake some of his confusion away.

The young woman blushed and giggled, before turning her head away.

"What did I say? Don't get all bashful on me."

The woman composed herself. "My name is Lilly. I began my training when I was eighteen. That was two years ago." She stared at Brock with a faint smile.

"What? Do I have soup on my face?"

Lilly touched the side of her head lightly and pointed at Brock. "Your hair is quite short. I have not seen a man with such hair before." She blushed.

Brock smiled. "I don't know what to say. It's just how Rachel styles it."

Lilly's smile faded. "Rachel is your wife?"

"Oh, no. I'm not married. Rachel is a stylist at the salon where I go."

Lilly cocked her head slightly and frowned then continued to feed Brock his soup without further comment. She worked quickly unlike the relaxed pace when she first arrived.

"Thanks for the soup, Lilly. By the way my name's Brock. It's good to meet you."

Lilly blushed again then removed the wooden chair she had pushed to the bedside. "You rest now."

"You know, Lilly, I could kill for a toothbrush. Any chance of getting me one?"

Lilly jumped back and touched her throat with her free hand.

"What'd I say?" Brock said, frowning. "What's the big deal about a toothbrush?"

Still keeping her distance, Lilly said, "I know not of a brush for teeth. I can get a chew stick if you wish." She turned quickly and was gone.

Brock's eyes grew heavy watching a man lighting candles in glass lanterns on the wall of the long room. Would Lilly and Isaac and Dr. Rush still be around in the morning? If not, where would he be and would he have a head injury and a bandaged arm when he woke up?

Initially, the name "Dr. Rush" had not registered. But after remembering that Isaac had said they were in Philadelphia at Pennsylvania Hospital, a twinge of recognition sparked, then faded. Lying in the gloom of the large room where every sound echoed off the walls, Brock tried to recall where he had heard of Dr. Rush. But it wouldn't come to him.

He anticipated a restless night given the strange environment and his paranoia. It was more than uneasiness; Brock was scared that he would still be in the old hospital in the morning.

CHAPTER 3   Oct 13, Saturday

The bright sunlight that streamed through high-set windows awakened Brock from his deep sleep. At first he welcomed the warming rays above his head despite their concentration of dust motes. Then anguish washed over him like an incoming tide as he realized he was still in the old hospital with its disgusting smells, less intense now but still nauseating.

It occurred to Brock that he didn't even know the supposed year of his hallucination. He turned toward the amputee two beds over. The man was quiet now and on his back, his remaining foot making a small teepee under the blanket. His eyes were open as he stared at the ceiling. "Hey, dude. It might be a strange question but what year is it?" The amputee did not move.

Brock pushed himself up on his elbow, turning more toward the other patient. He spoke louder. "Hey, guy. Can't you hear me? I can see you're awake." Still the patient didn't stir.

Terror flared inside Brock. He screamed toward the other end of the room. "Nurse! Nurse! Somebody! Something's wrong with this guy!"

At Brock's calling a middle-age nurse strode in his direction, her frown and slight snarl showing irritation rather than concern at the early morning racket. Half way to Brock's end of the room she held a single finger to her lips signaling for quiet. Brock frantically pointed to the fellow patient in the nearby bed.

The nurse stopped her charge at the amputee's bed and turned in his direction. She leaned over the man, putting her ear to his lips. Then she slowly straightened. With a gentleness that surprised Brock, she bent and closed the man's eyes. The nurse stood for a moment, head bowed, her hands clasped in prayer. She gently pulled the bed sheet up over the man's head and straightened it.

Brock stared at the scene so close but could not assimilate the obvious. His eyes were wide, his lips tight, as he lay back down, staring at the ceiling. The nurse's measured steps faded.

It was at least ten minutes before the nurse and two large men returned to the amputee. Using a wooden, flatbed wheelbarrow, they loaded the body unceremoniously and carted it out of the room. The nurse returned with more sheets and remade the bed in a routine manner despite the blood-stained pad that served as a mattress. Brock winced as he envisioned the pad underneath him.

The sudden death of the amputee and the matter-of-fact reaction by the staff horrified Brock. After all, he was a patient too. He lay half-turned toward the far end of the ward, alert to anybody that might approach.

Brock was shaking slightly when Isaac appeared at the doorway. Rather than attend to any of the other patients, he walked directly to Brock's bed. "I understand you slept through the night, Brock."

Brock's voice trembled. "Yeah, and I woke up with a dead man ten feet away! And nobody gives a shit. What kind of place is this?"

Isaac maintained his calm demeanor. "I suppose the trauma of losing his leg coupled with the spread of gangrene was too much for his body. It is unfortunate. The death will be a burden on his family."

The seemingly flippant attitude of the intern solidified Brock's decision.

"And how are you feeling this morning?" Isaac asked.

"I guess I'm better after some sleep. But can you get me some clothes? I need to get out of here."

Isaac smiled. "I was hopeful that you would recover quickly. I've some garments for you to borrow. I'll fetch them before I continue my rounds."

Brock said nothing, only nodded.

Moments later the young nurse from the previous day appeared at Brock's bed carrying some clothes. She separated the articles and laid them across Brock's blanket then looked at him out of the corner of her eye. "Will you need help with dressing?" She blushed.

"No, I can manage," Brock said. "By the way, Lilly, thanks for the chew stick last night. It was certainly different than what I'm used to, but it was better than nothing." The nurse nodded then walked away.

The crude long johns were baggy on Brock yet less so than the pants. Fortunately, the long, two inch-wide leather belt had enough holes to secure the pants. The scratchy wool shirt with its odd buttons fit him in the shoulders but had more than enough cloth to accommodate someone with a huge beer belly. The crude, leather shoes had no curvature to suggest a left or a right. Brock put them on anyway, learning they were too big but the heavy, knitted socks helped fill most of the excess space. The shoes would do until he could get out of the hospital and back to civilization.

On his way to the doorway Brock waved at Isaac near one of the beds at the other end of the ward. "These clothes," he pulled at the shirt waist to demonstrate the excess material, "was this the best you could do?" When Isaac only raised his hand in response, Brock continued, "Well, thanks anyway."

Brock moved out of the room and entered the hallway. He turned left toward a door at the end of the hall, hoping it was an exit. Before he reached his target door, he approached a stairwell, with muffled, yet horrifying screams of pain or madness or both rising from the floor below. The screams, some blood-curdling, grew louder as Brock passed the stairwell, causing him to tremble from the agony he heard and envisioned, while the staff moved about in the hallway with little reaction to the screeches. He stepped quickly toward the heavy wooden door.

The ornate doorknob turned easily but it took some effort to swing the door open where a blinding sun hit Brock full in the face. Instinctively, he closed his eyes and raised his hand to shield them. Several seconds passed before his pupils contracted to accommodate the full sun. Brock raised his head and through squinted eyes observed the scene in front of him. "Oh, s—," as he collapsed.

######

Brock could feel a cool cloth on his forehead. The young nurse, Lilly, was leaning over him. He jerked upward almost bumping her in the face. "Rest easy, Brock," Isaac said from the other side of the bed.

Brock was back inside the hospital ward on a bed just inside the door. His right elbow hurt but the pain was insignificant compared to his panic. "What the hell, Isaac? There's a brick wall outside the hospital. But I saw horses and buggies. More people dressed just like you and—"

Isaac interrupted, "Of course, Brock. Did you expect streets of gold? It's Philadelphia, not heaven." Isaac smiled at the nurse who looked at the intern but maintained her concerned expression.

Brock lay back down on the bed and closed his eyes. A soft moan escaped his lips.

The nurse moved away and Isaac leaned closer. "You seemed fit leaving the ward. Did you stumble and fall outside?"

Brock stared up at the intern. He hesitated before he spoke, his voice breaking, "Isaac, what year is it? Would you, at least, tell me that?"

Isaac hesitated and frowned slightly. "Why, Brock it's October, 1787. You will remember that the Philadelphia Constitution was signed only two months past?"

Brock pushed himself up on his elbow again and locked Isaac with his eyes. He whispered, "My last memory is of being in Huntsville, Texas. The year was 2029!"

Isaac's lips tightened and his eyes squinted as he shook his head ever so slightly. "My goodness! Your hallucinations have returned, I'm afraid. Did you hit your head again?"

"Forget my head. What's real is 2029! This hospital, this place, you people, this…this 1787 is the hallucination!" Brock looked to Isaac for answers.

Still standing beside the bed, Isaac placed one arm across his midsection, rested his other elbow on it and held his fist at his mouth in concentration. Seconds passed. "Brock, Dr. Rush will want to examine you further after this second fall. But he will not be in attendance until after dinner. If you feel strong enough, perhaps we could stroll outside a bit. Some fresh air and familiar sights may help clear your thinking."

The offer of help getting out of the hospital energized Brock yet he was slow to respond due to the fear of what he might find "outside." At last he said, "Okay," and swung his feet slowly off the bed to sit up. He looked up at Isaac. "You're gonna walk with me when we get outside?"

Isaac smiled. "Certainly, Brock. I shall accompany you."

CHAPTER 4   Oct 13, Saturday

Gathering clouds muted the sun's intensity as Brock and Isaac moved through the hospital door at the opposite end of the hall from Brock's earlier failed exit. Prepared for what he would see, Brock was, nevertheless, stunned as he stood outside the door at the top of the steps. A high brick wall stood at the end of the walk about fifty feet away from their position. Looking in both directions, Brock followed the wall to corners where it turned ninety degrees and continued out of sight beyond the corners of the building. From the elevation of the steps Brock could see over the wall to the fronts of narrow, two-story buildings sandwiched together across the way, smoke wafting from most chimneys. And through the open gate he saw a mounted horse clop along the cobblestone street. A woman, towing a small child, passed by in the opposite direction, peering through the opening but not slowing her pace.

Isaac led Brock down the steps, along the walk and through the open gate. The scene that met Brock amplified his shock. The pedestrians and riders all wore drab clothing, similar to what he had observed in the hospital. There were no cars, no bikes. Just a wagon pulled by horses in the distance. The lack of noise became apparent. Only the horse hooves on the stones and the occasional spoken word from a passerby broke the silence. No car noise, no music blasting, no drones humming above. Just soft quiet. Brock looked at Isaac's face for any reaction to the scene.

The intern's faint smile and slightly furrowed brow told Brock nothing.

"Come along," Isaac said then motioned that they should move along the narrow brick sidewalk, their faint shadows leading by a half step.

Brock followed slowly, stepping carefully in his ill-fitting shoes on the uneven walkway. After only a few paces he grabbed Isaac's coat sleeve. "Man, this cool air is doing a number on me. I've gotta piss like a race horse! Where can I take a leak?"

Isaac frowned then chuckled. "You speak in strange ways, friend. But I believe I understand you need to pass water."

"Whatever. Just show me somewhere quick."

Isaac led Brock back through the gate onto the hospital grounds and pointed. "The hospital privy is near the far wall."

A wooden enclosure with two doors stood thirty yards away. "You're kidding, right?" Brock said as he started toward relief, the fit of the borrowed shoes hampering his urgent mission. When Brock jerked opened one of the doors of the privy, the smell was like nothing he had ever experienced. Despite his reservations, he turned his face away from the privy, took a deep breath and stepped up into the wooden box.

Sixty seconds later Brock reappeared, gasping for air. "Damn, it's ripe in there. How do you stand it?"

Isaac only shrugged and motioned for Brock to follow.

Outside the wall again and a half block further along, an older man approached going in the opposite direction. He tipped his hat slightly before passing. Brock felt, however, that the man had stared at him an instant longer than he did Isaac. It was as if he knew Brock didn't belong.

Brock's eyes remained in constant motion. The narrow brick houses with no space between, all just a few feet from the narrow street. Riders on horses dominated the street with alert pedestrians scrambling to avoid both the huge animals and the abundance of road apples.

Brock winced as the smell of raw sewage mixed with the odor of fresh horse shit assaulted his nostrils. How could people live with this stench? He realized, however, that the hospital had absolutely reeked at first but then seem less noticeable this morning after he had been there overnight. He assumed it was the body's adaptation mechanism that allowed people to tolerate the horrific smells.

After ten minutes Brock's feet were killing him in the borrowed shoes. "Where are we going?"

"I thought you could meet my father and mother and we could join them for dinner. Our house is just in the next block."

The term "dinner" was odd to Brock for late morning but he didn't question it. He was starving. All he had eaten was the thin soup and the piece of bread the previous evening. "Yeah, some food would be good."

From the outside, Isaac's parents' house looked much like the others they had passed. It reminded Brock of Elfreth's Alley with its houses squeeze together in Old Town Philadelphia he saw during a family vacation. He hadn't realized the building style had been so dominant in the city's early years. The entrance to the three-story house was up a half-dozen steps with a single window to the left of the door helping define the width of the building, maybe twenty feet.

When Isaac opened the heavy wooden door, a delicious aroma emerged from the dim hallway beyond, lit only by the glass transom above the door. A pleasant-looking woman wearing a long dress and apron appeared at the end of the short hallway.

"Isaac, my son, what a surprise," the woman said. "Will you be taking dinner with us?"

Isaac moved toward the small but sturdy woman and hugged her. "Yes, Mother, if you have ample." He turned back toward Brock. "And, Mother, this fellow is Brock Sinclair. He is a patient of Dr. Rush at the hospital. I've invited him to dinner also, unless it will be an imposition."

The woman withdrew a half step back into the room at the end of the hall out of Brock's view and did not respond at first. Isaac motioned for Brock to follow him down the hall where they entered an area between the front room and the kitchen with spiral stairs leading to the upper floors.

Isaac's mother stared at Brock for a few seconds. "Welcome, Brock," she said at last without smiling as they moved forward into what had to be the kitchen. "Come sit at our table." She pointed to a sturdy wooden table with a straight back chair at each end and benches along both sides. She turned back to an open hearth with its small wood fire off-center to the right. A three-legged, cast iron pot hung at the edge of the fire from a metal support mounted to the side of the hearth.

The woman's hesitation to his presence was obvious. Was she pissed that Isaac had brought someone to the meal without notice? Or, was him being a patient of Dr. Rush the concern? Dr. *Benjamin* Rush! Suddenly Brock recognized the name. He had read something somewhere about Dr. Rush. He was renowned as the first psychiatrist in America but was a big believer in bleeding his patients. God knows what other torture he practices. If I'm one of his patients, Isaac's mom must think I'm a psycho.

Brock attempted to appear normal despite his circumstance. "Thanks. Mrs. ... aah. Sorry, I don't remember Isaac's last name," Brock said, blushing.

"Mrs. Jamison," she stated flatly. "And this is our daughter, Amelia." A slim, pretty teenager with similar drab clothes, her hair braided and pinned high on her head, stepped from the rear of the room. The girl's smile revealed uneven teeth but her large, pale blue eyes captured Brock's attention.

Mrs. Jamison spoke to her daughter. "Amelia, set two extra places for your brother and his friend."

"Yes, Ma'am," Amelia said as she began putting wooden spoons and crude mugs at seven positions around the table.

Brock felt like an intruder but his hunger and the lack of a polite exit told him to stay. Isaac directed him to the end of a bench across the table from where he sat down. The room's low, darkened ceiling and the limited light from the window in back and the barely flickering hearth fire caused Brock's heart to race. He began taking short, shallow breaths. Once seated, however, the claustrophobic sensation faded.

Amelia began pouring a pale yellow liquid into the mugs as two boys, one tall and thin, maybe twelve-years-old, the other, smaller and maybe two years younger, stomped down the spiral stairs Brock had passed on the way in. They stopped short of the table. Brock didn't know if it was his presence or house rules that had reined them in.

When the older boy saw Isaac, he ran to him and pounded his arm playfully.

"Duncan! Nathan! Mind your manners. We have a guest," Mrs. Jamison said in a tone that did not invite challenge. The boys quietly sat down, one on the far end of each bench.

As Amelia was setting a plate of hand-sliced, dark bread in the center of the table, the front door opened and closed. The sound of footsteps in the hall preceded a man, in his forties, into the kitchen. He was of average build, like Isaac, although heavier around the middle. He removed his tri-corner hat and coat before scanning the table.

Isaac said, "Father, I've invited someone I met at the hospital to join us for dinner. His name is Brock Sinclair."

The bench's position made it awkward for Brock to stand. As he made a half-hearted attempt to rise, he extended his hand. "Good to meet you."

Mr. Jamison stole a glance at his wife who stopped her stirring of the pot and responded with an almost imperceptible nod. He then grasped Brock's hand. "Welcome Brock. Your queer accent tells me you are not a Philadelphian. Pray tell from whence you hail?"

Brock hesitated. "I'm from…" His lips quivered and his eyes filled with tears. He sobbed softly as he sat back down and bowed his head, surprised at his lack of control.

"Father, Brock received a blow to his head in a recent fall and his memory has been affected. Dr. Rush is tending to him. I am hopeful that a walk and a change of scenery will be helpful."

Mr. Jamison's eyes widened as he watched Brock. "I see," he said as he sat down at the head of the table. He looked at Brock, composing himself, sniffling. "Welcome, young man. Perhaps some of my wife's venison stew will improve your memory." He nodded toward the hearth. "Edith, please serve, I must get back to the store. I have a delivery coming this afternoon. The *Albemarle* finally arrived in port this morning? I will have much inventory to settle."

Mrs. Jamison proceeded to ladle stew onto wooden plates that Amelia placed in front of Brock, then her father, then the rest of the table. When the steaming stew had been served, Mrs. Jamison sat down at the other end of the table from her husband, between the two young boys, and folded her hands prayerfully. Amelia, on Isaac's side of the bench did likewise as did the rest of the family.

"Let us thank the good Lord for this food and all that we have," Mr. Jamison said. The family members bowed their heads with Brock following their lead. Mr. Jamison offered grace in what sounded to Brock like a sincere, yet expedited manner then said, "Amen."

Brock found the prayer surprisingly soothing. He could not have repeated the words. But Mr. Jamison's tone, the thankful attitude, and the promise of hope gave him comfort.

In unison the family took up their spoons and attacked the stew. Brock really wanted to wash his hands after everything he had touched in the last twenty-four hours. But he saw no opportunity nor did anyone else appeared concerned with hygiene. He pushed his concern to the back of his mind and dug in. The stew with chunks of meat, potatoes, carrots and some chunks he didn't recognize was outstanding. He knew he was hungry but didn't anticipate how good the food felt reaching his stomach. No one spoke, only the sounds of slurps and chewing could be heard. Brock broke the silence, "Mrs. Jamison, this stew is awesome."

The young boys glanced at each other across the table, then giggled. "Hush!" Mrs. Jamison said to the boys with a stern glance to each, instantly restoring order. Amelia's grin at Brock's comment lingered then dissolved.

"Your speech is strange, friend," Mr. Jamison said conversationally as he took a slice of the bread and passed the plate to Brock. "Do you not remember anything about your life before your fall?"

Brock looked across the table at Isaac who met his eyes but gave no hint how to respond. He took a deep breath, "Well, I remember my father, Trip, and my mother, Laura. We live southwest of here in a place called 'Texas'."

Isaac smiled.

"'Texas'? I do not know of it," Mr. Jamison said. "Is it beyond Pennsylvania?"

"Yeah. It's probably a two-day drive from here."

"You traveled with a team then rather than on horseback?" Isaac asked, obviously pleased with this bit of information.

Brock felt like he was sinking in quicksand. Sweat trickled down his sides. "I'm afraid the details are fuzzy. Maybe more will come to me later." Both boys snickered.

"Give it time, son," Mr. Jamison said, as he gave stern looks at the two young boys who both quickly returned their attention to their food.

The meal continued with little further conversation. Brock had questions about the family lifestyle, so crude from anything he had ever known. But he remained quiet, concerned with exposing his situation.

The beverage that Amelia had poured was a weak beer. Despite its lack of any head and being at room temperature, the brew was pleasant in a lite beer sort of way. Brock emptied his cup in big gulps.

Mr. Jamison spoke briefly of the rumors of the *Albemarle's* narrow escape from privateers during its voyage from India. Apparently, the encounter and bad weather had delayed the voyage by a week. As a result, his inventory of cotton cloth at his store was down to three bolts he advised.

With Brock's hunger, his plate was soon empty. He turned toward Mrs. Jamison, "Is there more of the stew?"

Mrs. Jamison's wide eyes and a slight shake of her head signaled her husband at the other end of the table.

"All the stew has been served," Mr. Jamison said to Brock in stilted speech. "Perhaps another slice of bread will sate your appetite."

The look on Isaac's face was as if Brock had cleared his throat and spit on the table.

"I'm sorry, the stew was just sooo good," Brock said to Mrs. Jamison. "Thank you for sharing." He then nodded to Mr. Jamison.

Mr. Jamison soon rose and excused himself with a belch and promptly left to attend to the store.

As Brock stood to leave at Isaac's suggestion, he said, "Mrs. Jamison, again the meal was outstanding. Thank you for your hospitality."

Mrs. Jamison responded with a slight smile and nod but seemed relieved that Brock was leaving. Amelia peeked often at Brock while she cleared the table of the empty plates and cups. She had been stealing glances in his direction throughout the meal as well.

Brock had some questions about this Amelia.

######

As the two young men walked from Isaac's home back toward the hospital, Brock said, "I apologize if I insulted your mom by asking for more stew. It was just that I hadn't eaten much and was really hungry. And the stew was very good."

"You may not have taken note that, as a guest, you were served first and your plate contained the most. The remainder of the stew was then divided among the family plates."

"No man, I didn't notice. Shit, I feel like such an ass." Brock paused then looked at Isaac. "Is there some way I can make it up to your folks?"

"There is no need. You have already been forgiven."

Brock didn't understand how Isaac could know how his parents would be so gracious. He chose not to question Isaac further but the incident stuck in the back of his mind.

Moments later Brock changed the subject. I guess you don't live at home since your mother was surprised to see you."

"As an intern I sleep and generally take my meals at the hospital." He grimaced. "I visit my folks as often as my duties and studies allow, however." He paused. "To my father you claimed to hail from a 'Texas' yet you referenced 'Huntsville' earlier. Which might it be?"

"Yeah, I guess I did confuse you. I live with my folks in a city called The Woodlands in the state of Texas. But I was visiting a friend in the town of Huntsville, about thirty minutes north of there, when I apparently fell. Sorry about that."

"This 'Texas' is a state just like Pennsylvania or Virginia?"

Brock lets out a huge breath. "Exactly!" Isaac nodded slowly in response.

A block further on Brock made a decision and stopped. "Isaac, I've got to talk to you." The intern stopped and faced him.

Brock took a deep breath. "First, thanks again for allowing me to visit with your family and to share the meal." He continued with obvious hesitation. "I'm not sure what to do but I think I've got to trust somebody. You see, I don't want to go back to the hospital. I know about Dr. Rush. He was…is known for his treatments of his patients, both those who are sick and those considered to be mentally ill. He insists on bleedings as a treatment for everything. And I think I remember he also used mercury chloride as a laxative to purge his patients. Where I'm from doctors know that these treatments are bullshit and actually harm the patients. If I go back to the hospital, I'm afraid I'll end up in his psyche ward strapped to a bed with blood running out of my arm or my head. I just can't let that happen."

Isaac frowned. "How is it that you know Dr. Rush is such a staunch advocate for bleedings? I was not aware that such was common knowledge."

"I've read about Ben Franklin, including his autobiography, and I know that he and Dr. Rush were, at least, acquainted. Anyway, I've picked up a few bits and pieces about Dr. Rush, some good but most of it pretty horrible by the medical standards where I'm from."

"What books exist that address Dr. Franklin? And I was not aware he had published an autobiography."

"Oh, that's right. He was called Dr. Franklin after his honorary degree from Oxford. Most of what I've read was published long after his death in 1790."

Isaac frowned. "Dr. Franklin is certainly an elderly man. But how could you know that he will die in just a few years?"

"Because I live in the year 2029 and know much of the history of the country," Brock sighed. "I mentioned that date back at the hospital if you'll remember."

Isaac went quiet, apparently mulling what he was hearing. At last he spoke in a skeptic tone, "It seems your memory is returning rapidly. Perhaps you could tell me more of your past?"

A man and young girl approached. "Can we go somewhere private so we can talk?" Brock asked. "What I have to tell you will be hard for you to believe. Actually, I can't believe I'm here to tell you."

CHAPTER 5   Oct 13, Saturday

From across the street Brock had watched Isaac enter Pennsylvania Hospital to report he would be away for an hour. A light rain had begun, adding to the coolness of the fall air. Brock had closed his eyes briefly and remembered being at the cabin near Lake Livingston on cold, damp weekends with his dad. The clopping of a horse and rider approaching in the street brought him back to his 18th century environment. During the wait Brock half expected three or four burly guys to come running out of the hospital to take him back in and strap him to a bed.

Thankfully, Isaac reappeared after only a few minutes, alone. He said, "My superior was displeased with me but said I could work additional this day as recompense."

Brock sat across from Isaac at a small table in a dimly-lit tavern a block from the hospital. The rough-hewn walls and floor were not painted, adding to the room's darkness. Only a single window on each side of the door allowed meager light to enter. Maybe a dozen men and a young boy were spread among the few tables talking quietly, some eating. A Franklin stove stood in one corner partially defending against the autumn chill.

"Isaac, what I'm about to tell you will sound crazy," Brock said, leaning forward and speaking in hushed tones. "And I can't explain how this occurred. But you have to believe me that it's the truth."

Isaac folded his hands on the edge of the table. "I give you my complete attention."

"My name is Brock Sinclair. I'm nineteen years old and I was born in December of the year 2009." Isaac's eyes widened as he inhaled and sat up straighter.

Brock plowed on. "I live in a state called Texas, probably fifteen hundred miles southwest of here. A buddy of mine and I did some drugs that make you feel really good. I must have stumbled and fell and I guess I hit my head. That was Monday afternoon, October 8, 2029."

Isaac's compassionate expression disappeared to be replaced with one of concern and maybe disappointment. "Brock, some of this tale you shared previously. Perchance you are just remembering your hallucination, mistaking it for reality."

Brock slapped the edge of the table in front of him with his fingers. "No, Isaac!" He glanced around the room to see if he had drawn any attention but no heads turn in their direction. Looking at Isaac again, he continued, "I can tell you every detail of my life from childhood, through high school, one year of college, up to when I fell. I can list places I've been, things I've done, people I know. A hallucination couldn't have thousands and thousands of details like that." Brock was on the verge of tears. "And everything about living in the 18th century is unfamiliar to me. The buildings, the clothes, horses in the streets, everything."

Isaac stared at his patient from across the table. Then, with a grin he said, "Surely, healing in your year has advanced far beyond what I study. Can you speak of it?"

Brock felt like a very thin rope had been tossed to him from across the table just as he was falling off a cliff. He smiled than hesitated while he considered how to describe modern medicine to the 18th century intern. Before he could answer, a stout man, bearded and wearing an apron, approached. "Good day, gents. Will you be having a bumper of my finest ale?"

"Yes, two, please," Isaac said to the barman. The man nodded and turned toward a short bar at the other end of the room.

"Okay, Isaac, some basics," Brock said when they were alone again. "Modern medicine knows that many illnesses are from bacteria and viruses. These microscopic organisms get into our bodies and play hell with our immune systems. A lot of the symptoms you see are the result of our bodies reacting to the presence of these organisms. For instance, the reason people get diarrhea from drinking river water is because of the bacteria in it. But if you boil the water first to make coffee or tea, you kill the bacteria and then you don't get sick. The beer-making process does the same thing." Brock turned his palms up to emphasize the simplicity of what he was telling Isaac.

"Do you suggest that small organisms cause the flux?" Isaac said, scratching his cheek.

"Yes! What causes sickness are the tiny, microscopic life forms that are too small to see with the naked eye. Pure spring water is generally okay and so is rain water. But any water that gets contaminated with bacteria from the waste of animals or people can make you sick, again unless you boil the water first to kill it."

The barman arrived with two tankards and set them on the small table. "That'll be two pence."

Isaac raised an eyebrow then withdrew two small coins from his vest pocket and dropped them into the man's open hand. The barman moved away without further comment as both Brock and Isaac promptly took long pulls from their tankards.

Alone again, Isaac said, "Please go on."

"Well, keep in mind that I'm not a doctor; I only know what I read on the Internet or see on haloscreens."

Isaac's stare went blank.

"That's okay, just remember that I've had no medical training but I do read a lot."

Isaac nodded once, very slowly.

"When a patient gets sick, doctors have all kinds of tests they can run on blood, urine, tissue samples to help determine what's wrong. They also have many different machines that can look inside the body to see growths, see blood flow restrictions, blockages, and broken bones. Then, there are thousands of drugs available to fight a disease or help relieve patients' symptoms."

Brock watched Isaac to see if he was still paying attention before he continued. "The thing that would probably blow your mind are the techniques available to open up the body and repair stuff and even replace organs like kidneys, even hearts."

Isaac's eyes had grown larger and larger as Brock talked. "Please, you say physicians have replacement organs waiting to put into bodies?"

The excitement in Brock's voice dropped a notch. "No, the replacement organs are from people who die and donate their organs for transplant."

The look on Isaac's face was a mix of confusion and horror.

"People sign cards in advance that if they die of an accident and the organs in their bodies are healthy and not damaged, they can be harvested and quickly transplanted into a patient who is on a waiting list for an organ." Brock took a deep breath and sat back in his chair.

Isaac stared from across the table.

Brock couldn't tell if Isaac was considering the believability of his statements. Or, if he was deciding just *how* crazy the story teller was.

At last Isaac said, "Tell me of your life in this Texas." There was no grin, just an intense focus on Brock.

Brock's face met the solemn stare. "I don't know where to start. A lot about life in 2029 you wouldn't comprehend because technology has advanced so far since the 1700's." Brock did not want to lose his only potential ally with what might be seen as even more outlandish claims. "First of all, in the 1800's they figure out how to generate electricity. With that came the electric light and electric motors to drive machinery. Years later people started using electricity to cook food, heat and cool their homes, achieve global communication and other things that would be difficult for you to conceive."

Isaac's expression indicated Brock had exceeded the intern's threshold to visualize. He said in a hesitant tone, "You spoke of global communication. I do not understand."

Brock hesitated. "I don't think you're ready to hear about that just yet. But what you might understand is cars."

Isaac just stared at his companion.

Brock continued, "Remember that I told your dad I lived a two-day drive from Philadelphia? To get here from my home in Texas, I might choose to ride in a self-driving, electric car. I would get in this metal carriage with windows all around and comfortable seats. I would program the car to come here. I could then read, sleep, whatever, while the car traveled about eighty miles per hour over the highways. It would have to stop every six hours and recharge its batteries. I could then get out to stretch, take a leak, get some coffee, then I'd be off again. I'd probably stop for a few meals but even then I'd get here in a day or two."

When Isaac rolled his eyes, Brock knew he had lost him. "Look, Isaac. The self-driving car didn't happen overnight. At the start of the twentieth century, automobiles were slow, unreliable, horseless carriages powered by small engines. It took more than a century for the technology to evolve to what is now available."

Isaac leaned toward his cross-table companion. "Brock, you tell fascinating tales. And I will concede that you have an active imagination. But—"

"Jacob! Jacob! What's wrong, son!" a man shouted at a table halfway across the room. The man stood over a boy, about ten-years-old, slapping him on his back. The boy was holding his throat and even in the dim light Brock could see he was turning pale blue.

"Isaac, that boy's choking!" Brock shouted as he leaped from his chair. Both ran to the table.

Brock fidgeted as the man slapped the boy's back with no benefit. Isaac kneeled beside the boy, helping to hold him against his father's blows.

Customers from the other tables had moved toward the commotion, talking quietly or remaining silent.

"Let me try!" Brock said, pushing the boy's father out of the way. The man resisted but Brock continued. "Look, we don't have much time. Let me help him."

Without waiting for the man's response, Brock lifted the boy out of his chair by his arm pits. He held the boy's back against his chest and placed his left fist just under the boy's rib cage. With his right hand on top of his left, he gave a strong jerk back and upward that lifted the boy off the floor.

The boy doubled over from the thrust in his midsection but showed no sign of relief. Brock jerked again. No reaction.

"What are you doing?" Isaac yelled, standing close.

The boy's father grabbed Brock's shoulder. "Put him down. You're hurting my son!"

"Trust me. I know what I'm doing!" With that Brock jerked a third time, harder than before. The boy spit out a chunk of sausage onto the table and sucked in a deep breath, coughed, then took several quick breaths. He whimpered, tears running down his face as he panted and coughed more.

Brock eased the boy back into his chair. "I think you'll be okay now." The boy looked at Brock through his tears. Brock patted him on the shoulder and looked at the man, squatting next to his son. "He should be all right. He was choking on the piece of meat."

The boy's father held his son's shoulder. "Jacob, are you all right?" The boy nodded slightly as he wiped his tears with his coat sleeve.

The father stood and faced Brock. He extended his hand. "Thank you for what you did for my boy."

Brock shook the man's hand. "No problem. I was trained how to do that but I've never actually done it. I'll admit it was kind of scary there for a minute." He looked down at the boy. "His chest will probably be sore for a few days but I don't think I broke any ribs. You might want to get a chest x-ray just to be…Never mind."

A tavern customer approached and slapped Brock on the back. "Damnedest thing I ever seen." He shook his head and walked back toward his table. Another man spoke to the boy's father in hushed tones as they both nodded toward Brock.

Isaac, his eyes wide, followed Brock back to their table.

When Brock and Isaac were again seated, Isaac said, "Where did you learn how to revive the young boy?"

Brock was still shaking from the experience. "I've seen the technique demonstrated several times. It's called the Heimlich Maneuver, named after the guy who came up with…" Brock stopped, his eyes went wide. "Isaac, I don't know exactly when Heimlich developed that maneuver, but it was definitely sometime in the twentieth century. My dad said it was fairly new when he was a boy. It proves that what I've been telling you is not a hallucination."

Isaac did not respond immediately; he just shook his head ever so slowly. "I have never witnessed such as what just occurred. But, it does not prove that you lived in future years."

Brock met Isaac's eyes while he considered his response. His eyes dropped to the table as he struggled for his proof. None came to mind. Finally, his eyes brimming, Brock looked across the table. "Isaac, I could tell you about wars, catastrophes, inventions coming in the next two hundred fifty years. But you would have no reason to believe me."

Isaac's face reflected deep sympathy as he nodded slowly. He then straightened in his chair and said in a soft voice, "We must return to the hospital. Perhaps additional bed rest will aid your recovery."

Brock jumped up. "I can't go back to the hospital! Rush will want to strap me to a bed and drill a hole in my head to *let the bad blood out*." He put up his hands to ward off Isaac's suggestion. "I'll end up a vegetable or dead when he gets through." Brock had backed away from the table. The barman and a few others looked in his direction.

Isaac raised his hands in surrender. "What if I can guarantee you that Dr. Rush does not take you from the main ward?"

Brock swayed, near panic. "How are you going to guarantee that? No disrespect, but you're just an intern."

"I am the elder intern and responsible for releases from the main ward. That is why you were allowed to leave the hospital."

Brock hesitated. "If I say okay, can you prevent another bleeding? Can you make sure that doesn't happen?"

Isaac hesitated. "As you must know, bleedings are routine. Despite what you say, it may be beneficial to your improvement."

"No! The damn bleedings do nothing positive for patients. And using unsterile instruments risk introducing infection that can kill. Promise me no bleeding. Will you promise, Isaac?"

The intern studied Brock for several seconds then nodded. "I will intervene if an order for a bleeding is given." He stood up and spoke in a whisper. "But Brock, you must refrain from references about the year 2029 in the midst of others."

Brock nodded slowly and followed the intern out of the tavern and back toward the hospital. He realized he was trusting Isaac with his life.

CHAPTER 6   Oct 13, Saturday

Brock walked a half step behind Isaac as they climbed the steps to the main entrance of the hospital where a middle-aged man in a rumpled suit met them with a frown. "You are tardy for rounds, doctor. Do not let this become a habit."

"Yes, sir. I'll settle this patient and join you straight away."

Isaac led Brock to the empty bed at the far end of the ward where he had initially been found. "Brock, remove your garments and get into the bed. I will return after rounds." He watched the ward while his patient undressed.

After removing his shoes and socks, Brock took off the pants and laid them on the bed. He then removed his shirt and turned to lay it with the pants.

"What, pray tell, are the markings on your shoulder?" Isaac exclaimed. He grasped Brock by his left arm, turned him slightly and leaned forward, studying the deltoid.

Surprised at first, Brock grinned as he looked toward his shoulder. "Oh, the tat? I got that for my sixteenth birthday. A flag was about the only thing my dad would let me get. It's still pretty cool though."

"It appears to be a flag not unlike the banner flown in the states today. But the circle of stars is absent. Instead there is—"

Brock spun around and faced the intern directly. He grasped Isaac by the upper arms. "Isaac, that's it! The flag tattoo shows the fifty-one stars for the number of states!" He lowered his voice. "That's the number of states in 2029." He turned to give Isaac a better view. "Look closer. The flag's just like the Betsy Ross original with the same thirteen stripes and blue field, just more stars. It proves that what I've been telling you is true!" He fist pumped the air with both hands in celebration.

Isaac leaned even closer to the markings. He touched the tattoo gently with his finger tips and moved them over Brock's skin. "I have seen but few tattoos, most on jack tars being treated for injuries at sea or bearing sickness. They were on the men's forearms, initials in crude black or blue letters or numbers. The precise detail and the colors of this image on your skin are..." He shook his head and moved to face Brock.

Brock shook with excitement. "Now do you believe me? Technology to do this kind of ink won't come along for at least another hundred years."

Isaac's nostrils flared, his eyes bulged as he stepped back from Brock, trembling.

"What's wrong, Isaac? You look like you've seen a ghost."

Isaac's voice faltered. "This...This is the work of Satan."

Brock chuckled. "The devil's work? No, no, the tattoo was done by a girl at Elegant Ink out on Sam Houston Highway. The guys there are definitely strange but they're not demons."

Isaac paced in a small circle, his left hand cupping his chin, his eyes switching from tightly shut to wide open. Seconds later he reached for Brock's shirt on the bed. "Cover yourself! You must never let anyone observe the image! Your life could be at risk!" Brock slipped the shirt back on.

"You're serious about this devil thing?" Brock put up his hands. "What's the big deal, Isaac? It's just a tattoo."

As Brock buttoned the shirt, Isaac spoke quietly but firmly. "My faith is not as strong as that of some. And I question many of the teachings of the church. I do, however, know others that harbor strong beliefs and groundless fears of that which they do not understand. Were these markings to be revealed, your safety, indeed your very life, could be in jeopardy."

Isaac stepped closer. "I do not know who you are or why you are here." His frown disappeared. "But I feel I'm called to be your friend."

Brock, stunned by the warning, yet relieved to hear Isaac's support, answered in an uncertain voice, "Thanks for the warning; I'll be sure heed it." He grined. "And I already considered you a friend."

Quietly Isaac said, "I must attend to rounds." He moved away. After a single step he turned back slowly and spoke in a whisper. "Get into the bed. When I return, we will seek assistance." He then turned and continued across the room.

Brock got into the bed as Isaac had insisted. Still alarmed by the potential of being killed because of his tattoo, he was nevertheless, encouraged that Isaac had used the term "we" in reference to getting help.

While he waited, Brock kept an eye on the door to the hall for Dr. Rush. Fortunately, the activity in the ward was similar to the previous afternoon with only a few nurses milling about. At one point Lilly, the nurse from the previous day, approached his bed and asked if he needed anything. Her smile reassured Brock that he was safe for the moment. She stayed for only a brief time before moving on to tend to the other patients.

As Lilly walked away, Dr. Rush entered the ward. The man strode directly to Brock's bed, a sneer on his face. "How is our patient, this fine day?"

Although he did not trust the doctor, Brock was desperate to have the hallucination go away. "I feel okay."

"And do your hallucinations persist?"

Brock watched as Dr. Rush kneaded his hands. "If you're asking if this place is extremely odd to me, the answer is, yes. But my vision and my thinking are quite clear."

The doctor's shoulders slumped noticeably. He considered Brock's response then nodded in affirmation. Without another word Dr. Rush turned and strode briskly from the ward, ignoring a plaintive call from one of the other patients.

Brock did not know what to make of the exchange with the doctor or his abrupt departure. But what little hope he had in getting a cure from him had disappeared. If he had anything to say about it, this encounter with the doctor would be his last.

Looking toward the doorway, he wondered what was taking Isaac so long. Through the doorway two men emerged, one muscular, the other very tall but far from skinny. They both wore crude shirts and pants, unlike the other medical staff. They walked like men on a mission, moving toward Brock's end of the ward. When they were five feet from his bed, Brock held up his hands to halt their advance. "Whoa, fellows! What's going on?"

The beefy guy spoke in a coarse voice. "Dr. Rush said to bring you downstairs." He grasped Brock's blanket and pulled it off roughly. Brock leapt from the opposite side of the bed, landing on his feet. He jumped sideways into the space beyond the foot of the bed and from years of Taekwondo training and competition instinctively assumed a defensive posture. Tall guy moved toward Brock, his arms extended. In a swift, practiced move Brock kicked out and up striking tall guy in the crotch with a crushing blow. The giant folded like a beach chair and collapsed, moaning and gasping for breath.

The other brute snarled as he stepped around his fallen partner and turned his body sideways when he reached for Brock. From four feet away Brock whirled 360°, his right leg in a ferocious arc, catching the man on the side of his head with his foot. Despite his bulk, the man fell backward and hit the floor hard. He remained motionless while Brock waited, prepared for another counter.

Brock retrieved his pants and dressed quickly while keeping an eye on the two horizontal men and the nurse who had arrived to attend to them. He shrugged at the stares from patients and staff then hurried toward the hospital exit and away from Dr. Rush's chambers.

CHAPTER 7   Oct 13, Saturday

Brock needed to find Isaac but he had no idea where to look inside the multistory building. He hurried out the main door, assuming he was less likely to encounter more of Dr. Rush's orderlies outside. Through the perimeter wall and down the street he moved at a fast walk. Other than a woman he almost knocked over as he left the hospital grounds, nobody seemed to pay him any attention.

Wet leaves spotted the sidewalk, muffling his steps. After only a few blocks, fewer houses lined the street and the tree density in the open spaces increased. Even in the misty rain, the assortment of autumn leaf colors grabbed his attention. The observation surprised Brock. Under normal circumstances he wouldn't have given the natural beauty a second thought. Yet, in this very unusual and stressful situation he had noticed.

The brick sidewalks gave way to a packed dirt surface before he turned right at a corner, hoping to find something familiar to get his bearings. The number of houses and shops on the street soon increased but still he recognized nothing from his earlier walk to the Jamison family home. After maybe twenty minutes Brock's feet hurt in the damn shoes and he admitted to himself that he was lost.

The only landmark Brock knew was Pennsylvania Hospital. He figured he could get directions to it from just about anybody. But he didn't know what to expect if he showed up there.

As Brock stood assessing his situation, the sound of metal pounding on metal reached him. Through open double doors across the street a huge man was wielding a hammer against a glowing piece of metal on his anvil. The blows of the hammer sent shards of bright orange sparks in all directions, drawing Brock to the sights and sounds.

The blacksmith did not notice or chose to ignore Brock standing in the doorway, his focus on the chunk of orange metal held on the anvil with his tongs. To Brock the blacksmith's project looked like it had the potential to become an axe head.

When the blacksmith turned and plunged the metal into the glowing coals of the forge, Brock stepped forward. "Hello. How ya doin'?"

The burly man, maybe fifty years old, with massive bare arms turned his head slowly toward Brock while he maintained his rhythm on the long lever of the bellows fanning his forge. "What say ye?"

"Afternoon. I heard your hammer from across the street." Brock wrapped his arms around himself. "Could I watch you work while I warm up a bit?"

The man snarled. "Suit ya self. But I don't have no time for jawin'." The blacksmith turned his piece in the forge with the tongs. "And stay outta tha way."

"Okay. It's just that I've never seen a blacksmith actually work a piece of metal before. It's fascinating."

The blacksmith squinted and frowned at the statement, then sneered. "'Fascinatin', sheit. What it is is hard work. Hot, dirty work." He lifted the piece from the forge and turned back toward the anvil. "Move back!"

Glowing sparks of metal sprayed as the hammer struck the metal piece held on the anvil. There was a steady rhythm to the smith's hammer blows that Brock had not noticed from across the street. With each impact the smith repositioned his work piece on the anvil as it slowly yielded to his strikes. The smith never looked up from his work, the metal changing from bright orange to a dull glow as it cooled. After a dozen or more blows, the piece went back into the forge.

The blacksmith lifted a small shovel at the edge of the forge and piled the glowing coals on his work piece all the while pulling on the bellows. Brock stepped closer to the man and his forge, careful to stay out of the way. "This ain't your first day as a blacksmith is it?"

The grouchy blacksmith's face and voice softened. "Been smithin' since I was a pup. My daddy teached me. Said I had a knack for it, God rest his soul."

Brock didn't know what else to say. In the next instant the smith grabbed his tongs, jerked his work piece from the forge and turned back to the anvil. Brock stepped back as the heavy hammer struck powerful blows, sending more sparks in all directions.

When the work piece returned to the forge once more, Brock's curiosity prevailed. "Will that be an axe head when you're through?"

The smith looked over his shoulder. He nodded once. "I reckon it will be."

"Do you ever make double-bitted axes?"

The smith turned slightly, his hand on the bellows never stopping. "Ain't seen no double-bitted axe. What it be for?"

"Well, I'm no lumberjack. But my dad has one he inherited from his father in the garage. He said woodsmen kept one blade real sharp for felling trees. But the other blade was thicker and used for cutting roots or chopping through knots."

The smith appeared torn between his work and the conversation underway. "What be this gay-ragz where the double-bit axe be kept?"

Brock hesitated. "It's just a storage room for tools and such near our house." The smith nodded then turned back to his forge.

For most of an hour the smith transformed the chunk of metal into an impressive axe head. Apparently, satisfied with his work, the smith reheated the head to a bright red color in the forge. He then carried it quickly to a wooden barrel near the wall of his shop and plunged it into the water. A cloud of steam rose from the surface of the water then quickly subsided. The smith removed the axe head from the water and placed it on his anvil for close inspection. He filed some imperfections before motioning for Brock toward a bench not far from the forge.

Brock followed the man. "Dude, that axe head is awesome. You're good at this."

The smith turned to Brock and extended his rough, calloused hand. "I be Amos, not Dude."

Brock shook the formidable hand. "Amos, it's good to meet you. I'm Brock."

Once both men were seated on the small bench, the smith said, "Can you draw me that double-bit axe of your pappy's?"

Brock smiled at the sweating man. "Sure. I'm surprised a man with your skill has never made one much less having never seen one."

Amos shrugged and found a short, fairly smooth plank and a piece of charcoal for Brock's drawing.

Brock's limited artistry and the crude drawing supplies made the task a challenge. But he used the newly formed axe head as a model. He just drew the blade on both ends of his sketch. "He looked up from his sketch to the smith. "Amos, this is a pretty rough drawing but I think you get the idea."

Amos nodded and smiled.

Brock continued, "Look, I don't know much about this type of axe; I've just seen my grandfather's. But from an engineering stand point, I would think that balance would be critical; the weight on both sides of the handle would need to be equal."

Amos nodded his head with enthusiasm, a hint of a smile on his face. "When I finish fixin' Mr. Marshall's plow, I'm gonna make one of them there double-bit axes." His smile widened. "If I can make it, I might sell them to the farmers and woodsmen."

Brock nodded at the enthusiasm of the smith and was pleased that he had made a positive impact on the man. And maybe he had made another friend.

######

Brock had been gone from the hospital for over an hour. Was Isaac looking for him and was it safe to go back to find him? With directions from Amos, he made his way back to the hospital perimeter wall and peeked through one of the open gates. A few people were entering and leaving the building in a calm manner. There didn't seem to be lookouts watching for him.

The entrance to the hospital he and Isaac had used after dinner was on another side of the building. He found it and with caution made his way inside and to the ward where he had been found initially. As he entered the ward, Lilly walked in his direction frowning.

When she was face to face with Brock, Lilly said in a quiet but stern voice, "Where have you been? Dr. Rush and Isaac...Dr. Jamison have been searching the hospital for you."

Brock cupped Lilly's shoulders. He looked her directly in the eyes and spoke in a firm voice, "Look, Lilly. I need to talk with Isaac. Can you find him and have him meet me outside the hospital wall? And don't tell Dr. Rush." She opened her mouth to object. But Brock put a finger to her lips. "Shhh. I'll explain later but I don't think it's safe for me here. Will you just find Isaac and send him out the door on this side of the hospital?" He pointed in the direction of the exit he intended to use.

Lilly seemed torn between her duty and Brock's request. At last she nodded.

Brock kissed her cheek and smiled. "Thanks, Lilly. Now, I've got to go."

Lilly gently touched her cheek where she had been kissed as Brock moved quickly out of the ward and out of the building. Once outside the wall, he crossed the street and took a position behind a tree to watch for Isaac.

Moments later Isaac rushed through the gate, looking in both directions.

Brock stepped out from behind his tree and waved the intern to his side of the street.

Isaac paused to let two riders pass then crossed. When he reached Brock, he said, "Where did you go? Dr. Rush is frantic to find you."

"I bet he is."

Isaac grinned. "The staff reports that you disabled two of Dr. Rush's orderlies before you disappeared. Is there truth in that?"

"Dr. Rush sent those two apes to take me downstairs but I decided not to go with them."

"But how did you—?

"I'll tell you later." Brock grabbed Isaac by the arm and pulled him along the sidewalk. "Let's just get away from the hospital."

Isaac did not resist. "The nurses advised that Dr. Rush was most annoyed that you were not in the ward earlier today. They reported that he had planned a treatment for you this afternoon."

Brock shuddered and looked over his shoulder as he picked up the pace. "I was afraid of that when those two guys showed up. Nobody is going to drill holes in my head without a fight."

"But how were you able to overcome the orderlies?"

"You've probably never heard of Taekwondo."

"I beg your pardon."

"Later. More importantly, where can we go for now?"

Isaac did not immediately respond but led Brock south. A block further on the intern said, "Brock, I conjecture that your hallucinations are a result of head trauma. Nevertheless, that fails to explain your odd presence in the hospital, your unusual speech, your combat skills, the technique used with the choking boy and the distinctive image on your shoulder." He paused then smiled, "Inexplicably, your presence intrigues me."

Brock listened closely, uncertain about where the conversation was going.

Isaac continued, "It is my opinion that your behavior, despite your symptoms, does not indicate that you are insane as Dr. Rush might diagnose. Moreover, for some time I have doubted the benefit of the excessive bleedings prescribed by the doctor." He took a deep breath. "Rather than leave you to such treatments, we shall go to my older brother's house on Gaskill Street. Seth is an attorney whose counsel I hold in high regard. He's also an intelligent fellow who approaches issues with careful analysis."

"Thanks, Isaac, for helping me out. I know this is all weird as hell but I really don't have any other options."

A block further on Isaac said, "As your confidant, I believe I deserve to know how you were able to defend yourself with the two orderlies at the hospital."

"Okay. For eight years in Texas I practiced a method of self-defense called Taekwondo. It's a form of martial arts developed in a country called Korea more than two thousand years ago. Taekwondo concentrates on powerful kicks to disable an attacker or one's opponent. During the years I trained, I also entered competition with other students. I was able to earn a 4th degree black belt as a symbol of my skill level."

"How is it that I know not of this Tie-con-doe?"

"It's probably because you've never heard of Korea or much else from that part of the world. In the centuries from now the cultures of the earth will be shared globally. Taekwondo is just one example of what we've learned from these other countries in my time."

Isaac shook his head slightly. "Yours must be a violent world indeed."

Brock thought for a moment. "Unfortunately, there is much violence in the world. But that's nothing new. People have been killing each other throughout history. On the bright side, in the twenty-first century there's a lot known about saving lives and prolonging life. For a comparison, the life expectancy in the US is over eighty years in 2029, while it's probably only fifty years here in the 18th century. I believe life, in a lot of ways, is better in the future."

"I want to hear more about your fighting skills," Isaac said. "But Seth's home is near." He stopped and turned to face Brock. "Remember, you must never mention the tattoo or show it to anyone including my brother. You will surely be accused of witchcraft. The penalty could be death by hanging or worse."

Brock swallowed and nodded, his face ashen. The tattoo might be his ticket to convincing others to believe him, but it also might get him executed.

CHAPTER 8   Oct 13, Saturday

The two young men walked along with Brock still marveling at all he was seeing and smelling. The mix of wood smoke and waste, human and animal, still disgusted him. But the annoyance was fading. The brick houses, so close to the brick walks, continued to surprise him. After eight or nine blocks they stopped at a brick house much like many they had passed, wider than Mr. Jamison's but only two stories. Isaac knocked.

A black, middle-age woman, answered the door. "Why, Mr. Isaac. It be ages since you come by." She leaned to the side and eyed Brock on the step outside, her smile fading.

"Afternoon, Flora." Isaac gestured toward his companion. "This is my friend, Brock. May we come in?"

Flora backed up to let them enter. "Of course, Mr. Isaac. Miss Margaret in the parlor with baby Christopher. She be right happy to see you."

"How you doin'?" Brock said to Flora after he closed the door. The woman nodded with only a slight smile.

Isaac and Brock followed Flora as she turned off the hall to the front room of the house. Brock could see the kitchen beyond through a doorway from the parlor and another room further to the rear. The furnishings appeared to be a step lower in quality than at Mr. Jamison's house although it was hard for Brock to make an accurate distinction. What he did notice was that everything was dusted and orderly. He assumed that could be attributed to Flora's efforts. It surprised him that Isaac's brother could afford a maid despite being a lawyer.

On the far side of the parlor a woman, in her twenties, sat in a rocker cradling an infant. She smiled as she recognized her brother-in-law but held the side of a finger to her lips. "Hello, Isaac. Come sit," she said in a whisper. She pointed to a straight-back chair near her. Looking at Brock, she said, "Who is this with you?"

"This is a new acquaintance, Brock Sinclair," Isaac said, also in hushed tones. He turned to Brock and gestured toward the woman. "Brock, please meet Margaret, my brother's wife. That's Christopher she holds. Her son, Lucas, must be down for a nap. He's four."

"Glad to meet you, Margaret," Brock mouthed.

Isaac sat on the edge of the chair near Margaret and leaned toward her. "We do not want to wake the boy. In truth we've come to speak with Seth."

Margaret frowned. "Have you forgotten what day it is? Seth meets with other members of the Library Company at Carpenter's Hall every Saturday afternoon to peruse the books. But I suspect the debates among the members entice him more than any of the bound volumes on the shelves."

Isaac sighed, looked at Brock then back at Margaret. "I did forget. When shall he return?"

"Perhaps six, certainly before supper."

Isaac looked at his watch, then stood. "We'll walk toward Carpenter's Hall in hopes of intercepting him during his return."

"Urgent your matter must be," Margaret said, raising her eyebrows.

"Both Brock and I are indeed eager to speak with Seth," Isaac said nodding to his sister-in-law. "Good day to you."

When Isaac and Brock approached Carpenter's Hall, Seth was outside on the steps talking to another man in the twilight. Seeing Isaac, Seth concluded his conversation and hurried to his brother. "Little brother, what good fortune to see you." The two men did not embrace but shook hands vigorously and each clasped his left hand on the other's right forearm. It was evident they were close. They broke apart with Seth saying, "And who might this strapping fellow be?"

"Seth, let me introduce Brock Sinclair, a new friend. Brock, this is my dear brother, Seth." The two men shook hands firmly.

"Gentlemen, it will be supper soon," Seth said. "Please come along and join Margaret and me for some refreshment and evening repast."

"Seth, we were just at your house," Isaac said. "And Christopher had just gone to nap. Are you quite certain we would not be intruding?"

"Banish the thought, brother. Flora always prepares more than we could ever eat." He winked at his brother. "Just yesterday I procured some of Mr. Schmidt's finest ale from The Hitching Post Tavern. It would be my honor to share it with you and your new friend."

CHAPTER 9   Oct 13, Saturday

Seth had been correct on two accounts. Flora's supper was ample, simple but delicious. Brock thoroughly enjoyed the sliced meat, some cheese, bread, and cooked apples. And the ale was strong and good. Brock felt sated for the first time since waking up in the hospital.

After the meal Margaret carried the baby with Flora towing Lucas from the kitchen to the upstairs. While the men still sat at the table, Isaac took the opportunity to approach Seth about Brock's situation. He talked quietly, explaining about Brock being found in the hospital with a contusion on his head. He explained, "It appears the injury has erased Brock's memory, at least for now."

Seth nodded sympathetically at Brock.

"What is peculiar," Isaac said glancing at Brock then back to his brother, "is that in place of his memory are images of his life somewhere else and at a different time."

Seth sat up straight. "I see," he said without conviction.

Silence and tension surrounded the table. Brock fingered his mug in silence. On the walk over, Isaac had encouraged Brock to let him do the talking since he knew how best to manage his brother's moods. Brock was to join in only if Isaac asked him.

At last Seth clasped his hands in the edge of the table and looked at Brock. "So, you remember nothing from your past?"

Brock looked to Isaac than at Seth. He spoke clearly but in a soft voice. "Prior to being in your local hospital, I have not been in Philadelphia for at least five years. But I have never lived in this year or any year prior to now."

Seth rubbed his thumbs together as he blinked several times.

Brock continued, "What I do remember is a detailed life from childhood to my current age in a state called Texas." He paused. "And where the current year is 2029."

Seth stood up abruptly and rubbed his hands along the side of his head to the base of his short ponytail. He stared at Isaac with narrowed eyes. "Brother, I must insist that you take this man from my house. I also recommend that you return him to the hospital where he can get proper care. God in Heaven knows he's in need of it."

Isaac stood to face his brother. "Seth, I ask that you give my judgement its due. I have spent many hours with Brock today and have gotten to know him quite well. As a physician I feel strongly that this man is no threat to others or to himself. Was I skeptical at the outset? I can report a resounding yes. Am I still confused as to his origin? Again, a resolute yes." Isaac gestured toward Brock. "But I trust that this young man truly believes he is not from this place…or from this time."

Seth stood with his hands in his pockets.

Isaac pleaded, "Please sit and listen to what I have learned and why I resist turning Brock over to Dr. Rush."

Slowly, Seth sat but did not pull his chair up to the table.

Over the next several minutes Isaac explained that Brock knew about Dr. Rush's proclivities that only doctors working with him would know and that he claimed to have gained this knowledge from books printed in future years. He spoke of the short, yet accurate, hair style Brock wore. He pointed out that

Brock's clear thoughts and speech were unlike a person with mental problems. Seth was attentive but not necessarily convinced.

Finally, Isaac said, "Seth, earlier today in a tavern Brock executed a unique procedure to clear the throat of a boy who may have choked to death had he not intervened. It is not something in any of our medical texts and not a known procedure. Brock says it was developed in the twentieth century by a man named Heimlich. If this is true, how do you explain that Brock has such knowledge?"

Seth studied Brock closely. At last he narrowed his eyes and said, "If you have lived in the year 2029, you should have knowledge to substantiate such. Do you possess such knowledge?"

Brock looked at Isaac for support then back to Seth. "Much has transpired in the U.S. and globally from the 18th century to the 21st century: technology, wars, political change, social changes, space exploration, transportation, communication, and medicine." Brock nodded toward Isaac. "I could go on and on. But my knowledge of such wouldn't convince you that what I say is the truth. It's the same problem you would have if you visited 15th century London and tried to convince the English that you were from the 18th century."

Seth snorted softly and grinned. "Of course, I would display our advanced weapons. Our improved tools. Our—"

Brock interrupted. "But if you arrived in London naked with nothing else? Then, how would you convince them?"

"I would…" Seth looked at the ceiling, deep in thought, as he settled back into his chair. "I would need to give such a preposterous supposition considerable analysis before I could respond." He paused then sneered. "All right. Expound on the judiciary in this Texas."

Brock clasped his hands in front of him on the table. "The US Constitution established the three branches of the federal government including the judicial branch. That remains in place today…I mean in the 21st century. There are state courts, including the ones in Texas, and federal courts with appeal systems and supreme courts in both."

Seth winked at Isaac before looking at Brock. "I see. What are some of the major decisions of this federal Supreme Court?"

Brock blew out a breath. "I'm not a lawyer and certainly not an authority on the courts." Brock ran his fingers through his hair, giving him time to think. He could only recall a limited number of cases but needed to pick one or two that Seth might believe. "A few rulings that come to mind include the decision that states cannot segregate schools because of race. Another one is that if someone is charged with a crime, they have the right to an attorney even if they can't afford one. Also, abortions were legalized in another ruling." He paused. "One more I can think of said that the police must advise anyone who is arrested of their rights to have an attorney present when they're questioned."

Seth's eyes widened. "You suggest that Negroes attend schools with the white boys?"

"Well, yeah. And not just boys. Girls, both black and white, attend the same schools too."

Seth shook his head slowly. "And, the populace supported these decisions?"

"Bear in mind this occurred years before my time. In school we learned about opposition in the South to school desegregation. But it's not been an issue since I was born."

"Inconceivable," Seth said, looking at his brother. He turned back to Brock, biting his cheek. "Tell us more about your Texas."

Both brothers listened to Brock's tales of life in 2029, although Seth's facial expressions and body language clearly showed his skepticism.

At the reference to air travel Seth shook his head emphatically. "If God had wanted man to fly, He would have given us wings."

Brock controlled his temper. "Seth, man has learned how to build ships to travel on water and wagons to move over land. Why is it so unbelievable that in years to come he could not figure out how to travel through the air?" Seth tightened his lips and crossed his arms but did not respond.

"Please continue, Brock," Isaac said from the edge of his chair. "Earlier today in the inn you spoke of the use of electricity and something called 'global communication'. I would like to hear more."

Brock gave Seth a short look. "You're probably aware of experiments with electricity by Ben Franklin." He looked at both men as they nodded slightly. "Well, in fifty or sixty years scientists will build glass bulbs with very thin metal wires running through them. When they apply electrical current to the wires, they glow brightly. Thus, the electric light was invented. Electricity generating plants were built, powered by rushing water or coal to provide power to drive electric motors on machinery rather than using water, wind, or horses. The…"

Brock stopped. "Look, Isaac. The technology that has been developed to use electricity is very complex. That includes numerous types of communication including speaking to someone in another country. I can assure you it exists but it will be difficult for you to believe given the science of the day."

But both brothers displayed tiny grins, Isaac's supportive, Seth's unclear.

Over the next few hours Brock fielded the brothers' questions. They appeared both amused and amazed. His prompt responses were meant to lend credibility to his statements.

At one point Seth opened his watch and declared, "Gentlemen, I must retire. Daybreak and worship will soon be upon us." He extended no invitation for either Isaac or Brock to sleep there but instead moved toward the door to see them out.

"Good night, brother," Isaac said in a tired voice as he passed Seth on the way out.

Seth held the door and extended his hand. "Brock, I have enjoyed this evening's conversation. You are indeed an entertaining fellow. I wish you well."

Brock's polite smile vanished; Seth's comment had disappointed and offended him. Yet, as he broke the handshake, his only reply was, "Good night."

On the street outside Seth's house Isaac said, "Brock, I assume you have nowhere to sleep tonight."

Brock nodded. "Yeah, I'm not sure what I'll do."

"Come along. We shall both sleep at my parent's house. I was granted permission by the administrator to be away from the hospital tonight and tomorrow. But I'll have to repay my fellow interns over the weeks to come."

"Thanks, man. I'll be okay on the sofa. Anywhere to get out of the cold."

On the walk toward Isaac's house both Isaac and Brock kept their thoughts to themselves. The barely-lit streets and the lack of other people at this late hour made the walk seem longer than Brock anticipated.

A block further on Brock addressed the subject that had bothered him since leaving Seth's. "I don't think your brother believes I'm telling the truth. He said I was 'entertaining'."

Isaac did not respond immediately. Later he said, "Seth is a cautious, practical man. His faith is strong but he depends on facts and common sense to guide his decisions." He paused while they continued walking. "You must agree that your situation and your tales of the future are extraordinary. Seth can be quite the skeptic. Be not offended by his doubt."

Isaac, with Brock close behind in the darkness, moved silently through the Jamison family home and up the spiral stairs to the third floor. In a bedroom two small beds were positioned along opposite walls. In the shadows the two young boys in one of the beds, cuddled against the cold.

Quietly, Isaac removed his clothes. Brock spoke softly, "Where am I going to sleep?" The fog of his breath confirmed the room's chill.

"You will share my bed, of course," Isaac whispered matter-of-factly.

Brock's eyes, already open wide to maneuver in the dark, opened even wider. He looked again at the small boys spooning in the other bed. "Ah...No, I don't think I can do that." He nodded toward the empty space between the beds. "I'll be okay here on the floor."

Isaac shrugged. "You have strange ways, friend. But suit yourself." He then crawled into the empty bed.

Still fully dressed, Brock settled onto the woolen rug between the beds. Moving to one side, he flipped the other part of the dusty rug over himself. The hard floor and the cold predicted a long night. But he was inside and not out on the street. What would happen to him the next day? His mom and dad, where were they? And what did they think had happened to him? He sighed. Would he ever see them again?

CHAPTER 10 Oct 14, Sunday

It had been a long, restless night. Brock's hips ached from the hard floor and the dust from his rug blanket irritated his sinuses. No light shone through the small window when noises occurred downstairs. Apparently, the Jamison's day had started. The possibility of a warm fire, hot coffee, and a big breakfast with steak and eggs and maybe some pancakes had Brock totally awake in seconds.

Soon the door to the room opened and Mrs. Jamison, holding a single candle, stepped in almost like a drill sergeant in the movies. "It is the Lord's day; rise and shine. We mustn't be late for worship."

At her orders, Brock struggled to a sitting position. "Morning, Mrs. Jamison."

"Gracious!" she shouted in the gloom, stepping back. "Who might you be?"

"I'm Brock Sinclair, Isaac's friend from the hospital. He said I could sleep here last night."

"Then why are you on the floor?"

"I...ah...I'm used to sleeping on hard surfaces. I rest better. Besides, Isaac has more room in his bed this way."

Mrs. Jamison looked at Isaac resting on his elbows in his bed and thrust a hand into her apron pocket. "Isaac, you best get your brothers up and dressed for services. Breakfast will be ready soon." She turned and left the room.

To Brock's disappointment breakfast consisted only of bowls of bland corn meal mush and milk with cream floating in it. The Jamisons, however, ate with gusto and little conversation other than Mr. Jamison's inquiry as to where Isaac and Brock had been the previous evening.

Isaac said they had visited with Seth and lost track of time as they talked.

Brock felt he was in the way as the family scurried about getting ready to leave for morning worship services. Mr. Jamison insisted that Brock join them, all members of St. Joseph's Catholic Church, for Mass.

Without a religious upbringing, Brock's experience with church was limited to a couple of funerals and a wedding in Protestant churches in Texas. But, rather than appear impolite, he accepted the invitation to go along with the family.

St. Joseph's was hidden among other buildings off a small alleyway, prompting Brock to wonder why the church builders had chosen this obscure location. Inside, the church's layout reminded him of Philadelphia's Christ Church he had visited as a teen but with smaller dimensions. And the church was cold; if a heat source existed, he didn't see or feel it. The worshipers, fifty at most, wisely had their coats on as the Jamison family marched to the sixth-row pew, left side.

Soon after the Jamisons and Brock were seated, a robed priest entered following a teenage boy, also robed, carrying an ornate cross on a tall staff. An unseen organ provided somber accompaniment to their procession to the slightly elevated pulpit.

With a flourish the middle-aged priest began a series of songs and prayers, some prompting the congregation to respond. Unfortunately, the songs and prayers were in Latin so Brock had no idea what was being said. Random kneeling by those in the congregation further alienated Brock from the service. The confusing rituals continued until at last the priest began his sermon. To Brock's relief it was in English.

Rev. Molineux, according to the sign inside the entry door, announced that his message would focus on forgiveness. At first, Brock tuned out the priest, catching only bits of his message.

One aspect of the sermon caught his attention, however. The priest had said that holding onto hate only hurts the hater. "Forgiving, as Jesus taught" he said, "allows the hater to release those emotions that can otherwise contribute to his own unhappiness."

Brock had always believed that getting even was the best way to settle a score. It made you feel better and punished the other guy so he would have second thoughts about doing it again. In this sacred setting, however, he considered the potential wisdom of the priest's words.

Finally, the priest said, "Ite, missa est" and everybody stood. The service was over and all the congregants lined up to file out of the small church, each eager or obligated to shake hands with the priest at the door. Brock and Isaac were in line with the Jamison family as they made their way to the exit.

Brock had paid attention to Amelia on the walk over to the church. She cleaned up pretty good compared to lunch the previous day. Her plain dress hugged her figure nicely except for the full skirt. Shiny hair flowed down her back from a simple bonnet. In the line to greet the priest she turned around and glanced in Brock's direction. He caught her look but she turned back rather than allow eye contact.

Outside the church the entire Jamison family, including Seth, Margaret and Lucas, gathered around the infant Christopher, making silly noises at the child and watching his smiling reaction. Before the two households went their separate ways,

Mrs. Jamison asked Brock if he had enjoyed the worship and what plans he had for his stay in Philadelphia.

Caught off guard, Brock, nevertheless, recovered. "Ma'am, I've read about Christ Church and Independence Hall where the Constitution was signed by Washington, Franklin, and others. I'd like to visit both places if Isaac would serve as my guide."

Mr. Jamison frowned. "Christ Church is only blocks away. However, the Convention met in the State House. I know not of Independence Hall."

"My bad," Brock said realizing his oversight. "I meant the State House. I apologize for my error." He looked down at the ground. "My memory is still not what it was." Mrs. Jamison's maternal smile reassured him.

Mr. Jamison opened his arms to corral his family. "Come along, Edith, children. We should be getting home to dinner."

"Father, I should like to accompany Isaac as he escorts his friend about the city," Amelia said timidly.

Mr. Jamison stared at his daughter, surprise in his face as he looked toward Brock and Isaac. His expression was not one of approval. His wife touched his forearm gently and they exchanged a brief look. At last Mr. Jamison looked at Amelia with raised brows. "As long as Isaac accompanies you back to our home, I will allow you to go along." The Jamison family then moved off while a smiling Amelia kept her eyes on the bricks of the walk.

CHAPTER 11   Oct 14, Sunday

Brock felt awkward walking side-by-side with Isaac while Amelia followed a step behind her brother. He assumed it was a social order thing and Amelia didn't seem offended. She even smiled whenever he looked over his shoulder at her.

Christ Church was in exactly the same place as when Brock had visited Philadelphia with his mom and dad while on vacation. All the other buildings and the streets were different, of course. People filtering out of the church must have been stragglers from the recently-ended worship service. Their exit at the front of the sanctuary was different from the side door entrance/exit at the rear of the church, with its gift shop, that he and his parents had used. Inside things looked similar except more decorative, more lavish than before, actually centuries later. Burning candles were everywhere. The inscriptions on the burial slabs in the center aisle of the church were less worn than they would be centuries from now. Their presence comforted him. *If I can remember details like this, it's has to mean that I'm not insane. It also means that I really am in an earlier century.*

Isaac stood beside Brock. "Your posture suggests comfort with this holy place. Am I correct?"

Brock looked at his new friend than glanced to his right, noticing that Amelia was in the other aisle. He spoke softly, "I *have* been here. I was here with my family five years ago. I mean when I was fourteen. Some things were different then like electric lights but the church was much the same." Brock smiled. "Would you believe that services are still being held in this same sanctuary more than two hundred years from now?" He grabbed Isaac's arm and pointed. "About here is where Ben Franklin supposedly had his pew in the church. When I visited here with my family, there was a brass plaque indicating that it was the Franklin family pew. Tourists who visit the church all want to get to the pew to have their pictures taken."

Isaac stared at Brock for several seconds. "Confusion from your comments aside, my acceptance of your testimonials is fragile. As a student of science, I find it most difficult to reconcile your statements with mankind's limitations. Friend, I do not wish to offend, but express my honesty, I must."

Brock's enthusiasm for the church's familiarity faded as Isaac's words slapped him back to the present, the 18th century present. "I understand the skepticism, Isaac. But it's a huge downer after finding a place I could relate to my real life."

Isaac put his hand on Brock's shoulder and presented a stiff smile to his friend.

On the walk toward the State House Brock tired of Amelia trailing behind like a pull toy. He turned slightly and gently grabbed her upper arm. He guided her to a position between Isaac and himself. "I'm not comfortable with you walking behind, being left out of the conversation."

Amelia looked at her brother with questioning eyes. Isaac frowned slightly but nodded his acceptance of her new position. Amelia's face glowed at the change.

"Tell me, Amelia, do you go to school?" Brock said as they walked along.

Again Amelia looked to her brother, who nodded. "I attended adventure school last year to learn of music, dancing and needlework. But I wish to attend The Young Ladies Academy if father will permit it."

With Brock facing him, Isaac provided an explanation. "It is a school for girls that began this year with a curriculum supposedly similar to that provided in a boys' school." Isaac pursed his lips. "Dr. Rush is the founder. He *is* involved in many worthwhile pursuits."

Brock paused before turning the conversation back toward Amelia. "Have you studied reading, writing, and math?"

The girl continued to look straight ahead as they walked. She spoke as if she was self-conscious, "Mother and Isaac taught me my letters and I can write them." Then, with excitement in her voice she turned her head toward Brock. "But I very much want to learn more. Also, arithmetic."

To Brock, Amelia looked like she might be sixteen or seventeen. But she talked and acted even younger. Regardless, she was cute for a girl of the time.

At the State House no Independence Mall extended north. Much would change around the building in the next two hundred years. Brock and his companions walked around the State House to the front side but could not enter. Isaac speculated that, it being Sunday, representatives and government staff were with their families and the building locked to discourage miscreants.

The statue of Commodore Barry that would stand on a pedestal on this side of Independence Hall had not yet been erected. If I can remember something from the 21st century that does not exist now, does that also mean I have somehow actually traveled back in time? Or, is that just a detail of the illusion?

######

After dropping Amelia off at the Jamison family home, Isaac offered to treat Brock to a tankard of ale and maybe share a trencher at a nearby tavern. Brock readily accepted.

The innkeeper placed their mugs on the table and set an oblong wooden container half filled with what looked like stew and several slices of coarse bread in the middle of their small table. Isaac promptly broke off a chunk of the bread and plowed it into the stew on its way to his mouth. Startled at the serving technique, Brock, nevertheless, followed suit. In short order they cleaned the trencher and finished the bread.

Over the remainder of their ale Isaac broached the subject of Brock's future. "Friend, you apparently remain confused about your past. Yet, otherwise, you seem quite rational. Have you given thought to your intentions for the coming week? Will you seek to return to your Huntsville or Texas? Or, will you settle in Philadelphia?" When Brock didn't respond, he continued, "Tomorrow I must return to my duties at the hospital. And I am delinquent in my studies with examinations later this week. My available time for further discourse will be limited indeed."

Brock remained quiet. He studied his weak, flat ale then looked around the dark tavern as he considered his situation, fear and loneliness primary in his thoughts. But being home in Texas with his parents was the goal that he maintained. To think about other priorities was tantamount to giving up on that goal.

"Look, Isaac. I've got to figure out how I got here and how to get back. My life's in modern-day Texas, not here. At some point in the future this period of time will be referred to as the good old days. But I'll take the 21st century with all its problems over this anytime."

"What is so disappointing about the Philadelphia that I know?"

Brock hesitated, grinned, then put on a somber face. "I don't want to insult your city or your quality of life. But I miss my smart phone, hot showers, comfortable clothes, cold beer, music…not to mention better sanitation."

The confusion and disappointment on Isaac's face was plain.

"It's not anybody's fault. And I'm sure you're proud of America winning independence from England as well as the numerous other accomplishments of the day." He paused. "It's just that, like I said before, technology will advance so much in the next two hundred years that life then is really not comparable to now."

Isaac stared at Brock, expressionless for several seconds, then grinned. "What are 'hot showers'?"

Brock rolled his head back and sighed. Then smiling, he leveled his gaze at Isaac. "You get into this small enclosure maybe four by four feet covered with tile on the floor and walls. A spray of hot water comes out of a pipe at head level and hits you in the head and face. You then move around so the spray hits your body front and back. Using a body wash you scrub your hair and body, then rinse. Oh, I forgot. The water that runs off your body goes down a drain in the middle of the shower floor to a sewer system. When you're done, you feel clean and refreshed. And you smell a lot better."

"Only one person benefits from the water for washing?" Isaac asked with a frown.

"Yeah, you normally shower alone." Brock grinned. "Unless your girlfriend joins you in the shower. But that's another story."

Isaac's eyes widened then twinkled.

Brock continued, "The amount of water one uses in a shower is far less than it takes to fill a tub for a bath. So several people can take reasonable showers and not use any more water than used sharing the bathwater like you do now."

Isaac nodded while squinting slightly. "I think I can envision the 'hot shower'. It sounds pleasant."

Brock took a drink of his ale, set down his mug and straightened in his chair. "As I said, I want to get back to Texas but until then I can't just curl up in a ball and wait for a time warp or worm hole to appear. That's not how I was raised. I've got to eat and I don't have any money." He pulled at the front of the borrowed shirt and grinned. "I need some clothes that fit. And I need a place to stay. I can't mooch off your family forever. How do I go about finding some kind of work?"

Isaac smiled. "Perhaps my father could use some help in his store. Do you have experience as a merchant?"

"No, but how hard can it be? Hell, I'll do anything to make a few dollars," Brock said while wondering what an 18th century store in Philadelphia was like.

Isaac's eyebrows rose. "I can assure you that profanity will not be welcomed by my father's customers, nor him. And you will undoubtedly work for far less than a dollar."

"Okay. I'll watch my language." Brock's head hung slightly then raised. "Actually, thanks. I've still got a bunch to learn about here and now."

On the walk to the Jamison home Isaac indicated he would approach his father privately about the possibility of Brock working in his store. Accordingly, when they arrived, Isaac and his father stepped out the back door into the small rear yard. Brock's chest tightened as he awaited the outcome of the discussion. He felt that this potential job might be a small step forward. If it fell through, he'd be back at square one. It surprised him how quickly he had grasped at this tiny lifeline with no idea where it would lead.

Isaac and Mr. Jamison were outside at least twenty minutes. This had to be a bad sign with Isaac trying to convince his father and then both of them deciding how to say "no." When the two men returned, Mr. Jamison led the way across the kitchen to where Brock waited.

"Young man," Mr. Jamison started. "My son has confidence in your sanity and honesty. And although I respect his judgement, I have not had the opportunity to make my own assessment of your character."

Brock prepared for the rejection before Mr. Jamison could even finish his statement.

"Nevertheless, I am currently in need of a strong back to help in my store. Inventory needs to be put away and customers' wagons need to be loaded. I will pay you a fair wage if you give me a fair day's work. And you are welcome to sleep in the room with the boys and sit at our table for one month until you get on your feet. Is that agreeable?"

"Yes, sir!" Brock said without hesitation. He stepped around the table to shake Mr. Jamison's hand. "I'll work hard for you, sir. And thank you." He looked at Isaac. "And thank you."

CHAPTER 12   Oct 15, Monday

The Jamison household, including Brock, rose before dawn, all except the young boys. After the same bland breakfast as the previous day, Mr. Jamison and Brock walked together toward the man's store on Walnut Street. The cool, crisp air of the morning initially chilled Brock but the brisk walking pace soon warmed him. Mr. Jamison spoke to several men they passed along the way but said little to Brock, who found the lack of conversation uncomfortable. In Texas he and his friends were always BS'ing about something. But here he was the new hand; he'd let his boss take the lead on the chit chat.

Unlocking the door of the store, Mr. Jamison said, "Your first duty is to build a fire. Then, I want the entire store swept. The broom is inside the back door."

The cast iron stove sat in the middle of the store, elevated on a single course of bricks inside a wooden frame. A round metal pipe extended from the stove straight up through the roof. Brock could see spots of daylight around the pipe and wondered if water leaked in when it rained.

Growing up in the suburbs, Brock's fire-making skills were limited to starting the gas grill on the deck at home by pushing a button or drenching charcoal briquettes with liquid starter in a state park grill before lighting them with a match. He had watched a few survivor shows on TV where guys used dried grass and twigs to start a fire using primitive techniques. This was different. He needed something like paper and small kindling to get a fire started but he saw only a pile of split logs on the floor beside the stove.

Anyone watching Brock fumble around the stove would have recognized the novice. Mr. Jamison watched only seconds before saying, "Do you not build fires at your home?" He didn't wait for an answer. "I'll show you only once."

Mr. Jamison lifted a cast iron poker from the floor behind the stove. He opened the stove and used the poker to stir the ashes from a previous fire causing them to drop through the grate to the level below. He then pulled a small sheet of newsprint from a covered wooden box several feet from the stove and crumbled it before placing it in the stove's firebox. He carefully added half dozen small sticks of kindling from the wooden box to the crumpled paper. Finally, he added three of the smaller pieces of split wood to the top of the pile.

After opening the damper all the way, Mr. Jamison took an odd, foot-long stick from a closed metal container also in the wooden box. "These parlor matches are costly. Do not waste them." He struck the match on the brick hearth and gently touched it to the paper. The fire started slowly but grew quickly and after only a couple of minutes Mr. Jamison said, "Once the split wood is burning, close the damper halfway and add two larger pieces of firewood. That should be warmth enough for today and will spare the wood. Keep your eye on the fire throughout the morning and keep it stoked if the chill lingers. We'll decide if we need the fire after dinner."

"Yes, sir," was all that Brock could say, embarrassed but confident he could build a fire tomorrow.

"And keep the kindling box filled from the wood pile in the shed out back."

Brock nodded and said, "Yes, sir," before moving to the back of the store to start his next task. He found the crude broom with its thick handle in the back near two wooden coffins standing on their ends. It shocked him that such morbid items would be on display along with food and tools.

The only sweeping Brock had ever done was pushing a five-foot dust mop on the basketball court at his high school as part of detention. The wooden floor of the store with its rough boards and the cracks between them presented more of a challenge.

But Brock was determined to make a good impression on Mr. Jamison after the fire fiasco. He stabbed the broom into the corners and repeatedly brushed it along the base of the walls and counter bottoms to get at the stubborn dirt and spider webs. An accumulation of broom straws among his growing pile of dirt warned that a new broom could be needed by the time he finished. And his efforts were producing quite a cloud of dust which he chose to ignore.

From the front of the store Mr. Jamison coughed and yelled, "Blazes, boy! Do you intend to suffocate me with dust?"

Brock could see the frown on his boss at the front counter. "No, sir. I'm just trying to be thorough."

"Did you spread sawdust from the keg beside the broom?"

Brock's blank look was his only answer. Mr. Jamison looked toward the ceiling in frustration. "Dampen some sawdust and spread it around before you continue sweeping. And sweep to *move* the dirt not pummel it." Mr. Jamison turned back to his work still coughing. "And open the back door to clear the air."

Brock felt like a complete screw up. He jerked the back door open harder than he intended where it banged against a pile of sacks. Shit, I don't belong here. Strange ways, strange tools, odd way to talk, no electronics...I'm not ready for this.

The dust was only one cause of Brock's tears. He sniffed and was surprised that he did not hide his emotions from his boss.

The sawdust keg's contents included almost as much dirt and dried weeds as it did sawdust. He filled the metal cup in the keg and went outside looking for water. In an open wooden barrel he found a few feet of stagnant water with insects floating on the surface. He pushed back the floating bugs with the cup, then allowed a small amount of the foul-smelling water to wet the sawdust mixture. With a stick he stirred the sawdust then added a bit more water.

Brock shuffled back inside and spread the sawdust mixture over a large area of the store. He then resumed his sweeping using gentle, more-precise strokes. Sweeping with the grain of the rough floor boards moved the dirt more effectively and the damp sawdust helped with the dust. He checked regularly if Mr. Jamison was watching.

In time, Brock found the sweeping therapeutic. He felt he was finally doing something at least half-right. And I'm helping earn my keep. Odd how that phrase came into my head. I must have read it somewhere when studying Ben Franklin. *Learn to sweep to earn your keep.* He grinned. If Franklin didn't write that, maybe he should have.

Brock looked in Mr. Jamison's direction once more. The merchant nodded once in return but did not smile. Maybe he wouldn't get fired before the end of the day after all.

Through a front window Brock saw a wagon pull up and a man in well-worn clothes jump down. "A good day to you, Mr. Fisher," the merchant said with enthusiasm to the man when he entered. "What can I do for you?"

"And a good day to you, Mr. Jamison," the man replied. He pulled a wrinkled piece of paper from his pocket. "I've a list of items I'll be needin'. We brung two sacks of potatoes and a bushel of apples, picked yestadee."

"Well, Jedidiah, let's look have a look at your list." Mr. Jamison took the scrap of paper and smoothed it out on the counter top with the flat of his hand. Using a fat, wooden pencil, he scribbled numbers beside each item on the paper then added them. After a moment he said, "Your potatoes are always respectable. Are your apples red and sweet?"

"To be sure. We was blessed with summer rains."

Mr. Jamison nodded then rubbed his chin for a long minute. "Jedidiah, I can let you have only one grubbing hoe and only one bushel of salt. The balance of your list is satisfactory."

The man studied the merchant, both men refusing to break eye contact. At last the customer said, "It's a hard bargain. But fair, I guess." The two men shook hands.

Mr. Jamison turned to Brock. "While I gather Mr. Fisher's items from the shelves, unload the potatoes and the apples from his wagon. Put them along the east wall there, away from the stove. Handle them careful, particularly the apples. I do not want them bruised." He pointed to the spot he referenced then looked down at the farmer's list. "Then load one of those ten-quart kettles by the door, two sacks of flour, and one bushel of salt."

"Yes, sir," Brock said, propping his broom against the wall. The farmer stared as Brock moved out to the wagon.

Outside a young boy, maybe eight-years-old, stood holding the reins and stroking the neck of one of the two horses hitched to the beat-up wagon. His ragged clothes and lack of shoes suggested that life outside Philadelphia was even harder than in the city. Brock nodded to the boy. "How ya doin?"

The boy only looked in Brock's direction.

Brock found the potatoes in rough, open-weave sacks and the apples in a basket without the wire handles like he had seen at the farmers' market when he was a kid tagging along with his mom. It would take three trips to move the produce inside.

Despite his size and strength, Brock struggled to get the potatoes off the wagon. He gathered the loose material at the open end of the sack with one hand but then had to lift most of the weight up onto his shoulder with his free hand. There were no legible markings on the sacks but he guessed the weight at a hundred pounds.

On his first trip back inside Brock found the cast iron kettle where Mr. Jamison had nodded. The pot was heavier than he expected but didn't test his strength on its way to the farmer's wagon. On his next trip inside Brock addressed the flour to be loaded. He approached the large pile of sacks where Mr. Jamison had pointed but no markings confirmed the sacks' contents. Because his back was to his boss and the farmer, Brock felt they were probably watching with critical eyes. What else could it be besides flour? He hefted a sack onto his shoulder and turned toward Mr. Jamison who was weighing out coffee beans. "Two of these sacks, sir?"

Mr. Jamison looked up, maybe a little annoyed, and nodded.

Brock felt the fabric of the flour sack as he carried it to the wagon. It was much softer and finer than the potato sacks. Those sacks were similar to the material on a tree root ball. The flour sack material, however, reminded him of the flannel shirts his grandpa had worn in winter.

Loading the assigned "bushel of salt" provided the greatest confusion. Brock couldn't envision a basket like for the apples used for salt. He looked around the store hoping for a clue. But no baskets existed other than those for sale hanging above the counter. After Mr. Jamison finished weighing out some nails on the ancient scale, Brock interrupted him a second time. "Where are the baskets of salt, Mr. Jamison?"

The merchant looked in Brock's direction then at his customer who stood patiently waiting for his purchases. He grimaced and said to Brock, "Don't you see the sacks yonder marked 'salt'?" He pointed to another pile of sacks across the store from the flour. "Load one of those. And be quick about it."

The farmer nodded toward Brock then looked at Mr. Jamison. "Greenhorn, uh?"

The store owner smirked then raised his eyebrows in reply. "Real green." Then he grinned. "But strong."

Brock moved to the sacks as directed. As he got closer, "SALT" was stamped in small, black letters on the sides of the coarse sacks. The texture of these sacks was closer to that of the potatoes than the flour and he remained puzzled why the salt didn't spill onto the floor through the weave. When he lifted the small sack by the end to sling it over his shoulder, its significant weight surprised him. On his shoulder, he could feel chunks poking him through the sack material. The salt was coarse, maybe even rock salt. Still the "bushel" designation remained confusing to him.

With the sacks and the kettle loaded, Brock helped the farmer carry his remaining items out of the store. The farmer mounted his wagon and took hold of the reins of his team. The boy jumped into the back of the wagon and sat down on the sacks Brock had loaded. "Have a good day," Brock said before the wagon moved.

The farmer turned to look, hesitated, then made a single, stern nod before slapping the reins on the rumps of the horses. The wagon moved forward slowly.

Brock raised his hand in a high-five salute to the young boy and the kid raised his hand but only part-way in response. He did not smile but maintained eye contact, his expression blank, until Brock turned to reenter the building.

The remainder of the day passed with more farmers' wagons to unload and load. And an assortment of women passed through the store looking at the bolts of cloth, pots & pans, or even the funky little hats that were for sale. Mr. Jamison had Brock rearranging inventory, dusting with a feather duster and more sweeping when he wasn't loading wagons. Would the day never end?

CHAPTER 13   Oct 15, Monday

At the end of the day, Brock's hands were sore from his hours with the broom and from handling of barrels, kegs, and sacks. And his feet hurt from the shoes. He had been on his feet all day except for the brief time he sat at the noon dinner table with the Jamison family. That meal had been awkward since Isaac didn't come home from the hospital, leaving Brock without a confidant. The minimal table conversation had only added to his unease.

As sunset approached, shadows in the store increased. Three clocks for sale on a high shelf all said approximately five o'clock when Mr. Jamison said, "Brock, bolt the back door; we'll close for the day."

On the walk to the Jamison home, Brock broke the silence, "Mr. Jamison, I want to thank you for the opportunity to work in your store. I know I've got a lot to learn. But I should pick it up fast. My dad always said I was a quick study." Brock chuckled and added, "But he also said I could be hard-headed."

"I recommend you focus on the former and resist the latter," Mr. Jamison said without breaking stride. "How is it that you seem to have gained so little knowledge about store goods?"

"Well, sir." Brock paused to formulate his response. "At home we do not have much storage space. So Mom buys flour, salt, and other groceries in much smaller quantities. And we live not far from a store so she can go there often. In truth I rarely go with her."

"And what is it that you do with your time?"

"I attend...attended university near home."

Mr. Jamison turned his head toward Brock and frowned. "I see. Yet your bearing does not suggest you come from wealth."

Confused, Brock said, "I guess my dad does okay financially. But I wouldn't say we're rich. Dad did put away some money for my college fund."

"Hmm. And what are your lessons?"

"If you mean 'what do I study,' then the answer is mechanical engineering."

"You desire to be a builder, do you?"

"Not exactly. Mechanical engineering deals with machinery but not necessarily building it. Actually it's a really tough major that takes a lot of time and study. I'm not sure I can hack it. Besides, I'd just like to hang for a while." For an instant Brock had forgotten the timeframe and cultural differences between Mr. Jamison and himself. His boss nodded slowly with Brock suspecting the man had not followed the conversation but didn't care enough to address his confusion.

A block farther on Mr. Jamison said, "Earlier, you referenced your father. What can you say of the man?"

Choosing his words carefully, he said, "My dad's a manager for an engineering company near our town."

"He works with machinery then?"

He considered how to respond to end this conversation. "Not exactly, sir. He and his fellow employees design manufacturing processes for other companies." Brock ended his comment in hopes of changing the subject. Fortunately, the explanation appeared to appease Mr. Jamison.

Closer to the Jamison home, Brock asked what had been bugging him all afternoon. "How is it that a bushel of salt is in a cloth sack?"

Mr. Jamison glanced at Brock before responding. "A bushel, fifty pounds, is the measure for the sale of salt. I purchase salt from the seacoast works in New Jersey. I'm told that the crystals are heaped initially into fine baskets, allowing for drainage. Once dried, the salt is shoveled into sacks that are less costly and easier to stack in a wagon. Still, a sack contains fifty pounds."

Brock smiled at this tidbit of salt packaging history.

Later, when Isaac came through the door of the house for the evening meal, relief spread over Brock. He wanted to share his experiences and observations of the day with his only friend. But Isaac dampened Brock's mood with his announcement that he had to return to the hospital after supper to work on his studies.

When Isaac had gone, Brock remained at the kitchen table after supper mulling his situation and dreading the long evening. Mr. Jamison had disappeared upstairs with the two young boys, with muffled thumps and distant laughter penetrating the floor above. He considered going for a walk but his aching feet begged for relief.

Mrs. Jamison sat in a rocker in the parlor knitting something with a light blue yarn. Apparently she had sensed Brock's boredom. She called to him from the other room.

When Brock entered the parlor, Mrs. Jamison pointed to a small shelf on the wall across from where she sat. "Brock, if you can read, we have books for you to while away the evening."

Brock brightened. "Yes, Ma'am. I'd really like something to read." He hesitated. "If it's not too much trouble."

"It is no trouble. Mr. Jamison is proud of his small library. Choose whatever you like." Amelia, who sat on a small, padded bench near her mother, looked up from the thread-button she was sewing onto a shirt.

Brock moved to the bookshelf and looked at the spines of a dozen, leather-bound volumes. Most did not display the title on their spines, causing him to pull each, one by one, from the shelf to study the covers or even open to the first page. Not much of a choice. One book had a very long title including the words "Robinson Crusoe." The author was Daniel Defoe. If this was the story he recognized, Brock didn't realize it had been written so long ago. "If it's okay, I'd like to read this *Robinson Crusoe*. I think I know some of the story but have never actually read the whole book."

Mrs. Jamison nodded her approval.

Back at the kitchen table, Brock moved closer to the oil lamp. The light was pathetic and the font in the Defoe novel was small and ornate. But he had something to read; he'd make the best of it.

Moments later, Amelia rose from her seat and whispered to her mother. Mrs. Jamison looked up at her daughter, hesitated then nodded to the girl.

Mrs. Jamison spoke to Brock from the other room. "Brock, would you be so good as to read aloud from the book to Amelia? She knows her letters but has not yet learned to read. And the *Robinson Crusoe* story is one of her favorites."

Brock felt awkward about reading aloud and to a cute teenager no less. But he was a guest. "Sure, Mrs. Jamison. I'd be happy to." He waved to the girl. "Come sit at the table, Amelia, so we don't disturb your mother."

Amelia moved quickly to the table, her eyes shining, and sat across from Brock on the opposite bench. He cleared his throat and began, "I WAS born in the year 1632, in the city of York, of a good family,…"

CHAPTER 14   Oct 16, Tuesday

The next morning Brock's shoulders and back were sore from lifting heavy, unbalanced merchandise at the store and another night sleeping on the floor. And his feet still hurt from the awful shoes. But he rose with the Jamison family and walked with his boss to open the store.

Brock started the fire in the store's stove without incident. Although Mr. Jamison didn't acknowledge this success, Brock felt it was a sign that the day would go smoother. His boss directed Brock to chop kindling out back as his first assignment for the day. When he had completed the task, Brock was to continue to dust the inventory.

As the morning progressed, Mr. Jamison interrupted Brock several times to carry sacks and kegs to customers' wagons. Brock didn't mind the distractions since the various personalities and manners of speech were becoming interesting. Mostly, he learned, however, that the working people of Philadelphia focused on making their purchases but were not above a little gossip, primarily with Mr. Jamison.

The women shoppers were another matter. Their dresses were bulky and mostly drab. But generally there was at least an attempt at fashion. Many wore little hats over hair pinned-up on the backs of their heads and thin cloth gloves with small purses hanging from their wrists. Jewelry, if there was any, was hidden by long sleeves and high collars.

The ages of the women varied from young women with a small child or two, to middle-age and older women, mostly alone. One very attractive woman in her early thirties, who Mr. Jamison greeted as Widow Hawkins, had been in the store the previous day but didn't buy anything. Today she purchased several items in tins and a small sack of coffee. Although her bundle of goods was small, the widow asked Mr. Jamison if someone could walk with her to her house to carry her purchases. Mr. Jamison, with an odd smirk, instructed Brock to assist.

As they walked to Mrs. Hawkins' house, Brock solidified his earlier assessment that she was a nice-looking lady. Not beautiful by 21st century standards but certainly no slouch either. Unremarkable facial features were eclipsed by flawless skin that suggested no need for makeup. Her dress accentuated her full breasts and small waist but hid her lower body in yards of material that blossomed from her hips to the ground. And perhaps most distinctive of all was her fragrance. Brock had grown accustomed to the odors of people who seldom bathed. But the widow's freshness delighted him as if she had just stepped out of a shower with lots of floral body wash. He breathed deeply of her scent as they walked.

After a block, she said, "My name is Kathrine. I believe you are new at Mr. Jamison's store. Are you a relative?"

Kathrine's sweet voice in concert with her appearance and her scent gave Brock tingles. Good tingles! "Ah... No, my name's Brock and I'm a friend of Isaac. His dad was willing to give me work at the store. Do you know Isaac?"

"Why yes, I've met Isaac on occasion. A doctor, if my memory serves."

"Yeah, he is. And though I only met him recently, he's one of the good ones."

After ten minutes of minor chit chat, Kathrine and Brock, toting her small purchases in one hand, arrived at her house. From the outside the house was smaller than the Jamison's but looked well maintained. They climbed the few steps and entered.

"Please place the items there," Kathrine said, pointing to a sturdy table in the kitchen area. "Excuse me for a moment," she said before disappearing into another room.

Brock scanned the house from where he stood. Everything was neat and in its place. How does a widow manage without the financial support of a husband in this place and time? Yet Kathrine dressed as well as any woman he had seen thus far and the house was adequately furnished.

As he contemplated Kathrine's circumstances, she reappeared from a back room. The hat was gone and her hair was now down and flowing about her face. She had removed the white gloves and the shawl that had been around her shoulders. He did not remember it from earlier but her dress was now unbuttoned about three inches down from the top in front. She moved toward Brock and stopped about two feet from him. With a pretty smile she said, "I very much appreciate you helping me with my purchases. They may not be heavy for someone as tall and strong as you. But I would have struggled over the distance."

Brock felt himself blush despite efforts to prevent it. "Not a problem, Kathrine. I'm happy to help…any time."

Kathrine stepped even closer and put her hands gently on Brock's chest, her eyes locked onto his. "Since I live alone, it's important that there is someone I can depend on when I need something. I do hope I will see you again...soon. You and your beautiful, white teeth." Her hands slide slowly down Brock's chest and stomach before breaking contact.

After several seconds Kathrine slowly closed her eyes, then with a gentle toss of her head that made her hair flare slightly, turned away from Brock, brushing against him with her backside. She then turned back to face him. "Thank you, again."

Brock didn't know whether to shit or go blind. Still blushing and now blinking, he cleared his throat. "Well, I better be getting back to the store. Mr. Jamison will wonder what happened to me." He moved to get around Kathrine without making body contact. "I'll see you again," he said as he moved outside.

When he reached the bottom of the steps to the sidewalk, Brock looked back. Kathrine was standing in the doorway straddling the edge of the half-open door and caressing it with her hands as she stared at him. She then slowly closed the door.

Brock's mind replayed what had happened in Kathrine's house again and again as he walked back to the store. Did she really make a move on him? And should he have taken her up on her "offer?" What if he had responded but had misread her signals? He could still smell her fragrance and feel her touch. And he would remember those eyes staring into his for a very long time.

When Brock entered the store, Mr. Jamison's grin suggested he may know more about Kathrine than he had let on. "You certainly took you time to deliver a few items barely a stone's throw from the store."

Brock's blush returned. "I ah...it's several blocks to Kathrine's house and she walks slow. I hurried back as quickly as I could."

"Oh! You and Widow Hawkins are on given-name basis, are you?" Mr. Jamison's grin had morphed into a broad smirk.

Brock looked down at his feet then up at his boss before moving to where he had left off his dusting. "She...she's a friendly person, sir." He glanced up at Mr. Jamison then back down. "But I should get back to work."

"Well, son, you are not the first young man to hear the siren song. Just remember that it spelled doom to the mariners who heeded its call."

CHAPTER 15   Oct 16, Tuesday

When Brock and Mr. Jamison arrived home at the end of the day, Isaac was there. Seeing his friend boosted Brock's spirits. It had been a long, but interesting, day and he wanted to share some of it with Isaac.

While Mr. Jamison tussled with the young boys and Mrs. Jamison and Amelia finished cooking the supper, Isaac and Brock talked quietly in the parlor. Isaac spoke first. "I needed a respite from my studies which the walk home and the coming meal with family should provide. However, I must return to the hospital after supper."

Brock's spirits sank from the news but recovered, thinking about the highlight of his day. "Do you know who Kathrine Hawkins, the widow, is?"

Isaac displayed a slight smile and nodded. "Oh yes, I've met The Widow Hawkins. Did she, by-chance, come into my father's store today?"

"What are you grinning about? Yeah, she came in today. What's her story?" Brock said, trying to disguise his interest.

"Her husband, a major in the Pennsylvania Second, was killed at the Brandywine. The gossip is that she trifles with men, especially young men, but rejects them if they respond to her advances. For your own good, you should avoid her charms."

Brock nodded and changed the subject. "Anything new with Dr. Rush at the hospital?"

"It bears reporting that the good doctor is inquiring into your whereabouts. It should not be a surprise if he learns of your employment at my father's store. What actions, if any, he may take are uncertain."

The news disturbed Brock. "I guess in the back of my mind I've been worried about Rush and his 'assistants'. But really, I focus on work at the store and try to figure a way to get home."

Isaac nodded, his lips pressed tight. "There has been no improvement in your memory then?"

Brock's eyes narrowed but he made no response.

With Isaac having returned to the hospital after supper, Brock resumed reading about Robinson Crusoe's adventures to the attentive Amelia. At the conclusion of Chapter 4 he closed the book and rubbed his burning eyes. The expressions used by the author in the 17th century novel caused him to stumble often as he read aloud. If Amelia had detected his hesitation on some of the words, she hadn't let on. Her bright eyes had stared at him the entire time.

Earlier, Mr. Jamison had descended the stairs and quietly entered the parlor without speaking. He nodded at Brock then seated himself on the other side of the lamp near his wife and began reading a thick book.

Brock looked up but did not move from the bench when someone knocked hard on the front door. Mr. Jamison rose from his chair and went to answer.

A young boy, breathless and nervous, announced from the entry door, "Mr. Jamison, come quick! Isaac's been hurt at the hospital."

"What happened, son?" Mr. Jamison said, his voice shaking.

"I do not know, sir. Something about one of Dr. Rush's patients. Please hurry."

Mr. Jamison stepped back into the room and lifted his coat from its peg. "Edith, I will return as soon as I know anything." He looked at Brock, now standing. "Come, Brock. Perhaps you can help."

Brock hurried to follow. "Yes, sir."

Both Mr. Jamison and Brock walked at a hectic pace, the young boy jogging to stay ahead. Closer to the hospital, Brock's unease about Dr. Rush and his goons surfaced. But his concern for his new friend overshadowed his apprehension and never let his pace slow.

The young boy led the men up the steps to the hospital and in the front door before disappearing through a side door down the hall. An elderly man with a cane grasped Mr. Jamison by the arm. "Matthew, it's Isaac. He's taken a great blow."

Mr. Jamison swiveled his head in a futile attempt to locate his son. He jerked his arm away from the man. "Where is my son?" he shouted. "Where is he?"

The old man pointed his cane down the hall to the ward on the left. "Dr. Rush was still in the hospital when this happened. He's attending to Isaac even now."

Brock followed Mr. Jamison as he raced down the hall to the ward. In the dim light two men and a nurse were gathered around a bed in the middle of the ward. Patients in the other beds were straining to see what was happening.

Mr. Jamison moved toward the quiet group at the bed but then slowed his steps as if he feared what he would find.

As he and Brock approached, Dr. Rush looked up and immediately turned in their direction. "Mathew, I regret this unfortunate situation. One of our patients attacked Isaac. Before he could be restrained, he struck several blows with a stool, at least one to the head." Dr. Rush looked down at the floor and lowered his voice. "There was nothing I could do." He met Mr. Jamison's eyes and through tight lips said, "You have my sincere condolences." Rush then looked at Brock with narrowing eyes.

Mr. Jamison pushed the doctor aside and moved to the foot of the bed. Brock followed but remained a half step behind, dreading to look and feeling like an outsider.

Isaac lay on his back, the left side of his head badly beaten, his hair matted with blood. Brock sucked in a quick breath and fought his churning stomach. Tears filled his eyes as he struggled for composure. He had never seen anyone up close who had died only minutes before, much less a friend. And even though he had known Isaac for only a few days, he had, indeed, been a friend. He moved a step closer to Mr. Jamison and gently laid his hand on the man's shoulder as his father had done for him at grandpa Hank's funeral.

Brock stood with Mr. Jamison, the man fighting tears. After a nurse gently spread a blanket over Isaac's body and head, Mr. Jamison turned suddenly to face Dr. Rush. "How did this happen?" he shouted. He stepped closer to the doctor. "How could you let a mad man attack my son?"

Dr. Rush put up his hands in defense. "One of the patients became very upset and began screaming. Isaac was with other interns where they study and came to investigate. He was the first to arrive at the patient's room and he took it upon himself to unbolt the door and enter. It was there that he was attacked. When the attendants arrived, the patient was clubbing Isaac with a wooden stool. They subdued the patient and carried Isaac from the room." The doctor dropped his hands. "Matthew, I am truly sorry. If only Isaac had waited for others to help before entering the room."

Mr. Jamison's stare should have blinded the doctor. "I demand to know why you keep mad men in the same hospital as sick people. This is your fault, doctor." He pushed Dr. Rush aside roughly and stomped from the ward.

Brock glared at Dr. Rush before hurrying to catch up with Mr. Jamison.

Out in the hall Mr. Jamison stopped in his tracks, taking deep breaths. The old man who had intercepted them on the way in stepped forward. "Matthew, I will have Isaac's body brought round to your house in the morning." He paused. "Isaac was truly a good man and was becoming an exceptional doctor. His death is a loss to us all."

Mr. Jamison turned to look at the man. "Thank you, Mr. Chapman." He sobbed softly, "Yes, I'm very proud of my son."

Brock's tears began again.

Brock and Mr. Jamison walked side-by-side on the way back home. Neither spoke for several blocks. Finally, in a small voice Mr. Jamison said, "His mother's heart will be broken. And I can find no words to temper the dreadful news."

Brock could not respond. He didn't know what to say to the man who had just lost a son. And despite his compassion for Mr. Jamison and his family for their loss, Brock sensed a significant loss of his own. Isaac had not only been a friend, he had been his closest ally in 1787 Philadelphia.

CHAPTER 16   Oct 18, Thursday

Brock awoke Thursday morning dreading the day. He had slept on the floor for the second night since Isaac's death, not wanting to disrespect his friend's memory and hesitant to ask Mr. Jamison for permission.

Yesterday he had helped load a wooden casket from the store's inventory onto a neighbor's wagon. Then, he and Mr. Jamison had walked beside the wagon to the Jamison home carrying white funeral gloves from the store that Mr. Jamison explained would be worn by those attending the funeral mass.

Wednesday had also been a busy day of preparation for Isaac's funeral. Different from the mortuary services routinely used in Texas, family and close neighbors had done everything to prepare for the funeral. Women trained in preparing the body, shrouders Mr. Jamison called them, had done their gruesome tasks of preparing and dressing Isaac's body before placing it the casket in the front room for viewing. Neighbors and women from the church had helped Mrs. Jamison bake all day to feed the mourners that would be present. Only one outside service was hired; "warners" had been engaged to spread the news on Wednesday of the death and of today's funeral. Brock had generally stayed out of the way of those who were experienced in the tasks of preparing a funeral.

Today, in the early afternoon, as Isaac lay in the small front room, family, neighbors, church members, hospital staff, and even some of Mr. Jamison's customers filed through, viewing the body and paying their respects to the family. The mourners then moved quietly through the kitchen where food had been prepared for them, as was the custom.

Brock was completely out-of-place with the proceedings. Isaac's body lying so close to where people were eating and drinking freaked him out. And he didn't know any of the people gathered other than the Jamison family members. His only experience with funerals had been his grandpa Hank's in Texas and that had been in the 21st century.

Though there were dozens of people crowding the small house, Brock's presence raised no obvious questions from the diverse mourners. Amelia sensed Brock's discomfort and often stood near him as people mingled, talking softly. At one point she brought him a cup of beer outside the house where he had gone to escape the crush of people. "Please share the food inside. Everyone is welcome, including you."

"Thanks, Amelia. I'll get something in a little while."

She smiled, her lips tight, her eyes wide, before disappearing back into the house.

Sipping his beer, Brock scanned those outside the Jamison home. He recognized the sizable bulk of the blacksmith he had met a few days earlier standing alone at the edge of the crowd. The man may have been uncomfortable in clothes almost as shabby as Frank's but he stood straight, not shying from the stares of some of the other mourners.

Relieved to see the familiar face, Brock approached the man. "Amos, I'm surprised to see you here. You may not remember me but I'm Brock. We met in your shop last week."

Amos nodded and in a deep voice said, "I 'member you. You drew axe for me."

Brock's grief faded for the moment. "Did you make one?"

The blacksmith grimaced then pursed his lips. "Started one but it need more work. Balance not right."

"Well, keep at it. From what I saw at your shop, you can make just about anything." Brock motioned toward the house. "How did you know Isaac?"

"Isaac patched me up after a horse kicked me last year. Even come to my shop after a week to check on my leg. He was sure a good doctor."

"Yeah, everybody's saying good things about him."

"You family?" Amos asked while keeping his eyes on the others standing outside, talking quietly.

Brock hesitated. "No, just a friend. I met Isaac at the hospital." He liked Amos but chose not to share anything more about his presence in Philadelphia.

In mid-afternoon the priest from St. Joseph's in his vestments showed up at the house. Those in front of the house grew quiet with the priest in their midst and parted to allow him to enter. A man moved among the mourners distributing the white gloves. Everyone donned a pair, a sign to Brock that the funeral was about to start. Suddenly, his stomach felt uneasy. He looked at Amos for support but found only sad eyes.

Maybe ten minutes later the front door opened and the priest appeared first, followed by six men carrying the now-closed coffin. Six other men followed close behind, four of which carried the three-foot high, long wooden stand that had been under the coffin in the house.

Mr. and Mrs. Jamison and their children and Seth and his family were next in the procession. As they passed by those gathered outside the front of the house, Mr. Jamison reached out a hand to Brock. "Walk with us. Isaac trusted you." Brock nodded and fell in behind the family, tears rolling down his cheeks. Others joined the solemn procession along the street.

After two blocks the men carrying the coffin set it down with care on the stand that had been carried along. Then the second group of six men lifted the coffin and the procession continued to the church.

Inside the church a young boy, carrying a cross on a pole, took the lead to the front alter. The pall bearers placed Isaac's coffin on the small stand at the front and sat together on one side of the sanctuary.

The priest began the funeral mass with ceremony much like he had done at the Sunday mass except he also sprinkled water on the coffin as he sang Latin phrases.

From his seat in the pew directly behind the Jamison family Brock paid little attention to the proceedings or the message. His thoughts were on the friend he had lost. Isaac's whole life had been in front of him. A life of healing and helping others. A life that probably would have included a wife and kids. A life with such potential, now tragically wasted.

And Mr. and Mrs. Jamison had to be suffering terribly. He could only imagine their pain. He thought again of his own father and mother and the grief for their son who…who had disappeared. Tears spilled onto his cheeks.

Following the abbreviated service the procession moved out of the church to the adjacent cemetery where an open grave awaited. There the coffin was laid next to the grave on two long ropes that were stretched across the grave to the other side. The family and mourners gathered around the gravesite, some sniffling quietly.

The priest sprinkled more water on the coffin and said more prayers in both Latin and English then moved aside. He nodded to the pall bearers who then lifted the coffin using the ropes. They moved it over the grave and slowly lowered it. They then removed the ropes, coiled them and stood aside. The priest turned to Mr. and Mrs. Jamison and quietly offered his condolences then followed the boy with the cross out of the graveyard.

As if a signal had been given, the family turned and parted the crowd to exit the graveyard by the same route they had entered. The other mourners followed close behind. As the distance from the church increased, mourning gave way to chit chat, then to laughter. By the time the group reached the Jamison's house, a party atmosphere had developed.

Beer, wine, other spirits flowed freely well into the evening. Apart from some toasts to Isaac early in the festivities, it felt like a neighborhood block party with heavy drinking and joking. Brock looked for Amos among the partiers but never found him. It was near midnight before the stragglers finally staggered out the door.

Mr. Jamison and Brock were the only ones in the household not in bed when the quiet returned at last. The aggrieved father sat down heavily on his kitchen chair. He sighed then spoke in a quiet voice, his words slurring slightly from a combination of alcohol, exhaustion and grief. "Brock, even though Isaac is gone, I intend to honor the agreement I made with you. You may continue to work at the store and you may sleep in the boys' room." He paused. "I believe Isaac would approve."

Brock had consumed several cups of the strong beer during the celebration but was far from drunk. Unconsciously, he had restrained himself from his usual indulgence back in Texas. He stared back at Mr. Jamison, not sure how to respond to this man who was hurting so much. "Thank you. You're most kind. And Mr. Jamison, if I may say so, it's clear where Isaac learned to be a gentleman. I commend you, sir."

There was a pause in their conversation with Brock not knowing what else to say.

"Did you know that Isaac was going blind?" Mr. Jamison said, without looking in Brock's direction.

Brock stiffened. "No, sir. I had no idea. How bad was his eyesight?"

"He mentioned it to me perhaps six months past in the strictest of confidence. He said it was gradual and did not yet hamper his studies or his training. But he shared his condition with no one for fear his future as a doctor would be in jeopardy. I told no one, not even his mother."

"I only knew Isaac a short time but I saw nothing to suggest he had a problem. It had to be hard for him with all the required reading. He had extraordinary determination to continue to pursue his career. You've got to be very proud of him."

Mr. Jamison sighed. "I *am* proud of my son." He paused. "I'm proud of all my children." With effort he rose from his chair. "But now we should sleep. Good night, Brock."

"Good night, sir."

Brock lay in Isaac's bed in total darkness, hearing only the soft breathings of the two young boys in the other bed. He felt sorry for Duncan and Nathan, knowing that they would not have their older brother to teach and guide them as surely Isaac would have done.

He reflected again on his own situation and considered his choices for a confidant who would, perhaps, believe him and agree to help him as Isaac had done. Unfortunately, he could think of no one. His grief and his desperation only added to the cold, darkness of the room.

CHAPTER 17   Oct 19, Friday

The morning after Isaac's funeral the Jamison family members moved like they were in a trance as they gathered for breakfast with no one speaking and or making eye contact. Mrs. Jamison fought tears as she stirred the mush and spooned it into the bowls. With everyone served, she dropped heavily into her chair. She pushed the mush around in her bowl for a few seconds then looked at her husband with tears in her eyes before she hurried upstairs. Everyone at the table watched her go.

Nathan, the younger boy, said, "Is Mama all right?"

Amelia looked at her brother. "Never you mind. Eat your breakfast." She looked sideways at her father at the far end of the table. Mr. Jamison spooned some of the mush into his mouth and with flooded eyes and trembling lips attempted to swallow. Everyone followed Mr. Jamison's cue and one by one started eating. No one at the table spoke.

When Mr. Jamison had emptied his bowl, he rose and went upstairs quietly. Amelia and Brock exchanged a glance from their positions diagonally across the table. Brock wanted to provide some comfort to Amelia and the boys but didn't know how. He just stared at the table and his now-empty bowl.

Moments later Mr. Jamison descended the stairs. He approached the table and addressed his children. "Listen to your mother and don't make a racket today." He turned toward the door. "Brock, we best be going."

Mr. Jamison and Brock walked to the store in silence, the latter enjoying the cooling sensation in his lungs and the warmth of the bright sun on his face.

At the store Brock again found success building a fire but Mr. Jamison didn't seem to notice. Brock tried to stay busy by moving the dust around on the inventory with the feather duster, mindful of any cloud he might create. The morning wore on with Mr. Jamison speaking only when necessary. The few instructions he gave to Brock were in subdued tones. To Brock the man was just going through the motions of his business with his mind absorbed in his loss.

Though the customers were fewer than the previous days, each had words of condolence for Mr. Jamison or praise for Isaac. Mr. Jamison was gracious yet reserved. Thus, the day proceeded much as it had before with even fewer words spoken between Brock and his boss.

######

That evening after supper Amelia carried *Robinson Crusoe* to the kitchen table, preparing for Brock to continue reading the novel.

Brock said, "I need to go for a walk to sort out some things in my head. Maybe later." Her pout and sad eyes made Brock feel guilty but he had a mission.

On the dark streets of Philadelphia Brock struggled to remember the route to Seth Jamison's house. After several wrong turns and some back tracking, he arrived at the door of Isaac's older brother. Was he intruding too soon after Isaac's death? His hesitation lasted only a moment before he knocked.

Flora answered the door wearing her coat and hat as if she was leaving. "Evenin', Mr. Brock."

Surprised that the woman remembered his name, Brock said, "Good evening, Flora. I wish to speak with Seth. Is he home?"

"Yes, sir. He be here."

Before Flora could turn, Seth appeared in the hall doorway

"Mr. Seth, Mr. Brock come to visit," Flora said as she moved out of the way and toward the door. "If you not be needin' me anymore tonight, I's be headin' home." Flora nodded to Brock as she squeezed past him in the hallway.

"Fare thee well, Flora. We'll see you tomorrow," Seth said.

Seth motioned for Brock to come in. "Welcome, Brock. Come sit at the kitchen table, surprised I am to see you." Once seated, his smile suddenly disappeared. "Is anything the matter at my father's house?"

"No, nothing's wrong. Of course, they're both still pretty down about…Isaac. But I think they're coping with it as good as could be expected." Brock paused and straightened in his chair. "Seth, I've come to ask a favor."

Seth frowned slightly.

Brock continued, "Do you know Ben Franklin?"

Seth's frown deepened. "Well, I've met Dr. Franklin on occasion at Carpenter Hall. It is doubtful, however, that he would remember me by name. Why do you ask?"

Brock chose his words carefully. "I'd like to talk to him about some scientific matters that I think would interest him."

Seth's tone changed. "And just what is the nature of these 'scientific matters'?"

Intimidated by the lawyer's challenge, Brock hesitated a few seconds. "I've read about Franklin's interest in electricity and I know he has done some experimentation. An inventor in England is toying with the concept of an electric light design and I have some basic knowledge of it that may appeal to Franklin. Perhaps with his intellect, he could improve on this work." Brock watched for Seth's reaction and not seeing an immediate dismissal of the idea, continued, "All I ask is for an introduction."

Seth shook his head. "First, the man's title is *Doctor* Franklin and should be accorded due respect. Secondly, if this electricity light you reference is one of your tall tales, I will have no part of it. And lastly, even if I did condone your requested meeting, I am not in a position to make the introduction."

"I certainly meant no disrespect to Dr. Franklin. I'm sorry for the oversight."

Seth nodded in response but maintained his stoic demeanor.

Brock continued, "Would you write a letter of introduction that could be delivered to Dr. Franklin. Maybe that would at least get my foot in the door."

Seth bristled. "I have no time for such folly. My brother has just been killed and I should devote any available time to the support of my parents and my brothers and sister." He stood, suggesting the conversation was over. "Now, I have much work to do before I turn in. I bid you a good night."

Brock moved toward the door. "Good night, Seth. And thank you for your time." He shook hands at the open door. He then brightened. "What if I drafted a letter for your signature? A letter from you, a prominent lawyer and someone who regularly attends Carpenter Hall, would have more weight than one coming from an unknown such as me." Brock held Seth's eyes.

Seth frowned but seemed to be relenting. Instead he spoke firmly, "I will not allow myself to be drawn into a bizarre scheme involving electricity lights. And I suggest that you desist from any harassment of Dr. Franklin. Now, be gone."

Brock moped back to the Jamison house, dejected but still hopeful. As he arrived, he stood in the dark outside the door and reminded himself that even if he could talk with Dr. Franklin there was no guarantee he would help. Getting back to where he belonged was the real goal. A goal that was a long way off.

CHAPTER 18   Oct 20, Saturday

At the store the next morning Brock approached Mr. Jamison. "Have I earned enough wages to buy a few sheets of writing paper? And maybe I could borrow one of those fat pencils you use at the counter?"

Mr. Jamison frowned. "And for what purpose might you need writing paper?"

"I want to write a letter to Dr. Franklin asking for a meeting to ask some questions about electricity."

Shaking his head, Mr. Jamison, nevertheless, said, "The paper I will deduct from your wages. The pencil you may borrow."

At the noon dinner time Brock asked if he could stay at the store and work on his letter with benefit of the good daylight.

Again, his boss agreed. "Perhaps I will carry a biscuit back for you."

"That would be great, sir. But don't go to any trouble; you've already been more than kind to me."

In the quiet of the store Brock positioned the writing paper on the counter and carefully drafted the letter he had been working on in his mind ever since leaving Seth's house the previous evening:

Dear Dr. Franklin:

Please allow me to introduce myself. My name is Brock Sinclair and I am from an area far southwest of Philadelphia. I apologize for the use of pencil in this letter but, although I have significant formal education, I am not adept at the use of a quill.

Sir, I am quite familiar with your career in printing, politics and as an inventor. It would be accurate to say that I have studied your achievements since my early youth and am a true admirer. And since I have a background in science, it would be an honor to meet with you and discuss some of your inventions and experiments, particularly those with electricity.

Sir, I do not wish to occupy a significant portion of your time. However, I am convinced that the insights I have to share will pique your interest.

Should you be so gracious as to grant me a few minutes of your time, please send word to me at Mr. Jamison's general store on Walnut St. at Ninth St. My schedule is flexible, thus I am available to meet most any time.

Highest regards,

Franklin Brock Sinclair

When he held the letter up for review, the writing was not evenly spaced and tended to trail down the page rather than straight across. All his life he had relied on lined paper to keep his calculations or hand-written notes neat with ninety-nine percent of his writing being done on a tablet or at a computer. The letter's amateurish appearance did not represent him favorably.

He found a crude framing square Mr. Jamison had for sale and drew faint lines an inch apart on a fresh page. He then rewrote the letter on the lined paper, trying to be as neat as possible with his printing, having never learned cursive writing. He then folded the letter and sealed it with candle wax as he had watched Mr. Jamison do.

Brock then rushed the folded letter toward where the Ben Franklin Post Office had been on Market Street when he visited Philadelphia with his folks. He had written the man's name on the outside but didn't know what the procedure was to have the letter get to its intended recipient.

Instead of the expected post office, Brock found a three-story, brick house on each side of a wide vacant lot. There were no indications of the historic post office anywhere. But in the rear of the vacant lot stood another three-story house, more impressive than those on Market Street. It appeared to Brock that this structure stood about where he remembered the "Ghost House", a 20th century artist's creation, had been erected to depict where Ben Franklin's home had once stood.

Apprehensive, yet determined, Brock approached the house. He took a deep breath before banging the ornate door knocker three times then moving back a step.

A moment later a dark-haired man in his late twenties or early thirties answered the door. His clothes were fancier than most Brock had yet seen. He snarled. "What is it you want?"

Brock straightened to his full six foot-two height but controlled his voice. "Good afternoon. Is this the Franklin residence?"

"Exactly who is it that wants to know?" the man said in a coarse tone and with hands on both side of the doorway as if to block any attempted entry.

"I've brought a letter for Dr. Franklin." He held out the folded letter where the recipient's name could be seen. "If Dr. Franklin lives here, would you see that he gets it?"

"My grandfather is resting and cannot be disturbed." The man snatched the letter from Brock. "If he has an opportunity later, he *may* choose to read this. Now be gone with you."

Brock looked down at his shabby clothes and opened his mouth to respond but controlled his temper rather than risk his mission. In a syrupy tone he said, "Thank you very much."

On the way back to the store Brock stewed about the asshole at Franklin's door. He knew Temple Franklin lived with his grandfather and had apparently become protective of him.

Off and on during the afternoon at the store Brock wondered if Dr. Franklin actually got the letter and if he would respond. And if so, how soon? The letter was a long shot but at the moment he felt it was the only one he had.

Closing time arrived with no notice regarding the letter. Dr. Franklin probably had a lot on his plate. And if he did get to the letter, it might be days before he responded even if he intended to do so. Still, Brock was disappointed.

At the Jamison home Brock went alone to the bedroom he shared with the boys. Despite being tired from being on his feet all day sweeping and loading wagons for customers, he felt he should do some ab work and some pushups; it had been almost two weeks since he'd worked out at the gym in Texas.

He started with some planks, did a set of push-ups, then started fifty sit-ups. The repetitions took his mind off his wait for a response from Dr. Franklin and his situation in general.

A knock on the door followed by Amelia's timid voice broke his spell. "Brock, pounding on the floor can be heard below. Is anything the matter?"

"Come on in. I'm just finishing up some ab work."

The door moved slowly revealing a hand and then Amelia's surprised face in the small opening. "I've only got twenty more to finish," Brock said, his voice straining with the exertion. "I'll be downstairs in a few minutes."

Amelia, her eyes wide and her face flushed, lingered in the opening for several more seconds then withdrew slowly and closed the door.

At the supper table Mr. Jamison leveled his gaze at Brock. "Amelia reports you were lying on the floor of your sleeping room sitting up then lying down again? May I ask why?

"Yes, sir. It's called sit-ups."

Both of the Jamison sons laughed aloud while Mrs. Jamison and Amelia smiled but kept their eyes on their plates.

Brock grinned at the reaction to his comment. "The exercise strengthens your abdominal muscles. It's one of several exercises to strengthen your core which helps to protect your back from injury when lifting."

Mr. Jamison studied Brock for a long minute. "And you conduct these 'exercises' frequently?"

"I should do them more often than I have been doing. But several times a week is best." Brock looked at Amelia, her mother, then back to Mr. Jamison. "Such repetitive movements also help to reduce one's stress. At least I find them helpful."

"I understand neither 'repetitive' nor 'stress'," Mr. Jamison said. "What do these words mean?"

Brock put down his spoon. "'Repetitive' simply means to do something over and over or repeat it. And 'stress' means the tension or worry or frustration in one's life." He paused. "Like you were worried about the ship being late getting to the port. That's an example of stress."

"Where did you learn such words?" Mr. Jamison said with apparent interest.

"These are common words where I'm from," Brock said holding his hands just above his plate, fingers knitted together.

Mr. Jamison nodded very slowly then returned to his meal.

Across the table Amelia's grin had been replaced by something more sensuous. Brock blinked and returned his attention to his food.

After the meal Brock remained at the kitchen table to continued reading *Robinson Crusoe* to Amelia when the kitchen was returned to order. The girl whispered to her mother who then looked directly at Brock. After a brief pause, Mrs. Jamison spoke to Brock. "Amelia would like to look at the words in the book as you read. Would you permit her to see the pages also?"

"Well…sure," Brock said, sitting up straighter. He looked at the smiling Amelia and patted the bench beside him. "I'll follow along with my finger so you can see and hear the words at the same time."

Amelia moved quickly to sit about six inches from Brock on the bench at the table. The look Mrs. Jamison gave her daughter was a clear warning to behave.

Mrs. Jamison moved her stare to Brock and held it there for several seconds. She then moved to the front parlor to do hand work from a chair where she could easily see into the kitchen.

The dim light and the ornate font were no easier to read than during the earlier sessions. Brock's grasp of the unfamiliar prose had improved only marginally. And keeping a finger moving on the page for Amelia to follow was a pain. But the engaging story and the closeness of Amelia softened the effort.

More than once Amelia interrupted his reading to pronounce a word just before he read it. She *was* paying attention.

After an hour Brock marked the book with a tiny scrap of paper and closed it. Amelia's pout caused Brock to grin. "How about we do some math?"

The girl frowned. "What is math?"

"You know, mathematics … arithmetic. Your numbers."

Amelia's smile lit up the room. "Yes, could we?"

"Do you have scrap paper and a pencil we can use?"

Her eyes fell to the table. "Papa would never allow us to use paper. He uses it only for very important business."

Brock rubbed his hands together. "Okay. We'll figure something out. For now let's start with counting. How high can you count?"

Amelia beamed. "I once counted to fifty."

"Okay. Let me hear you do it."

She sat up straight and cleared her throat. "One, two, three, four,.." She continued until she got lost at thirty-seven with Brock then helping her get back on track.

For the next half hour Brock had the girl count by tens, then fives and finally by ones again. His patience exhausted, Brock said at last, "You're doing pretty well. But that's enough for tonight. We can do some more another time."

Amelia's enthusiasm about learning made the process bearable although Brock suddenly had great appreciation for what teachers do. He didn't think he had the patience to teach but working with the cute teenager made the job tolerable.

Sleep did not come easy to Brock that night. He continued to focus on hearing back from Dr. Franklin. What would he say to the man to gain his trust before he revealed his situation? He tried to recall all that he had learned about Ben Franklin over the years and during that family trip to Philadelphia. Somewhere in his recollections, sleep prevailed.

CHAPTER 19   Oct 21, Sunday

With no particular interest in religion, Brock, nevertheless, attended worship services with the Jamisons Sunday morning out of respect for the family and Isaac. Immediately after the Sunday dinner he excused himself, claiming he had an important matter that needed his attention. Mr. Jamison frowned but did not question him. And Amelia's face clearly showed her disappointment.

Despite the death of Isaac and Brock's attempts to enlist Dr. Franklin's help, the image of Kathrine and her seductive ways kept resurfacing in his mind. He remembered the warnings from both Mr. Jamison and Isaac but he couldn't dismiss the possibility that she considered him special. And her fragrance! He could still smell her, particularly when he got into bed at night. Each day since the funeral he had wished she would walk through the door of the store giving him a chance to see her again. Her absence had only enhanced his memory of her and stoked his imagination.

Brock walked slowly toward Kathrine's house, rehearsing what he would say when she answered the door. He could say, "I was in the neighborhood and stopped to see if you needed anything." Or, "Since it's Sunday, I wondered if you would like to take a stroll." And he considered if she did welcome him into her house, how far was he willing to go with Kathrine?

What Brock did not anticipate was seeing Temple Franklin leaving Kathrine's house. Brock moved to the shadows in case Temple looked in his direction. From nearly a block away he could see the asshole slink down Kathrine's steps, turn in the opposite direction and move away. His disappointment was so intense his stomach ached.

Brock turned west, walking slowly with no destination in mind. If Temple somehow knew that he had walked Kathrine home and gone inside, it might explain the guy's resentment. It still didn't give Temple the right to be such a prick.

As he walked, Brock's thoughts gradually turned from Kathrine to his primary objective, getting home. The hours he had spent over the last week trying to think of something he could make as proof of him living in the 21st century had not been productive. Still, he brainstormed with himself as he walked. His depression, always just under the surface, further dampened his mood.

Brock didn't feel like going back to the Jamisons to sit in the gloomy house all afternoon. He walked determined to explore somewhere he had not been before.

The streets of Philadelphia were different than during the week. Few wagons were out and couples, families and groups of young men, were walking, most in there better clothes. Sunday priorities were clearly different than weekdays. Brock wondered when in the future, this change had occurred. In lots of ways back home, Sunday was just another day.

Walking further west, Brock toured the city where he might be trapped for the rest of his life. He had never really been on his own before. His mom and dad had always provided the necessities of life, something he had taken for granted. Without their love and support, he felt vulnerable and lost.

The further west Brock walked, the more rural the area became. Dirt trails at right angles to each other seemed to mark future streets. But there were few buildings to identify this area as a city. Some homes appeared abandoned, partially dismantled and scavenged. Who would have been so destructive and why?

In what would become city blocks in the future, stands of trees had been clear cut, apparently for building materials or firewood. Some of these blocks showed evidence of crops having been planted during the growing season. Further west the blocks were even less defined as stands of hardwood, as yet uncut, dominated the landscape.

After more than a mile Brock arrived at a slow moving river. It was maybe a hundred yards wide with a rickety, floating, wooden bridge to allow passage. Brock could see only a few, small structures on the other side. But there must be some level of civilization over there. Otherwise, why the bridge?

With the sun dropping lower in the southwestern sky, Brock headed back toward the Jamison home, having achieved little other than getting some exercise and some fresh air. The extended walk had spawned no ideas to persuade Dr. Franklin.

Just before sundown Brock arrived at the Jamisons. His legs were tired and his feet hurt. He craved a glass of ice water but knew it was neither available nor wise to drink. Amelia offered him some of the weak beer which he gratefully accepted.

It then occurred to Brock that he could make cold water from the local well if he boiled it first. "Mrs. Jamison, do you have a container with a lid that could be used to store water for drinking?" he asked.

"Brock, it is unwise to drink water because of the flux." Mrs. Jamison shook her head.

"Back home if we have water that's not safe to drink, we boil it first to make it safe," The lie didn't really feel like much of one. "If you were to boil some water when you have the fire going, then pour it in a container and put it outside to cool, we would have cool water for drinking later. The container would just need some sort of lid to keep dust and bugs out."

Amelia, who had been listening to the exchange, said, "Mother, I would taste the water if Brock does." She smiled at her tutor.

Mrs. Jamison smirked. "All right. When we make supper, I will boil some water to set aside." She gave a stern look to Amelia. "You will wait 'til morning before tasting the water to see if Brock is stricken by the flux."

Brock's confidence in his plan faded as this experienced mother cautioned her daughter about what he understood to be diarrhea. And with only an outdoor john, diarrhea would be a bitch. Yet Brock wanted to make a point to the Jamison family. And to himself.

CHAPTER 20   Oct 22, Monday

At breakfast the next morning Brock remembered the boiled water set outside the night before. He figured with the cool night, the water could be refreshing.

He found the ceramic jar on the step outside the back door and was relieved to find no bugs floating when he removed its lid. Back in the kitchen his courage wilted when he observed the slight cloudiness of the water as he poured it into his mug.

With all eyes watching, Brock tentatively sipped the water. He swished it around in his mouth to give it a fair trial. In truth bottled water at home put it to shame. But at least he didn't gag.

Amelia spoke first, enthusiasm obvious in her voice. "How does it taste, Brock?" She then caught her father's stare and lowered her eyes.

Brock was sure that the hint of mud and the bland taste would not impress anyone. At the same time these people didn't drink water. They may not know what it was supposed to taste like. He smiled and passed his mug across the table toward Amelia. "Try a sip."

Amelia reached for the mug, hesitant.

Before the girl could accept the mug, her mother interrupted, "Do not drink that, Amelia!" In a calmer voice she said. "We agreed to wait to see if Brock contracts the flux."

Amelia withdrew her hand from the mug and turned her eyes down. "Yes, ma'am."

"In for a penny, in for a pound," Brock quoted as he took a longer drink from the mug with his eyes on Mr. Jamison.

"You either possess a strong constitution or are quite daft," Mr. Jamison said, shaking his head and continuing his breakfast.

With the longer drink from the mug Brock realized that his taste test was a distant second to the real test. He really hoped he didn't get the runs.

At the store that morning every time Brock strained to lift something heavy, he feared the worst from the morning water. But the uncontrollable runs never came. He figured the longer the time since he drank the water, the less likely he would be affected by it. If he didn't get the trots, might Mrs. Jamison believe what he had said to her?

The work at Mr. Jamison's store was coming easier to Brock. He had learned the names of most of the inventory. And he had learned the common shopping routine of the farmers vs. that of the women who came into the store in ones and twos. A few of the women returned, having been in the store earlier in the week. One pair giggled as they glanced at Brock going about his chores. Brock nodded back and smiled. More giggles.

He recommended purchases to the customers as he loaded their wagons or baskets. He pushed the fresh apples and the other produce. He made positive comments on the color of the cloth or the quality of the tools to potential customers. Mr. Jamison scoffed at Brock's tactics but didn't object to the additional sales.

Late morning from the back of the store Brock heard the front door open and close and a voice, "Good morning. I am Temple Franklin. I understand I can find a Brock Sinclair at this establishment. Is this correct?"

"Good day to you, Temple," Mr. Jamison said. "And how is the health of Dr. Franklin? I've not seen him in many months."

"His health wavers. Currently, he appears to be improving slightly each day." He paused. "Can I not find Brock Sinclair here, sir?"

Brock's first reaction was to rush out and see if Dr. Franklin had agreed to meet with him. But with Temple's condescension at Dr. Franklin's door and the sight of him leaving Kathrine's house still lingering, Brock forced a slow walk to the front. "I'm Brock Sinclair."

Temple's eyes surveyed Brock. With no hint of a smile, Temple turned his nose up slightly. "*You* are Brock Sinclair?"

Brock nodded.

Temple continued to stare. At last he spoke as if he had no choice. "Dr. Franklin has agreed to meet with you at two o'clock today in his library. He, however, would not expect his guest to appear in garments suitable for farm chores. And be prompt; I do not want my grandfather to be kept waiting." He turned to Mr. Jamison. "Good day to you, sir."

Brock restrained himself from lashing out. "I'll be there." Temple didn't react to the comment, just walked to the door and left. Brock wanted to say something sarcastic to Temple about the powdered wig he had on today. But he didn't want Temple to be more of an obstacle to meeting with Dr. Franklin.

When Temple had left and with no one else in the store, Brock said to Mr. Jamison, "Is he always such a prick?"

"Watch your tongue, young man!" Mr. Jamison's stern look lasted only seconds followed by a slight grin. "Yes, he can be." Brock smiled in return.

On the walk home to dinner Mr. Jamison said, "Perhaps you could wear Isaac's Sunday clothes when you see Dr. Franklin later today. You are a tad taller than my son…was. But his clothes may be more suitable for your visit."

"Are you sure, Mr. Jamison? I don't want to disrespect Isaac or you."

"Nonsense. You have the need and the clothes lie idle. Isaac would want you to use them." Mr. Jamison's eyes filled with tears as they walked on.

Excited about his afternoon meeting, Brock didn't have much of an appetite for the dinner Mrs. Jamison had prepared. But he needed the protein in the meat stew and certainly didn't want to insult her cooking.

As they ate, Mr. Jamison grinned and said, "Edith, we have something of a celebrity amongst us."

Her reply was a blank stare and a frown.

"Brock has a meeting with Dr. Franklin at his house on Market St. this afternoon."

Both Mrs. Jamison and Amelia looked at Brock with quizzical expressions.

"Oh, it's nothing really," Brock said, blushing. "I've read about his science experiments and wanted to ask him some questions. He was good enough to give me a few minutes this afternoon. That's all."

Amelia's raised eyebrows suggested she was impressed, a reaction Brock appreciated.

The suit Isaac had reserved for Sundays and funerals fit Brock acceptably in the body since it had been baggy on Isaac. But the sleeves and pants were a little short. Nevertheless, it was a significant improvement over the loaned clothes he had been wearing for more than a week.

Brock estimated the walk from the store would take him ten minutes. But he left even earlier to be sure he was on time. At Dr. Franklin's door he straightened his clothes then knocked. No one answered. After a minute he knocked again.

Temple opened the door slowly. His scowl left no doubt as to his strong disapproval of Brock's presence. "My grandfather is in his library; I will lead you there. Do not upset him and do not stay more than a brief period."

Brock narrowed his eyes but nodded slightly then fell in behind Temple. The walk through the house mesmerized Brock. The rich furnishings, the elaborate wall coverings and paintings, even the handmade rugs suggested close attention to detail by a wealthy owner.

As they entered the library, Brock sucked in a quick breath. The man sitting in a large chair with an ottoman *was* Benjamin Franklin. The large, balding head, the bifocals, the frilly shirt showing through an open coat, even the knee-length pants and black boots seen in portraits. It was all there.

The man struggled to his feet with the aid of a cane. "Welcome, young man. I am B. Franklin. May I assume you are Franklin Sinclair?

Brock stepped forward, his mind trying to remember how to form a sentence. "Yes…yes, sir. But I'm called Brock Sinclair." He quickly extended his hand to shake the one offered by his host. The man's grip was firm and warm. Brock could not break eye contact. "It's really you!" He shook his head. "I mean, it's an honor to meet you, sir."

Dr. Franklin motioned to an armchair to the right of his overstuffed seat and then sat back down. Temple, who had remained silent during the greeting, chose a chair on his grandfather's left. When all were seated, Dr. Franklin said, "The name Brock is quite unusual. There was a burrowing animal that the Frenchmen called a 'Brock.' It was a muscular, low-slung beast with distinctive white markings and a reportedly inhospitable temperament."

Brock grins. "Sir, I'm not familiar with this 'Brock' animal although your description suggests it could be a badger." He clears his throat. "My full name is Franklin Brock Sinclair with 'Brock" after my great grandfather. My grandmother said I reminded her of her dad and always called me 'Brock'. So, I guess the name stuck."

Dr. Franklin's eyebrows rose slightly. "Well, Brock, your letter suggested you have studied my career since you were a boy. Might I ask what sources were at your disposal for such scholarship?"

Brock looked at Temple's constant sneer then to his host. "Dr. Franklin, your career is the stuff of legends. Your work with electricity, the Franklin stove, lightning rods, your establishment of the first library in Philadelphia, the fire company, the University of Pennsylvania, and of course your distinguished political career in the states and abroad are all remarkable. In particular you were instrumental in getting the U.S. Constitution signed by the Convention members and ratified. I've read newspapers and heard many accounts of your accomplishments."

"Your flattery I recognize but your foresight for the ratification of the Constitution by the thirteen states contains considerable optimism. Pennsylvania should vote soon and I am informed that Delaware and New Jersey are leaning to support, but no state has yet to actually ratify."

Brock blushed. "I misspoke, sir. I meant to infer that your efforts to unify the states through the Constitution are quite notable. And I can assure you that in time all thirteen states will, indeed, ratify."

A middle-aged woman entered the room. "Father, I apologize for the interruption, but Temple's presence at the State House is requested. Some documents apparently need his signature."

Temple groaned at his conflict of priorities. "The clerks have certainly taken their sweet time." He rose and turned to his grandfather. "If you will excuse me, it is important that I attend to these matters without delay." He turned to Brock with narrowed eyes. "Do not annoy my grandfather with your inane questions.

And limit your stay to no more than a few minutes." Temple then followed the woman from the room.

Dr. Franklin waved a dismissive hand at the back of Temple then faced Brock. "You mentioned newspapers. Is the Baltimore American a newspaper you favor?"

Brock felt trapped. "Sir, I've read a lot of newspapers. To acknowledge one source over another would be misleading."

Dr. Franklin was losing his enthusiasm. "Well then, what might be your questions for me, son?"

Brock leaned forward in his chair and braced himself with his hands on his knees. "Have you experimented with making light with electricity?"

"Why, yes, I have observed electricity fire in some experiments. Intense sparks provide light but the duration is decidedly brief. Why do you ask?"

"What if I told you that work is being done to create an electric light using a glass bulb with a thin, coiled wire inside that glows brightly?"

Dr. Franklin grasped the arms of his chair. In a confrontational tone he said, "Who is doing such experimentation and how did you learn of it?"

The moment of truth for Brock had arrived. He took a deep breath. "Dr. Franklin, I respectfully ask that you indulge me while I explain my background."

Dr. Franklin's expression did not change but he resettled in his chair and nodded.

"My home is in a place called Texas. If one was to travel there on horseback, it would take weeks." He put up his hands to forestall an interruption. "I know I said in my letter that it was a two-day ride. That's also true. If you'll hear with me, I'll explain the difference."

Dr. Franklin's brows now showed curiosity rather than consternation.

"I was with a friend in Texas and while walking along a street, I fell and hit my head and was knocked unconscious. When I regained consciousness, I was in a bed at Pennsylvania Hospital here in Philadelphia."

"Who carried you to Philadelphia and why?" Dr. Franklin said, obviously confused.

"I don't know how I got here, sir. But what is more confusing than being in Philadelphia is that the year is different than when I fell in Texas."

"Pray tell, what is the year in your Texas?" Dr. Franklin said with a grin.

Brock hesitated, trying to decide whether or not to proceed. "Sir, when I fell the year was 2029."

Dr. Franklin laughed aloud and continued until he was coughing violently.

When the coughing had slowed, Brock said, "Sir, I can prove what I say."

The smile on Dr. Franklin's reddened face had faded. "You can prove that the date is 2029 in a place called Texas?"

"It is, sir, but proving it is difficult. I believe that somehow I've been transported back in time to this place and this year. I can't explain how, but I can tell you a lot of things that will happen in the next two hundred and forty years."

"I'm quite certain that you can." Dr. Franklin cleared his throat again as he moved the ottoman away from his chair, preparing to rise.

"I've read your autobiography that will be published after your death."

Dr. Franklin halted at the edge of his chair. "Well, it is no secret that I am writing my memoirs. And perhaps it will be published after I depart this world."

Brock interrupted, "Part 1 of your autobiography is written to your son, William, and early on you say that you've had a good life but given the chance to live it over you would do so but would do some things differently."

Dr. Franklin frowned deeply. "How could you know such things? The manuscript resided with a local attorney until reclaimed by me this past year and remains in my possession."

"Sir, I've read the entire book, three regular-length parts and a short fourth part. I guess it was published after your...a few years from now."

Dr. Franklin pushed himself back into his chair and stared across the room, seeming to be in deep concentration. "An enterprising young man could have gained access to accounts of my undertakings for the purpose of a ruse yet may not have gleaned details of my personal life. Do you, young man, fit this characterization?"

"In your autobiography you write that when you landed in Philadelphia as a young lad, you had little money. You used it to buy several loaves of bread which you carried down the street eating. You saw a young girl in a doorway who you felt was not impressed with your appearance. It turned out the girl would eventually be your wife, Deborah Read. Another incident in your autobiography is where you and your friends took some building stones to construct a bridge in a swamp area. You got caught and received a reprimand from your father."

"It was a marsh that flooded at high tide where we caught minnows." Dr. Franklin coughed again and looked pained. "I must ponder all that you have said." He grimaced then yelled, "Sally! Sally, come see this young man out."

The woman must have been close for she entered the room on his last word. "Father, try to relax. I will return directly." She spoke to Brock, "Follow me, please. My father must rest now."

Before the front door closed behind him, Brock said, "Can I see Dr. Franklin again sometime soon?

"He will make any such decision. Now good day to you," she said in a polite, yet urgent, tone then closed the door.

A depressed Brock walked slowly back to the store. Hope for help from the famous Ben Franklin had vanished and he could see no other means of gaining help. Brock even questioned his own sanity: maybe all his memories of a life in Texas were just his imagination. But if they were, where had he lived and who had he lived with for the last nineteen years here in Philadelphia? And was he really nineteen? Or, was he imagining that too?

Before supper Brock's mood rallied when Mrs. Jamison asked about the flux and he could report that he had no symptoms. He drank more of the water then offered his cup to Amelia and her mother.

Mrs. Jamison shook her head and declined.

Amelia reached for the water but took only a sip then made an ugly face. "It has no taste. Why would anyone choose to drink this?"

Brock tried to sell his accomplishment. "If water is clean and ice cold, it can be very refreshing. Water caught while it's raining would taste better than this I'm sure."

Later, his despondent mood returned even while reading and working with Amelia on adding some simple numbers. He just couldn't shake his funk.

CHAPTER 21   Oct 23, Tuesday

Brock remained despondent the next morning, the disillusionment with Kathrine on Sunday and his hasty dismissal by Dr. Franklin on Monday still consuming him. He swept the rear of the store without his usual enthusiasm. His mind replayed his conversation with Dr. Franklin again and again. How could he have handled it differently so the man actually paid attention to his plight?

Mid-morning the woman Dr. Franklin had called Sally entered the store, a cloth purse hanging from her arm. Brock recognized her from the rear of the store but his embarrassment from being dismissed at the Franklin house kept him in the back. The woman perused the merchandise on her way to the counter where Mr. Jamison greeted her.

"Good morning, Mrs. Bache," Mr. Jamison said to the woman. "What can I get for you this fine day?"

"In truth my primary reason for coming today is to speak with Brock Sinclair. Would such be possible, sir?"

Mr. Jamison's smile partly masked his disappointment that a sale was unlikely. "Of course, Mrs. Bache." He stepped toward the back room just as Brock emerged. "Oh, Brock, Mrs. Bache wishes to speak with you."

Brock walked toward Mrs. Bache, his eyes at her feet, expecting to be chastised for annoying Dr. Franklin.

"Hello, Brock. We were not properly introduced yesterday. I am Sarah Franklin Bache, Dr. Franklin's daughter. But everyone calls me Sally."

Brock met her eyes but spoke in a soft tone. "Good morning, Mrs. Bache."

"My father dispatched me to find you and invite you to dinner today." She looked at Mr. Jamison, her eyes pleading. "That is if Mr. Jamison can allow you to interrupt your work."

Mr. Jamison looked at Brock for an instant. He then turned back to the woman. "Certainly, he can attend."

Sally scanned Brock's clothes. "Your work clothes are acceptable. This will not be a formal meal. Can I inform my father that you will join him at noon?"

Brock felt his entire face smile. "Yes, ma'am, I will be there. And thank you."

Temple Franklin answered the door when Brock knocked just before noon. He stepped out onto the stoop and pulled the door closed behind him. He moved toward Brock and glared at him. "I do not know what you said to my grandfather after I left the room yesterday. He would not share your cock and bull tale but insisted that you join him for dinner today."

Moving closer and into Brock's personal space, Temple pointed his finger between Brock's eyes. "My grandfather is an old man. I will not stand for some charlatan deceiving him! It is my duty to protect his name and his resources. You will not return after today. Is that understood?"

Brock placed the flat of his hands on Temple's chest and pushed with a short, forceful stroke, causing Temple to stumble back against the closed door. "Get out of my face. You weren't the one who invited me to come here today." He pointed at the door. "Now, are you going to let me in? Or, do I need to explain to Dr. Franklin that you threatened me?" His aggressive behavior was reminiscent of how he would have reacted back in Texas. It was unlike the more tolerant demeanor he had developed while in Philadelphia. But this guy pissed him off to no end.

Temple's stare bored into Brock's face with the intensity of a high-speed drill. Yet, he turned slowly and opened the door and entered the house. Brock followed a few steps behind, keeping alert to any sudden movements as they walked to a different room than the previous day.

Dr. Franklin sat at the head of a long dining table. Two places had been set, one in front of the host and one at his right hand. "Welcome, Brock. Please join me," Dr. Franklin said from his dining chair. "Temple, please excuse us. I intend for our dinner conversation to be private."

Temple snorted and disappeared.

Brock smiled as he sat down adjacent to Dr. Franklin. "Sir, I will admit that I was both surprised and delighted to receive your invitation to lunch. Thank you."

"Lunch is a term with which I'm not familiar. Is not the midday meal *dinner* from whence you hail?"

"I'm used to a smaller meal at midday called lunch and eating a more substantial meal in the evening. I didn't mean to confuse you."

A woman of about sixty carried bowls and plates of food to the table and placed them where they were within easy reach. "Shall I serve, Dr. Franklin?'

"Never mind, Mable. We will help ourselves as we talk. Would you pour the wine before you go?"

With the wine poured, the two men served themselves slices of meat, bread, cheese and warm, fragrant, cinnamon apples. Finally, they were alone. "Brock, I apologize for my lack of hospitality yesterday. My afflictions cause me great pain at times and until relief occurs, I regret that I can be rather uncivil."

"Is it the gout that pains you, sir? Or, the bladder stones? I understand you had…or have both ailments."

Dr. Franklin, still holding his knife and fork, dropped the heels of his hands to the edge of the table and stared at Brock. "I am surprised further at your knowledge of my personal affairs. You know of my health?"

Brock hesitated as in their earlier meeting. "As a founding father of the United States, you are revered, sir. Many biographies have been written about your life as well as a multitude of books about your accomplishments. My father is a particular fan of yours and he encouraged me as a child to learn about you and your values."

"But only my family and my doctor are aware of the stones. How could you—"

Brock cut him off. "You might find this interesting. Bladder stones are essentially little chunks of minerals that form in the urinary system. The treatment available in my time is to apply a localized blast of sound in the area of the stones to pulverize them into smaller pieces so they are easier to pass." Brock took a bite and smiled.

Dr. Franklin put down his fork. "Now see here, young man. Do not play me for a fool. I invited you into my home for stimulating conversation for you appeared an intelligent sort. Now you repay me by making sport of my age and my infirmities. I will not tolerate such insolence."

Brock put down his fork also and wiped his mouth with his napkin. He put his hands in his lap and turned toward his host. "Dr. Franklin, in no way would I *ever* think of disrespecting you. You've been an influence on my life since childhood. Because of some bizarre circumstances my parents experienced before they were married, I was actually named, Franklin, in your honor." Tears formed in Brock's eyes. "I've turned to you as my last hope in resolving the mystery of my situation. If you turn me away, I don't know what I'll do."

Dr. Franklin pondered then leaned forward in his chair. "We should not waste this table Mable has prepared. Might I suggest we delay conversation concerning your presence in Philadelphia until we withdraw to the library? As we dine, perhaps you can amuse me with the details of bladder stone treatments."

Brock sniffed, smiled, and picked up his fork. "Sure. But remember, I'm not a doctor and can provide limited details about stones. But I'll tell you what I've read." He smiled.

The meal proceeded with Dr. Franklin listening more than talking. Brock explained about high pitched sounds being able to shatter a wine glass with vibrations.

Dr. Franklin's eyebrows rose. "My boy, I heard of such demonstrations while serving in France. I assumed they were only illusions used to entertain."

"No, it can be done if the voice is at the right pitch and with enough power on delicate glassware." Brock then extrapolated to the use of sound at a certain frequency to vibrate the stones inside the body.

Dr. Franklin appeared fascinated. After asking several questions on the subject and hearing Brock's attempts at answering them, Dr. Franklin smiled broadly. "My boy, I surmise that you are either who you claim or you are a master story teller. Now it befalls me to determine which."

"I only ask that you consider what I tell you to be the truth. It's my hope that your renowned analytical mind can find an answer to my problem so I can get back to where I belong."

######

For two hours in Dr. Franklin's library Brock shared bits of the future of the United States, a few early technological achievements and some of his life growing up in Texas in the 21st century. He was careful to slip in references to bridges, highways, museums and the $100 dollar bill that had been named in honor of Benjamin Franklin. His host reacted enthusiastically and interrupted frequently with questions or asked for clarifications. Brock could not tell if the man's interest was real or if he was just entertaining himself.

To prevent telling a totally rosy vision of the centuries to come, Brock mentioned some natural disasters, world wars and climate change. Without some negative aspects of the future, his credibility might be at risk with the man who had seen much in his lifetime.

While Brock attempted to explain the modern postal service and fire departments, Dr. Franklin yawned. The conversation was winding down. "Dr. Franklin, it's been a long afternoon. Maybe I should leave and let you get some rest."

"Perhaps that is best, young man. I profess that I am indeed weary. Mable will see you out."

Brock panicked. "Dr. Franklin, would it be possible for us to meet again?"

Another yawn. "My schedule is quite full for the next several weeks. Perhaps next month we can have a short visit."

"So, you don't believe anything I've told you! Is that it?" Brock was standing now, his fists clenching and unclenching.

"Son, I am reminded of a work by Samuel Madden, *Memoirs of the Twentieth Century*, if my memory is sound. This was preceded by Johnathan Swift's *Gulliver's Travels*. Both contained abundant fancy. Your tale is distinctly more complex, requiring a very prolific imagination and delivered with a credible performance. I rather enjoyed the experience."

Brock tensed as he turned in a tight circle. He stopped and leveled his eyes at Dr. Franklin. "What if I can show you something that doesn't exist today? Would you believe me then?"

All traces of humor left Dr. Franklin's face. "Should such evidence be brought forward, I would consider its merits. Now good day, Brock." He called toward the room's doorway, "Mable, please come show this young man out."

Brock left Dr. Franklin's house deflated even more than on the previous visit. This time, however, determination overlaid the disappointment. He would find some way to convince the old fart that he had knowledge of the future that no one else in this time had. A lot of thought had already gone into some kind of proof with no revelation. He would have to think harder.

That evening after reading to Amelia, Brock took another walk along the streets of Philadelphia. He had no destination, only quiet and cool air in which to think. He paid attention to the stone sidewalks, the brick houses, the gas street lights, the wharf, the wooden ships tied up at the dock. He mentally walked through his science classes in high school and his coursework at UT for inspiration. Nothing spawned an idea.

CHAPTER 22   Oct 24, Wednesday

With business slow in the store, Brock got permission to run an errand, though Mr. Jamison cocked an eyebrow at the request.

Brock walked along the streets of Philadelphia rethinking his strategy. There was a risk with what he planned to do but he also felt it was his best option at this point. At his target address he knocked firmly on the heavy door.

Soon, Sally Bache opened the door. "Oh! Brock Sinclair! I was not aware that my father was expecting you. He has just settled for a nap."

"Actually, it's you I'm here to see, Mrs. Bache. And ask for your help."

She blinked several times. "This is quite a surprise, Brock." She stood aside. "Do come in. We can sit in the parlor."

When they were seated across from each other in the ornate parlor, Brock cleared his throat. "Mrs. Bache—"

"Please call me Sally."

"Yes, ma'am." Brock squirmed in his chair. "Sally, I have the greatest respect and admiration for your father. Believe me when I say I would never do anything to offend or discredit him."

Sally tilted her head, nodded. "Thank you. Please continue."

"Did he speak of our conversation yesterday afternoon?"

"No, when I inquired about the subject of his meeting with you, he declined to comment saying it had been a confidential conversation. I pressed him no further."

"Sally, I can share that we discussed a variety of issues. But we disagreed on a certain topic. Thus, my presence here today"

Sally sat up straighter in her chair. "I do not get involved in my father's affairs unless he requests my assistance. To do so without his knowledge would be quite inappropriate."

"I would certainly not ask you to do anything that Dr. Franklin wouldn't approve." Brock swallowed. "In conversation with your father I stressed that I have acquired some unique knowledge at my home many miles southwest of here. The examples I shared intrigued him, but I'm afraid he believes I am a fraud whose objectives are unclear."

Sally frowned and crossed her arms under her bosom. "Are you a fraud?"

"Certainly, not! I only seek Dr. Franklin's keen intellect to address a personal matter that I explained to him in confidence."

Sally rose from her chair.

Brock pressed, "Please just listen to what I propose and why I am requesting your help."

Sally sat back down but on the edge of her chair.

"One of the things I have learned at my home is that there are tiny organisms called bacteria all around us, in the air, soil, and water. Most are harmless and some are actually helpful in digestion. But some are harmful. Although all bacteria are too small to be seen with the naked eye, these bacteria can get into an opening in the skin through a scratch or cut and can cause infection." Brock leaned forward in his chair. "Surely you've seen the redness and swelling that sometimes develops at a wound. Or at the site where someone has been bled by a doctor. That swelling is the body fighting the bacteria. Sometimes the body wins and the wound heals leaving only a small scar. But sometimes, depending on the type of bacteria, the organisms get into the blood stream and make the patient very sick, occasionally with deadly results."

Sally had remained expressionless during Brock's explanation. Now she looked puzzled. "Despite my ambivalent reaction to your claims, why involve me in your conjecture?"

"I want to conduct an experiment to demonstrate the presence of these bacteria. If you observe the experiment, your credibility may convince Dr. Franklin that the results are valid."

"This is most unusual," Sally said, shaking her head slowly. In the ensuing silence she looked at Brock. At last she said, "What would be my participation?"

"Mainly, I want you to be a witness to what I do." Brock held her eyes. "And maybe help supply a few items that I'll need, such as a small amount of whiskey, a sharp knife, and some clean strips of cloth."

"Tell me exactly what you expect to do," Sally said. "And what results you hope to achieve."

During the next ten minutes Brock laid out, in detail, the procedure he intended to follow. Sally winced at one point but did not turn away.

When Brock had finished his explanation, Sally stood and walked slowly across the room. She paced for a moment, keeping a close eye on Brock. Finally, she stood behind her chair. "I am quite certain my father would not approve of this arrangement. However, your sincerity seems genuine. I will, therefore, consider your request in the interest of science."

Brock smiled broadly and wanted to hug Sally but restrained himself, not sure if such was acceptable. "Thank you so much."

In a less enthusiastic tone Sally said, "I will send word to you at Mr. Jamison's store when I have made my decision." She then walked him out. "Good day to you, Brock."

Sally had said only that she would consider his experiment. Still, it gave Brock hope.

CHAPTER 23   Oct 25, Thursday

Late Thursday morning Mr. Jamison sent Brock to the Harbor Master's office to see if there was any news about the pending arrival of the *Empress of China*. According to Mr. Jamison the vessel was two weeks past due.

A block from the store Brock was intercepted by a man who identified himself as a city warden. Two other men, carrying pistols, moved to either side of Brock. And the two orderlies he had confronted at the hospital stood grinning only feet away. The warden barked, "Dr. Rush has issued a sworn statement that you suffer from lunacy and are a menace to the people of the city. My watchmen and I have been directed to deliver you to Pennsylvania Hospital."

Brock considered taking on the men until he felt one of the pistols pushing against his ribs. He said, "Is this really necessary?" as the warden applied crude handcuffs tightly on Brock's wrists. He got no reply other than a snort from one of the orderlies.

With the warden leading, the watchmen marched Brock toward the hospital. Residents along the way stared and whispered as they moved aside for the men and their captive.

Minutes later Dr. Rush met the group at the door of the hospital. "Mr. Sinclair, I've been waiting for you," he said with slight grin.

"Homer, you and Nicholas escort our patient downstairs to his room and put him in shackles and fetters before the warden removes his restraints. And remember to watch his feet; you know what happened last time."

The more muscular of the two orderlies put his arm around Brock's neck from behind in a vicious choke hold. "We'll see to it, doctor." He pulled Brock backward causing him to stumble back against the brute. While Brock tried to regain his feet, the tall orderly kicked them out from under him then quickly lassoed Brock's ankles with a short rope and pulled it tight. He then lifted Brock's legs and he and the other orderly carried their prisoner to the nearby stairwell and down to the floor below. Dr. Rush, the warden and his watchmen followed.

In a room the men forced Brock into a sitting position against a stone wall. With his knees bent they secured his ankles to the wall with fetters and short chains. They then removed the handcuffs and attached shackles to his wrists with chains attached to the wall above his head, leaving his arms almost straight up, his hands about four feet apart. Brock guessed he could probably stand to give some relief to his arms. Otherwise, his movement was severely limited.

Dr. Rush thanked the warden and the watchmen for their help in apprehending the dangerous man and they left, verbally patting themselves on the back for a job well done.

With no one else around other than the orderlies, Dr. Rush addressed Brock. "Mr. Sinclair, you created quite a stir at the hospital with your attack on members of my staff. Fortunately, neither suffered permanent injury." The doctor paced. "But your actions confirmed my suspicions that you suffer from a degree of lunacy. Upon my return from Baltimore yesterday, I learned you had pestered Dr. Franklin at his home. It is time to remove you from the streets of our city and cure you of your condition for the benefit of society."

Brock raised his voice in frustration, "I went to Dr. Franklin's home at his invitation. But I guess you didn't ask him about my visit?"

The doctor shrugged and moved toward the door. "After I attend to other matters, we will begin your treatments. Do not fret, my reputation for treatment of the insane is unmatched on this side of the Atlantic."

"Wait, you can't do this!" Brock struggled to a standing position as he shouted and strained at his chains.

Dr. Rush did not react to Brock's plea. Without another word he and the orderlies left and locked the room.

Alone, Brock tested the security of the shackles and fetters. Any hope of defeating the heavy iron hardware and chains vanished. By grasping the chains above his head, he lowered his body back to the floor but the strain on his arms returned. He realized he would be able to stretch his legs and give some relief to his shoulders while standing but nothing else. Even crossing his feet while seated was not an option.

Despair, greater than before, settled over Brock. He had been worried about getting back home to Texas. But his situation had taken a turn for the worse. Much worse. The possibility of death or mental mutilation at the hands of Dr. Rush was very real.

Later, it must have been midday, the taller orderly entered the room holding what Brock assumed was his dinner. Instinctively, he wriggled to his feet despite aching shoulders and stiff knees.

The orderly carried a metal plate of beans with a wooden spoon and a hunk of bread on top and a cup of liquid. He approached Brock cautiously and set the items on the floor in front of Brock about four feet from the wall.

Brock glared at the orderly. "How am I supposed to reach that with these chains?" he said, frustration clear in his voice.

The orderly stepped forward and landed a brutal punch to Brock's midsection. Brock grunted and doubled over to the limit of his chains, trying to breathe.

"For kicking me in me balls," the orderly said as he unlocked the shackle on Brock's right hand. He then quickly moved back a couple of steps and chuckled. With Brock still struggling to breathe, the orderly walked out and locked the door.

Through tears of pain Brock watched the orderly leave. Minutes later he regained his composure and contemplated the beans and bread. It didn't look appetizing but his hunger was real and who knew when he might get something else to eat.

Brock stretched the chains and his joints to their limits to reach the plate and the cup. He dragged them toward the wall and squatted down beside them. Using only his right hand he was able to feed himself the undercooked beans and the coarse bread. He drank the weak, room-temperature beer. In his Texas life he would have rejected this gross food. Here, in this place, in this time, he took advantage of the nourishment.

When he had finished eating, Brock used his free hand to examine the lock on the other shackle but he could see no way to release it. He settled back onto the floor to wait, helpless and more afraid than he had ever been in his life.

######

The clank of the door lock startled Brock before the two orderlies, trailed by Dr. Rush, entered. With his left arm essentially useless from the constant stretch and his knees stiff from his sitting position, it took a major effort to stand to confront the doctor and the orderlies. Pain shot through his left shoulder and wrist when the tension lessened.

Dr. Rush approached but stopped several feet in front of Brock. He held a small, wooden-handle knife in a sheath and a small metal pan. "Mr. Sinclair, it is necessary that we remove some of your bad blood. We will again draw from your arm. If that is unsuccessful, we will choose other sites." He turned and motioned for the orderlies to move closer. "Now, will you cooperate? Or, must these gentlemen restrain you?"

Brock struggled to maintain his composure. "Look, Doc, if I thought the bleeding would help, I'd gladly submit to it. But, in fact it doesn't help and you'll leave a contaminated wound that will probably get infected."

"Hold him," Dr. Rush said to the orderlies with a frown. The muscular one slammed Brock against the wall with his body and simultaneously pulled on his left arm, pulling it to the limit of the shackle chain.

Brock screamed at the pain, certain the shoulder would dislocate from the force being applied. The tall orderly grabbed Brock's right arm above the elbow and at the wrist and pinned it to the wall.

Dr. Rush approached and pushed up Brock's sleeve as he withdrew his knife. "Hold him tightly. I want no blood on my garments."

Brock strained against the orderlies and the chains as he felt the knife slice open his forearm just below the elbow. Blood ran from the cut, off his arm and dripped into the pan the doctor held. Brock stopped his struggles with the belief that doing so would somehow slow the blood flow.

"Desist! Put down the knife!" boomed a voice from just inside the door.

Dr. Rush turned to face the intruder. "What is the meaning of this? This is my hospital and my patient. Who dares to interfere with my treatments?"

A heavy-set man, about fifty, stood in a posture of authority. "I am John Givens, Justice of the Peace." He waved a document. "This is an order, signed by his honor, Judge Marshal Thompkins. It stipulates that you are to immediately release Brock Sinclair, into my charge."

Mr. Jamison and his son, Seth, stood just inside the room, conviction clear on Mr. Jamison's face.

Dr. Rush maintained his position with the blood continuing to flow. "As any simpleton can see, I'm bleeding this man to help rid him of his madness. Do not interrupt my work, sir!"

The Justice of the Peace spoke louder, "The judge's order says 'immediate release'. Now stanch the bleeding and release the man."

Dr. Rush sighed heavily. He then pulled a rag from his coat pocket and pressed it to the wound. "Hold this," he said to the tall orderly at Brock's right arm. The other orderly also released Brock and stepped away. "Unlock his restraints," the doctor said.

The doctor stomped up to the Justice of the Peace. "I will speak to Judge Tompkins about this personally. You *will* see this patient back in the hospital where he belongs." The doctor hurried to the door. "Mark my words; you will see," he said to the Jamisons as he passed, then disappeared.

Brock groaned when the orderly unlocked the shackle from his left arm, which fell loosely to his side. Mr. Jamison stepped forward to hold the rag to Brock's bleeding arm while Seth steadied him. "Are you able to walk, Brock? We must leave here before the doctor returns. A hired carriage awaits."

Stiff from the experience yet relieved, Brock said, "Yeah, I can walk." He cringed and held the rag on his still bleeding arm. "Can you tie something around the rag to hold it in place? That should help stop the bleeding." Mr. Jamison nodded and took his handkerchief from his coat pocket and secured the rag.

As Seth helped Brock into the carriage, Mr. Jamison spoke with the Justice of the Peace. "Sir, your authority prevented potential harm to this young man. Thank you."

The official shrugged. "Only did what the judge ordered. I would watch out for reprisal from the good doctor. He don't take kindly to his authority being questioned."

Mr. Jamison pursed his lips and nodded.

CHAPTER 24   Oct 25, Thursday

After the short carriage ride to the Jamison family home, Brock sat at his usual spot at the kitchen table with Mr. Jamison at the head and Seth in Isaac's spot. Mrs. Jamison and Amelia had herded the boys upstairs to give the men privacy.

Brock sipped a cup of the now-familiar, weak beer. "How did you know I was at the hospital?"

Mr. Jamison spoke up. "When you did not return from the Harbor Master, I set to worry. Directly, Mr. Chapman from the hospital entered the store. He told of what he had seen and heard when the warden and the watchmen arrived with you in handcuffs. I locked the store, collected Seth and we went straight to Judge Thompkins. His father and mine were life-long friends. When we explained that Dr. Rush had no authority to seize and hold you, he signed the order for your immediate release pending further details from the doctor."

"Sir, I can't begin to thank you for your involvement." Brock teared up. "I was really scared while chained to that wall." Mr. Jamison reached and patted Brock on his shoulder.

Seth had hardly spoken during the entire ordeal and fidgeted as they sat at the table. He looked at Brock then at his father. "I think there is more that you do not know about Brock." His serious tone concerned Brock.

"Do you refer to his belief that he left the future to be among us?" Mr. Jamison said straight-faced.

Brock jerked his head toward Mr. Jamison.

"How did you know, Father?" Seth asked in disbelief.

Mr. Jamison displayed a faint smile. "Isaac shared a discussion he had with Brock before he asked me to take him on at the store." He stared at Brock and nodded.

"I had no idea, sir." Brock frowned. "But you never let on that you knew." He spread his hands apart.

Quietly, Mr. Jamison said, "It was my belief that when you trusted me, you'd tell me what you had shared with Isaac."

Brock lowered his eyes, blushing. When he finally looked up, he found disappointment but kindness in Mr. Jamison's eyes. He responded with a weak smile accompanied by watery eyes. "I'm sorry, sir."

Brock turned his focus to the immediate problem with Dr. Rush. He looked from Mr. Jamison to Seth. "Something Dr. Rush said while I was chained to the wall caught my attention. He said that I had pestered Dr. Franklin. How would he know I'd met with Dr. Franklin and had dinner with him?"

Mr. Jamison shrugged.

Seth's face showed a slight grimace then nodded. "Gossip in the courthouse suggests that Temple Franklin was spouting off about a young man attempting to swindle his grandfather. Supposedly, he vowed to intervene."

"That asshole!" Brock blurted then saw the severe frown on Mr. Jamison. "Opps. I'm sorry."

Brock continued, "It's just that Temple seems dead set to keep me away from Dr. Franklin. You saw how he behaved in the store a couple of days ago. I don't trust him any farther than I can throw this table." He pounded the surface to make his point.

Mr. Jamison looked squarely at Seth. "Son, what should we expect from Judge Thompkins after Dr. Rush assails him?"

"It's difficult to predict," Seth said, shaking his head. "Dr. Rush is a recognized authority on lunacy. His diagnosis will undoubtedly hold considerable sway with the judge."

"Does that mean I'll be thrown back into Rush's prison after he talks to the judge?"

Seth's look of resignation answered Brock's question. "I'm afraid we have few options," Seth said. "We can seek another recognized doctor to certify that you are not mad. Or, we could try to hide you until Dr. Rush and Temple Franklin have forgotten your existence." He looked at his father. "Father, neither of these choices assures success, however."

Mr. Jamison rubbed his chin. "What say you, Brock?"

Brock fidgeted on the bench. "I'm not going to let them take me back to that basement. That's a death sentence."

Seth interrupted. "You could flee the city."

Brock jammed his hands into his arm pits. "You mean just get on a horse and ride away? I don't know where I'd go or how I'd survive when I got there." He blushed again. "And I've never actually ridden a horse."

Both Seth and Mr. Jamison stared at Brock, then looked at each other and grinned lightly.

Seth turned back to Brock and spoke with a degree of hesitation. "If you were to admit that you contrived the tale about the future to gain attention in the city, all might be forgiven."

Brock frowned and shook his head slightly.

"Or, perhaps you could claim that you no longer remember this *Texas*, only Pennsylvania," Mr. Jamison said, his face lighting up. "You could claim that after the second bleeding by Dr. Rush you're cured. The flattery alone may get Rush to dismiss the issue."

Brock stood quickly, the bench scraping on the floor. He held the crude bandage on his arm as he paced. Both Seth and Mr. Jamison watched him without speaking.

"Those ideas make sense," Brock said. "But I'd be lying in both cases. And my problem of how to get back home to Texas would still exist."

Seth shrugged. "Is avoiding Dr. Rush's treatments not worth a bit of prevarication? Although as an attorney, I could not participate in a known misrepresentation of the truth."

Brock shook his head. "I don't know. If I went before the judge and tried to say I'm cured, he would want to know where I'm really from, how I got to the hospital, where my parents are, and on and on." He crossed his arms. "And I don't have those answers. At least answers he would believe."

Seth shook his head while Mr. Jamison nodded slightly.

"Dr. Franklin! I've got to convince him to help," Brock said, his jaw set, his posture straight. "He can call off Temple and I'd bet he can convince Dr. Rush to let this go." He leaned on the table. "I just have to persuade him to help somehow."

Mr. Jamison tapped his fingers together. "Brock, you've met with Dr. Franklin for only brief periods. How do you expect to convince him to become your advocate in this situation?"

A smile came to Brock's face. "There just might be a way."

######

Mr. Jamison rose from the table, saying he needed to return to his store. He suggested that Brock stay at the house for the remainder of the day to recover from his experience.

Brock insisted that he was okay and could return to work. "Sir, I've already screwed up your day. If I can help at the store, I want to do it."

"Very well. Come along." He turned to Seth as they all moved out the door. "Son, thank you for your assistance this day. Isaac too would be most grateful you helped rescue his friend." They shook hands warmly before Seth walked away in the opposite direction.

With only two hours left before closing time, Brock set about stacking some kegs to make room for the goods expected from the *Empress of China*. In the process his right arm started bleeding again. Brock's concern did not faze the shop owner. Mr. Jamison merely untied the bloody handkerchief used at the hospital and replaced it with a length of cloth he had been using to wipe off his inventory. He snugged it up, pleased with his medical care. Brock cringed at the lack of sterile dressing but did not know how to voice his concerns without insulting his boss. He let it go for now.

After supper at the Jamison house, Brock did not feel like working with Amelia on arithmetic. He wanted to rest and think about his next move with Dr. Franklin. But the teenager's excitement about a slate tablet she had borrowed persuaded him to reconsider. "Okay, I want you to write the numbers 1-25."

Amelia began writing the numerals on the slate with what she called a slate pencil. The screeching caused Brock to cringe. He had heard the expression "fingernails on a chalkboard" from his grandmother but had never actually experienced it. Until now!

Clenching his jaw, he clamped his hand over Amelia's to stop the sound. "Holy…crap! That's awful!"

Amelia dropped the slate pencil and folded her hands in her lap, looking down. "Am I doing it wrong?"

Brock recovered when the screeching stopped. "No. No, it's nothing you did. It's the sound of the slate pencil. Don't you have any chalk?"

She frowned. "I don't understand 'chalk.'"

Brock sighed. "Okay. Go on with the numbers. Maybe I'll get used to it." He braced as Amelia brought the slate pencil back to the tablet then winced as she formed the numbers.

In addition to the unnerving screech, the marks made on the slate by the pencil were faint; he could barely make out the numbers as Amelia proceeded.

For the next hour, sitting side by side, Amelia marked and Brock wiped the slate as they moved from writing numbers to simple addition. Gradually, Brock found a level of tolerance to the pencil screeching.

Brock discouraged his pupil from counting on her fingers, instead teaching her to memorize the standard addition tables used in the twentieth century. At first she was overwhelmed. Soon, however, she got the gist of it and delighted at Brock's praise for her progress. The satisfaction he felt pleased and surprised him. The evening flew by.

Only minutes after Mrs. Jamison called bed-time for the boys, Brock excused himself and made his way to his bed. He was tired and sore from his hospital "stay." In the cold bed he tried to concentrate on his plan for Dr. Franklin but found it impossible as the bed warmed. He didn't fight the needed sleep.

CHAPTER 25   Oct 26, Friday

Brock's duties at the store the next day did not prevent him from developing his plan. He needed to get to Dr. Franklin as soon as possible. Any delay might land him back in the hospital if Dr. Rush successfully appealed to the judge.

Getting past Temple Franklin was the first major hurdle. Of course, he also needed Dr. Franklin to agree to meet with him. His best chance was to get Sally Bache to run interference for him. But getting to her and convincing her to help without encountering Temple and, by extension Dr. Rush, could be a significant challenge.

Brock opted for another letter to Dr. Franklin. But getting it into the famous man's hands could be a challenge. He'd deal with that later. He composed the letter in his head as he worked:

Good day, Dr. Franklin,

First, let me express my gratitude for you meeting with me initially and then inviting me to dinner last Tuesday. You are both a kind and generous man. And, of course, your intellect is well known on both sides of the Atlantic.

Sir, when we last met, you agreed to consider meeting with me again if I could provide proof of what I have told you in confidence. I would like to offer such proof for your consideration. But I must do so in person.

I am at your disposal. However, I ask that we meet soon. I was recently held captive by Dr. Rush at Pennsylvania Hospital. And I suspect that your grandson, Temple, may be complicit in my seizure. My release from captivity was achieved only via written orders from Judge Thompkins. I fear, however, that further efforts to apprehend me and to perform atrocious surgery upon me are forthcoming. I beg you to receive me, sir.

Please contact me at Mr. Jamison's store at your earliest opportunity.

Respectfully,

Brock Sinclair

With Mr. Jamison's continued support and writing supplies, Brock wrote his plea to Dr. Franklin during the mid-day dinner break. Brock showed Mr. Jamison the letter when he returned from his dinner.

"May I ask the 'proof' to which you refer?" Mr. Jamison said, biting his lip.

Brock hesitated. "Sir, no disrespect, but I'd rather keep it confidential for the time being." Mr. Jamison tightened his lips and slowly turned away. Brock felt bad about not leveling with the man who had helped him in so many ways. But Isaac's warning about the tattoo still registered with him and Mr. Jamison *was* a devout Catholic. Losing Mr. Jamison, his only real ally, because of a baseless fear was not worth the risk.

He returned to his work while considering how to get his letter delivered to Dr. Franklin. If he hand-delivered it to the house and Temple answered the door, the letter might just get burned before Dr. Franklin saw it. He couldn't take that chance.

Sally Bache's husband, Richard, had become head of the American Post Office after Ben Franklin retired from that position. If Brock took the letter to the post office, wherever it was, maybe Richard would hand deliver it to his father-in-law.

All afternoon, Mr. Jamison had not spoken to Brock except to give specific orders. He remained silent on the walk home. Brock broke the ice. "Sir, I apologize for not sharing what I hope is proof of my situation. I do not mean to offend and I hope to be more forthcoming soon."

Mr. Jamison stopped and faced Brock. "By welcoming you into my home and providing you employment I have demonstrated significant trust in you. I would have thought that your trust would be reciprocal."

Brock felt terrible. "Mr. Jamison, the conversation I had with Dr. Franklin included some details I did not have the opportunity to share with Isaac. I also revealed to Dr. Franklin aspects of his life that are not well known in this time but will be made public in the future. As such, we agreed to keep our conversation in the strictest of confidence. If I'm able to convince Dr. Franklin of the validity of my situation, I would then be able to share all with you. I hope you can understand."

Mr. Jamison held Brock's eyes. But he did not respond verbally, and, in time, only nodded slightly.

"Thank you for your patience, sir. And also thank you for everything you and your family have done for me."

Further along in their walk Brock chanced seeking advice from Mr. Jamison. "I'd like to get the letter you saw into Dr. Franklin's hands without Temple intercepting. If I took it to the local post office, do you think Richard Bache might deliver it to Dr. Franklin?"

Mr. Jamison considered the question then nodded. "Your approach may have merit. That is, if you can find Mr. Bache."

As they walked, Mr. Jamison explained that the post office was on Market St. between 2nd and 3rd. Brock then received permission to leave the store in the morning just long enough to take the letter there.

When the supper dishes were cleared from the table, Amelia immediately produced the writing slate and the slate pencil. She had replaced her interest in *Robinson Crusoe* in favor of arithmetic. Initially, Brock was annoyed that she just assumed he would continue to tutor her every evening. But the truth was he did not object to the opportunity.

Amelia moved onto the bench beside Brock, careful to leave a small gap between their hips. The lesson began with Brock giving his student simple, two-digit, addition problems to write and solve. Both the slate pencil's screech and its feeble marks on the tablet annoyed Brock more than the previous session. In the dim light he could hardly distinguish the numerals Amelia was writing. "Would it help to wipe the slate with a wet cloth?"

With a clean slate Amelia attacked the addition of the digits one through six with ease. Digits above that slowed her responses yet she remained error free. Each time Brock told the girl that her answer was correct she quickly wiped the slate and prepared for the next problem.

Amelia was ready for something a little more difficult. He neatly wrote the multiplication table for the digits one through five on the slate and had the girl start to recite the answers out loud. After three passes, he erased the answers and had Amelia tell him the products of the multiplications. She faltered a few times but made good progress.

Brock concluded the session with Amelia agreeing to work with the slate during the next day.

"After my chores tomorrow, I will study the arithmetic," she said, her eyes sparkling. "I promise to be perfect for the next lesson." Her gains were small in Brock's mind but he was proud of his student anyway.

CHAPTER 26   Oct 27, Saturday

Saturday morning Brock found the post office in a nondescript building where Mr. Jamison had said it would be. A stocky Richard Bache greeted Brock without enthusiasm. "The delivery from New York is late and will compromise the day's entire schedule. I have little time for interruptions."

"I understand, sir," Brock said. "But if you could just deliver this letter to Dr. Franklin when you return home, it would really help me out." Brock reached into his pocket for the coin Mr. Jamison had given him to pay for the postage and offered it to Mr. Bache. "I hope this will cover the cost of the delivery."

Bache smiled and chuckled. "A halfpenny?" He put up his hand to reject the coin. "I suppose I can burden myself with the delivery. Who are you by the way?"

Brock hesitated. "My name is Brock Sinclair." He quickly added, "I've met with Dr. Franklin a couple of times recently. I believe he anticipates this correspondence."

"Dr. Franklin lives just yonder." Bache pointed in the direction of Dr. Franklin's house. Can you not deliver it yourself?"

Brock rubbed his hand on his pants leg nervously. "In truth Temple is not exactly one of my supporters. I'm afraid he'll intercept the letter and it's important that Dr. Franklin gets it." His eyes pleaded with the man.

Bache pursed his lips, then nodded before tucking the folded sheet with its seal inside his coat pocket. "I'll see that he gets it."

After the dinner hour a young boy ran into Mr. Jamison's store with a small sheet of paper. He spoke to Mr. Jamison. "Sir, I was told to deliver this to Brock Sinclair. Would he be about?"

Brock rushed from the back of the store. "Here. I'm Brock Sinclair." He took the paper from the boy who turned and ran from the store. The boy's hasty exit surprised Brock. He broke the seal and unfolded the paper and read while Mr. Jamison watched.

"What is it, Brock?"

Brock smiled at his boss. "It says Dr. Franklin will receive me at three o'clock today."

######

When Sally showed Brock into Dr. Franklin's library, the old man looked up over his spectacles but made no effort to stand. "Brock, come in."

"Thank you for meeting with me again, Dr. Franklin. I believe you will find today's conversation quite interesting."

Dr. Franklin pointed to the chair where Brock had sat previously. He then spoke to his daughter, "Thank you, Sally. Please leave us and don't permit Temple to enter should he return." Sally turned and left the room.

Dr. Franklin looked directly at Brock. "I observe that you arrive empty-handed. But before we get to your alleged *evidence*, I want to hear your claim of being apprehended and mistreated at Pennsylvania Hospital."

Brock felt as if he was on trial by this man whose life he admired. "The truth is that men with pistols and two of Dr. Rush's orderlies surrounded me on the street. They put me in handcuffs and led me to the hospital. There Dr. Rush's men chained me to a wall where one of them punched me in the stomach. Later Dr. Rush came in with the two orderlies and proceeded to hold me against the wall while Rush bled my arm supposedly to let the bad blood out." Brock's eyes flared as he described the incident.

Dr. Franklin focused on every word. "You are aware, of course, that bloodletting is a recognized treatment for numerous ailments and is, indeed, a common practice. Nevertheless, continue your account."

"While blood flowed down my arm into a pan, Mr. Jamison and his son, Seth, who's a lawyer, and a justice from a Judge Thompkins' office broke in and called a halt. Rush objected but eventually his brutes released me. The Jamisons got me into a carriage and took me to Mr. Jamison's house. In discussions there I learned that Temple had been spreading rumors that I was trying to swindle you in some way and he was going to take steps to stop me." Brock's voice had become more forceful as he finished.

"Do you insinuate that Temple played a role in your apprehension?"

Brock hesitated for an instant. Clearly angry, he said, "Temple has been belligerent to me from the start. He made it clear that he did not want me in your house or talking to you. I don't know why he resents me but it's obvious that he does. And yes, I suspect he had a part in me being kidnapped and taken to the hospital."

Dr. Franklin sat back in his chair, deep in thought. "Temple *did* speak of your visits with intense cynicism." He paused. "I will speak with him concerning any animosity he may harbor."

Hearing that Dr. Franklin had detected something in Temple's attitude bolstered Brock. He took a deep breath to improve his self-control. "And, sir, if you have any sway with Dr. Rush, maybe you could put in a good word about my sanity."

Dr. Franklin mulled this request. "Perhaps the good doctor and I will have a chat."

"Thank you, sir."

"Well, son, your note said you could share something that confirms your earlier statements," Dr. Franklin said, tapping his fingers on the arm of his chair.

Brock leaned forward. "Sir, before I show you my proof, I want to clarify a couple of things."

Dr. Franklin frowned but nodded.

"Having made several sea voyages, you undoubtedly observed ink markings on the arms of some of the sailors, right?"

Dr. Franklin looked puzzled and was slow to respond. "Yes, I observed crude drawings and numbers marking the forearms of seamen. What of it?"

"Bear with me, sir. You used the word 'crude' in reference to the tattoos and I bet they were black or dark blue. Is that correct?"

"As I recall, yes."

"Okay, now hold that thought. Before I show you my evidence, I want to understand your religious beliefs. From what I've read a Deist believes in God but does not condone organized religion or such teachings. Is that correct?"

"I do not intend to debate religion with you," Dr. Franklin said, his patience fading.

"And I have no interest in debating religion with you, sir; I'm quite certain I would lose that contest. It's just that the one person who witnessed what I'm about to show you warned me not to show it to anyone else or risk having it labeled as witchcraft. Respectfully, does your intelligence hold you above such pagan beliefs?" Brock's tone was dead serious. He stared directly into Dr. Franklin's eyes. His stomach ached knowing that this could be his last chance with the man.

Dr. Franklin returned the stare. Finally he answered, "My beliefs are firmly grounded in morality and nature."

"I take you at your word, sir." Brock stood and unbuttoned his shirt.

Dr. Franklin reared back in surprise.

With his shirt lowered from his left shoulder, Brock turned slowly to Dr. Franklin. "Sir, the flag you see is similar to the one currently being flown in the thirteen colonies, ah…the thirteen states. It has the same thirteen red and white stripes to represent the original number of colonies. What is different is that instead of thirteen stars in a circle on the blue field, there are fifty-one stars in a rectangle to represent the fifty-one states in the year 2029."

Dr. Franklin squirmed forward in his chair and pushed himself up with the aid of his cane. He stepped around the hassock, leaned close to Brock's shoulder and raised his chin to peer through his bifocals. At last he drew in a breath and released it. "Unbelievable!"

Brock turned slightly to see Dr. Franklin's face. "Sir, the electric needles and inks used to draw tattoos with these colors and this level of accuracy won't be developed for another century or more."

Dr. Franklin's wide eyes met Brock's before he used his free hand to grasp Brock's arm for a better view. He ran his fingers over the flag image, along the stripes and in circles among the field of stars before stepping back to his chair. He fell into it and remained silent, staring at Brock's shoulder.

Brock slipped back into his shirt and sat in his chair, watching his host. He could not restrain his fidgeting and after what felt like hours, said, "Well, do you believe me now?"

Dr. Franklin slowly turned his head to look at Brock. "My scientific knowledge does not permit me to comprehend how you could have lived in another time. But my experience, particularly as a printer, confirms that the markings on your skin cannot be achieved with current methods. Thus, the quandary." He never broke eye contact with Brock, apparently looking for any reaction that would give him a clue to the truth.

This was another critical juncture in his plea for Dr. Franklin's help. "Sir, I am also at a complete loss as to how I got to Philadelphia and to this year. But I can explain the existence of the tattoo as if it was yesterday."

"Please do."

"When I was sixteen, getting tattoos was a popular trend and had been for many years. I asked my parents to let me get one for my birthday. My conservative father, probably from your influence, agreed but would only allow certain design choices and only in a non-conspicuous place. I settled on the flag because…well, it was colorful and not controversial.

"Since I wasn't eighteen, it was illegal to get the tattoo without a parent's signature. Dad went with me to a tattoo shop near our home in Texas where I chose the flag tat and had it done there. The girl used an electric tattoo machine that had several small needles that injected the ink just under the skin. It was a bit painful but tolerable. I had to make two trips because of the different colors that touched each other."

"I want to know more about the flag. You indicate that there are fifty-one stars and fifty-one states?"

Hope swelled within Brock. He grinned, his excitement building. "After the first thirteen states, the country expanded south to the Gulf of Mexico and west to the Pacific coast. This happened mostly in the 1800's, with a few more states added later."

Dr. Franklin's eyes sparkled. "America extends to the ocean of Balboa?"

Brock shrugged. "My history and geography aren't the best. But yes, America stretches from the Atlantic to the Pacific and now includes Alaska and the Hawaiian Islands far out into the Pacific Ocean."

Dr. Franklin's smile continued for a minute then faded. "It is my opinion that analysis of this matter by committee may have more benefit than that of one man alone. With your concurrence I will endeavor to assemble some trusted colleagues to join us in subsequent discussions and examination."

Brock hesitated. "I don't know. What about the warning I received about the tattoo being seen as witchcraft? If your associates want to burn me at the stake, how open will they be to consider my story?"

Dr. Franklin pursed his lips before he spoke. "Your point is worthy of consideration. Nevertheless, I will choose my associates based on their analytical thinking but with your concern in mind. Perhaps we can gather here tomorrow at two o'clock if you are in accord?"

"Without a doubt, sir. And thank you for your indulgence."

Brock left Dr. Franklin's house almost skipping as he hummed "I Gotta Feeling", a twenty year-old song that popped into his head.

CHAPTER 27   Oct 27, Saturday

The rest of the daytime and that evening Brock's enthusiasm did not diminish despite the continuing pain and swelling in his right arm at the recent bleeding site. At the supper table he commented about the weather, Dr. Franklin's home, even how nice Sally Bache had been to him. Mrs. Jamison allowed herself a grin at Brock's non-stop chatter.

After the meal Brock did not wait for Amelia to raise the issue of study. He was helping her and her mother clear the table when he said, "What say we tackle some more math tonight, Amelia?"

The girl's instant smile gave Brock his answer. "Yes, please. I've practiced my numbers many times." She looked at her mother who nodded in response as she bent to wash the supper plates and mugs.

With the kitchen tidy, Mrs. Jamison moved into the parlor with her darning while Brock moved an oil lamp to the kitchen table and sat in his usual spot. Amelia brought her slate and pencil and sat beside him with Brock feeling her hip touch his lightly. Was it intentional or just a coincidence? Regardless, he enjoyed the contact.

"Let's start with your multiplication tables," Brock said. "I want you to write the two's, the three's, the four's and the five's. Then we'll go from there. Okay?"

Amelia hurriedly moved her slate into position and started writing the number combinations. Clearly, she had practiced writing the digits; the handwriting had improved noticeably from their previous session. After only a few minutes her calculations filled the slate. She laid the slate pencil on the table and crossed her arms, indicating satisfaction with her accomplishment.

"Good job!" Brock said, patting Amelia on the arm. "Now, let's move on to the rest of the numbers."

Brock wrote the multiplication products for six, seven, eight and nine for all the digits 1-9. He then had Amelia point to and recite each simple equation he had written. But did she understand what she was looking at?

Amelia shook her head in frustration. "I cannot memorize all the numbers in the world. There are just too many."

"If you memorize these remaining numbers on the slate, that's all you need to memorize."

Amelia frowned at Brock. "I do not understand."

Brock smiled. "What's the biggest number you can imagine?"

"One hundred!" she said with little hesitation.

"How about a bigger number like 13,542?" Brock saw her puzzled look. In the corner of her tablet he wrote the number then read it aloud. "Would you agree that's a big number?"

"Yes, very big," her eyes larger than before.

"Well, notice that you already know all the digits in that big number. Once you memorize the multiplication tables, you can multiply any number by any other number. And next time I'll show you exactly how to do it."

Amelia clasped her hands in front of her like she had just been given a present. She then turned toward Brock, wrapped her arms around his upper body and kissed him on the cheek. Then, as if Brock was on fire, she jerked her arms away and jumped to her feet, blushing. With her slate and pencil still on the table, she ran up the spiral stairs.

Brock froze. Amelia's reaction had surprised him, leaving him unsure about what had just happened. He gathered his wits and dared a sideways glance into the parlor to see if Mrs. Jamison was aware of what had transpired. With relief he saw that she remained focused on her hand work. But she had to have at least *heard* Amelia run up the stairs. Should he say something to her? Explain what had happened? But what had happened?

CHAPTER 28   Oct 28, Sunday

When Brock arrived at Dr. Franklin's house at two o'clock on Sunday and was shown into the library by Sally, several well-dressed men stood talking with their host.

Dr. Franklin welcomed Brock with an outstretched hand and a smile. "Please join us, Brock. I want to introduce you to my distinguished colleagues. He gestured to each man as he made the introductions. "This is Mr. Jared Ingersoll, an attorney; Dr. John Jones, my personal physician; and Mr. Thomas Mifflin, a prominent merchant before distinguishing himself in the Continental Army and more recently in politics." Brock nodded to each man in turn as he shook their hands.

"Gentlemen, this young man is Brock Sinclair. He is a visitor to Philadelphia with a very unusual situation. As I indicated with my invitations, it is my hope that using our collective powers of analysis and problem solving, we may offer Brock some insight to his circumstances."

Dr. Franklin gestured for everyone to be seated with Brock at his right hand. He turned to Brock. "I am confident that these gentlemen are open-minded, not judgmental and, above all, trustworthy. Therefore, I encourage you to be forthcoming with them as you have been with me.

"And to you, gentlemen," Dr. Franklin addressed the three men seated in an arc across from him and Brock, "Be mindful that I have heard Brock's assertions previously and find them quite astounding. Nevertheless, I would not have troubled you to assemble today if I did not think further scrutiny had merit. I implore you to hear Brock out and to earnestly consider his account and the physical evidence he will share in due time."

Dr. Franklin turned back to Brock, "You have our full attention. Please proceed."

Brock had been excited about having his problem analyzed by Dr. Franklin and some of his learned associates. Now, however, facing these obviously busy men, who were not expecting to hear anything like what he was about to share, unnerved him. Would they laugh at him, ridicule Dr. Franklin for playing a joke or just walk out? Dr. Franklin had expressed his support in front of these men. And he *is* Dr. Franklin. So, maybe they will at least give his claims deliberation in deference to their host's reputation.

"Gentlemen," Brock said after clearing his throat, "thank you for taking time from your schedules to meet today." A few heads nodded in response.

"As Dr. Franklin said, my name is Brock Sinclair. I am nineteen years old and find myself in your fair city without family or resources. My home is in a place called Texas, hundreds of miles southwest of here. I'm certain you have not heard of it because it is much farther southwest than any of the states."

"Son, that would be unexplored wilderness," Mr. Ingersoll said with exasperation. "No one inhabits those lands except the natives and perhaps an occasional trapper."

"That is probably quite true, sir,...at this time," Brock said, uncertainty in his voice.

Eyebrows rose on all three men.

"Brock, I suggest you start from the beginning," Dr. Franklin said with an encouraging nod.

Taking a deep breath, Brock began. "My home is in the state of Texas, approximately fifteen hundred miles southwest of here. I grew up there, went to school there and have completed one year of college at the University of Texas in Austin. When I was last there, the year was 2029." The looks on the faces of the three men caused Brock to pause before proceeding.

Dr. Jones broke the silence, grinning. "Benjamin, with all due respect, do I detect a lark?"

Dr. Franklin leveled his gaze first at his physician then at the other two men. His voice conveyed no conviviality. "I summoned you here in good faith. As I prefaced my remarks, young Brock's assertions are quite extraordinary. But I implore you to hear him out." He nodded for Brock to continue.

Before Brock could speak Mr. Ingersoll, the attorney, interrupted. "There was chatter this week in the taverns about a new type of axe, one with two cutting heads made by one of our local blacksmiths. The tattle is that the smith got the inspiration from a blond stranger named Brock who had visited his shop recently. Supposedly, the smith said this stranger had seen such an axe stored at his father's house." Ingersoll narrowed his eyes at Brock. "Are you, by chance, the originator of the axe rumor causing a stir in our city?"

Brock blushed. The news of the axe surprised him and he wasn't sure whether this revelation would help him or hurt him as he tried to convince these men to take him seriously. "Sir, I did speak with a blacksmith, Amos, several days ago and we did talk about a double-bitted axe that belonged to my grandfather. Amos indicated that he would try to make one. Whether or not he was successful, I do not know. It sounds like he was." Brock tightened his lips.

Dr. Franklin cleared his throat and looked at Brock. "I believe it is best for you to start your account at Pennsylvania Hospital."

Brock wiped his smile away and nodded. "Yes, sir." He faced the three men across from him. "Gentlemen, almost two weeks ago in my home state of Texas, I apparently fell and hit my head, losing consciousness. When I came to, I was in a bed at Pennsylvania Hospital where Dr. Benjamin Rush had already bled me from my left arm. I have no idea how I traveled fifteen hundred miles from Texas or moved from the year 2029 to this century. But my memories of life in Texas are complete and detailed from a young age until the time of my fall. Lastly, I have no memories of a life in Pennsylvania or being in this century prior to my discovery in Pennsylvania Hospital."

"Certainly, your memory has been altered by your head injury," Dr. Jones said. "You should be in the care of Dr. Rush. No one knows better than he about the appropriate treatments."

Dr. Franklin stared at his physician. "Doctor, you may not be aware that Dr. Rush and his assistants took Brock from the street by force and restrained him with chains in the hospital. There they attempted to bleed him against his will until the procedure was interrupted by a judicial order."

Dr. Jones just rolled his eyes and crossed his arms.

Jared Ingersoll addressed Dr. Franklin. "Sir, I believe we are all aware of the challenges with which Dr. Rush contends. Some of his mental patients are, unfortunately, not cooperative and a few, I presume, are violent. Thus, he must take measures to protect his staff as well as those patients while treatments are administered. It may seem harsh to many but is necessary for the good of society."

Dr. Jones nodded in agreement. "Indeed."

Dr. Franklin held up his hand to suppress further comment and looked his guests in the eyes while he gestured toward Brock. "Does this young man appear mad? Or violent? Confused perhaps but certainly not a danger to our citizenry. Hear him out."

Brock waited a few seconds then cleared his throat again. He wanted to show his nearly-healed cut and his infected cut to the men but felt the timing was wrong since he had no proof of bacteria. Maybe later. "Gentlemen, life in years to come will be very different from what you know." He paused. "Technology has grown rapidly during this century, wouldn't you agree?"

The assembled men nodded as they glanced from one to the other.

"In the next two hundred and fifty years technology will advance at a rate beyond your imagination. Choose any topic and I'll try to tell you what it's like in 2029."

The three men looked at Dr. Franklin expectantly then at each other.

"Surgical procedures!" Dr. Jones said with another smirk and crossed his arms again.

"Shipping!" Mr. Mifflin said in a raised voice, grinning.

Mr. Ingersoll stood. "Gentlemen, we will be here until dark hearing this young man's fanciful tales. Let us agree on a single topic that will be of interest to all and may expose this pretext for what it is. Shall we?"

The three men rose and faced each other, talking in hushed tones. Mr. Ingersoll, the attorney, spoke up. "Dr. Franklin, we would like to speak with you in private before proceeding. Could you ask the young man to leave the room while we discuss this matter?"

Dr. Franklin gave Brock a pleading look. "Would you be offended to wait in the parlor until we call? Your agreement to do so may serve as a measure of legitimacy for these gentlemen."

Brock rose without hesitation. "Sure. Just yell when you're ready." He left the room and closed the door.

As Brock walked toward the parlor in the front part of the house where he had visited previously with Sally, she appeared from the dining room.

"Brock, your departure from the conference is quite sudden."

"Oh, hi, Mrs. Bache. No, I'm not leaving." Brock paused. "At least I hope I get invited back to the meeting. They wanted to talk alone to respond to a challenge I made to them."

"Again, please call me 'Sally'." She indicated for Brock to follow her to the parlor.

When they were seated across from each other, Brock said, "Sally, the demonstration I talked about may not be necessary."

Brock rolled up the sleeve on his left arm and leaned forward. "This cut to bleed me was made two weeks ago when I first arrived in Philadelphia. Notice how the scar is smooth and there is little redness. And though there is still a tiny bit of tenderness, it's almost healed."

He then pushed up the sleeve on his right arm and removed the bandage. "This cut was made when I was restrained…in the hospital on Thursday, three days ago." He pointed with his left hand. "This site is red, the arm swollen and very sore. It's infected with the bacteria I told you about earlier. Unless I get some treatment soon, there is a chance the infection will spread and cause serious damage, even death.

Sally covered her mouth with her hand. "Gracious, Brock! Your arm is swollen and looks quite painful. Have you not been to the hospital for a doctor's assessment?"

"No, I don't trust the doctors since they don't understand what's wrong. I plan to treat it myself tonight with Mr. Jamison's help." He nodded in the direction of the library. "But I may show Dr. Franklin and the other men my arms first."

CHAPTER 29 Oct 28, Sunday

Both Sally and Brock turned at a noise in the hall. Brock stood up when Thomas Mifflin approached. "Brock, please rejoin us in the library."

When Brock and Mr. Mifflin had returned to their seats, Dr. Franklin faced Brock. But before he could speak, Mr. Ingersoll interrupted. "Dr. Franklin, would you allow me to pose our challenge to the young man?"

Dr. Franklin hesitated. "Very well."

Mr. Ingersoll's smirk was obvious as he addressed Brock. "History will undoubtedly record our recent achievements at the Constitutional Convention. But how the states will vote is as yet undetermined." He glanced at Mr. Mifflin and Dr. Jones then turned back to Brock. "What results can we expect from the states?"

The question about the Constitution caught Brock off guard. He had expected the men's questions would be about some aspect of technology or scientific advancements. Changing mental gears, the order of the states' ratification was surprisingly clear.

"Mr. Ingersoll, gentlemen, first of all, I am *not* a historian. And although I have studied the life of Ben Franklin, rather, Dr. Franklin, I have not been particularly interested in history."

Mr. Ingersoll grinned at Dr. Franklin.

Brock continued, "I *can* tell you that Delaware, to be known as the First State, will lead the ratifications in early December with Pennsylvania and New Jersey also ratifying before the year ends. The next eight states, beginning with Georgia and Connecticut, will ratify next year." Not understanding how he knew this information, Brock continued. "North Carolina and Rhode Island will be hold-outs with the former ratifying in '89, the latter in '90."

Mr. Mifflin lifted an eyebrow. "Most of the delegates would predict that Delaware and Pennsylvania would ratify first. The rest of what you say is no more than conjecture. It is encouraging, however, that you predict that all will, indeed, ratify."

"I knew that the hard-headed Country Party in Rhode Island would be stubborn," said Dr. Jones. "They offer so little to the nation yet serve as a perpetual thorn."

Dr. Franklin interrupted. "Doctor, your statement suggests you give credence to Brock's account."

The man blushed. "Sir, my position is only that the young man's prediction is quite plausible." He turned to face Brock and in a sarcastic tone said, "Young man, when did this state of yours, this Texas, ratify?"

Brock paused to consider the perceived challenge. "Sir, Texas won its independence from Mexico in 1836 after the Battle of San Jacinto. Nine years later in 1845 it was annexed by the United States to become the twenty-eighth state."

"Blazes, Dr. Franklin! Are we to accept such twaddle? Twenty-eight states, indeed!" Mr. Ingersoll was on his feet gesturing toward Brock.

Dr. Franklin grasped the arms of his chair as if he was going to rise. Instead, he responded calmly, "Jared, is it your prognostication that the new nation will stagnate along the sea coast? Will it not in future years explore the vast lands to the west and likely settle them? Certainly, I cannot confirm the number of states young Brock professes. But logic would suggest there will be more than thirteen states in the future."

Dr. Franklin turned to Brock. "I cannot explain how I know this, son, but is not the 'Mexico' to which you refer, now known as New Spain?"

Brock nodded. "I think that's correct, sir." He wanted to correct the apparent perception that the country had only twenty-eight states, but waited.

"And what are to be the fourteenth and fifteenth states?" Mr. Mifflin said, breaking his silence.

"I don't know the history of all the states, sir," Brock said. "The only reason I know about Texas is because I grew up there and we studied state history in school. If I had to guess at the next states to join the union after the original thirteen colonies, I'd say something in New England or to the south of South Carolina."

The room went quiet while the three men stared at Brock.

Mr. Ingersoll broke the silence. "Brock, our second question is also related to the Convention. There were proposals supported by the Anti-Federalists that a list of individual rights be included in the Constitution. While such is not in the final writing, the compromise was to consider amendments to enumerate these rights when the First Congress comes to session. We would like to hear your version of the outcome of these proposals."

Brock faced Mr. Ingersoll, nodded, then scanned the others. "The first ten amendments, added relatively soon after ratification, are called the Bill of Rights. And if I remember correctly, this is something Thomas Jefferson pushed for but James Madison actually provided the first draft. The first amendment addresses free speech, free press, assembly and religion. The second provided the right to bear arms." None of the men spoke, seemingly focused on Brock's words. "Another indicates that any rights not assigned to the federal government by the Constitution are given to the states and the people."

Dr. Franklin looked first at Mr. Ingersoll then to Mr. Mifflin. "Gentlemen, you were also at the convention. Does this sound familiar?"

Mr. Ingersoll said, "Dr. Franklin, of course there was some brief discussion on delineating the rights of the people but little detail expressed—"

Mr. Mifflin cut him off. "Jared, the proposals that young Brock listed along with no quartering of troops, right to a fair trial, and prohibition against unlawful search and seizure were also bandied about." He looked at Brock. "How could you know this? There were no written records of those discussions."

"Sir, for me the Bill of Rights is a document that's over two hundred years old. I'm embarrassed to say I cannot recite or even outline the Bill of Rights for you." He blushed. "In my defense I'm only a student and not a politician. And there are now twenty-seven amendments which I have not memorized."

Dr. Jones pounced again. "You cannot identify these supposed amendments?"

Brock set up straighter in his chair. "Sir, no I cannot tick off all twenty-seven. But some *are* more memorable than others."

Brock looked to Dr. Franklin for support but saw no response. To Dr. Jones he said, "One of the amendments abolished slavery and another protects the rights of all people including people of color to vote." Mr. Ingersoll coughed then glanced at Dr. Franklin. The other men glanced at each other, shaking their heads slightly.

"Another amendment gave women the right to vote," Brock said.

A collective gasp went up from the three men.

Brock grinned then continued, "In the early twentieth century an amendment prohibited the drinking of alcohol but it didn't last too long. A few years later another amendment repealed that law. The only other one I remember is a limit of two terms for the president."

Dr. Jones and Mr. Mifflin leaned toward each other, whispering. Mr. Ingersoll sat with his arms crossed, staring at Brock.

Turning to Brock, Dr. Franklin said, "Son, I believe it is time to show these gentlemen what you presented to me on Friday and what I especially want them to see."

Brock's lips formed a tight line before he nodded to his host. He then faced the three men. "Gentlemen, what I share with you now I do at some personal risk. I was warned by an individual, for whom I have great respect, that by my reveal, I may be subjecting myself to serious persecution. I asked Dr. Franklin to assemble open-minded men and I trust he has done so."

With some hesitancy all three men nodded.

Brock continued, "And I ask that you keep what I am about to show you in strictest confidence."

Standing, Brock slowly pulled his shirt from his left shoulder. With the garment slack on his body, he turned his side to his audience.

A soft gasp escaped from one of the men.

"Saints preserve us!" Dr. Jones said as the men got to their feet and approached.

"My God!" Mr. Ingersoll said. "Those markings!" His hand shook as he made the sign of the cross.

In a calmer voice Thomas Mifflin said, "The figure has a resemblance to our own ensign!"

Brock felt the light touch of fingers on the skin of his shoulder. He grimaced as Dr. Jones pinched his skin roughly.

"Gentlemen, you're looking at a tattoo of the American flag. It was done in Texas when I was sixteen-years-old." Brock paused. "That would have been in the year 2026." He pointed at the tattoo with his right hand. "Note that the flag has the same thirteen red and white stripes as your current flag. The big difference is the stars on the blue field number fifty-one to reflect the number of states after Puerto Rico joined the union."

Dr. Franklin's eyebrows rose as he sat straighter in his chair. "The islanders fought bravely in the far south during the war." He smiled. "Statehood would seem an appropriate award. It is curious why it took so long."

Dr. Jones interrupted. "But how…how is this rendering on the young man accomplished?" His tone no longer defiant.

"Doctor, there are many uses of electricity starting in the nineteenth century and expanding exponentially thereafter. An electric tattoo machine drives several needles in and out of the skin, each carrying ink that permanently mark the lower layers. Different colors of ink are used to create an image such as mine."

Dr. Jones shook his head. "But who knows how to do this and where did the devices originate?"

"John," Dr. Franklin said to his physician. "That is precisely the point young Brock is attempting to convey." His smile reassured Brock who was pulling his shirt up on his shoulder.

Mr. Ingersoll sat down heavily, trembling as he stared at Brock. "God, have mercy on our souls."

"Jared!" Dr. Franklin admonished the attorney's distress. "What reason exists to suggest the markings on this young man are demonic? We have already heard evidence that Brock bleeds just like any man. Would a demon do as much?"

Dr. Franklin stared over his glasses at the attorney. "Brock claims it is only ink that we see under his skin. After I observed the markings, I took an opportunity to visit a sea captain with whom I am acquainted. When I described Brock's markings in strictest confidence, he responded that in all his years he had seen nothing even remotely similar. He added that he doubted the markings were genuine but rather an effort at trickery using paint or ink on the skin."

Dr. Franklin looked first at his physician then turned to Brock. "Son, would you allow the good doctor to scrape your skin to see if the image can be removed?"

Brock's eyebrows went up, but a stern look from Dr. Franklin suggested this was a critical test of Brock's claim. Still he cringed at the thought of the 18th century quack scraping his shoulder with a dirty blade. Nevertheless, he nodded.

Dr. Jones rose and pulled a folding knife from his pocket while Brock slowly removed his shirt from his shoulder. As the doctor applied the blade, Brock tried not to flinch despite the pain. He felt sure he was bleeding.

As the doctor backed toward his chair, he announced, "Gentlemen, I see only skin and some blond hair on my blade. I see no evidence of paint or ink on its edge."

The doctor wiped his blade between his thumb and forefinger and closed his blade, a bitter smile on his face.

Brock sighed and put on his shirt once more.

Dr. Franklin addressed his associates. "We need to apply our collective analysis and logic to understand how a young man such as this can be among us with such apparent knowledge of the future and so little knowledge of the present. And, of course, the markings on his shoulder should weigh heavily on our deliberations."

Silence dominated the room. All the men except Dr. Franklin stared at the subject of their challenge. Brock looked toward the men but purposely avoided sustained eye contact. He wanted to present a humbleness that motivated these men to help him. He felt they represented a small hope for a way to return home.

Mr. Ingersoll spoke to Brock in a quiet, yet still somewhat defiant voice. "When you spoke of your Texas earlier, you indicated there were twenty-eight states. Yet you say the markings on your shoulder represent fifty-one states. Which is it?"

"Sir, to be clear. Texas was the twenty-eighth state in 1845. The year when I fell was 2029. In the years since Texas became a state many more were added as the country expanded west to the Pacific Ocean. In 2029 there are indeed fifty-one states."

Dr. Franklin gestured to the wall behind the three men. A crude, framed map that roughly outlined North America with the thirteen colonies barely identifiable hung on a near wall. The men turned and studied the map then one by one turned back, apparently already familiar with it. "Jared, consider all that territory west of the thirteen states. Can you not envision many more states once this vast land is settled?"

Mr. Ingersoll made no further comment only lowered his gaze and shook his head slowly.

Dr. Franklin closed the discussion. "Gentlemen, I propose that we reassemble Tuesday at two in the afternoon to share our individual deliberations."

Mr. Ingersoll spoke up. "Dr. Franklin, I will be in court Tuesday and Wednesday. Perhaps we could meet Thursday instead?" The other men considered the suggestion then indicated their agreement.

Dr. Franklin's three colleagues then rose and in turn shook their host's hand before departing. None shook Brock's hand and only Mr. Mifflin nodded in his direction to acknowledge his presence.

When Brock rose to follow the three men from the house, his host spoke, "Brock, a word before you depart."

Brock turned back.

"The electricity light of which you spoke days before. Perhaps you would assist me in an experiment to replicate what you reported?"

The solemn expression on Brock's face disappeared, replaced by an all-encompassing smile. "Hell, yes!" He blushed. "I mean, certainly, sir. It would be an honor."

Although Dr. Franklin appeared tired, he motioned for Brock to return to his chair. "Please describe in some detail the electricity light that you claim will be developed in the coming years."

"The incandescent light bulb I referenced was one of the earliest types of electric lights. Later more efficient lights that produce little heat and last longer were developed, leaving the incandescent light somewhat rare."

"I do not understand 'incandescent light bulb'."

Brock paused to think. "Incandescence just means something glowing like the embers in a fire. And the early electric lights were shaped a little like a flower bulb."

The two then discussed what would be involved in setting up the experiment and what materials would be needed. Brock's frustration grew as Dr. Franklin did not understand some of the explanations and said some suggested materials were not readily available.

As they talked, Brock asked what they would use as a source of electricity.

"I am fortunate to have a battery that, once charged, should provide the lightning for our experiment."

Brock was puzzled at the term "battery". "Could I see your battery, sir? I'm having a hard time envisioning what it might look like."

Dr. Franklin removed his glasses and pinched the bridge of his nose. In a tired voice he said, "Brock, it has been a long day and my strength is sapped. I should rest now. I have appointments until Wednesday, but perhaps you can join me then for dinner at which time we can further discuss our experiment."

Brock's smile faded. "Sure. I understand, sir. I'll be here at midday."

Dr. Franklin's brows pulled down in concentration. "Son, our discussions this afternoon have been extraordinary. Our guests may indeed contemplate all they have heard and seen. And they may offer suggestions. However, I advise that you restrain your expectations from these deliberations." He smiled weakly. "In my life there have been things which I desired to change but could not. And I have learned that when I accept such circumstances as unalterable, I am more successful at matters which I can influence."

Fighting frustration, Brock said, "Are you saying I should just accept a life here and give up trying to get home to my real life and family?"

"Only you can decide what is best for you. Every road has its own ruts and streams to navigate. As always, one should use one's mind and heart in making difficult choices." Dr. Franklin grimaced. "Now, if you will excuse me."

Brock trudged back toward the Jamison house, Dr. Franklin's sobering advice having all but erased the enthusiasm he had felt following the group discussion. *If I'm honest with myself, those guys, including Dr. Franklin, don't have a clue about who I am, much less how to help me.*

As he walked on, however, his depression dimmed and his determination flared. *I can't give up my family, my life in Texas. I might be stranded here, but I don't have to like it.*

CHAPTER 30   Oct 28, Sunday

When Brock arrived at the Jamison house and despite his disappointment with Dr. Franklin's advice, he was determined to treat his infected right arm where Dr. Rush had bled him during his recent confinement at the hospital. He asked Mr. Jamison if he would help with some preparation and the actual procedure.

"Brock, you should go to the hospital for treatment. I'm not a doctor."

Brock sighed. "Unfortunately, the doctors don't understand the cause of the infection. I believe with your help we can do what is needed with a higher degree of success." His eyes pleaded with the man. "Please, sir."

With some hesitation, Mr. Jamison agreed.

They heated a sharp knife in the fire for sterilization and brought Mr. Jamison's strongest rum and a few strips of clean cloth to the table. After Brock washed his hands and his wounded arm with soap and warm water and had Mr. Jamison wash his hands, they were ready.

Despite the intense pain from the infection as well as the knife wielded gently by Mr. Jamison, Brock held still while the wound drained so he could then apply the rum. Finally, he had

Mr. Jamison tie one of the clean strips around his arm securely to stop the bleeding and to keep the wound clean.

"All the washing and the waste of the rum seems unwarranted," said Mr. Jamison. "Are you sure it's essential?"

"Sir, without those steps we might be introducing more bacteria into the wound than if we did nothing. But we had to do something. Otherwise, I could lose the arm."

Mr. Jamison rose from the table and returned the rum to the cupboard, his lips tight, his head shaking.

######

That evening after the supper dishes had been cleared and the boys dismissed, Mrs. Jamison and Amelia returned to the table where Mr. Jamison had requested Brock to remain seated. Brock had interlocked his fingers on the table and studied them as the women worked, trying to anticipate what this was about.

Mr. Jamison cleared his throat. "My wife and I have observed your tutoring of Amelia with the reading and her numbers."

Brock could feel the blood rushing to his face. He knew that Amelia had touched him on the arm a few times during recent sessions and that she had recently narrowed the gap between their hips. But Brock didn't think her mother or her father had noticed. And he certainly had seen no reaction from Mrs. Jamison after Amelia's peck on the cheek the night before. The expected reprimand from the protective father was a total surprise. And that Mr. Jamison would chew them both out at the same time struck him as unusual. Why not reprimand him privately at the store?

Mr. Jamison continued, "Your knowledge and patience seem well-suited as a tutor. Would you consider tutoring Duncan and Nathan as well as Amelia?"

Brock released the breath he had been holding and tried to breathe normally without the change being noticed. "I...don't know, sir." He paused and worked at cleaning a fingernail then looked at Mr. Jamison. "I've just been sharing some of what I know with Amelia. I'm not really qualified as a teacher."

"As you are aware, Duncan attends the nearby Quaker school. Although he is a bright boy, he tends to distraction and his marks reflect disappointing progress. We are hopeful that a spate of tutoring may augment his development. For Nathan we are hopeful an introduction to grammar and his numbers now will bode well when he attends school next year." Mr. Jamison paused and looked at his wife before continuing.

"I would relieve you from your work at the store two hours early three afternoons each week to perform tutoring until supper. You would continue your wages of three shillings per week. And you can continue to live under my roof as long as the children make progress in their studies."

Brock considered the offer while not trying to make eye contact with anyone at the table. The opportunity to do something rather than sweep and load wagons was tempting. And not having the fear of eviction would be a huge relief. But working in the poor light with no manuals, paper or pencils would be frustrating. "Sir, would you provide some writing slates and pencils for Amelia and the boys to help with their work?"

The merchant considered the request with a frown until he spotted the stare from his wife. "Yes, I believe a few slates and pencils could be made available. Are we in agreement?"

Brock, bolstered by his negotiations, said, "Are there beginner reading books that could be available for our use? Maybe from a school or library."

Mr. Jamison emitted a long exhale. "I suppose a copy of *The New England Primer* would be in order. Is that all?" he said with mock frustration in his voice.

Brock grinned. "Then, we have a deal, sir. When do you want me to start?"

"I see no reason that tomorrow could not be the initial day."

Brock swallowed and nodded. He was not expecting to get started this soon. He had no idea how to go about teaching three students at three different levels.

CHAPTER 31   Oct 29, Monday

Brock did not sleep much Sunday night because his arm hurt and he continued to reflect on Dr. Franklin's advice. How could he just forget his 21st century life? He missed the technology, the food, his friends, his parents, hot showers. He missed so many things.

All morning at the store Brock could hardly focus on his duties. It had taken three tries just to get a fire started in the stove. A cold wind had blown in from the northwest overnight and with no fire in the stove on Sunday, the store had been frigid when they arrived.

When Mr. Jamison had commented that Brock seemed distant, Brock shared some of his doubts with his boss. "Mr. Jamison, late yesterday afternoon Dr. Franklin suggested that maybe I should just forget about living in my time and accept that I am here. That I might be better off focusing on my current life."

Mr. Jamison stepped closer and squeezed Brock's shoulder. "Certainly, Dr. Franklin's wisdom is well known and should not be discounted. But he cannot see inside you, nor direct your life." He sighed. "Nor, can I, Brock. But know that I have grown to respect you like a son and that you have my support in return for your trust."

Brock extended his hand and shook Mr. Jamison's. "Thank you, sir. That means a great deal."

At 2:30, true to his word, Mr. Jamison withdrew two writing tablets from a shelf and two slate pencils and laid them on the counter. "Ensure the boys treat these with care. They are indeed costly," he said with a stern look.

"Yes, sir. We'll be careful."

On his walk to the Jamison house Brock's worry moved from Dr. Franklin's advice to his new challenge: tutoring.

######

When Brock arrived, the three young Jamisons, without prompting, hurried to their usual seats at the kitchen table. Brock moved to Mrs. Jamison's chair to help establish his authority with Duncan and Nathan. He then had the boys swap seats on the benches and directed Amelia to sit in Brock's normal eating spot at the other end of one bench. His strategy was to emphasize this was a teaching situation rather than a meal and they should behave accordingly. Brock intended to move from one end chair to the other since he planned to teach the beginner-level boys separately from Amelia who had mastered the alphabet and knew a little math. Although Duncan attended school and should be more advanced than Nathan, he wanted to see for himself what each boy knew.

The boys displayed boundless energy as they squirmed and made faces while slapping at each other's hands across the table.

Brock clapped his hands loudly. "Boys, sit still with your hands in your laps!" He rose and loomed over Nathan then Duncan trying to intimidate them with his much larger size. "Your father is paying me to teach you to read and to write. But it will take effort to accomplish anything. I intend to do my part."

He looked from one boy to the other. "I expect you to do your parts. If you do not pay attention and do as I say, your father will hear about it when he gets home. At which time I feel sure he will address any issues. Is that understood?"

The two boys suddenly became breathing statues. Amelia was grinning from the other end of the table. When Brock winked at her, she blushed and looked away.

"Now, when we are at this table to learn, you will refer to me as 'Mr. Brock'. Is that clear?" Brock's intense stare at the boys generated a nod from both. Amelia's grin disappeared.

"There will also be some fun as we learn. But *I* will decide *when* and *how much* fun. Until then you will concentrate on your assignments."

Brock took one of the writing tablets and placed it in front of himself. He then looked at each boy as he spoke. "Nathan, Duncan, watch what I write on the tablet." In large, block, capital letters he wrote A B C D E. "These are the first five letters of the alphabet. The alphabet is nothing more than twenty-six of these letters we use to write everything in the English language. Once you learn all the letters and how to put them together, you can write stories, books and important papers for business. And, of course, you'll be able to read anything once you know the words."

The boys looked dazed but remained silent.

Brock pointed to the first letter. "This is the letter 'A'. A common word that starts with 'A' is apple. Together let's say 'A is for apple.'"

Nathan and Duncan recited the phrase along with Brock. The introduction to the other four letters followed similarly with Brock pointing to the letters in turn as he and the boys repeated the respective mantras several times. Each time the boys pronounced the words with more confidence.

Brock reached his right hand out over the table, his palm facing the older boy, and held it there. "Put your hand up like mine, Duncan." Cautiously, the older boy complied.

Brock pushed his hand together against Duncan's with only minor impact. "Good job!"

Duncan looked surprised but smiled.

"Okay, let's do it again. But this time you move your hand to gently slap mine. And when the hands meet we'll both say, 'Good job!'"

Duncan, a quick learner, produced a satisfying slap between student and teacher. "Good job!" they both said aloud.

Duncan's smile felt good to Brock who immediately turned to Nathan. The younger boy had been paying attention and met Brock's hand with an eager, if poorly aimed, slap.

"Good job!" Nathan bellowed.

Brock smiled but put a finger to his lips and pointed to the front room where Mrs. Jamison sat peeling potatoes.

Both boys were now bouncing in their seats. Brock rose and told the boys to stand. He moved away from the table and put his hands on his hips. "Watch what I do," he told the two youngsters. With that Brock put his hands on his hips and squatted to the floor, then stood back up. Looking from one boy to the other, he did it again. "Now you do it with me."

As Brock squatted the third time, the boys, both using terrible form, squatted and rose back up unevenly. "Keep your back straight and don't lean forward. And go down and up slowly." On the next squat the boys improved marginally.

"Okay, do ten more while I work with Amelia," Brock said as he moved toward the other end of the table.

"How much is ten?" Nathan said, clearly confused.

The question surprised Brock.

"One for each finger," Amelia said from her seat.

"I'll count for us," Duncan said. "I know my numbers."

Brock nodded to the older boy. "Okay. Take your time and go down and up slow."

Brock's teaching career was off and running. Teaching wouldn't be easy but the boys were eager. Keeping them engaged would be the challenge.

Amelia was another matter. Working close to her might be a distraction for both of them.

After a couple of hours of "school," Brock told his students that they were done for the day. Duncan scrambled to his feet and to Brock's surprise said, "Thank you, Mr. Brock."

CHAPTER 32   Oct 31, Wednesday

The presence of Sally Bache and her husband, Richard, at the Wednesday dinner table with Dr. Franklin surprised Brock. He had expected that he and Dr. Franklin would eat alone to talk freely. During the casual meal Richard asked Brock about his background and his relationship with Dr. Franklin. Brock deflected the questions as best he could. Thankfully, Dr. Franklin steered the conversation to his current cause, the abolition of slavery. Brock knew this issue was important to Dr. Franklin despite the man having owned a few slaves earlier in his life. But due to his lack of insight into Sally and Richard's position on the topic, Brock mostly just listened.

At the conclusion of the meal Dr. Franklin rose with the aid of his cane. "Brock, shall we proceed to the laboratory?"

Brock got to his feet. "Yes, sir." As he moved to follow his host from the room, a folded, single-page newspaper lay on the sideboard. Under the paper's banner was the date October 27, 1787, the previous Saturday. October 27th was the date of Wally's bachelor party "back home." The thought that he had missed the bash that he had spent so much time planning took the edge off his enthusiasm for the work in Dr. Franklin's lab.

Brock did a quick mental calculation then blurted, "Today's the thirty-first. Happy Halloween, Dr. Franklin!"

The man stopped and turned back. "I beg your pardon."

"Halloween? Trick or Treat?" Brock said, splaying his hands.

The slight shake of his host's head and his blank expression told Brock the treat-giving "holiday" did not extend back to the eighteenth century. And any explanation might distract from their work. "Never mind, sir. We can discuss it later."

At the top of a stairway to the third floor Dr. Franklin unlocked a single door but before entering turned to Brock. "During discussions in my library one week ago, among a litany of future events, you mentioned 'world wars' without elaborating."

Brock nodded. "Yes, sir."

"Will there be wars in the future that encompass all nations?"

"I'm sorry to say so, but yes there will be devastating wars in the future of the United States. Two world wars in the twentieth century will kill millions in Europe, Africa and the Far East. Before that, in less than one hundred years from now there will be a civil war that will threaten to tear apart this country you helped build. And it will be fought over the topic of slavery versus its elimination. More than a half million Americans will die in this war, lasting four long years."

Dr. Franklin put his fist to his mouth. "And what will be the outcome?"

Brock allowed himself a small smile. "The country will be reunited and slavery will be abolished."

Dr. Franklin calmed then said, "But five hundred thousand lives."

"Even with the abolishment of slavery it will take generations for the discrimination to subside with pockets remaining still. I'm no historian, but we should sit and discuss this sometime. I'll tell you what I do know."

"I would welcome the exchange," Dr. Franklin said as he opened the door to a room that he called his laboratory.

Inside the room on a heavy table stood a large, open-top, wooden box, about eighteen inches tall. The interior of the box was divided into thirty-five equal compartments, about three inches on a side, arranged in a five by seven matrix. In each compartment stood a tall glass jar that extended above the top of the box. Each jar was about half full of a liquid and fitted with a cork stopper. A metal wire ran through each cork down into the liquid. The other ends of the wires were then connected by means of metal rods. A single metal rod then ran toward a simple, hand-crank device at the far end of the table.

"This is my Leyden Jar assembly. By connecting the jars together, I can create a larger spark than from a single jar. I call this a battery since, like cannons massed together for a concentration of firepower, the collection of jars provide a greater concentration of the electricity."

Brock studied the jars in the wooden box. He was aware that a Leyden Jar was one of the earliest forms of battery to store static electricity but didn't know how it actually worked. "How do you charge this thing?"

Dr. Franklin moved to the other end of the long table and where the wooden frame device held a large glass ball mounted on a horizontal spindle near its top. It appeared that by turning the handle attached to a large wooden pulley, a rope belt would rotate the spindle and the attached glass ball which would rub against a wool pad. Metal fingers touching the glass ball would rub against it also as it turned. Brock deduced that the metal fingers would carry a static charge to the battery.

The workmanship on the contraption impressed Brock. Intricate polished wood components, some turned on lathes, and the whole thing assembled with wooden pegs. "Does this thing really work?" Brock said, fidgeting as his eyes roamed the device.

"Perhaps it would be best to demonstrate the static machine." Dr. Franklin connected a thick, bare wire from the machine to a metal rod on the battery. "Please, turn the handle clockwise to send the electricity to the battery."

Brock rotated the flywheel with some difficulty, slowly at first then faster until Dr. Franklin said, "Maintain that pace but do not increase the effort." The only sounds generated by the static machine were the rotating parts in the frame and the soft shushing of the glass ball on the wool.

After five minutes Brock's arms were tired. "How much longer do I need to turn this thing, Dr. Franklin?"

The 18th century scientist looked at the open pocket watch he carried in his hand. "Only for a brief time, son. I will advise when to cease."

Brock continued to turn the flywheel for another two or three minutes until Dr. Franklin said, "That should be sufficient." Brock slowed the flywheel to a stop and wiped his brow.

He moved to the battery to get a closer look at its design. Curious to see how the tops were attached to the Leyden jars, he leaned over the nearest one and reached to touch the glass.

A blinding flash erupted, lifting Brock off his feet, sending his body flying back across the laboratory.

END OF PART I

PART II

CHAPTER 33   Oct 31, Wednesday

Brock becomes aware of a rhythmic chirp, like a bird but with no variation in pitch or tone. He's on his back on a cushioned surface, still in the slow process of regaining consciousness. A distinct chemical odor is familiar yet unidentifiable.

The effort required to open his eyes shocks Brock but at last his lids part slightly, revealing a low level of light. As his eyes adjust and his focus improves, he identifies four large rectangles of pale yellow light in the flat ceiling.

With his head and shoulders elevated several degrees, Brock turns his head slightly to his right, stopping at a large, rectangular window. Despite the tint in the window he can see a line of white, puffy clouds in the distance moving slowly. The elevation of his head and the Spartan décor suggest he's in a hospital room. But what hospital and where? Certainly *not* in eighteen century Philadelphia! The pace of the chirping increases slightly.

Responding to movement on his left, Brock turns his head in that direction as someone quietly enters the room. The outline of the approaching individual, backlit by strong light through the doorway, suggests it's a woman. But the prominent ears, high on its head, imply otherwise. He cringes at the soft rustle of clothes and the faint squeak of footsteps as it moves closer where its slanted eyes and a black-tipped nose are visible. Fear supersedes the confusion he felt when he first awoke.

"Brock, you're awake!" the cat woman whispers as she leans beyond his field of vision at the head of his bed. The chirps grow faint followed by an increase in the room's level of light.

The cat woman moves back into his field of vision, tapping on a small device on her wrist. She then leans down close to Brock and in a soft, yet animated, voice says, "Welcome back, Brock. I'm Nurse Sybil. Just lie still. Dr. Keller will be here any minute." Her smile, framed by painted whiskers, broadens. "Happy Halloween, by the way."

Brock exhales then smiles at the well-done, feline makeup.

His fear abated, his confusion reemerges. Is he in Philadelphia? Or, home in The Woodlands? Or, somewhere else? And how did he get here from 1787?

The door swings open again and a dark-haired man, graying at the temples, hurries in. "Sybil, what is it?" the man says, panting.

"Doctor Keller, the patient opened his eyes. He has not spoken yet but appears responsive."

The doctor raises a silver tablet he carries at his side and studies it. With pursed lips, he nods.

Brock does not recognize the doctor, though that's understandable since he only knows their family physician and Dr. Ellis, the doctor that had consulted with his high school sports teams.

The doctor leans in close. He wears a crisp, white smock over a pale blue shirt with a red tie. His eyes are smiling. "Son, I'm Dr. Keller. Don't try to talk just yet. If you can understand me, blink once."

Brock hesitates but blinks, one time.

The doctor's face glows. "Excellent." He points a pen light in first one eye then the other. "Both pupils are equally reactive to light." He returns the light to his smock pocket.

With a stethoscope from a side pocket, the doctor listens to both sides of Brock's neck then his chest, his face a mask of concentration. "Brock, I don't want you to try to speak just yet. It's important that we take things in a specific order. Blink if you understand."

In response Brock blinks once but frowns.

Dr. Keller continues. "Dr. Baum, a speech therapist, is on the way." He puts ups his hands to deflect Brock's sneer. "I know your throat is very dry and you want a drink of water but you need to hang in there for just a few more minutes. When the therapist is through, then hopefully you can have a sip of water. Let's go ahead and raise you more upright."

Brock blinks and the soft hum of the hospital bed coincides with Brock feeling the movement of his head and shoulders. Minor dizziness leaves him just as quickly as it came.

As if she was waiting outside the door for stage direction, a woman in a white smock enters the room. "Dr. Keller, you paged?"

"Thanks for getting here so quickly, Dr. Baum." He points to the bed. "This is Brock Sinclair. He's been in a coma for twenty-two days but is now alert and ready for a sip of water. Can you work your magic and get him some relief?"

Hearing "coma" and "twenty-two days," Brock's eyes bulge. He makes a grunt sound deep in his throat.

The therapist moves in close to Brock. "Relax, big boy. I know you want to ask questions but you need to work with me. I'm Dr. Baum and I'm here to get you to swallowing and talking and maybe some water. Blink if you think you can follow my instructions."

Brock nods slightly and blinks.

For the next few minutes Dr. Baum carefully leads Brock through her procedures to ensure he can swallow without choking before giving him a small amount of a thickened fluid from a straw. When that goes down successfully, Brock finally gets just a sip of cool water. It's the sweetest water he's ever tasted. His smile rewards all three medical professionals watching his reaction.

Next, the therapist gets Brock to do a series of simple voice exercises to determine if his speech mechanisms are functional then has him say certain words. She turns to Dr. Keller. "He's all yours, Roger. I want him to keep his voice low for the rest of today. His vocal cords are still somewhat rigid." She turns back to the patient. "You did good, Brock. But no loud talking or whispering today; both are hard on the vocal chords. By tomorrow your throat will guide you."

Brock smiles at the therapists then croaks, "Thank you."

Dr. Baum pats his arm. "You're welcome." She then slips from the room.

Dr. Keller continues his exam. "Now that you can respond to my questions, let's find out how you're doing. Just relax, son. You haven't moved in a while. It'll take some time for you to loosen up. Just take a few deep breaths." The doctor grasps Brock's hand and turns the palm up.

Brock looks down at the hand the doctor is holding and notices a clip on his index finger with a green wire from it disappearing over the side of the bed. He assumes it's a pulse meter or something. Before Brock can ask about the clip, the doctor says, "Can you move your fingers?"

Brock understands the question but wonders why it's important. Is there some doubt he can move? Has he been in an accident? Brock hesitates to move his fingers. What if he can't?

Something sharp pokes the side of Brock's pinky. He closes his fingers feebly. "Uh!"

The doctor beams, the nurse releases a soft sigh.

Inwardly, Brock joins the medical people in their minor celebration as Dr. Keller moves to Brock's feet and scrapes a pen across his soles with similar results.

Brock mutters, "Wa...ter."

"Sybil, give him a tiny bit more."

The doctor stands at the foot of the bed and looks directly at his patient. "Brock, you must have a thousand questions. And we'll get to all of them. But it's important that you concentrate on *my* questions first. Will you do that?"

Brock nods with effort then blinks one time.

Dr. Keller makes entries on the polished tablet he's holding. "Can you tell me your full legal name?"

"Frank...lin Brock Sin...clair." His voice is scratchy, but intelligible.

"Good, Brock. Now, how old are you?"

"Nine...teen."

"Your parents names?"

"Trip. Laura."

Dr. Keller fingers his tablet again. "What is the last thing you remember before waking up here?"

Brock knows what he wants to say but forming the words is a struggle. Slowly, he mumbles, "Doc Frank...lin's lab. Big bat...tre."

The excitement on the doctor's face fades to a frown. "And who is Dr. Franklin?"

Brock had raised his head off the pillow to look directly at the doctor. But in frustration and from weakness he lets it drop back. He takes a couple of quick breaths. His voice is weaker now. "Ben...Frank...lin...after dinner."

With the fingers of his right hand the doctor repeatedly taps the tablet he's holding. His brows knit as he looks back at Brock. "Okay. That's enough for now. We'll talk about Dr. Franklin after you get your strength back." The doctor drops the tablet to his side and smiles. I'll be back very shortly. I need to notify your parents that you're awake."

Brock blinks once. "What is…this place?"

"This is Memorial Herman in The Woodlands." The doctor steps to the bedside as he makes another tablet entry.

Brock nods then turns his head to look directly at the doctor. "What day…is it?"

"Why it's Wednesday, Brock, the 31st of October," the doctor replies. "Is that important, son?" The doctor looks at the nurse, grins then back at Brock. "It's Halloween."

Brock's head drops back, his eyes squeezed tight in concentration. He remembers the newspaper on the sideboard at Dr. Franklin's dining room. From it he had calculated the day was Halloween. He remembers mentioning that before going upstairs with Dr. Franklin to work on the experiment. He doesn't remember what happened and he doesn't remember leaving Dr. Franklin's house.

"Been here twenty-two days?" Brock's eyes plead with the physician.

Dr. Keller glances at the nurse holding Brock's water container then back down at his patient. "Yes, but don't worry about that now." He raises his hand to forestall Brock's next questions but it's ineffective.

Brock's shaking his head, eyes squeezed shut. "No! Was in Philadelphia…Jamisons."

"You undoubtedly have some confusion and lots of questions. And we will get to all of them. I promise. For now I want you to focus on the fact that you're safe, your vital signs are good and that your folks will be here soon." He looks at nurse Sybil then back to Brock. "How about a refreshing smoothie?"

Brock sighs, closes his eyes, then nods.

Dr. Keller tells the nurse that Brock can have a nutrition smoothie and they agree on the strawberry flavor. "Remember, he sips. I want the bottle to last thirty minutes. Then, wait another thirty minutes before lowering his head slightly so he can sleep if he wants." He looks back at his patient. "Brock, I need to make some calls. Just rest for now. I'll be back soon."

Both the doctor and the nurse leave the room, the nurse returning in a moment, shaking the small, bottled smoothie. She twists the top off and inserts another flexible straw. As with the water, she holds the straw to Brock's lips. "Take just a sip to see how it goes down."

The cold, sweet liquid is like velvet in Brock's mouth. He swallows with minimal pain and tries to take more. "Whoa, fellow! Dr. Keller said to go slow. We'll wait a couple of minutes than you can have another sip."

To Brock it is forever between sips and too soon there's a slurping from the bottom of the small bottle.

"You got it all, Brock. Now we wait thirty minutes to lower your bed a fraction so you can rest."

Even is his near-sitting position Brock's eyes grow heavy. He doesn't know how he got to this hospital or even why he's here but the room is warm and the bed is comfortable. As he drifts off, Brock's confusion grows about being in Philadelphia with Dr. Franklin, Mr. Jamison, Amel—

CHAPTER 34   Oct 31, Wednesday

On only his first full week back at work, Trip Sinclair's wrist phone shrieks with a message from Dr. Roger Keller, "**BROCK AWAKE! COME!**"

Speeding north toward The Woodlands branch of the renowned Memorial Hermann hospital system on the far north side of Houston, Trip joins what he normally considers the "infuriating speeders." In his need to get to his son as quick as possible he weaves around the few, annoying vehicles moving only ten miles per hour above the speed limit, grateful that the five lanes of I-45 are not crowded. A few hours later traffic will be moving at only a crawl.

Trip punches a button on the steering wheel. "Call Laura," he shouts, louder than necessary. Seconds later he hears his wife's voice. "Trip! Are you on your way to the hospital?"

"Yes! I wanted to make sure you got the message from Dr. Keller."

"I was in the shower but I'm almost in the car. I'll meet you there." She pauses. "Do you know anything more?"

"No, I assume you got the same message." Frustration is clear in Trip's voice. "I'll meet you at Brock's room." He terminates the call then slams the heel of his hand against the steering wheel. Why did she have to shower in the middle of the afternoon? She'll be late just like every other time we need to be somewhere. It's her fault I'm not at the hospital right now. It's only been three weeks since Brock fell. But she insisted that I take some time away from his bedside.

Despite his fixation with getting to the hospital, Trip remembers that he hadn't even told his administrative assistant he was leaving as he raced to the elevator. He would call later; she'd understand.

The idea that he would think of the office during this critical moment in his son's life exposes the lake of guilt Trip has been treading ever since his son entered the coma. His focus to succeed at the company and the long hours he gave to it over the years had robbed him and Brock of a relationship. Trip had always told himself and Laura that his commitment to the job was for financial security for his family. And that Brock understood his presence at every little league game and high school sport event wasn't really necessary.

But during his grief these past three weeks he had reordered his priorities. But was Brock really at the top of the list? Tears cloud Trip's vision as they had done almost daily since the incident. He wipes them on his sleeve not from embarrassment but to help ensure he reaches his son as quickly as possible. He promises he will make it up to Brock. Unless his son is... The tears continue to flow.

At the hospital a familiar nurse on the day shift approaches Trip just inside the entrance. Her ever-present, smile is intact. She focuses over Trip's shoulder through the glass doors to the walkway Trip had just jogged over. "Mr. Sinclair, I believe that's your wife coming across the parking lot."

Trip turns to see Laura hurrying toward the entrance. He watches as she pushes on the automatic door, impatient with its opening speed, and moves to where he and the nurse are standing. She grasps his hand with a fierce grip.

"I was at work," Trip says to the nurse. "She came from the house." His pleading eyes meet the nurse's. "Is Brock...?"

The nurse gently grasps Trip's arm above the elbow and smiles. "Brock woke up! But I don't have any details. Dr. Keller just said to meet you here and bring you to the conference room near Brock's room. He said it's critical that he speak with you before you see Brock."

Trip rushes toward the elevator, the nurse pulling on a still-panting Laura to encourage her to keep up.

On the fourth floor Trip speed walks to the familiar conference room where they had met with Dr. Keller and other specialists several times since Brock's accident. Laura and the nurse are only a few steps behind.

Dr. Roger Keller is seated at the conference table facing the door with his ever-present, tablet open in front of him. He rises as the Sinclairs enter. "Laura, Trip, please sit." He gestures to the chairs opposite him then says, Thank you," to the escort nurse who closes the door on her way out.

Trip pulls a rolling office chair away from the table and sits but does not roll back up to the table. His tense expression and constantly moving hands suggest he is struggling to maintain control. Laura is more subdued, almost numb.

Dr. Keller sits back down and faces the couple. "I'll get right to it." He looks at his watch. "Approximately, forty-five minutes ago Brock woke up. As you might expect, it is a slow process for someone to fully assimilate from a three-week coma."

Using his hands, Dr. Keller punctuates his words. "His vital signs are good and we allowed him a few sips of water and a nutrition smoothie. My preliminary exam showed normal physical responses."

Trip is now swiveling his chair from side to side, facing the door more and the doctor less on each half- rotation. "Why are we in here? I want to see my son!" He jumps to his feet.

Dr. Keller removes his glasses and places them on the table. "Mr. Sinclair, I can understand your urgency to see your son. And you *will* see him in just a few minutes. But first you need to be aware of his delicate mental state at this critical time." The doctor waves his hand towards Trip's chair. "Please sit. I'll make this as brief as possible."

Trip reluctantly drops back into his chair.

"When I asked Brock some basic questions like his name, his age, your names, his responses were understandably slow but spot on. However, when I asked him to tell me what was the last thing he remembered before waking up here in the hospital, he said something about being with Ben Franklin in his lab."

Trip splays his hands as he rears back in his chair. "Why is that a surprise? He's had Ben Franklin's history pounding in his head twenty-fours a day for weeks."

"The audio stimulation apparently helped Brock respond to the treatment. And the Ben Franklin approach, which you suggested by the way, may have been critical to his response to the drug." Dr. Keller takes a deep breath. "But there is undoubtedly some level of confusion with Brock. We must recognize this confusion and allow him to process what is real and what he may have experienced while in the coma."

Trip exhales deeply before nodding to the doctor.

Dr. Keller looks back and forth between Trip and Laura. "I advise you not to be alarmed. Remember that there are a lot of unknowns working here, the head trauma, the fentanyl, the APX207 and, of course, twenty-two days in a coma. To expect Brock to wake up thinking clearly with no confusion and just walk out of the hospital would be unreasonable."

Laura and Trip exchange a look before the doctor continues. "We need to give Brock time. We must exercise patience and let him resolve his confusion at his own pace."

Trip leans forward and bangs his elbows on the table then drops his head into his hands. In an instant he snaps his head up. "Are you saying we can't talk to him or ask any question?"

"Not at all, Trip. Talk to your son. Ask how he's doing. Be his parents." Dr. Keller holds up his palms. "But if he says something that's odd or doesn't make sense, don't make a big deal of it or try to probe him. I will assemble my team for a group assessment most likely Friday morning. Even then we will move slowly. Before then we need to do tests and imaging to compare to his baseline." Laura gently nods in agreement. Trip less noticeably.

Dr. Keller stands, the Sinclairs follow suit. "You can see Brock now. Mind you he just had the smoothie I mentioned. And it's common for patients coming out of a coma to sleep off and on for the first day or so. Be patient and let him wake up on his own." After the doctor rounds the table, he puts his hand on Trip's shoulder. "I know you love your son. Just make sure *he* knows it."

CHAPTER 35   Oct 31, Wednesday

With a gentle caress of his right hand, Brock slowly opens his eyes. His mom is standing beside his bed, eyes closed, her head bowed. Despite her being his mom, he is struck by her casual beauty, the stylish cut of her hair framing her face. Brock detects her fragrance, so fresh compared to the women he encountered in Philadelphia. He smiles despite missing his Philadelphia friends.

His mom looks up and draws in a breath, covering her mouth with a hand. "Oh, my God! Trip, he's awake." She leans closer to Brock's face. In a soft voice she says, "Sweetheart, it's your mom. Can you hear me?"

Brock continues to smile and nods to reassure his mother.

Trip jumps to his feet from a recliner at the far wall and moves to the other side of the bed. "Son, are you okay? If you can't talk, just nod."

Excitement, yet concern, is obvious in his dad's face. He looks older than Brock remembers with dark bags under his moist eyes. Tears form in Brock's own eyes at the sight of the parents he feared he had lost. In a weak voice he says, "Mom! Dad!" He looks from one to the other, each gripping one of his hands. "What…happened? Why am I in the hospital?"

Trip turns to his wife before answering. "Son, you had a fall on the Sam Houston campus and hit your head. The paramedics brought you here." He pats his son's hand. "How do you feel? Do you want me to get the nurse?" He shifts his weight to the foot closer to the door, eager to help.

Brock moves his head back and forth as he speaks slowly. "No, I'm okay. Just weak. And sleepy. So sleepy."

Trip nods. "Dr. Keller said to expect that. He said it's normal."

Laura looks first at her husband, who shoves his free hand into his pocket, then to her son. "Honey, what can you remember about your fall?"

"I remember going to Wally's in Huntsville. We were going to discuss his wedding plans and talk about the bachelor party." He pauses. "I remember getting there on my bike but…not much else until I woke up in Philadelphia."

"Philadelphia?" Trip says, louder than he should, catches himself then glances at Laura as his face relaxes. With a forced smile he continues in a controlled voice, "Son, you must have had a dream while you were…asleep."

"No, I was there, Dad." Brock shakes his head. "I was in the hospital there and spent more than two weeks trying to figure out how I got there and how to get back home." His mother is biting her lip, her free arm wrapped around her body.

Trip runs his fingers through his hair. "Dr. Keller mentioned that. He wants to hear all the details a bit later." Trip releases Brock's hand and shoves his other hand in his pocket. "Can we get you anything?" He laughs nervously. "The standards? Gum, magazines, toiletries?"

Brock grins uncertainly at his dad. "I'm okay. Maybe later."

Laura swivels her body and gently sits side-saddle on the bed near Brock's feet and leans toward her son. "Sweetheart, we're anxious to get you home. As soon as the doctors release you, we'll take you out of here and let you start getting your strength back. Being in this bed and on a feeding tube is a big change from your normal eating and exercise routine."

Brock's eyebrows pinch together. "The head injury, is it serious? Is there something else?" He shifts his gaze to his father.

Trip clears his throat. "Son, you were unconscious after the fall. The ER doctors were concerned about why you fell." He looks at Laura before continuing. "They did their exams and, because you remained unconscious, they took blood and urine samples. They found several things in your system. Alcohol, marijuana and…" Trip's eyes move from Laura to his son. "They also found traces of fentanyl."

Brock struggles to push himself up onto his elbows. "Fentanyl! I don't remember what happened at Wally's. But I would never take fentanyl!" He falls back on the pillow. "Dad, Mom, you know that my friends and I drink a few beers now and then. And now that pot is legal, we've been able to score a little weed on occasion. But, I swear, I've never used anything stronger. That's the God's truth."

Laura comes to his defense. "We believe you, son. But it's been in the news lately that there's some black market pot in the state that's laced with fentanyl. There's even been several overdoses from it." She looks at Trip before continuing. "Maybe that's what you got into."

Brock blinks rapidly. "Am I going to be all right?"

Trip stands with his arms folded across his chest. "Brock, the doctors were very concerned early on. But now that you're awake they're optimistic that you're going to be okay." His tone becomes less sympathetic. "But we've been worried as hell while you lay here in a coma with your brain scrambled, maybe permanently. And Dr. Keller still can't assure us that there won't be any lasting effects." Trip clenches his fists before turning and storming out of the room.

Brock watches his father leave then frowns at his mom. "Is Dad okay?"

Laura leans forward and grabs her son's hand again. "You know how your father can be. And he has hardly slept since your…accident. He blames everybody for this: whoever got you the pot, you, the doctors, friends,…most of all himself." She stops. "He's been so worried that you might—" Tears flood her now-smiling eyes and in a halting voice she adds, "You waking up today is what I've prayed for ever since you got here. I'm going to be positive about your complete recovery. You've got your whole life ahead of you."

Brock takes his mom's hand in both of his. "If I caused you and Dad to worry, I'm really sorry. I didn't mean to put you through such anguish."

Laura dabs at her eyes and wipes her nose. She smiles at Brock. "I know you didn't. Let's just focus on you getting better. We'll get through this together. All of us."

Brock's brow furrows. "Mom, did Wally get sick too? You remember his wedding is on November 17th?" His lips form a straight line. "I guess I missed the bachelor party Saturday night. Did you hear anything about it?"

Laura's eyes fill again as she stands. "Oh, Honey." She hesitates. "They found Wally beside you on the sidewalk. He had pushed the panic button on his cell then apparently blacked out. The police used his cell GPS to locate you both."

"But he's okay?" Brock pushes himself up on his elbows.

Laura shakes her head very slowly. "No, son. They rushed him to the hospital too but…he didn't make it." She struggles to get the words out.

Brock lowers himself back onto the pillow, his eyes directed at the ceiling but with a blurred, far-away focus. Finally, his voice cracking, he says, "He was my best friend, Mom." Tears flood his eyes. "That's the second good friend I've lost recently."

CHAPTER 36   Oct 31, Wednesday

When Brock collects his emotions, his mother speaks quietly, "What do you mean 'Wally's the second friend you've lost'?"

"Mom, I can't explain what happened to me since I went to Wally's apartment. I understand that I was supposedly here in a coma after I fell. But I would bet my life I was in Philadelphia in the 1700's, 1787 to be exact." Brock rises up on his elbow to face his mother directly. "I woke up in this ancient hospital where I met this intern, Isaac Jamison. I leaned on him for help and we became friends. Unfortunately, a few days later Isaac was killed."

"That's awful, Brock! I wonder why his death was in your dream or whatever it was."

His mother makes a slow turn to the foot of the bed then turns back to her son. "There's probably an explanation for what you remember, but I think it's better for the doctors to fill you in. Their treatment protocol is pretty technical and I might only confuse you more." She steps closer. "Dr. Keller did say you might have some dreams during the coma. You must be remembering some of it."

Looking at his mom, Brock says, "No, I'm not remembering some of it. I remember *all* of it. I could give you a minute-by-minute account from the time I woke up in that hospital until I was in Dr. Franklin's lab." Brock stops. When he told the people in Philadelphia that he had a full memory of his life in Texas things didn't always go well. This time he would need to be cautious about who and what he told of his Philadelphia experience. He trusted his mom but maybe the less said the better for now.

As Brock considers what he should share with his folks, his father reenters the room, his eyes on the floor. "Son, I'm sorry I lost my cool." With liquid eyes, he looks up to face Brock. "It's just that I've been so worried about you. Afraid we'd…lose you."

"It's okay, Dad. I'm just sorry I put you through this."

For the next half hour Trip and Laura bring their son up to date on current events particularly the three Texans games Brock had missed. No further mention is made of Brock's accident or his coma dream.

At four o'clock Dr. Keller enters saying that he needs to examine Brock further and asks his parents to say their goodbye's and give their son a chance to rest. He advises that they are welcome to return the next day. Brock gets a hug from his mom and a firm handshake from his dad before they leave, vowing to return to see him tomorrow.

Dr. Keller and a nurse proceed with a more comprehensive exam than Brock received earlier. In addition to measuring his vitals, blood is drawn, his vision is tested and an EKG test is performed.

Alone with Dr. Keller after the nurse leaves to deliver the blood sample to the lab, Brock asks the doctor for his assessment.

"Well, your vitals are good and the EKG is normal for someone your age. We'll know more after the blood work up." The doctor smiles. "But I don't expect anything abnormal."

"What about my mind, Doc? Has there been any damage to my brain from the fall or the fentanyl?"

"You know of the fentanyl?"

"My folks mentioned it but no details."

Dr. Keller pulls a chair to the side of the bed and sits, facing his patient. "Brock, by law you are an adult. So I don't need your parents' permission to outline your condition or your treatment." He removes his glasses. "When you were found unconscious, the paramedics took you to Huntsville Memorial, the closest hospital. They diagnosed a mild concussion, by itself no cause for great alarm in a healthy, young male. But when they discovered fentanyl in your system and you had not regained consciousness, the decision was made to transfer you to us where we have certain assets they don't."

The doctor clears his throat. "Keep in mind that I'm giving you the Cliff Notes version of what transpired. Anyway, after serious consultation with a team of physicians here and at the main hospital in Houston and with the approval of your parents, we administered a drug called APX207. This drug, although experimental, has shown remarkable success in head trauma patients where complications are present. APX207 induces the brain to create a narrative that has shown to be effective in brain stimulation for, otherwise, healthy patients. Its benefit involving a foreign substance such as fentanyl is unknown."

Brock raises his head from the pillow. "Was it effective?"

Dr. Keller smiles. "Well, first, you awoke from your coma in a reasonable length of time. That's positive. Second, you seem okay physically though it's still a bit early. And your basic mental functions seem intact." He paused. "You tell me, do you feel like it worked?"

Brock hesitates, remembering his mom's reaction to his telling her about the hospital in Philadelphia and the doctors there. He wonders if the APX207 altered his brain such that he can no longer distinguish between reality and fantasy. And if he's adamant about his time in 1787, will they diagnose him as mentally impaired? And what would that mean?

"Did you hear me, Brock?"

"Yes, Doc. I feel okay, maybe a little tired. But I'm confused about my time in the coma."

"What do you mean 'confused', Brock?" With no immediate response, he continues, "Do you mean the impression you had of meeting Ben Franklin?"

His shining eyes lock on the doctor. "Yes, sir. I guess that's it. Is that normal for someone with my injury and the APX…drug?"

Dr. Keller crosses his legs. "There is an explanation concerning your experiences with Ben Franklin."

Brock pushes himself up on his elbow, eyes widened. "What's that?"

"A few, previous cases with APX207 suggested that aural stimulation during the coma by material that interests the patient can be beneficial. Our team felt you were a prime candidate for this. Your father recommended Taekwondo, given your accomplishments in that sport. But we rejected that suggestion because we felt that, while the sport requires mental discipline, it's more of a physical skill. As an alternate, he suggested you had done some reading about Ben Franklin in your youth and had shown a level of interest in that period of history, especially during a vacation to Philadelphia.

"We decided to go with that and acquired audio recordings of Franklin biographies and a vast assortment of related materials. We played that for you non-stop while you were in the coma."

A slow smile grows on Brock. "That explains the Colonial setting and Ben Franklin and his family members?"

Dr. Keller shrugs. "I assume so."

A frown develops on Brock. "Where did all the other people I met come from?"

"Brock, I can't answer that. Unfortunately, there is no normal for APX207. Every case has been different and in truth there haven't been that many." The doctor stands. "But I wouldn't worry about it too much. Friday my colleagues and I will spend some time with you to try to understand what you remember. And why. Perhaps that will give us some insight."

Moving the chair back to the wall, Dr. Keller says, "Your supper will be here soon. The meal will be liquid; we don't want to challenge your swallowing just yet. Maybe tomorrow, if all goes well, maybe some soft food and then work up from there."

Brock nods. "I'll try, Doc. But at the minute I'm not really hungry, just sleepy."

"Well, that part *is* normal. My guess is that you'll probably sleep ten hours or more tonight." He pats Brock's foot. "I'll see you tomorrow."

"Doc, one more thing." He blushes. "What about this tube in my…penis?"

Dr. Keller turns back. "If we remove it, you'll have to use a bed pan until you can stand and walk safely to the restroom." He nods to the room in the corner. "If you want it pulled, we can?"

Brock hesitates. "Yes, sir. Let's get it out."

Dr. Keller turns toward the door. "Okay. I'll have the nurse take care of it."

CHAPTER 37   Nov 1, Thursday

Brock awakens, smelling food. Confusion about his surroundings lasts only a few seconds; he's still in his room at The Woodlands hospital. The door to his room opens and a nurse carries a tray toward his bed with a smile.

"Good morning, Brock. Breakfast is served." She places the tray on his bed table but pushes it out of her way. "I need to get a blood pressure first."

After rehanging the blood pressure cuff, the nurse says, "Do you want to use the bed pan before you eat?"

"I'd rather try going to the restroom."

The nurse nods. "If you feel strong enough, let's give it a shot. I'll get someone to help me."

Minutes later, Brock is back in his bed. "Washing my face and combing my hair felt wonderful. Thank you very much for the help."

Brock had felt a slight dizziness when he first stood but it had passed quickly. His wobbly legs and his general loss of strength surprised him but with the nurses' help he made the round trip to the restroom without incident.

At the restroom mirror he had been relieved to see someone had shaved him recently; his blond, scraggly facial hair had never supported a beard. His hair was longer than normal and matted. Maybe he would be allowed to shower soon.

When the nurse and the breakfast tray are gone, Brock activates the retractable haloscreen in the bed's footboard to learn what's going on in the world. He watches a morning show and is surprised how warm the weather is in the country this late in the year. The measures to mitigate global warming, although significant, are still lagging. On a sports channel he realizes that in addition to the three Texans' games he missed while in the coma, he missed three Longhorns' games. He wonders what their record is now. As soon as he gets his phone, he can answer that question and others. But somehow those questions don't seem as important as they once did.

Brock is continuing to scan channels when his mom arrives.

Laura moves into the room, allowing the door to close, and takes a position on the window side of her son's bed. She bends and kisses him on the forehead then smooths the hair off his forehead. "Did you have a good night?"

"I slept like a cat in the sun." Brock looks toward the door. "Where's dad?"

"He went to find Dr. Keller to get an update. Has he been in this morning?"

"I don't know. But I've only been awake for about an hour.

"Did you have breakfast?"

"Yes, ma'am. Well, sort of. It was mostly liquid. Dr. Keller said to expect that for a while. My hunger was substantial and I ate every morsel." Brock looked thoughtful. "I guess I got used to bland food while—"

A stout, brown-skinned orderly, maybe thirty, enters the room with a wheel chair and a smile. "I'm sorry to interrupt but Brock is due downstairs for an fMRI and an MEG." He speaks to

Laura. "He'll be gone almost two hours if you want to get a coffee in the cafeteria." He shrugs. "It's not Starbucks but it'll help keep you awake."

Laura wrinkles her nose and faces Brock. "We didn't have breakfast yet. I'll go get your father and we'll find something to eat." She winks at the orderly. "But maybe not in the cafeteria?"

"Good choice, ma'am."

As Laura shuffles from the room, the orderly addresses Brock, "I'm Miguel. You ready to go for a ride?"

After getting Brock into the wheelchair, Miguel wheels him to the elevator and down to the second floor. They move out of the elevator to the right and down the hall to a wide door marked "IMAGING" with warning signs plastered all over. Miguel pushes the door open and calls, "Angela? You here?"

A slim blonde, no more than twenty-five, steps from a small enclosure inside the room. "Where else would I be, Miguel?" she says, feigning irritation.

Miguel smiles as he pushes the door open wide and rolls Brock inside. "Your nine o'clock is here."

Angela is stunning even in blue scrubs, with little makeup but a bright smile. Her short ponytail, dances as she approaches. She reads from a tablet she carries then looks up. "You must be Brock Sinclair. Welcome to my chamber." She grins and points to the open fMRI in the middle of the room.

Brock's nervousness from never having had an fMRI is compounded by the presence of the very attractive technician. Yet Angela's relaxed demeanor and efficient movements suggest he's in good hands.

After verifying Brock's wrist band matches the test order on her tablet, the technician helps the orderly get Brock up onto the machine's sled. When Angela is satisfied he is correctly positioned, she tells Miguel to come back in about thirty minutes. He issues a small salute and leaves.

Angela refers to her tablet. "Okay, Brock. Have you had an fMRI before?"

"No, and I'm not excited about tight spaces either."

"Well, I've never lost anybody yet in my Ultra Image 6000." She pats him on the arm. "You'll be fine."

Angela proceeds to verbally walk Brock through the procedure for the fMRI.

Thirty minutes later Brock, relieved to be out of the machine, sits on the side of the sled. He smiles at Angela, who's making entries onto her tablet. "This ain't your first day is it, cowgirl?"

The technician looks up from her tablet with a wry smile and puts a hand on her hip. "Actually it is. I usually work down in the morgue. The normal tech is sleeping off a hangover. He said to just push the red button and let the machine do its thing. By the way, what were we supposed to be examining? Head? Back? Knee?" She waves a dismissive hand. "Never mind. It's doesn't matter." She punches Brock gently in the arm and grins. "You did good, cowboy."

Angela opens the door to find Miguel in the hall sitting in the wheel chair. "Get your lazy butt out of that chair and take handsome here wherever he's supposed to go."

Miguel moves at a glacial pace rising from the chair then bows to the technician. With a broad smile he says, "Si, Senorita," his Spanish accent obviously forced.

As Miguel pushes Brock down the hall to another room, he assures his passenger that the upcoming MEG will be a snap compared to Angela's "torture chamber." He then leans close to Brock's ear and speaks softly. "The downside is the MEG technician has the personality of a bedpan. Trust me, you'll see."

As advertised, the overweight, middle-age, male technician in the MEG room provides neither a smile nor a calming word. His ragged, week-old beard and barber college haircut suggest he's a vagrant rather than a medical professional. And his extra thick, wire-rim glasses only add to his freakish appearance. He's all-business as he checks Brock's wrist band then roughly pulls a tight-fitting, synthetic cap with elecctrical connections onto Brock's head and adjusts it. He and the orderly then get Brock from the chair onto the gurney in a sitting position where the tech attaches a series of long leads from the console to Brock's cap.

"All right, now lie down and stay still until I say you can move. I don't want to have to do this a second time. They jammed so much into my schedule today there's no room for screw ups." The tech then drops onto a swivel chair that groans when forced to move his bulk closer to the console.

Looking for an ally, Brock's eyes move to where Miguel stood after they entered the room. Whether from hospital procedure or self-preservation, the orderly had escaped to the hallway. Brock is now alone with Dr. Jekyll, who's fingering the keyboard at the console, muttering incoherently.

With a grunt the tech stands. "We're ready to scan. I'm going into my hot, little booth until the test is done. The mild sedative they gave you after breakfast will help you relax so the scan can see you both awake and asleep. Just don't move anything until I come back in the room. Got that?"

"How long's this gonna take?" Brock says, a note of concern in his voice.

"Fifty-eight minutes if you do as I say." The tech then disappears into an enclosure at the end of the room.

Despite not having permission, Brock shifts his arms and legs slightly into a more comfortable position in the hope that he will fall asleep. He waits for some signal that the test is starting. But he hears nothing from the tech or the equipment. He waits. And waits. And waits.

Brock hears the geeky tech say, "We're done." Brock had fallen asleep but has no idea when or for how long.

The tech lumbers forward and yanks the cap from Brock's head. "Okay, I'll get the orderly to help you down to your chair."

Seconds later Brock is back in the hall with Miguel pushing the chair toward the elevator. "You warned me the tech was not Mr. Congeniality. But damn, Miguel, that guy's a real scalawag."

Miguel leans close again. "I'm not sure what a scalawag is. But I know he's a certified asshole!" They both chuckle quietly as they board the empty elevator.

In the ride up to his floor Brock changes the subject. "Tell me about Angela."

Miguel chuckles. "What about her?"

"Well, for one thing, do you know if she's in a relationship with anyone?"

"I guess you could say that."

"Is it serious?"

Miguel snickers this time. "The truth is she has been dating my sister, Maria, for about two years."

Brock turns his head and shoulders to see Miguel's face. He receives a sympathetic shrug and a grin from the orderly. "Well, shit fire and save the matches," he says, turning back around.

Miguel laughs aloud.

When they return to Brock's room, his parents are not yet back from their food search. Miguel helps his patient back into bed and asks if he can get him anything, but Brock declines.

Before he leaves, Miguel says, "Brock, I'm glad to see you're recovering from your coma."

The comment is strange to Brock coming from someone he just met.

Miguel continues, "I'm just helping out today. I normally work the night shift. And I confess that I took a couple of my breaks here in your room when the staff lounge was crowded." He points to the recliner near the foot of the bed. "Both times I wanted to crank that bad boy back and just enjoy the quiet. I looked at those fancy ear buds they had on you and wondered what they were playing and if you could hear anything. You never moved though. But I thought I could see your eyes moving under your lids." He chokes up a bit. "I was really pulling for you to get better. Young guy like you. You had your whole life ahead of you."

Moving closer to the bed Miguel sticks out his hand to Brock. "You take care, man. I'll see you around."

Brock takes the hand but doesn't know how to respond other than, "Thanks, Miguel...for watching out for me."

CHAPTER 38   Nov 2, Friday

Although dozing, Brock looks up when the door to his room opens and his mom and dad enter, smiling broadly.

"Good morning, sunshine," his mom says.

"What do you mean 'morning', Laura? Hell, it's almost time for lunch," his dad says with fabricated aggravation. His wife gives Trip a pseudo, stern look.

Laura turns back to her son. "We came back yesterday before noon but you were asleep. The nurse said you had more tests in the afternoon and we remembered Dr. Keller had said to let you sleep. So, we left and went on home."

"I thought you might be the source of the magazines I found. Thank you." Pushing the control button, Brock raises the head of the bed to face his parents. "All I did for the tests yesterday was to sit or lay down. But for whatever reason, I was exhausted. It was probably the sedative they gave me to relax for the fMRI or the MEG."

His parents move closer. Trip says, "Dr. Keller said it's quite normal to get tired easily after a coma. Apparently, your body atrophies quickly when you don't move for a period of time."

Brock nods. "I guess so."

"Listen, Honey," Laura says. "There's a session scheduled for 10:00 o'clock this morning in a conference room down the hall. Dr. Keller and some specialists, up from the main hospital in Houston, want to interview you about your experience. And, of course, we'll be there too. Do you feel up to it?"

Brock looks at the clock on the far wall then back at his parents. "I'm kind of sleepy but I'm eager to talk about what happened. Perhaps it will help me understand." He yawns. "Looks like I've got time for a short nap before the session. Will somebody wake me for it?"

His dad says, "I'll come get you when it's time."

Laura bends and kisses her son on the forehead. "See you in a little while."

Brock is already lowering his bed to a near-flat position. In a sleeping voice he says, "Thank you…for everything."

#######

At 9:30 a.m. Trip and Laura join Dr. Keller in the hospital's fourth floor conference room. Also present are three other men and a woman.

Dr. Keller sits at the head of the table and does the introductions. "On my left are Laura and Trip Sinclair, Brock's parents. Since they will be present during the panel review, I want them to be aware of the protocol we'll follow."

He gestures to his immediate right. "Dr. David Chen, is board-certified in head trauma and has been a key member of our team from the start." Dr. Chen nods in response.

"To his right is Dr. Nancy Alstead. She is an MD as well as a clinical psychiatrist."

"Good morning, Mr. and Mrs. Sinclair," Dr. Alstead says.

Dr. Keller continues, "Next to Dr. Alstead is Dr. Henry Singh, head of the hospital's Procedure Review Committee. And on the end is Mr. J. B. Crane, an attorney at Apex Pharmaceuticals, the developer of APX207."

Trip frowns. "Why is an Apex attorney here?"

Dr. Keller clears his throat and looks down the table at the attorney, then leans forward to face Trip. "Apex has invested years and millions in the development of a series of neurological drugs including APX207. Mr. Crane is here strictly as an observer to protect their interests."

"But do the HIPAA rules permit non-hospital personnel access to our son's medical condition and treatment?" Trip says.

Mr. Crane's lawyer tone is no-nonsense. "Mr. Sinclair, I understand your concerns. However, the release you signed for Brock to receive the APX207 allows Apex to have access to the clinical aspects of his treatment and the results. I assure you we hold the information in the strictest of confidence. Such data gathering as this meeting is one method we have to help develop and refine our products."

Trip leans back in his chair and contemplates the situation before sitting up straight again. He looks at Dr. Keller. "I guess it's okay. I just didn't expect an attorney to be involved."

"Very well," Dr. Keller says. He then looks across at Dr. Alstead. "Nancy, you requested this early review session. I'll turn the floor over to you."

Dr. Alstead looks left, right and across to ensure the attendees recognize that she is addressing everyone. "Brock has experienced a rare combination of a powerful opioid, head trauma, an experimental pharmaceutical and a lengthy coma. His brain, including his memory and his perception of reality, has been severely tested. We must all keep this in mind as he shares his experiences with us. At this early stage in his recovery it is imperative that we do not question his memories. If he says he ate some green cheese from the moon, don't scoff or challenge him. Based on the handful of other subjects who've received

APX207, none of which had ingested fentanyl by the way, it is difficult to predict the extent of Brock's confusion and his rate of recovery. We do know that we should accept and support him rather than correct him." She faced each participant in turn. "Are we absolutely clear?"

CHAPTER 39   Nov 2, Friday

When Brock moves slowly into the fourth floor conference room just before 10 o'clock on a walker, with his dad holding his elbow in support and his mom trailing, five chairs are already occupied at the long table. Dr. Keller rises from his chair at the head of the table. "Come in, Brock, Mr. and Mrs. Sinclair and have a seat." He pulls out the chair to his left and directs his patient to it.

After the Sinclairs are seated, Dr. Keller makes the introductions for Brock's benefit. He then nods to the group at large. "Be advised this session and any subsequent sessions will be video-recorded for future analysis." Dr. Keller then identifies all the attendees for the video.

"For the record, Franklin Brock Sinclair, age nineteen, was found on a city street in Huntsville in the early evening of October 8th, 2029. He was unconscious and suffering from head trauma. He was transported initially to Huntsville Memorial then to Memorial Herman - The Woodlands after fentanyl was detected in his system.

"Our subsequent blood analysis confirmed the fentanyl as well as the presence of alcohol and cannabis. After a thorough review of his condition and in consultation with our doctors here and those at the Texas Medical Center in Houston and with the concurrence of Brock's parents, we were granted permission from Apex Pharmaceuticals to administer their experimental drug, APX207, on October 10, 2029. Twenty days later, on October 31st, Brock regained consciousness."

Glancing down at his tablet, Dr. Keller continues, "Tests thus far suggest that Brock is in excellent physical health with no lasting physical effects from his injury or the drugs that were in his system upon arrival or those we administered. We are here to take the first step in evaluating Brock's mental and emotional health since he regained consciousness. And to learn the impact APX207 may have had on his coma memories."

The doctor gestures toward Brock. "The patient indicates he has a detailed memory of the entire time he was in a coma. This has not occurred in any previous use of APX207 and rather than burden Brock from retelling his lengthy memories numerous times, this evaluation committee has been assembled.

"Before Brock begins and for the record I want to stipulate that audio stimulation of Brock began on October 11th. We applied for and received approval for priority access to the Library of Congress' document-to-audio conversion process developed two years ago. We requested materials related primarily to Ben Franklin focusing on the 1780's rather than his entire lifetime to avoid what the Apex developers call 'scatter'. The Library of Congress used biographies, reference materials, personal correspondence, relevant texts, published writings of the man, etc. In all over 20,000 pages were converted to audio and transmitted to us. We played this audio through special ear buds Brock wore. In all we used approximately 90% of the material before Brock's abnormal brain activity ceased on October 31st and he came out of the coma. We're grateful to the Library of Congress for their priority handling of our request."

Dr. Keller turns to Brock. "Son, you have the floor. Take your time. If you need a break, we can stop to let you rest. If we need to reconvene another time, we can arrange that too. Please start from your earliest recollection after your fall in Huntsville."

Brock leans forward and puts his forearms on the edge of the table. "Let me preface my comments by saying that on the afternoon of October 8th, I remember drinking a few beers and smoking some cannabis. However, I do *not* remember the fall referenced by Dr. Keller."

After clearing his throat, Brock continues, "I realize that what I'm about to share with you will be hard to comprehend. I don't understand it myself. But the experience is...was so real that I'm convinced it was more than just an enhanced dream." He pauses. "I'll start with my first memory and proceed in more or less chronological order."

Brock sits up straight in his chair. "I awoke in the afternoon of October 12th in a building that looked hundreds of years old from its design and furnishings. I later learned I was in Pennsylvania Hospital in Philadelphia where the year was 1787."

One of the doctors stifles a near-audible breath.

Brock proceeds to detail his reaction to the hospital, his confusion and fears and his initial encounter with intern Isaac Jamison and Dr. Benjamin Rush. He describes the street scene on his walk the following day to the Jamison home with Isaac and sharing of the midday meal with his family.

Scanning his audience, Brock says, "You cannot imagine the impact on your psyche to suddenly be dropped into such a time warp. The 18th century architecture, the clothing, the horses, the lack of everyday sounds was beyond weird. It felt like I was in one of those old *Twilight Zone* reruns. And the smells! Oh my God! Everything smelled awful, even the people. I learned bathing was a seasonal event at best. But as the days passed, I was surprised how quickly I got used to it. Maybe because I'm sure I was getting pretty ripe myself."

Smiles and chuckles cross the table as his mother pats his arm, grinning.

Following a sip of water, Brock continues. He tells of sharing his true history with Isaac in a tavern and the intern later seeing the flag tattoo on his shoulder and issuing a stern warning.

Laura slowly moves her hand to clasp her son's. She notices Dr. Alstead staring at her. In response she shakes her head ever so slightly as the doctor makes a note on her tablet.

"Later, I was back in the hospital while Isaac was on rounds and Dr. Rush visited me again and apparently ordered another bleeding. Two orderlies showed up to bring me somewhere else in the building. Fortunately, I was able to escape from the hospital until Isaac came out later, worried about my safety."

Tears form in Brock's eyes and he pauses to collect himself. "I'll never forget Isaac's compassion for me despite his obvious doubts about my sanity. He befriended me and went out of his way to help while struggling with his failing eyesight. Unfortunately, Isaac was killed during an attack by a mental patient at the hospital only a few days later. I don't think I will ever forget him and what he did for me."

Brock continues his account, the doctors occasionally making notes on their electronic tablets. When Brock takes a break to sip on a bottle of water, Dr. Alstead says, "Brock, aside from the audio material that was played for you during your coma, have you pursued an interest in American history particularly the 18th century prior to your fall?"

"No, Ma'am. I took U.S. History in high school like everybody else. But I read only what was required. I was more interested in science and math." He pauses. "Oh, I forgot. We did take a family vacation to the east coast when I was fourteen or fifteen, including some time in 'Old City' Philadelphia. Dad bought a small paperback on the life of Ben Franklin while we were in Philly and insisted I read it. I also read a biography of

Franklin that Dad had on the shelf. Beyond that, I never studied anything about Colonial America."

Dr. Alstead continues, narrowing her eyes. "And why did your father encourage you to read about Ben Franklin?"

Brock looks toward his parents then back to the doctor. "He said it was because of a man named Franklin he and my mom met before they were married. Apparently, the guy had a lot of the same qualities of Ben Franklin that my parents thought I should learn about and consider. I'm told I was named after this Franklin fellow."

All the attendees look at Trip and Laura, no doubt expecting an explanation.

Trip is stone faced. "That's true. We did meet a special gentleman maybe twenty years ago that was like Benjamin Franklin in many ways. Sadly, we lost contact with him but not before he made a lasting impression on both of us."

Dr. Alstead makes a note in her tablet then folds her hands.

"Are you ready to continue, Brock?" Dr. Keller asks.

"Sure." Brock organizes his thoughts. "Before Isaac was killed he let me sleep in the room he shared with his younger brothers. He also convinced his father to let me work at his general store for room and board and three shillings per week."

"What would three shillings buy?" Dr. Keller says smiling.

Brock contemplates his response. "Well there were twelve pennies in a shilling and you could get a pint of ale for a penny at a tavern. Most everything else was more costly but I didn't need to buy much since I took meals with the Jamisons and I had the borrowed clothes." The doctor nods in response.

"I worked at Mr. Jamison's store during the day and read *Robinson Crusoe* to his daughter, Amelia, at night. Gradually, I began tutoring her in reading and math. She was an eager student. Eventually, Mr. Jamison asked me to tutor his boys also and agreed to give me a few afternoons off from the store each week to do it while still maintaining my wage."

Brock stops his recollection. "Maybe I'm providing disproportionate detail. Should I jump ahead."

Dr. Alstead folds her hands on the table and looks directly at Brock. In a quiet voice she says, "Brock, you have our attention and we are not in a hurry. I don't think we need to hear what you ate at every meal or daily meteorological reports. But if you think something is important, take your time and tell us."

After taking a deep breath, Brock continues. He explains meeting Ben Franklin in the hope the man could help explain what had happened and how to get home. Or, at least explain why he believed he was in Philadelphia.

Brock turns to his right. "Dad, you would have been blown away. The man was exactly like his sculpture in Signers' Hall at the Constitution Center. Rotund, balding, granny glasses, moved with a cane. And sharp as hell even at his age."

Over the next hour Brock walks those at the table through his ups and downs with Dr. Franklin and the efforts of Temple Franklin to keep him away from his grandfather. He details his capture and imprisonment in the hospital basement with his second bleeding being stopped only by the efforts of Mr. Jamison and his son Seth and an officer of the court. "Chained to that wall with blood running down my arm I was sure I would die there."

Brock's mom covers her mouth with both hands, her eyes glassy. "I—." Laura collapses back into her chair with Trip jumping to his feet to keep her from sliding to the floor.

Dr. Keller jabs a key on his tablet and speaks loudly. "Fourth floor Control! Bring a gurney to the conference room STAT!"

CHAPTER 40   Nov 3, Saturday

Laura Sinclair remains groggy from the sedative Dr. Keller administered the previous afternoon. Yet, after sixteen hours of sleep, hunger drives her to the kitchen where her best friend sips coffee. "Hi, Sheila. I guess you're the day nurse?"

Sheila rises from her chair and moves to hug her grinning friend. "Yeah, Trip called and asked if I could come over while he's at the hospital this morning. How you feeling?"

"I still feel tired but now I'm ravenous. I woke up thinking about eggs, toast and coffee."

"All right! You sit. I'll pour your coffee and fix some eggs."

When Laura had polished off the scrambled eggs, toast and jam, she pushes her plate to the center of the kitchen table. "That really hit the spot, Sheila. Thank you. And thank you for coming."

Sheila waves off the acknowledgement.

Laura takes a long sip of coffee then scratches her cheek. "You know, Sheila, something's different about Brock since he came out of the coma."

"What do you mean 'different'?"

"He's been through a lot. I know that. And he may be confused about what happened since his fall and the…"

"Laura, I know about the fentanyl in the weed." Sheila splays her hands and rolls her eyes. "You know how word gets around. I'm sure he didn't know the weed was spiked."

Laura nods while she runs her finger along the rim of her cup. "What I notice about Brock that's different is his patience and politeness. Don't get me wrong. Brock's always been a good son. He just seems different in some ways."

"That doesn't sound like a problem to me, Laura," Sheila laughs. "Besides maybe Brock's experience, which Trip mentioned on the phone, has him treading lightly until he fully recovers."

Laura shakes her head. "It's not like he's apprehensive or unsure of himself. He's still self-confident. It's like he just completed an advance course in maturity and manners. He uses 'sir' and 'ma'am' when addressing the doctors; he's never been that formal." Laura extends an index finger. "The other thing I've noticed is his vocabulary. He's using words like *anguish, costly, converse* and *privy* for the bathroom. That's very unusual. I guess it could have come from all the reference material they played for him while he was in the coma." Laura then explained about the Library of Congress recordings.

Sheila looks down at her coffee. "Laura, please don't take this the wrong way. But is it possible that Brock is making up the Philadelphia thing?" Suddenly Sheila's eyes widen and her tone becomes more insistent. "Or, may-bee he did have a dream that he's now embellishing it for some reason."

"Oh, Sheila! Why would Brock do something like that? What would he hope to gain?"

"I'm not saying he's making any of this up. I'm just saying it's a possibility. And who knows why he might be doing it. Remember, he's been through a lot with the fall, the drugs and all. It might not even be intentional."

Laura listened to her friend, not wanting to accept her supposition. It didn't make any sense. Did it?

CHAPTER 41   Nov 4, Sunday

After his semi-solid breakfast Sunday morning Brock's father calls and reports that he's coming to visit after he gets Laura up and fixes her breakfast. He reports she's feeling much better but will continue to stay home and rest for another day.

While waiting for his dad to arrive, Brock watches the news on the haloscreen. He's bored and anxious to get out of the hospital. Dr. Keller had indicated that if all goes well he should expect to go home by Wednesday.

The door to his room opens part way and he hears a man's voice. "Brock Sinclair?" Brock turns in that direction and sees a man, the size and build of an NFL linebacker, dressed in a sport coat over a white shirt and tie carrying a white, rancher style, cowboy hat. Another man, similarly dressed, follows through the doorway. As the first man approaches Brock's bed, he opens his coat to display a silver "star in a wheel" badge pinned to his shirt. The western cut of their clothes, the big belt buckles, their short haircuts and the no-nonsense demeanors of these men clearly distinguish them as Texas Rangers.

Brock, like most Texans, knew of and had heard tales of Texas's iconic lawmen but had never actually encountered any. Caught off guard by their presence, his stomach begins to churn.

He pushes himself up on his elbows. "Yes, I'm Brock Sinclair. What's this about?"

The lead man says, "Morning, I'm Lt. Garcia." He thumbs toward the other man. "This is Ranger Warner. We're with Company A of the Texas Rangers."

Lt. Garcia continues, "We understand that you just recently regained consciousness and we recognize that you're still recovering. But we've spoken with Dr. Keller and he approved a short visit." The Ranger gently lays his hat, crown down, on the visitor chair at the foot of the bed and takes out a small notebook. "We know it's Sunday, but we've been waiting for more than three weeks to talk with you about what happened the day you were hospitalized."

Lowering himself back onto the pillow, Brock hesitates to respond, not knowing what he should and shouldn't say about what happened that day. "Lieutenant, I'll tell you what I can. But unfortunately I don't remember much about that day." Brock summons his courage. "I'm confused. Why are the Texas Rangers interested in my medical condition?"

"Brock, you were found unconscious on the street in Huntsville with Walter Brutonski a few feet away, apparently both victims of a drug overdose. We need to know how this happened and who might be responsible."

"Officers…I mean, Rangers, all I remember was riding to Wally's apartment near the Sam Houston campus. We—." Brock stops, realizing that both he and Wally were underage to be drinking beer and vaping weed. "We drank a couple of beers and played some video games. I don't remember much after that until I woke up here a few days ago."

"So you don't remember taking any drugs or smoking cannabis while in the presence of Mr. Brutonski?" The Ranger's tone doesn't sound accusatory.

"Like I said, that afternoon is a blur. But I've never taken any drugs."

"What about cannabis?" the Ranger's stare is penetrating.

To Brock the room is suddenly quite warm.

When Brock doesn't respond immediately, the Ranger continues, "Look, we're not here to investigate a couple of underage college students smoking a little weed. After all, cannabis has been legal in Texas for a few years now…at least for folks twenty-one. We want to know the source of the cannabis, legal or illegal, that may have contributed to Mr. Brutonski's death."

Brock figures the Rangers already know he and Wally had weed and fentanyl in their systems. "Okay, I vaguely remember we smoked a vape pen Wally had. Because it was a vape pen, I just assumed the material was legal weed. But he never said and I didn't ask."

"Did you ever buy cannabis yourself, Brock?"

Brock hesitates, wanting to cooperate but fearful of incriminating himself. Finally he says, "I remember one time last year I asked Wally to sell me a small amount of weed to take back to school."

"I see. And where did Mr. Brutonski acquire this cannabis?"

"That was not something we talked about. He did say that the product we smoked at his apartment that afternoon was from a new source." Brock sits up again. "That's the only time he ever mentioned anything about where he got his weed."

Lt. Garcia looks at Ranger Warner then back. "And how much of this new cannabis did you and Mr. Brutonski smoke?"

"I can't be sure. I guess we each took a couple of hits. After that my memory is really fuzzy."

Lt. Garcia refers to his notebook. "You attended the University of Texas in Austin last year but aren't registered this semester. Why is that?"

More concerns arise in Brock. "My grades weren't that hot at UT and I decided that engineering wasn't for me. I planned to take a semester off and figure out what I would do next."

"I see." Lt. Garcia says as he makes an entry in his notebook. "A new Harley Davidson softail was registered in your name in June. We have to wonder where a college student gets the money to buy an expensive bike like that."

Beads of sweat appear on Brock's brow. He is visibly shaking. "Ranger, should I have an attorney present?"

Lt. Garcia grins. "I don't know. You're not under arrest." He looks over his shoulder at Ranger Warner. "We're just asking some questions here. If you've done nothing wrong, I don't see the need for an attorney. But, you tell me if you need one."

Brock realizes he's at a disadvantage dealing with these experienced Rangers. But he knows he's not a criminal. "Look, Lieutenant. My grandfather died earlier this year and left me some money. I took part of it to buy the bike." He raises his voice. "Is that a crime?"

The expressions on the Rangers soften. Lt. Garcia says, "It's not if the money used to make the purchase was acquired legally. What was your grandfather's name?"

"Hank Prescott, my mom's dad, in Nacogdoches. He had been the county sheriff there for years before he retired." Brock swallows. "He died suddenly in February of a heart attack." Lt. Garcia jots something in his notebook.

"I see." Lt. Garcia looks out the window then back at Brock with a slight smile. "That's a nice bike. Have you taken any road trips yet?"

Brock couldn't see how divulging his trip details could hurt him. "I went to Austin to see a couple of friends at UT when they returned for fall semester. I then rode up to Waco to look at the Baylor campus. I'm thinking about changing schools; UT was just too big for me. Then I rode back home."

"When was this trip?"

Brock searched his memory. "I'm pretty sure it was the weekend after Labor Day."

"And how many days were you gone?"

Brock is apprehensive; that the questions are leading somewhere. He hesitates. "I spent a night in Austin and a night in Waco. Then back home. Why does it matter?"

"Just routine info for our records, Brock. By the way, what are the names of the friends you visited in Austin?"

Brock squirms in his bed. "Why do you need to know? They're just guys I got to know when I was in school at UT."

"At this point I don't see any need for us to contact these fellows. But if you tell us the names now, we might not have to come back for them later."

Eager to avoid another session with the Rangers, Brock says, "Mark Stipple and Chandler Biggs."

"And addresses?"

"They live in Roberts Hall on campus. I know where it is but I don't know the address."

The Ranger nods then pulls a business card from a small leather case in his jacket pocket and hands to it to Brock. He slowly lifts his pristine hat from the chair, inspects the crown for any contamination that may have occurred then carefully smooths the brim. With eyes fixed on Brock's he says, "That'll be all for now. We've got a few things to follow up on."

The Ranger leans his head forward slightly and precisely positions his hat on his head and reengages Brock's eyes. "Son, we've had a number of recent deaths in the state from cannabis spiked with fentanyl. And we aim to get to the bottom of this problem with or without your help. And know that we *will* be back. Maybe your memory will improve by then. In the meantime if you remember anything that could help us, give me a call." He nods toward the business card. "All my contact information is on the card."

The ranger and his partner turn to leave. "You have a speedy recovery now."

Brock sinks back into the bed, staring at the closed door as if the Rangers might reenter. He realizes he's shaking and wonders if the Rangers had noticed it, supporting their suspicions. Flat on his back, Brock's stare moves to the ceiling. He dreads another session with the Rangers. He takes a deep breath. If it had been their intent to intimidate him, they had done one hell of a job.

But despite his agitation, Brock considers just what the Rangers' jobs really are. They're trying to catch the people who're putting people's lives at risk with fentanyl just to sell their weed. And one of those lives was Wally's. Brock then realizes his own life was at risk and that he may have long-term effects from the drug. Suddenly, Brock is pissed. He picks up the business card Lt. Garcia had handed him and studies it. Unfortunately, he can't remember anything that might help the Rangers find the source of the weed.

CHAPTER 42   Nov 5, Monday

The medical review panel reassembles Monday morning at ten, as scheduled, in the same conference room.

"Laura sends her apologizes for the scene she caused on Friday," Trip says. "She's feeling better this morning but chose to stay home for another day."

Dr. Keller shakes his head. "No apology is necessary. Both of you have been under extraordinary stress these past weeks. Let's all hope she recovers quickly." He nods to Dr. Alstead.

"Good morning, all. The gentleman next to me is Professor Thomas Grant. He holds a PhD in American History from Yale and is head of the History Department at the University of Houston. He's also a long-time associate who may be helpful in the review of Brock's experience from a historical perspective." She then introduces all at the table to her associate.

Dr. Keller says, "Mr. Sinclair, I hope you're okay with Professor Grant being here. He's already signed our confidentiality agreement that prohibits him from sharing anything he sees or hears without written permission."

Trip hesitates then nods. "If it will help our son, then fine."

"Well, let's continue where we left off yesterday," Dr. Keller refers to his tablet. "Brock had just detailed the horror of his brief imprisonment at Pennsylvania Hospital by Dr. Rush and his subsequent release aided by Mr. Jamison and his lawyer son." He nods to Brock. "I'll let you pick it up there."

Brock sits forward in his chair. He tells of being taken to the Jamison home where both he and Seth are surprised to learn that Isaac had told his father of Brock's claim to be from the year 2029. "We then brainstormed how to avoid another apprehension by Dr. Rush but came up dry. Then, I remembered my tattoo."

Brock rubs his hands together. "I guess Isaac's warning against showing the tattoo to anyone caused me to put it out of my mind. But I decided to use it to try to convince Dr. Franklin that I was telling the truth."

Brock tells of showing the tattoo to Dr. Franklin and the subsequent meeting with three of his associates, responding to their questions and showing them the tattoo.

Turning to face his father, Brock says, "After the men left, Dr. Franklin asked me if I would work with him to replicate the 'electricity light' I had mentioned in an earlier discussion. Can you imagine actually getting to work with Ben Franklin on an experiment? I was giddy at the prospect." He chuckles softly.

"Anyway, since he said he was tired, I agreed to come back in a couple of days for dinner and further discussion on the experiment." Brock hesitates. "Before I left that day Dr. Franklin gave me some advice that stung. He recommended that I consider making a life in Philadelphia and not focusing on Texas or the distant future. He suggested that doing that might provide me with a better quality of life with less disappointment. Trust me when I say that hearing such advice from someone I respected was hard to take.

"Anyway, when I joined Dr. Franklin, Sarah and her husband for dinner the following Wednesday, I saw a copy of the Pennsylvania Journal and Weekly Advertiser dated Saturday,

October 27th, four days prior, lying on the sideboard. The date caught my attention because of my friend Wally's bachelor party was planned for October 27th." Brock takes a deep breath.

"After the meal Dr. Franklin and I went upstairs to his lab where he had this elaborate Leyden jar battery set-up. I knew about Leyden jars but didn't actually know how they worked. At Dr. Franklin's direction I cranked the flywheel on this fancy static generator for what seemed like forever to charge the batteries." Brock pauses. "I remember a bright flash of light then nothing else until I woke up here in the hospital." With his forearms still on the table, Brock spreads his hands to indicate he is finished. "That's about it for a condensed version of my memories. The bizarre thing is that I can remember thousands of details over the two and half weeks I spent in Philadelphia. Despite the time that's passed since awakening here, it's all still crystal clear."

The attorney, Mr. Crane, seems caught up in Brock's account. "Did you and Franklin really get a light bulb to work?"

"I don't know, Sir. Like I said, my memory stops with the flash of light."

"Thank you, Brock," Dr. Keller says. Then, to those across the table he says, "Questions, comments?"

The visitors glance from one to the other before Professor Grant speaks, "If no one objects, I'll start. Brock, although I was not here on Friday, Dr. Alstead shared the highlights from that session with me. She also indicated that you had not studied the Colonial period in any significant detail. As such, I would be interested in some of the smaller details of your...experience. Could you, for instance, describe the tavern across from Pennsylvania Hospital where you and the man you called Isaac spent time together?"

"Sure." Brock closes his eyes for a few seconds. "Well, the room wasn't large, maybe twenty by twenty. It was rather dark with the only light coming from the two hazy windows on either side of the door. There was an oil lamp hanging from a rafter but it wasn't lit when we were there. The room had rough, unpainted walls and an exposed-beam ceiling with rough boards for the floor. Wide boards maybe ten inches or more. A Franklin stove in the corner kept the room reasonably warm although it wasn't a particularly cold day."

Brock swallows and closes his eyes to focus. "There was a simple bar in the rear with no mirror behind it like you see in the old cowboy movies. A doorway out the back of the room led to the kitchen I suppose. The room had maybe eight sturdy but unfinished tables with two or three chairs at each. The chairs were of a simple, straight-back design with no padding and actually not very comfortable." Brock paused. "I don't know what else I can tell you other than it was similar to another tavern I visited about a week later."

Professor Grant frowns. "Brock, I understand you listened to a lot of narrative from the period during your coma. But if you haven't studied drawings of that time, how do you explain knowing the details of the tavern and its furnishings?"

Brock shakes his head slowly. "I don't know. When we made our family trip to Philadelphia, we did visit Independence Hall with its period furnishings. But I don't remember being in a tavern." He looks at his dad for confirmation but receives only a shake of the head. "Like I said in my opening statement on Friday, I feel like I was actually there. The details are still quite vivid even now."

######

The morning review session broke up at 11:30. Brock had been excused and taken back to his room to rest. Trip insisted on staying to hear the analysis from the doctors.

Professor Grant is the first to share his observations. "Brock's details about the tavern he claims to have visited are quite convincing. However, he indicated nothing that couldn't have been gleaned from study of writings or drawings of the period." He looks directly at Trip. "Mr. Sinclair, I believe your son has spent considerable more time than he indicates studying Benjamin Franklin and the period in which he lived."

"If that's true, it's news to me," Trip replies as he folds his arms across his chest.

"Is there anything Brock shared that would be difficult, if not impossible, to learn from the recordings?" Dr. Alstead asks.

Professor Grant shakes his head slowly. "I will admit that the breadth of his basic lifestyle knowledge is unusual for a student with his stated lack of interest in the subject. But again the narrative information provided during the coma may have been quite comprehensive."

"What do you mean 'impossible for him to learn', Doctor?" Trip says to Dr. Alstead.

Prof. Grant looks at Dr. Alstead. "If I may, Nancy?" He then turns to Trip. "Well, he speaks of Ben Franklin's house off of Market Street in Philadelphia. We know where the house foundation is but there are no accounts of which I am aware that detail the layout of the residence, specifically the laboratory on the third floor. And I did a search last night for the grave of an Isaac Jamison at Old St. Joseph's Catholic Church. No such name is listed. Bear in mind that such records are known to contain errors and omissions. However, I did find a Jamison burial plot in the church records but no details of who is actually interred."

Dr. Alstead changes the subject. "I knew of the tattoo earlier but have not seen it. Is Brock's account of its origin correct, Mr. Sinclair?"

Trip clears his throat. "Laura and I aren't tattoo fans. But when Brock was sixteen, he begged to get one. Rather than have him go behind our backs and get something he'd regret later in life, we compromised on the small, unobtrusive flag tattoo. That's been almost four years ago and I'm not aware of any other *body art*," Trip says using air quotes and a sneer.

The room turns quiet as the doctors glance at each other and their tablets. Trip breaks the silence. "Is it your collective opinion that what Brock remembers is nothing more than an elaborate dream perhaps facilitated by the drug and the audio material?"

"Unless other details arise to the contrary, that would be my preliminary opinion, Mr. Sinclair," Dr. Alstead states quietly.

CHAPTER 43   Nov 6, Tuesday

Trip and Laura are standing at the foot of Brock's bed. Trip's fists clench and release repeatedly, his whole body tense. Laura clutches a handkerchief used to dab at her eyes and nose.

Trip takes a deep breath, apparently trying to control his temper. "What the hell is going on, Brock? The police come barging into the house this morning with a search warrant, scaring the crap out of us! Then they tear the place apart looking for drugs, guns, money and God knows what else. I've lost all patience with this situation. What the hell are you mixed up in?"

His mom is crying now. "Brock, I feel so violated. The police looked in every drawer, every cabinet, every closet, all the boxes stored in the garage and in the attic. The house is a disaster. It'll take months to put everything back in its place. I can't take this on top of worrying about you for the last month."

Brock sits up. "The Rangers never hinted about searching the house. You've got to trust me, I'm not mixed up in anything!"

Trip is pacing between the door and the bed. Finally, he stops at the side of the bed and stares his son in the eye. "You must have said something to the Rangers to fire them up. What did you tell them?"

Red in the face, but meeting his father's eyes, Brock flashes to the conversation with the Rangers. "I told them what I remembered about being with Wally that afternoon. I said that I didn't know where Wally got the weed." He paused. "They wanted to know how I could afford the Harley. I said that Grandpa Hank had left me some money that I used to buy it. They asked if I had taken the bike out on the road, and I told them about riding to Austin and then on to Waco before coming back home." He looked at his mom then back to his dad. "You both knew about that trip."

"What else, Brock?" his father asks accusatorily.

Nervous but trying not to leave out any details, Brock concentrates. "To one of their questions I said I had bought a little of Wally's weed last winter."

"Jesus Christ, Brock! Do you have your head up your ass? Using illegal drugs! Buying drugs! Are you selling too? Don't you know what this could do to your future?" Trip slams his hand onto the rolling table adjacent to the bed, spilling a cup of water. "Damn it, Brock!"

Brock knows he had not hidden any money or guns in the house. However, the small amount of weed with a pipe and lighter in the bottom of his toolbox in the garage is a concern but decides not to ask if the police found it. He looks to his mom for some relief. "Mom, who did the search? Was it the local police? The DEA? The Rangers? Who?"

Trip's nostrils flare. "What difference does it make, Brock? They had a search warrant that a judge signed based on probable cause. What did you do that gave them probable cause?"

Frustrated now, Brock fires back. "I don't know, Dad! I've already told you what I told the Rangers."

Trip smirks. "Well, one good thing that came from this is that they impounded that damn bike of yours." He sighs. "But they also wrecked the garage and all that stuff stored in the boxes. What a mess!"

The tendons stand out in Brock's neck. "Did they take anything else beside the bike?"

Trip continues to pace, shaking his head. Laura speaks at last, "Brock, they took some items in a couple of evidence bags but wouldn't tell us what they had. A detective from the Montgomery County Sheriff's office left his card for us to call in a few days if we had questions or if they damaged anything." She blushes. "They even took the edibles and the terpenes your dad and I had in the freezer."

Trip blares, "That I bought as an adult from a legal store!"

Brock looks from his mom to his dad. "What happens next? Am I just supposed to lie here and wait for the Rangers to return with their guns drawn and handcuffs ready?"

Grimacing, Trip says, "You should have thought of that before you got mixed up in illegal drugs."

CHAPTER 44   Nov 7, Wednesday

Dr. Keller checks his watch then looks across his desk. "Okay, what's so urgent that we needed to meet this morning?" He glances at Professor Grant sitting beside Dr. Alstead.

The psychiatrist replies, "Roger, there's some startling information Professor Grant's discovered." She turns to her friend. "Fletcher, it's your discovery."

"Sure, Nancy." Professor Grant straightens in his chair. "Dr. Keller, after our interview with Brock Sinclair on Monday, I did some digging into some of the things he referenced. As I said in the summation meeting, there are no records of an Isaac Jamison being buried at Old St. Joseph's Catholic Church. What I did find was a single reference to a general store on Market Street in Philadelphia run by a Matthew Jamison during the late 1700's. From my extensive resources for the period, the single reference I found would be accessible to perhaps only a half-dozen, fully-accredited researchers in the country. It is extremely unlikely that Brock would have had knowledge of that detail." He shrugs. "Unless it was included in the audio material played for him."

Dr. Keller frowns. "If it's not, then, how do you explain the 'Mr. Jamison' referenced by Brock? Is that just a coincidence?"

"Perhaps." Professor Grant turns to Dr. Alstead then back. "However, there's another even more exceptional reference to consider. I've been in contact with a colleague who's a recognized expert on Ben Franklin and who has done extensive research on the man and his life. He shared that the Yale library has the only known copy of a diary that belonged to Sally Bache, Ben Franklin's daughter. He's been granted access to the fragile diary once in thirty years and then only with special permission."

Professor Grant pauses to clear his throat. "My colleague indicates that there's an entry in the diary from October 31st, 1787. Part of the entry tells of a young man, whom Bache identifies only as FS, being 'struck by electricity' during an experiment in her father's laboratory. Unfortunately, the next page is missing. And there's no other mention of the incident later in the diary or anywhere else. My colleague, who has searched for a confirmation of the accident for years, could only assume that the person's identity and the extent of his injuries are lost forever. Mind you the date matches but the initials in the diary do not."

Dr. Keller pales. "You will remember that Brock's legal name is Franklin Brock Sinclair. So, the initials FS do add an element of peculiarity." He shakes his head. "If access to this diary is as restricted as you say, how could Brock have included this detail in his narrative?" He shakes his head. "But he must have learned of it somehow."

"That's just it, doctor. My colleague says there's no plausible way Brock could have had access to this diary. Moreover, nothing's been published about it because it's an incomplete reference." He shakes his head. "But I agree with you that there must be an explanation."

Suddenly frowning, Dr. Keller looks down at his tablet. "I'll be damned! You said October 31st was the date of the incident referenced in the diary. That's the same date Brock regained consciousness!" The doctor slowly shakes his head. "There's no way Brock could have kept track of the calendar while he was in a coma. Doing so would be…completely unprecedented!" He rubs the back of his neck.

Dr. Alstead puts down her tablet and aggressively attacks her phone. "Hold on. What if…" She looks up, brow furrowed, at first the doctor then the professor. In a whisper she says, "The calendars match?"

"What do you mean the calendars match?" Dr. Keller says, his eyes narrowing.

"The calendar for 1787 is identical to the calendar for 2029." She looks at Dr. Keller but with no focus. "If Brock's memory of his time in the coma is as accurate as he claims, he could believe he tracked his time during the month of October, 1787. In reality he was following the calendar for 2029."

Dr. Keller folds his arms across his chest. "Hold on! It's unheard of for a patient to track time while in a coma. And, Brock couldn't just decide to rouse himself from a coma on the date he chooses."

Dr. Alstead puts a finger to her lips. "Could the knowledge of a shock on a certain date in Ben Franklin's lab be enough for Brock's brain to 'restart'? Don't forget, Roger, that we don't have much data from APX207 patients and their recovery scenarios. And, the fentanyl is a wild card in all this."

Dr. Keller takes a deep breath and knits his hands on the edge of his desk, his eyes seeming to search the room for an answer. "If Brock knowing of that incident allowed his brain to restart, then he had to get the information somewhere." He scratches his head. "What do you propose?"

Dr. Alstead says, "We need to find out if the audio material we played for Brock can be searched for that specific date. If so, we should ask for a search of *Bache diary* and the date *October 31st, 1787*."

"I'll have IT get on it right away," Dr. Keller says. "Since the audio originated from written sources, maybe there's a word search capability."

"Doctor, I recommend you have them include the name 'Jamison' in the search also," Professor Grant says.

Doctor Keller nods and makes a note on a paper tablet.

Professor Grant is energized. "Good. I'll have my researchers do some in-depth digging into death notices just after the October 31st date and into the diaries of Richard Bache, Dr. Jones, Franklin's personal physician, Dr. Rush and anybody else who may have had knowledge of an incident. All those sources have probably already been searched, but I want to make sure."

Professor Grant continues, "I would also like to spend more time with Brock. Get him to provide additional details about his dream. Ask him some follow up questions, particularly about the Bache diary incident and the date."

Doctor Keller grimaces. "Professor, I don't know if the other members of the panel have the time or the inclination to listen to more of Brock's story."

"That's just as well. It might be tedious for anyone who's not interested in history to sit through a session such as I envision. And if I had my druthers, I would prefer to be alone with Brock and perhaps one other attendee to take notes. I want to build a rapport with the young man, gain his confidence. I would hope to get him to open up about the basis of his unique knowledge of the period. That failing, maybe I will detect flaws in his story to help establish or refute his credibility."

Dr. Keller leans back in his chair and steeples his fingers. "Although Brock's physical health is improving, I think his emotional health is still vulnerable. I have concerns about an interrogation regarding the details of what he remembers at this early stage of his recovery."

The historian puts up his hands. "I understand your apprehension, doctor. And I assure you I had no intention of conducting an inquisition. Rather I recommend a casual, yet detailed, conversation. I believe it is crucial to capture Brock's memories while they're fresh. The longer we delay a more thorough debriefing, the more chance we'll lose content."

Dr. Keller says, "Nancy, you're the psychiatrist. What do you think? Would we be putting Brock at risk?"

Dr. Alstead leans forward. "My impression of Brock thus far is that he's a strong-willed young man. And he appears quite stable. If we conduct the session as a conversation, I believe he'll be fine." She nods her head and turns to look at Professor Grant. "Fletcher, I'd be willing to sit in as an observer and note taker if Dr. Keller agrees to your suggestion."

"Another issue I foresee is that Mr. Sinclair will want to sit in to protect his son," Dr. Keller says. "Will that be a problem?"

Professor Grant squirms in his chair. "If he has to be there, I guess I'll have to accept it. But frankly, I would prefer that it just be the three of us." He motions to himself and Dr. Alstead.

"I'll see what I can do," Dr. Keller stands to dismiss his guests. "But understand that Trip can be quite insistent when it comes to his son."

"Dr. Keller, I strongly recommend that we keep the unexplainable details in Brock's dream confidential. I wouldn't want him to get his guard up prior to further interviews. And I would certainly think it best to keep this from getting into the public domain at this early juncture."

"I completely agree."

CHAPTER 45   Nov 8, Thursday

Eight days after waking from his coma, Brock's tolerance for tasteless hospital food is long gone and the walls of the hospital room are closing in. The boring hall strolls and the seemingly endless tests, most concerning his comprehension, have him considering an escape. But Dr. Keller has pushed his release until Friday, saying he wants to run a few more tests and to be sure Brock is ready for different surroundings and new stimulations.

The bland, hospital breakfast taunts Brock from the tray. The runny scrambled eggs, the dry toast, and the oatmeal with the consistency of paste only serve to spoil his appetite. He wants some food with salt and spices and texture like…well like real food. And yet he hasn't complained to the dieticians during their daily visits. It would be wrong to do so. They're just doing their jobs and are only concerned with his recovery. He nibbles at his toast to avoid insulting the kitchen staff.

At 9:00 a.m. Dr. Keller arrives. "Good morning, Brock. Let me have a look at your charts from yesterday and last night." He studies the tablet he carries, occasionally touching the surface or swiping it with his finger. "Young man, I don't see any reason why you can't go home tomorrow. Do you feel up to it?"

Brock smiles broadly. "Yes, sir! I'm ready to leave *now*!"

Dr. Keller grins. "I suppose that's a good sign. But I notice you've hardly touched your breakfast."

"I guess I'm just not hungry this morning," Brock suggests. "By the way doc, when will you remove the feeding tube from my stomach?"

"Is it bothering you?"

"No, it doesn't hurt. I'd just like to get it over with."

"Okay. I'll have the nurse do that this morning. You'll have to avoid eating anything for a while before and after the removal then gradually return to the diet you have been on. And no carbonated beverages for a couple of days." He waves off any further questions. "The nurse will give you all the details about managing the dressing and such."

Dr. Keller closes his tablet. "We'll get another fMRI today and unless it shows something unexpected, you're out of here tomorrow afternoon."

There's a firm knock on the door as it moves inward slowly. In the widening gap, the shape of a large man with his distinctive cowboy hat and western clothes appears. The breath involuntarily leaves Brock's lungs before his head drops back onto his pillow.

Removing his hat, the man says, "Dr. Keller? I'm Lt. Garcia of the Texas Rangers. The nice lady at the nurses' station said you'd be in here. You'll remember we spoke on the phone last week before our visit with Brock." He thumbs toward another man now also moving into the room. "This is my partner, Ranger Warner. We need some time alone with Brock if that's possible." His tone suggests a demand rather than a request.

Dr. Keller hesitates before looking at Brock. "Are you strong enough to answer the Rangers' questions?"

"I doubt I have a choice." He waves the Rangers in. "It's okay, Doc. I can talk to them."

"I'll schedule the scan for 11:00 o'clock so we don't compromise your lunch."

"No, I wouldn't want to miss that." Brock rolls his eyes.

As Dr. Keller passes the rangers on his way out, his glare at Lt. Garcia shows his annoyance at the intrusion. The Ranger responds only with a faint Bogart smirk.

With the door closed Lt. Garcia places his hat on the guest chair as he did during his first visit and opens his small notebook. "Mr. Sinclair, we'd like you to tell us again what happened in the afternoon and evening of October 8th."

"Rangers, no disrespect, but we went through all this when you were here before. Do we really need to do it again?"

Lt. Garcia leans closer. "Actually, we do. If there's the slightest chance your memory of that afternoon has improved, we want to collect any new details. Start from the beginning and don't leave out a single thing. If you and Mr. Brutonski ate Cheetos rather than pretzels when you got the munchies, we want to know about it. If you watched the haloscreen, we want to know what shows were on. If you work with us to reconstruct that afternoon, perhaps something of value will come out. Will you give it a try, Brock?"

"Yeah, I'll try." Brock then shakes his head slowly. "I've been trying to think of anything I didn't remember when you were here last time. I really want to help you catch the bastards that killed my friend and put me in a coma."

Lt. Garcia nods. "That's the spirit, Brock."

Brock starts from his phone call to Wally asking if his friend wanted to hang for a while. "When I got to his apartment, Wally came out and looked at my bike before we went inside." For several minutes Brock retells of his visit to Wally's, drinking maybe two beers (Shiner Bock) each, catching up on the past month, Wally complaining about school work and Brock bitching about his dad.

"I asked Wally if he wanted to get high and he said 'sure'. We lit a joint I brought and we both took a couple of tokes. When the joint went out, he said, 'Let's try some new bud I just got.'

He said he hadn't tried it yet but it was supposed to be primo. He went into the kitchen and returned with his vaporizer and loaded it with this finely-ground bud."

Ranger Garcia interrupts him. "Describe the container with the new cannabis."

"It was like the ones used at the weed stores except the label looked homemade like on a laser printer rather than done professionally." The Ranger makes another entry in his notebook.

"Continue, Brock. You're doing just fine."

"Well, we each took a couple of hits from the vaporizer. In like seconds I got super high. I remember Wally saying something like 'This shit's awesome! That Goddamned Hector was right.'"

Brock shakes his head. "I remember being light-headed and disoriented and even nauseous. It wasn't fun at all. I needed some cool air and a soda to help settle my stomach. So, we left for a convenience store down the block." He pauses. "I vaguely remember leaving Wally's place but after that everything is a blank." He looks directly at the Ranger. "That's all I remember, I swear. Three weeks later I woke up in this bed."

Lt. Garcia stares at Brock then slowly makes a note.

Brock does not tell the Rangers of his time in Philadelphia. Their issue is the fentanyl and he can't see how his 1787 experience would be relevant to their investigation and would only cause confusion.

"You said before that you did not know where Mr. Brutonski got his cannabis," Lt. Garcia says.

Brock shakes his head vigorously. "That's right."

"In all the times you and he were together he never mentioned a name, a place he went to buy cannabis, how much he bought or how much he paid?"

"Lieutenant, Wally and I were close in high school, you know? But last fall I left for UT and he went to Sam Houston. We didn't see each other after that except during holidays. He had a construction job all this past summer, plus Wally could be pretty private sometimes."

"I can't believe he never uttered anything about where he bought his cannabis." Lt. Garcia walks a slow, small loop in the open space of the room, seeming to record every detail.

"Lieutenant, if Wally said anything other than the name 'Hector' that one time, I don't remember it."

Lt. Garcia makes another loop but in the opposite direction. As he passes Ranger Warner, Brock notices a barely perceptible nod from Garcia's partner.

Back at Brock's bed Lt. Garcia's tone becomes less threatening. "Son, you may not have heard the news yet, but yesterday there was a coordinated raid on a warehouse in Bellmead. That's on the outskirts of Waco. Eight individuals are in custody and several more suspects remain at large. Significant quantities of cannabis and fentanyl were seized along with a handgun and tens of thousands in cash.

"This organization has been a major supplier of illegal cannabis for most of North Texas and southern Oklahoma. In recent months, to compete with the high quality of legal cannabis, they have been importing fentanyl and spiking their low quality weed. As a result, drug overdoses and deaths have skyrocketed. They were also expanding into southeast Texas."

Brock's mouth falls open as he listens to the ranger.

"When we searched Mr. Brutonski's apartment after his death, we found a small vial of cannabis tainted with fentanyl. Chemical analysis of that fentanyl matched that of cannabis purchased by undercover agents from the suspects in Bellmead in the weeks leading up to yesterday's raid." Lt. Garcia looks down at his notes and then back at Brock. "Based on the small quantity of cannabis at Mr. Brutonski's residence and no other evidence, we do not believe he was part of the drug ring in Bellmead. It's likely he was an unknowing victim of their deadly enterprise."

Brock lets out the breath he had been holding as the ranger talked. "I couldn't imagine Wally dealing drugs." He pauses. "Other than…like I told you before." He looks away as his face turns a faint pink.

Lt. Garcia clears his throat. "I assume you're aware that a search of your parent's home was conducted recently."

Brock nods weakly.

"We found a small container of suspicious cannabis in a toolbox in the garage." A hint of a grin forms on the Ranger's face. "You wouldn't know anything about that would you?"

Brock blushes again as he hesitates. "Exactly what kind of toolbox, Lieutenant?"

"Come on! Let's not do a Texas two-step here. Ranger Wagner and I are busy people. You know which toolbox."

"Okay! I had a tiny bit left from what I got from Wally that I was saving for a rainy day. I'd hope you'd consider that a pretty puny stash."

The ranger looks down at his notebook then back to Brock. "1.37 grams to be exact." He pauses. "And yes, we tested it for fentanyl and lucky for you it came back negative. For now we'll hold on to the cannabis as evidence."

Lt. Garcia puts his notebook in his jacket pocket and clips his pen in his shirt pocket. "You seem like a standup guy, Brock. Would you be willing to testify in court to seeing Mr. Brutonski in possession of the material that caused his death? And to the medical effects of the material on yourself when the members of this drug ring go to trial?"

Brock considers the request. He sure as hell wants to do what's right for Wally. But what would be the risks from the drug gang and their "associates? "I don't know Lieutenant. Can I think about it?"

Lt. Garcia nods. "Sure. We'll be in touch. Until then if you remember anything else about that afternoon, give me a call. You already have my card."

The Ranger recovers his Stetson from the chair. His jaw set, he looks down at Brock. "I hope you've learned something from this experience. Wait until you're twenty-one if you choose to consume cannabis and if you do, get it from a registered retailer."

A faint smile comes over Brock's face but does not answer.

Lt. Garcia then extends his large hand to Brock. "Good luck. I'm sorry you lost your friend." The Ranger smiles. "I really mean that, son."

As Brock shook the Ranger's hand, he decided the tone in the man's voice was genuine.

CHAPTER 46   Nov 12, Monday

Brock is not eager to return to the hospital for his meeting with Dr. Alstead and Professor Grant four days after his release. He's had enough of the place to last a lifetime. But getting out of the house even for an Uber ride to the hospital is a welcome reprieve from his mom's hovering. He has told her numerous times that he doesn't need to be pampered but she continues.

His energy level has increased quickly in the last several days such that he would rather be outside on a walk or doing some light Taekwondo. Instead he sits across from the doctor and the professor in the same conference room where he had already given accounts of his experience in the eighteenth century.

The fall sunshine beams into the room causing Brock to squint despite the electronic-tint windows. Is his position at the table facing the windows intentional? An assortment of energy bars and protein wafers rests on an orange, pumpkin-shaped tray in the middle of the table along with an insulated carafe of water and a half-dozen glasses.

Brock's father is not able to attend today due to critical meetings with the Board of Directors at his office. He has been promised a briefing by Dr. Alstead as soon their schedules allow.

Dr. Alstead says, "Brock, this is intended to be a casual discussion of your memories during the period of your coma. We are not recording today so you can relax and approach this session as if you're telling your experience to a couple of close friends. We're not here to judge but for you to clarify some things for us and perhaps for yourself." She pauses. "Okay?"

"Yes, ma'am. There were lots of smaller details of my weeks in Philadelphia that I didn't cover during those earlier sessions. Maybe going back and talking about them will be helpful."

Dr. Alstead nods, "Then, let's get started." She gestures to the snacks on the table. "Help yourself. Fletcher, rather Professor Grant, insisted that we have snacks. I've also arranged for some civilian food to be delivered at mid-day." Brock and Professor Grant both grin at the reprieve from hospital fare.

Dr. Alstead continues, "We'll take our time and see where this goes." She nods toward her colleague on her right. "Professor Grant will most likely be asking for clarifications along the way. After all he's the history expert. I expect mostly to be the scribe."

Professor Grant nods. "Brock, why don't you begin at the initial meeting you had with Isaac's family in their home? Tell us as much as you can remember about the house, their clothes, the food, everything."

Brock nods. "Okay. I'll start with Mrs. Jamison's greeting after Isaac ushered me through their door." Without interruption Brock describes in intricate detail the midday dinner he experienced with the Jamison family up to the point where he and Isaac left to return to the hospital.

In addition to the items Professor Grant requested, Brock elaborates on the layout of the room and what he could see beyond; the table setting; the room lighting; the demeanor and comments of each individual at the table; his reaction to the food and the weak beer.

Professor Grant cringes. "How was the beer, Brock?

Brock smiles at the professor's reaction. "Well, I wouldn't put it up against a cold Shiner Bock. But since I was really thirsty, it wasn't too bad. In the time I was in Philly, I grew to appreciate the weak beer and the ale served in the taverns. But the room-temperature thing takes some getting used to."

When Brock finishes his comments about the meal with the Jamisons, Dr. Alstead raises a single eyebrow and shakes her head. "Brock, I'm surprised. I couldn't have described dinner with my husband and son two nights ago in the same amount of detail. Are you always that observant?"

"I guess so. Like last week when we met here, you sat in that chair." Brock points to the chair where Professor Grant now sits. "You wore a navy suit with a pale yellow blouse, open at the neck with a small silver triangle at your throat. Your earrings were silver studs with small diamonds. Your hair was similar to today's but with maybe a bit less mousse. Your lipstick was more of a rose than today's pink."

Dr. Alstead blushes and absently pushes her hair back around her left ear before glancing at Professor Grant then back to Brock. "I don't know what to say. I can't verify that everything you say is accurate, but I did wear a navy suit one day last week."

Professor Grant smirks. "Well, Brock you are indeed full of surprises. But let me just say it's easy to stare at an attractive woman like Dr. Alstead for a few hours and come away with a detailed description. But—"

"On Thursday, Professor Grant, you wore black slacks with a narrow black belt and a brown and black check, two-button sport coat. Your necktie was almost black, tied in a half-Windsor with no clip. Your watch had a gold band with dark face and analog hands. It was five minutes fast compared to the clock over the white board. And you hadn't shaved for two or three days. And just to be clear, I agree that Dr. Alstead is certainly easier to look at than you are." Brock grins.

The professor stares at Brock as he slowly pushes his sleeve up to expose his watch. He glances down at the timepiece then up at the clock at the end of the room. "I'll be damned!"

Dr. Alstead leans back in her chair. "Brock, your recall of intricate details is most unusual. Is this a new ability?"

"It doesn't feel unusual to me. It feels normal."

Dr. Alstead says, "Let's try something. Tell us what your friend Wally was wearing the day you arrived at his apartment."

Intending to further demonstrate his recall skills, Brock responds quickly, "He was wearing…jeans…" Brock hesitates. "I mean I guess he was wearing jeans; he always did. He had on a gray 'Sam Houston' sweat shirt. No, maybe it was black." Flustered Brock says, "I'm not sure. We got stoned soon after I got there."

Dr. Alstead pulls her lips in. "That's fair. Okay, let's go back a little further to a time before your coma. You told us earlier that you rode your Harley to your friend's apartment the day you fell. Did you buy the motorcycle from a dealer?"

"Yes, ma'am. Northside Harley on I-45."

"Describe the salesman that sold you the bike."

"Well, Fred's about forty. Heavyset with a beard." Brock makes a noise in his throat but says nothing more.

Professor Grant says, "What color are his eyes? What was he wearing on the day of your purchase? How many bikes were in the showroom?"

Brock rubs the back of his neck and does not initially respond. "His eyes are maybe blue. He had on a black HD tee shirt like the one I bought. But I didn't count all the bikes; I was only interested in the softails." His voice rises as he speaks.

Professor Grant continues, "Can you tell us how you got to the Harley dealership that day?

"My mom dropped me off."

"And what was she wearing that day?"

Brock closes his eyes while he tries to remember. At last he says softly, "I don't know. Probably shorts."

"You don't remember the intricate details of the dealership, the salesman or your mom?" Dr. Alstead says.

Staring blankly out the window, Brock says, "No, I guess I don't." He changes his focus to Dr. Alstead. "What does that mean, Doc?"

Over the next several minutes Dr. Alstead asks Brock about other situations to test his memory. Brock's comments suggest that before the fall and his coma his powers of observation and memory were not nearly as remarkable as what he demonstrated from several days prior.

"Was it the drugs or the head injury that caused this, Doctor?" Brock asks. "More importantly, is it permanent?"

"I don't know, Brock. I'll need to do some analysis and research before I can make a determination." Dr. Alstead pauses then speaks softly. "Would you like it to be permanent?"

Brock is silent at first. "I kind of like it. But some of the things I notice and remember disturb me."

Professor Grant looks at Dr. Alstead, who nods, then turns to Brock. "Like what, Brock? What's something you observed and remember that's disturbing?"

Brock hesitates. "I keep seeing my friend Isaac lying on the bed at Pennsylvania Hospital, his face bloodied, his head bashed in. That horrible image is just as vivid now as it was weeks ago when I was standing there with his father looking down at him. I can't get it out of my mind."

For over four hours, including a working lunch of sub sandwiches, coleslaw and chips, delivered from a highly-rated local chain, Brock shares more details of his memory of 18th century Philadelphia. Professor Grant appears especially fascinated with any details about Dr. Franklin, his house and its furnishings. Brock wonders if the professor's priorities are perhaps more academic than analytical to his coma experience.

At 2:00 p.m. Dr. Alstead calls a halt to the session. "I've got a meeting with a client this afternoon." She interlaces her fingers and turns her palms outward. "Besides, my hands are aching. My schedule is fairly full for the next few days. I assume you gentlemen won't object if we schedule another session for Friday. Same time, same place?"

Professor Grant squirms in his chair then faces Dr. Alstead. "Can't we meet sooner? I want to get as much information from Brock as soon as possible."

Brock stares at Professor Grant. "There's no rush, Professor? I'm not going anywhere for a while."

"The content of your experience may be vitally important to Dr. Alstead's analysis. I would hate to lose anything critical just because we delayed our sessions."

Dr. Alstead shakes her head. "Fletcher, I see little risk in waiting a few days. Besides, Brock may need a chance to adjust to being out of the hospital, to stretch his legs so to speak. We'll go with Friday at ten."

CHAPTER 47   Nov 15, Thursday

An autumn sun streaks the southern windows at the Sinclair residence north of Houston as Brock relaxes with the afternoon news on his phone following his return from a short run in the neighborhood. "I'm pooped, Mom. That's only the third time I've worked out since maybe Labor Day when Wally and I did some lifting in his garage. It's amazing how out of shape I've gotten. And the instructor at the dojang yesterday is seriously hard-core."

"Son, I remind you again that you need to take it slow. Remember, you didn't move for three weeks...after your fall."

"Mom, I dosed on fentanyl. Unknowingly, mind you. But that's what really happened. You don't need to tip toe around the subject with me. Okay?"

Laura Sinclair, purses her lips and nods. "All right, son." She fingers her blond hair back over her head with her right hand and smiles. "Changing the subject. When you go up to visit Stephen F. Austin next week, you're not planning to ride your bike are you? It'll make me feel better if you drive your car in the cool weather and after...'the dosing.'"

Brock grins at the phrase. "Thanks, Mom. I was planning to drive the Mustang because I'm sure I'll pick up a bunch of folders and manuals from the tour and the admissions office. That would be a hassle on the bike. And Accurate Forecast says there's at least a fifty percent chance of rain on Monday."

The doorbell rings, interrupting their conversation. Brock, although stiff from his recent exercise, jumps to his feet with a low groan. "I'll get it, Mom."

When Brock opens the door, Lt. Garcia of the Texas Rangers looms on the stoop. The Ranger's presence including his pristine hat and polished badge jolts Brock back to the serious nature of his previous visits.

The Ranger removes his sunglasses and says, "Good afternoon, Brock. Could I have a few words with you?" Looking over Brock's shoulder at Mrs. Sinclair standing in the vestibule, the Ranger touches the brim of his hat, "Afternoon, ma'am." Changing his focus back to Brock, the Ranger says, "Can we speak in private?"

The queasy feeling Brock experienced on both previous encounters with Lt. Garcia returns, but despite his apprehension, he sees no way to avoid the Ranger. "Sure, Lieutenant." Brock steps aside and opens the door to allow the Ranger to enter. "Come in."

Lt. Garcia removes his Stetson and steps through the doorway, his polished boots clacking on the tile floor. He nods to Brock's mother, "Good afternoon, Mrs. Sinclair. I'm Lt. Garcia with the Texas Rangers. We haven't officially met but I saw you in the hall at the hospital." He extends his hand which is accepted. "I certainly don't want to intrude but I need to speak with Brock for only a few minutes if I may."

Laura Sinclair's eyes widen as she looks toward her son.

Brock smiles at his mother. "It's okay, Mom. If we sit in the family room, will we be out of your way?"

Laura turns slowly toward the back of the house, "I'll be in the kitchen if you need anything." She looks at the Ranger. "Coffee, Lieutenant?"

"No Ma'am. I'm good. But thank you."

With Brock seated on the sofa and Lt. Garcia in an armchair to Brock's left, the Ranger is the first to speak. "Brock, it's good to see you up and around. You've got more color in your face than when I saw you in the hospital."

"Yes, sir, I'm getting my strength back...slowly."

"Good." Lt. Garcia leans forward to lay his Stetson on the end of the coffee table. He lowers his voice. "Brock, I told you at the hospital that I may want you to testify in the fentanyl case we discussed at that time. I'm here to talk to you about that."

Brock takes a deep breath and lets it out. "Lieutenant, I've thought some about what you said at the hospital. Actually a lot." Brock's eyes move away from the Ranger to the floor near his own feet. "I've got to be honest. The idea of drug dealers or gang members seeking revenge on me and my folks scares the crap out of me, if you'll pardon the expression."

The Ranger pushes himself to the back of his chair. "I understand. But before you make a final decision, let me fully explain the situation."

Brock nods and turns only slightly toward his guest.

"The fentanyl operation in Bellmead, was a business enterprise started by two brothers who grew up in that area, Fernando and Jose Flores. They handpicked talent from the local market and imported a few guys from Mexico. They ran the operation like a corporation. They paid salaries, hiring bonuses for key people, and the sellers worked on commission. There was no gang or gang affiliation that has been identified. They sold only in areas that were not gang-controlled to avoid confrontations and, from what we can tell, they avoided violence altogether. In fact, there was only one hand gun confiscated in the raid of their operation."

"Okay, but—"

"Let me finish, Brock. "During the raid, we arrested Fernando and Jose along with their accountant, a materials buyer and four workers. Their dealers were not at the location but warrants were issued for their arrests and two have already been picked up. We got the leaders, so the heavy lifting is done." Lt. Garcia leans forward. "Brock, the commanders of Ranger Company F in Waco and Company A here in Houston are both convinced reprisal is unlikely from the prosecution of the Flores brothers. They were the masterminds of the operation, and pretty good business men by the way, but have no gang affiliation. They saw a business opportunity and were good enough entrepreneurs to seize it.

"I'm telling you this to say that we believe you and your family would be at very little risk of any revenge from the defendants or their associates."

Brock nods. "I'm not committing to anything. But what is it that you would want me to do?"

"The Flores brothers and eight of their accomplices have been arraigned and await trial in the McLennan County jail. The judge denied bail, considering all the defendants to be flight risks. As you may know, the court system can be slow. So their trial, to be held in Waco, won't likely be scheduled for months, perhaps not until the second quarter of next year. We won't need you for that. We have the evidence that they were making and distributing the fentanyl-spiked cannabis. That includes the material in the vape pen we found in Mr. Brutonski's apartment."

"Then why do you need me?"

"After their conviction, there will be a sentencing hearing at a later date. That may be as much as four to six months later. The District Attorney needs your testimony to link the spiked cannabis to Mr. Brutonski's death and your near-fatal exposure. If you agree, we would take a video deposition in the next month or so to have on hand for the sentencing hearing. When the time comes, the prosecutor may decide that the video deposition would be enough without you actually testifying at the hearing."

Brock runs his finger through his hair. He again recalls incidents in the news of witnesses being shot, their homes burned, families harassed or even killed to prevent testimony. He shudders. "I don't know, Lieutenant. I'm trying to move on with my life. If I get accepted, I plan to start school at Stephen F. Austin in January. If I had to miss class to drive to Waco to testify, it could jeopardize my studies."

"Brock, as I said back in the hospital I felt like you were a standup guy. Maybe I misjudged you. But I believe you want to see the men who caused your friend's death pay for their crime. Not to mention putting you in a coma."

The Ranger's words stuck with Brock and he *did* want to help put those guys in prison for a long time. "But what if a judge gives those guys five years in jail? What's to prevent them from looking me or my parents up to get even when they're released?"

"Brock, I think it comes down to a matter of trust. I, my Ranger commanders and the assistant DA all feel the case against the Flores brothers is rock solid. If they're convicted and tied to Mr. Brutonski's death, they will serve sentences of twenty-five to life. Moreover, I'm telling you that they are not hardened criminals just opportunists who didn't consider the serious risks they were taking. I truly believe vengeance is not in their nature. And that the risk to you and your family is extremely small."

Brock stares at the dried flowers on the coffee table as the Ranger's words swirl in his head. Finally, he looks the Ranger in the eyes. "Lieutenant, if I was your son, would you advise me to testify?"

The Ranger's encouraging smile wavers as he stares in the direction of his hat. His response is slow in coming, but finally he looks up. "Brock, first consider that I am a career law man and have spent my adult life working to see justice served. Know also that my son had some serious health issues when he was young, so he is very special to me and my wife." He pauses. "In all honesty my son would probably have the same reservations as you. But if he was in your situation, I would certainly encourage him to cooperate. And if he did choose to testify, it would be one of my proudest moments."

Brock's lips form a straight line. He then looks the Ranger in the eyes. "You're very persuasive, sir." Brock shakes his head slowly. "But I just don't know. I'd like to talk to my mom and dad about it since they have a dog in this hunt too."

Lt. Garcia slowly retrieves his hat from the table as he stands, a disappointed smile on his face. "I understand, son. You know how to contact me." The Ranger turns toward the door and steps in that direction. "Please tell your mom that it was nice to have met her."

Brock rises also and meets the Ranger's eyes. "Lieutenant, I'd like to think that if it was my decision alone, that I'd agree to cooperate. Trust me, I'll be persuasive when I approach my folks about this."

"Thank you, Brock." Lt. Garcia and Brock exchange a firm handshake before the Ranger strides out the door.

CHAPTER 48   Nov 16, Friday

As Brock drives his Mustang to the hospital for his 10:00 a.m. session with Dr. Alstead and Professor Grant, his apprehension builds. He trusts that Dr. Alstead has his interests as a primary focus. Professor Grant is another matter. Brock's gut tells him that the noted professor, with his busy academic schedule, is spending far more time on this effort than someone who is just a friend of Dr. Alstead. Brock doesn't know what it is that bugs him about Professor Grant but his senses are on alert.

He arrives early to the session and purposely takes a seat at the table with the windows and the sun at his back. When Dr. Alstead arrives, she greets Brock with enthusiasm and asks how he feels and how he's adjusting.

"I feel pretty good, Doc. I've been working out some and feel like my strength is coming back. Plus, my mom is trying to fatten me up," he says with a chuckle.

"And how is your recall of the events during your coma?"

"You know, Doc, it's interesting. We talked last time about my power of observation and recall. I've been testing myself regularly on the details of places I've visited over the past several days. It feels like I'm not noticing as much detail as I did right after my coma. Oh, I remember the obvious things like the weather two days earlier or how many students are in the Taekwondo class. But smaller details are much more fluid. On the other end of the spectrum, even the smallest details of Philadelphia and of the people I met during the coma and even the first few days after I woke up are still crystal clear. Can you explain that?"

"I can't say with confidence until I perform more analysis. But it might be that the APX207 enhanced your observation and recall abilities as long as it was in your system. But as the drug dissipated, its effects on your observation and memory may have declined as well."

Brock puts his hands on the table, his fingers interlaced. In an emotion-choked voice he says, "Will my memories of Philadelphia eventually fade?"

Dr. Alstead's lips form a straight line. "I really can't say. Remember, you're a special case of a limited number of trials. But my guess is that since you were 'living' in Philadelphia for that time, your memory will last much like any real experience would."

In the immediate silence, Professor Grant rushes into the room. "Damn I-45! Traffic's a bitch just south of here." He slams his briefcase down on the table and looks at Dr. Alstead. "Why are we sitting on this side of the table today?"

Brock pipes up, "Does it matter?"

Professor Grant taps the tabletop with his index finger, staring at Dr. Alstead. "No, it's fine. Let's get started."

When Grant is seated and Dr. Alstead is poised to key her tablet, Brock asks, "Should I start where we left off last time?"

Professor Grant's response is immediate. "Let's move to the end of your time in Philadelphia and work backward. It may be more productive and less prone to fabrication." He suddenly raises his eyebrows and looks across the table at Brock. "Look, no offense intended. But if your account in Philadelphia is a high percentage of details your mind created with the help of the APX207 rather than being based on facts you heard through the ear buds, having you tell your experience in reverse order may open a window of understanding for us. And for you."

Brock scowls at the professor. "Your use of the term 'fabricated' seriously offends me. It implies that I'm making up some or all of my experience in Philadelphia." He squeezes the edge of the table with all his strength, his jaw clenched. "Every detail I've reported is exactly what I saw or heard while in my coma. You can believe it or not. I really don't care."

Dr. Alstead attempts to mediate. "Brock, I'm convinced that everything you've relayed to us you genuinely experienced. Some of it was based on information you received from the audio and some of it your mind created to develop the narrative. But I firmly believe it was very real to you."

The professor puts up his hands to deflect Brock's scorn. "I apologize. My choice of words may not have been the best. I'm just trying to determine the basis of your details. If you say the streets were paved with bricks, was that something from the audio or readings you had done prior to the coma? Or, did your mind conjure it up as part of your prior experience? I see determining the difference as part of my focus."

"And why is that so important?" Brock says, his temper subdued but still volatile.

Professor Grant hesitates. "From a drug performance point of view, if you were able to hear, apply and remember the information from your ear buds, it might suggest that the APX207 has potential as a learning agent. Also, your recovery may benefit if you understand what was fact-based and what was based on your personal priorities or from your real-life experiences."

Brock faces Dr. Alstead. "Do you agree with the approach and potential benefits the professor claims?"

"Fletcher, we did not discuss this line of analysis. On the surface it appears it could result in some valuable data for Apex. But it's not clear to me how it will benefit Brock in any appreciable way."

Professor Grant rolls his eyes slightly. "Can we just give it a try for a few minutes? If it appears to be ineffective or counterproductive, we can revert to the chronological approach."

Dr. Alstead looks at Brock. "I'm okay to try for a short while if you are, Brock."

Nodding slowly, Brock straightens in his seat as he glares at Professor Grant.

"Okay," Professor Grant says. "Brock, let's start with the electrical experiment in Ben Franklin's lab. Leave out nothing. Tell us every detail. Then, we'll go to the meal just prior that you shared with Franklin and others. Be as detailed as possible."

Brock squints and furrows his brow. "I went over this in a fair amount of detail at the first session. I'm not sure what's to be gained by focusing on it again at this point."

"Start at the point where you left the meal," Professor Grant said. "Where were you in the house and what was your path to Franklin's lab? Did you proceed down a hall? Did you climb stairs? Was anybody with the two of you? What did you see along the way? That level of detail may be important."

For several minutes Brock describes his movements through Dr. Franklin's house to the lab. He details the layout of the lab on the third floor including the equipment with particular attention to the hand-cranked generator and the Leyden jar battery setup. "I was getting tired cranking the generator when Dr. Franklin finally said the battery was charged. Sweat ran down my face and my hands were damp as I walked the few steps to the Leyden jar assembly. I wanted to get a close look at the interconnections between the jars. The last thing I remember was leaning over the strange battery. Then there was a gigantic flash of light! After that my next memory is waking up in the hospital bed here."

"And you say there was no one else in the room with you and Franklin?" says Professor Grant.

Brock shakes his head. "No, like I said before, it was just Dr. Franklin and I."

"Did you trip or stumble before you were shocked?" Professor Grant asks.

Brock hesitates before he responds. "I never said that I was shocked. Why are you making that assumption?"

Biting his lip, Professor Grant glances sideways at Dr. Alstead then back to Brock. "I'm wondering if a strong stimulus such as the perception of an electrical shock could be what triggered the end of your…your 'experience'."

"Are you comfortable with his supposition, Dr. Alstead?" Brock says with a tilt of his head toward the doctor.

Dr. Alstead swivels in her chair to face Professor Grant directly. Her frown is stark. "Fletcher, where are you going with this? You're a historian not a psychiatrist. You have no credentials regarding Brock's neurological functions? You seem laser-focused on the specifics of the scene with no consideration of Brock's concerns or impressions of his situation at the time. Don't forget what our mission here is."

Professor Grant puffs out his chest. He then takes a deep breath and lets it out. In a calm voice he says, "Okay, I may have made an assumption. But I firmly believe that if we can pin down what triggered Brock's subconscious to end his allusion, we may better understand how to help him."

Brock rises from his chair and confronts Professor Grant. "I agreed to these sessions to both advance knowledge of the experimental drug and perhaps better understand my situation. Now you're off into conjecture. And to be clear, Professor, I trust the doctors involved in my care. You, however, do not have my trust nor do I want your help."

He turns to Dr. Alstead. "Doctor, you can contact me if you have concerns that I should hear or should you need to question me further." He faces Professor Grant. "However, I will not submit to further manipulation by someone whose agenda is suspect." Brock turns and leaves the room.

CHAPTER 49   Nov 18-22, Sunday-Thursday

Sunday afternoon before Thanksgiving Brock drives north to Nacogdoches to Granny Prescott's house. She had insisted that he spend the night at her house so he could make his appointment early Monday morning at the admissions office at Stephen F. Austin University. When he arrives, his grandmother wants to hear all about how he's doing after his hospital stay and about his plans to attend SFA. Since they had not really talked one-on-one since grandpa Hank's funeral in the spring, there is a lot of catching up to do. They talk on and on before and after a fabulous roast beef dinner granny serves.

Brock had been given the assignment by his mother to convince Granny to come down to The Woodlands for Thanksgiving rather than be alone at home for the holiday. The seventy-year-old is resistant due to the perceived heavy traffic and not wanting to intrude. Brock assures her that the traffic had not been bad on the way up and she would certainly not be intruding at their home. Rather, he says she would add to the festivities. Before Brock leaves for his appointment at the college, granny caves to the pressure to drive down the day before Thanksgiving. Mission accomplished.

In the Admissions office of SFA Monday morning, Brock clarifies his interest in attending the James I. Perkins College of Education with a goal of eventually teaching at the secondary level. The admissions officer who interviews him expresses preliminary optimism about his acceptance based on his exceptional high school grades and his SAT scores. She cautions that his transcript from UT is not flattering but could be discounted since he is changing his field of study.

Leaving the interview, Brock's life has a clear direction if he gets accepted. He wants to get his bachelor's degree then start on a master's. He can hardly wait to work with high school or even junior high students, teaching math or science. He's sure he can communicate with them despite his limited experience with younger people. And the compact campus, nestled among evergreens and the hardwoods with their fall colors, sold itself.

On the drive back from Nacogdoches, Brock evaluates the wisdom of owning the expensive Harley as a college student. Use of the bike during winter would be problematic and with nowhere to safely store it near the dorm at SFA, it would be vulnerable to theft and vandalism. As such, when he returns home, he sells the bike back to the dealership, taking a significant, but manageable, loss given the bike's pristine condition. He will depend on the used Mustang his parents bought him as a junior in high school. It's more practical for the two-hour drive to SFA than the bike.

True to her promise Granny Prescott drives down from Nacogdoches on Wednesday before Thanksgiving. On Thursday, around the table filled with traditional Thanksgiving fare, there is a mix of emotions at the Sinclair house. Certainly, there is thankfulness that Brock is out of the coma and appears to have no ill effects from the experience. And Brock expresses his optimism that he will be accepted at Stephen F. Austin.

On the negative side of the ledger all lament the first Thanksgiving since Grandpa Hank died. His absence weighs heavily on Granny Prescott, who's in tears occasionally during the meal. Brock also remembers Wally aloud who did not survive the fentanyl episode and expresses his sorrow for his family.

When the meal is completed, the table cleared, the dishes done, Granny Prescott goes to the guest room to lie down for a while. In the family room Brock is sitting beside his mother on the sofa with his dad in an easy chair at the end of the coffee table. The room is quiet with only some faint groans, blamed on the feast.

Brock turns on the sofa to face both his parents, "Mom, Dad, I need to talk to you about something important."

Laura and Trip rally from their digestive stupors, concern clear on their faces. "What is it, son?" Trip says.

"You remember the Texas Rangers visited me in the hospital and one even came to the house to see me?" Both parents nod. "I didn't want to share all that he said until I had a chance to think. Well, today I guess I made up my mind about something."

Laura frowns at her son. "I'm lost, Brock. What's going on?"

Brock takes a deep breath before starting. "As you know, the guys who made and sold the fentanyl-laced weed to Wally were busted near Waco several weeks ago. And the cops caught them with lots of evidence in the raid. But the Rangers and the DEA also want to charge them with second degree murder in Wally's death. To make their case, they want me to testify, probably via a video deposition that Wally died after smoking their weed."

Trip frowns. "Why the hesitation, son?"

"The concern I shared with Ranger Garcia is potential retaliation by the drug guys' associates. Or, if these guys get out of jail on a technicality or escape, would I or you be at risk? The Rangers and the other law enforcement agencies see this as a very low probability since they found no indication of any gang affiliation. The guys who started their drug enterprise hired people to work for them just like a legitimate business. As such, the Rangers expect no retaliation."

"Oh, Trip! This scares me!" Laura says, turning to her husband, her eyes widening. "What if the Rangers are wrong?".

"Son, are you saying you don't want to testify?" Trip says.

"No, dad. I've thought about it a lot in the last few days. And I want the guys to pay for Wally's death. I'm willing to testify, but I figured you and mom should have a say into the decision."

Trip stands and paces across the room and back. Staring at his son, he spreads his arms wide, stretching. "I can't help but think that all this could have been avoided if you hadn't been smoking weed illegally in the first place. You wouldn't have been in a coma for weeks. Wally would be alive. And we wouldn't be at risk from members of a drug gang." Trip drops back into his chair.

Brock leans forward, clenching his hands together. "Dad, we've been through this several times. I screwed up! I know that. I've said I'm sorry over and over. I don't know what more I can do to make it up to you and mom." He pauses then continues in a calmer voice, "What I *can do* is help get justice for Wally." Tears pool in his eyes. "Then, maybe I can forgive myself for my part in his death."

Trip stares at his son for a long minute then rises slowly from his chair and moves to the sofa and sits down, Brock now flanked by both parents. He puts his arm around his son. "Brock, I say 'get those bastards'."

"Thanks, dad," Brock says, returning the embrace.

"I'm terrified for you, Brock," Laura says, shaking her head slowly as tears spill to her cheeks. Then a faint smile comes to her face as she nods her agreement. "But I've never been more proud of our son."

CHAPTER 50   Nov 28-29, Wednesday & Thursday

With free time on his hands until early January, Brock's mom wants him to stay active and productive and encourages him to recommit to Taekwondo at the dojang he'd found on the south edge of Conroe. She also invites him to volunteer at the Montgomery County Memorial Library in Conroe where she has been the director for the last three years. However, Brock rebuffs the idea of shuffling around the library with "old ladies whispering and little kids screaming."

"But Brock, we have a room full of heavy boxes with books that were donated during the recent book drive. I need them moved to a sorting area where volunteers can see what's usable at any of the county libraries and which should be recycled. The unusable books will then need to be moved to the recycle bin in the parking lot. We need a *strong, young man* to move the boxes." She produces an exaggerated pout. "Won't you pleeeese come help for a few hours?"

With reluctance Brock agrees to his mom's request and is awarded with a kiss on the cheek. "How about your favorite chicken tacos for lunch, mister?"

Brock settles into the routine of 5:00 o'clock Monday-Wednesday-Friday adult Taekwondo classes at Master Kim's dojang. Despite his skill being more advanced than the other class participants, Master Kim ensures Brock is challenged. In just a half-dozen sessions Brock's proficiency nears that of his 4th-degree black belt status.

After class in the third week Master Kim approaches his rising pupil. "Brock, you are most accomplished student. Is joy to teach. I have offer for you."

Brock is surprised and pleased at Master Kim's comments but has no idea what he is about to propose.

Master Kim continues. "I travel to Seoul to attend urgent family business third week December. I do not want to close dojang. Many students yearn for class. Nephew to teach tikes class and young student class. Need instructor for Monday, Wednesday, Friday, 4:00 o'clock teen class and 5:00 o'clock adult class while gone. You teach?"

Brock's eyes widen and his brows rise to their limits. "I don't know, Master Kim. I'm flattered but I've never taught before. And I don't even know how your teen class is structured."

Master Kim waves away an invisible gnat between them. "No worry. You be assistant until I go. You learn teen class quick. Lead classes until I return." He holds up a hand with three fingers extended before Brock can respond. "I give you free classes - three months!"

The opportunity to teach the teen class intrigues Brock, prompting a grin. "That sounds like a reasonable deal, Master Kim, if I was going to be here after December. You see, I plan to start college in January in Nacogdoches."

The enthusiasm Master Kim had shown throughout their brief conversation evaporates.

Brock smiles, "But we can probably work something out."

Brock agrees to attend the next teen class that meets right before his adult class to observe how Master Kim manages the different ages and skill levels and to meet the students. But he reserves his final decision on leading the class in December. He and Master Kim shake hands with Brock both excited and apprehensive about the opportunity to teach.

As Brock leaves the dojang, a boy, maybe twelve or thirteen, rides off on an old bike, distinctive by its mix of colors and copious amounts of rust. The boy or, more accurately, the bike had been noticeable through the window of the dojang during the last few adult classes. The boy struggles either from the bike's bent front wheel or his legs being too long for it or both. Why had the thin boy caught his attention?

######

Thursday Brock relents and helps his mother at the library. He figures he can work at the library for a couple of hours moving boxes as a bit of exercise since he doesn't have a Taekwondo class that day.

The work at the library is not as boring as Brock had anticipated. The employees and volunteers are friendly and excited to have someone help with the heavy boxes. As soon as Brock moves a few boxes to a sorting area, they jump to the task of sorting, stacking the usable books and throwing unusable books into empty boxes on a flat dolly for movement to the recycle bin outside.

Brock notices that many of the books being tossed look to be in very good condition. He nods to the boxes of rejected books and asks one of the women doing the sorting, "What's wrong with those books? Some look to be almost new."

The woman smiles. "There either older printings of books already on the shelves, they're out of date reference books or their content is unsuitable for the library."

"Damn, it seems a waste to throw away perfectly good books," Brock responds.

"I tend to agree," the woman says. "But the problem is identifying which libraries outside of our system might want the books and getting them into their hands. Until a process exists to do that, the unwanted books become a storage problem. At least they get recycled rather than sent to the landfill."

Brock nods. "I guess you're right. I just never thought much about the issue."

After Brock fills the sorting area with two dozen boxes, he agrees to return another day to move the remaining ones. But before he leaves, he makes a short tour of the library to see the changes his mother had mentioned with pride.

In the patron computer area Brock recognizes the boy he had seen at the dojang window. He leans close to the boy and speaks in a quiet voice. "Dude, did I see you on a bike outside Master Kim's dojang yesterday?"

The boy turns abruptly in his chair and pushes away from Brock. "I didn't do anything wrong!" he says in a voice too loud for a library.

"Whoa," Brock whispers. "I didn't say you did anything wrong. I just noticed your bike's front wheel looks bent. What happened to it?"

"I don't want to talk about it. Besides, what's it to you? Are you the bike police or something?"

Brock straightens up and steps back, his hands up to deflect the reaction. "Okay, forget I said anything. I know a little about bikes and was willing to help. That's all." Brock turns and walks back to the front of the library where his mom is working at the reception desk.

Before Brock can tell his mom goodbye, she says, "What was the commotion back in the computer area?"

Brock explains what had transpired with the boy. "I just thought I could give him a hand."

Brock's mom leans forward. "I first noticed him early last week. He comes in every day, generally right after school. He's either on one of the computers or at a work table always on what looks like homework assignments. Seems like a nice kid, keeps to himself though. Always parks a rusty old bike on the rack outside the side door."

Brock shrugs half-heartedly. "Yeah, that's the bike I saw him on outside the dojang. But it looks like he doesn't want my help." He pinches his lips together. "And that's fine with me."

CHAPTER 51   Nov 30, Friday

Despite his confidence in his Taekwondo skills, Brock is nervous attending the teen class for the first time. Master Kim introduces him as his assistant who will be helping with individual attention so the students can progress faster. To cement Brock's credentials, Master Kim asks him to execute the black belt form Pyongwon for the students.

The Pyongwon is far more advanced than any of the forms practiced by the class members of various color belts. Understandably, the students are mesmerized by Brock's smooth, rhythmic, yet powerful movements. At his conclusion he bows to enthusiastic applause, including Master Kim.

Brock's earlier anxiety quickly dissipates as the young teens seem in awe of their young, skilled assistant instructor. The boys show off their skills for him while the few girls in the class hide their nervous giggles. By the end of the session, Brock could have led them off a cliff if such existed in southeast Texas. Master Kim's grin confirms *his* satisfaction.

Despite his focus on his students during the class, Brock notices the boy again sitting on his bike peering through the window of the dojang. When the teens are leaving for home or punching their phones while awaiting their rides, Brock steps outside the door to speak to his not-yet and maybe-never friend. "If you want, come inside and observe the adult class starting in just a few minutes. Master Kim doesn't encourage it but it *is* allowed." A slight forward lean and a glance back through the widow suggest Brock's sharing confidential information. "If he encouraged it, maybe he'd get more students." Brock nods toward the interior of the dojang. "I've got to get to class. Come in any time you want."

The boy shrugs half-heartedly. "Whatever."

In the adult class the students, all who have observed Brock's skills in previous sessions, are advised that until he returns to college in the New Year, Brock will be assisting Master Kim in the class. A smattering of nods suggests a mixed reaction to the news. Brock recognizes the skepticism and commits to earning their respect, knowing it will take time.

During the adult class a middle-age man enters the dojang and takes a seat in one of the chairs along the wall. Moments later bike-boy slinks in and sits in the chair closest to the door. Brock makes eye contact with him and nods slightly but the boy breaks the eye contact without responding. He continues to concentrate on perfecting his form but in the back of his mind he wonders if he can connect with the boy.

Even before the class is over bike-boy rushes out the door and Brock sees him mount his bike and ride off. He is bummed that the boy left without speaking. He thought he had been making progress.

In his street clothes and carrying his gym bag, Brock hurries through the moderately lit parking lot to the Mustang waiting in the partial shadow of a live oak tree, its small leaves still securely attached unlike most deciduous trees in December. As he arrives at the car, the boy walks his bike into view.

"You said you know about bikes. Do you know how to straighten a wheel?"

Brock stops at the approach of the boy and slings his gym bag over his shoulder. "I'm not an expert but I've done some repairs to my bikes in the past." He looks down at the boy's bike. "What happened?"

"That's not important." The boy smirks. "You said you could fix it. Can you?"

Somewhat shocked at the boy's response, Brock, nevertheless, remains patient. "Well, first of all we need to introduce ourselves." He puts his hand on his chest. "My name's Brock. What's yours?"

The boy looks at the ground, apparently weighing if getting his bike fixed is worth sharing his name. "Okay, it's Duncan. Now can you take a look at the bike?"

Brock is startled, since "Duncan" was the name of the older of the two boys in Jamison's family. Hell of a coincidence. But the thought passes as he unlocks the Mustang with a beep and throws his gym bag on the seat. From the center console he removes a small flashlight and walks to where the boy waits. He studies the boy's face looking for any sense of recognition, but finds none. "Good to meet you, Duncan." The boy nods slightly as Brock squats at the bike's front wheel. "Let's take a look."

Brock lifts the front of the bike off the paved surface and rotates the wheel which rubs against the front fork on each revolution. He then steps directly in front of the bike and sights down along the wheel looking for the cause of the problem. He clicks off the flashlight. "Duncan, it looks like somebody kicked or stomped on your rim. I really doubt that I can true it."

Duncan's hands fiddle with the bike's worn handlebar grips. His eyes suddenly reflect the filtered light before he sniffs. He abruptly turns the bike away from Brock and swings his leg over to mount the seat. "Thanks for nothing." He then stands on the pedals and forces the bike forward.

"Hold up, dude!" Brock calls. "There's options." The bike stops after it has moved only a short distance.

Standing astride the bike, Duncan looks over his shoulder. "Like what?"

Brock moves closer, trying to organize his thoughts. "Well, for one thing I could loan you my bike while I try to fix yours. Or, we could go to a bike shop and see if they can fix the wheel or sell us a used one."

"Why would you do that? You don't owe me anything. You don't even know me."

Brock puts his hands in his jeans pockets. "You're right I don't know you. But I know a little bit *about* you."

"What do you think you know about me?"

"I know you're at the library almost every day doing homework. That suggests you're a good student. You're interested in Taekwondo because I've seen you at the dojang several times. You must want to learn self-defense." Brock looks for a reaction but gets none. He continues, "You probably live not too far away since you ride your bike everywhere."

Duncan, still sitting on his bike, folds his arms. "That still doesn't explain why you would take the time to help a stranger?"

Brock shrugs before swallowing hard. "In another city some people, who didn't know me, helped me when I was…alone there. That may be why I feel like I'm supposed to help you. I don't know, maybe it's something to do with a balance in the universe." Brock grins and offers his hand. "But if you'll let me, I'd like to help."

Duncan hesitates then reluctantly invites a fist bump. Brock accepts the greeting as he nods to his new acquaintance.

CHAPTER 52   Dec 1 & 3, Saturday & Monday

As Brock removes the bike from the ceiling hangers in the garage where it had hung, untouched for the last two years and begins wiping it down, he fondly remembers the day his grandfather delivered it. Later he had bragged to his friends about the new, lightweight, single-speed bike that incorporated some of the latest technology. And he had put lots of miles on it. But the enthusiasm wore off after a couple of years when he convinced his parents to buy him a used Mustang to drive to school. The bike had been mostly ignored ever since.

Brock reflects again on the conversation he'd had with Duncan outside the dojang, and smiles at the look he anticipates on the boy's face when he sees the high-tech bike. It hadn't been in Brock's nature to really care about anyone except family and a few close friends, much less a stranger. But for some reason he's drawn to give Duncan a hand. And yet Brock knows practically nothing about the boy and doesn't know if he can trust him or earn his trust.

The help he received while in 1787 Philadelphia by Dr. Franklin and, particularly by the Jamison family, is still fresh in his mind. He's convinced there's a link between that kindness and his wanting to help Duncan.

Brock's reflection on those he met during his coma reminds him of Dr. Alstead's warning that the details of his "dream" may fade with time. He grins at the prediction since his memory of every minute in Philadelphia is as precise and complete as it was when he woke up in the hospital. He realizes, however, that the powers of observation he had right after the coma have, indeed, diminished. He could live with that.

######

Having borrowed his dad's pickup, Brock takes his rarely-used bike to his Monday Taekwondo classes. During the adult session he's relieved to see Duncan at the window of the dojang again, but is disappointed the boy doesn't come inside.

When the class concludes, Brock changes into his street clothes and gathers his belongings before hurrying out the door. Duncan waits on the strip center's walkway, twenty feet from the dojang entrance. Brock approaches the boy. "Hey, Duncan."

Astride his old bike, his eyes sparkling in the artificial light, the boy says, "Did you bring it?" His arms are crossed as if he expects to be disappointed.

"I said I would. You've got to have some trust, Dude." Brock nods toward the spot where he normally parks his Mustang. "Come take a look."

Brock and Duncan cross the lot toward the pickup, the latter straddling his bike and taking long strides, easily keeping pace. At the pickup, Brock leans over the side of the truck bed and flings off a tarp used to shield the bike from view. He then effortlessly lifts the lightweight bike and lowers it to the asphalt.

Duncan's wide-eyed, slack-mouth expression is even more rewarding than Brock had envisioned. As the boy stares at the bike, he does not speak. But a smile slowly forms when he faces his grinning benefactor.

"Go ahead. Give it a try," Brock says holding the bike upright with his hand.

Duncan lays his old bike on its side in an empty parking spot and moves hesitantly toward the Raleigh single-gear city bike. Brock cautions, "It's got a hand brake, not like your coaster."

The young teenager takes the handle bar from Brock and throws his right leg over the Raleigh, his foot landing on the pedal. He jumps to transfer his weight to the raised pedal and the bike shoots forward. When Duncan settles onto the saddle, only his toes reach the pedals of the much larger bike, yet he zips through the near empty parking lot. After a circuit, he returns to Brock and the pickup. "Hot damn, Brock! This bike's awesome!"

"Looks like we need to lower the seat a bit and adjust the handle bar. I've got wrenches in the truck. Hold on a minute."

After Brock ensures the bike is not too big for Duncan, he makes some adjustments to accommodate the boy's dimensions. In a voice intended to be friendly yet authoritative, Brock says, "You need to be careful until you get familiar with the bike. Don't take chances just because you can go fast with less effort. You could get hurt or worse." Brock turns back to the cab of the truck then returns to Duncan. "Here, I want you to wear this bike helmet. It's been cleaned and it might save your life."

"Aw, man. I don't need a helmet. I've been riding for years without one and never got hurt."

Brock makes strong eye contact and speaks in a steady voice. "There was a guy in my high school whose bike got hit from the side by a car that ran a stop sign. When his head hit the hood of the car, he suffered severe brain damage and will be an invalid for life. The doctors said that if had been wearing a helmet, he would probably have had only a concussion." Brock touches the handle bars of the bike. "You were riding a kid's bike before. This is an adult bike. And smart adults wear helmets. Promise me you'll wear it."

Apparently afraid that Brock will take the Raleigh back, Duncan slowly relents. "If you say so." He takes the helmet from Brock, puts it on and adjusts the chin strap. "Satisfied?"

"I'll be satisfied only if you wear it every time you get on the bike. And one more thing." Brock hands Duncan a titanium combination bike lock. "This piece of paper has the combination. You'll need to secure the bike to something solid whenever you get off it. Otherwise, it will probably be gone when you come back for it."

Duncan meets Brock's eyes, and nods. "No problem, man. I'll take good care of your bike. You can trust me."

Brock smiles at Duncan. "I do trust you. Treat it like you own it."

Duncan frowns as he looks down at his old bike. "Do you really think you can fix that thing?"

"I'll take it home and give it a closer look in the daylight," Brock says, having already decided that the old bike is not salvageable. "Come by the dojang next week and I'll let you know if it's worth fixing. But you can keep the Raleigh at least until we decide what to do with your old bike."

Duncan's nod is hesitant yet when his gaze returns to the Raleigh handlebars, a small smile forms on his face. "Cool, Brock." He blinks really hard. "You know, except for my folks, nobody ever did something special like this for me." He slowly extended his hand to Brock. "Thank you."

Eyes glassing, Brock grasps the boy's hand feeling a rare bond between himself and another individual.

After a quick good-bye, Brock watches Duncan pedal across the parking lot and disappear in the low light. He wonders if he's done the right thing. The boy could get hurt trying to protect the bike from bullies, or he could wreck it and be seriously injured. The concerns pass. Absolutely, he'd done the right thing.

CHAPTER 53   Dec 5, Wednesday

Brock remains pumped from the acceptance notice he received the day before. He was going to Stephen F. Austin! Normally a new student would have much to do to before "going off to college." But it hadn't been that long since he returned from a year at UT. He knows what to pack and what he took before that he didn't need. And he still has four and a half weeks before classes start.

When Granny Prescott learns that Brock has been accepted at SFA, she again offers for him to reside at her house. She promises he can have his own room and bathroom, his own key and come and go as he pleases.

Brock knows Granny Prescott is lonesome in that "big old house" since Grandpa Hank died. And the home cooked meals she would prepare each day were a powerful inducement to live with her, not to mention the financial benefit.

But Brock doesn't want to be a commuter student. He wants to be fully engaged in campus life, not like the hermit he morphed into at UT that only came out of hiding to drink with a few friends on weekends. The three hours of study per hour of class time had been too much on subjects that held little interest for him. Brock had already requested a dorm assignment when he registered despite his anticipation that Granny Prescott would offer for him to live with her. He promises himself and her that he will visit often since she lives only a few miles from campus. They can stay in touch and he can still get some of her home cooking occasionally.

######

After his Taekwondo class on Wednesday Brock notices Duncan circling the parking lot on the Raleigh and approach the Mustang. The boy stops near the car. "I'm afraid to ask. But what's the decision on my old bike?"

Brock maintains a solemn expression. "Well, Duncan, I've got some good news and some bad news. Which would you rather hear first?"

Duncan hunches forward and begins picking at his nails. "I guess the bad news first. I'd rather get it over with."

"Well, your old bike's not worth fixing. It may mean a lot to you but it's really a low-end bike that's seen a lot of abuse."

"That bike's nothing special. It was just outside the trailer my dad and I rented when we moved here a few weeks ago. The guy at the trailer park said the people before us left it behind. I was just using it to get around." Duncan met Brock's eyes. "What's the good news?"

Brock stifled a grin. "You can keep the Raleigh."

Duncan's eyes blossom. "No way!"

Smiling, Brock says, "Yep, it's yours!" His smile hardens. "Unless I catch you riding it without a helmet. Agreed?"

"Agree? Of course, I agree." Duncan dismounts from the bike and steps closer. "I'll just say it. Thank you, Brock." He reaches out his hand to shake.

Brock grips the hand firmly. "You're welcome, Duncan."

After the handshake, Duncan says, "I'm not sure how to ask this. But would you mind coming by the trailer soon and tell Dad that I didn't steal the bike. He trusts me and all but he couldn't believe someone would loan an expensive bike like this to me, particularly someone I didn't even know. Now, if I go home and tell him you *gave me* the bike, he'll be even more suspicious." Sad, puppy eyes go to work. "But if *you* told him that the bike was mine to keep, he'd know I was telling the truth. It would be one less thing for him to worry about; he's had enough on his mind the last month or so."

The request catches Brock off guard. He doesn't relish getting into another family's affairs. He had just wanted to help Duncan out a little. But since he set this situation into motion, he doesn't see how he can say "no."

"Duncan, you said you and your dad moved here a few weeks ago. Where did you live before that?"

Hesitant, Duncan says, "My dad and I drove down from Philly so he could take a job at Big Jake's Lumber and Hardware here in Conroe. My mom, my older sister and little brother are still in Philly. Once the house there is sold and we find a place here, they'll move down too."

Brock's mouth opens, but no sound comes out. Finally, "You lived in Philadelphia until recently?"

Duncan's eyes narrow. "So?"

"And you have a sister and brother still at home?"

In an uncertain tone Duncan says, "That's right. Why?"

Brock shakes his head slightly, trying to dismiss the surprising coincidence. He struggles to return to a conversational tone. "Wow. That's a long move. I hope you and your family will like Texas."

"Well, my dad wanted to get away from Philly anyway. First my older brother was killed in October. Then when—"

"Your older brother was killed? How?"

Duncan looks down at his hands. "There was an accident…"
He pauses, his chin quivering. "I don't want to talk about it."

Brock frowns. "Hey, I didn't mean to upset you. It's none of
my business anyway."

Duncan looks up, his composure returning. "Anyway, when
the Big Jake's store where Dad worked announced it was closing,
they offered him the manager's job here in Conroe. Dad and
Mom decided to say good-bye to Pennsylvania with its cold
winters. The problem was that Dad needed to report here
immediately because the local manager had been let go. I didn't
want dad to come all this way by himself and live alone for
however long it takes until Mom moves down. I asked if I could
come with him and he and mom agreed."

"That's very noble of you, Duncan." Brock struggles for
what to say next. "You had to leave your school in Pennsylvania.
So, where do you go to school now?"

"Armstrong Elementary is only about a mile from the trailer
and it's a breeze with the Raleigh." Duncan's voice faded. "But I
walk sometimes too."

Brock touches the bike's handle bar. "Is there a good place
to lock up the bike when you're in class?"

Duncan breaks eye contact and is slow to answer. "Yeah,
there's a couple of bike racks. But…never mind."

Brock senses that Duncan is not telling him the whole story.
"Why would you not ride the bike to school most days?"

"It's the same group of boys that hassled me about the old
bike being a piece of junk. They now sit on the Raleigh in the
rack and keep me from getting on it. One even kicked the tire but
I don't think it hurt anything. It's just easier to leave the bike at
home and avoid the aggravation."

Brock had never been bullied in school. He had seen other
kids get bullied but never got involved; it wasn't his problem. But
this was different. "Did you tell the principle or your teacher
about the guys bullying you?"

"No! Those assholes already pick on me at lunch too. If I report them, it will just make things worse. I'll be okay. It's just that I'm the new kid." Duncan's eyes are tearing, but none escape to his cheeks.

"Is there anything I can do?"

"Well, you could talk to my dad about the bike."

Brock stifles an eye roll. "Okay, when and where?"

"Sunday is dad's day off. How about some time in the afternoon? We'll be there watching football like we always do."

Running his hand through his hair, Brock says, "And what's the address?"

When Duncan has shared the address and the trailer number, he thanks Brock again for the bike. He then says he needs to get home and rides off.

Brock stands in the glow of the parking lot lights and ponders Duncan's statements about his brother's death and his siblings back in Philadelphia. The similarities to his Philadelphia experience are unreal.

CHAPTER 54   Dec 7- 9, Friday-Sunday

Arriving early for the teen Taekwondo class on Friday, Brock notices Duncan siting astride the Raleigh staring through the dojang window as Master Kim is wrapping up a regular, one-on-one session with a college student prepping for his black belt test. Unnoticed, he approaches Duncan as he walks from the Mustang.

"What's up, Duncan?" Brock says as he steps onto the curb fronting the line of businesses.

Duncan stiffens then jerks his head around in Brock's direction. "Damn! Why'd you sneak up on me like that?"

"I wasn't sneaking. You must have been concentrating on the session inside." Moving closer, Brock notices a bruise on Duncan's face just below his left eye. He touches his own face in the same general area. "What happened?"

"It's nothing. I tripped on the stairs at school. That's all." Duncan turns back to the window.

Speaking to the back of Duncan's head, Brock says, "Are you sure, man?"

Duncan is staring at Brock now. "I said I tripped! Let it go, will you?"

Brock puts up his hands, defending the rebuke. "I'm just trying to help. That's what friends do."

Breaking eye contact, Duncan looks down toward the bike's handle bars. "If you have to know, I got into a tussle with Roy Bemis after school yesterday. He demanded I unlock the bike so he could show everybody how good he could ride it. I told him 'no' again and again until he shoved me. When I fought back, I guess he got in a lick or two before a teacher broke it up."

"Damn, Duncan. Did he get into trouble for starting it?"

"We both got three days detention. The school doesn't care who started it. If you're involved, you get punished."

Brock shakes his head. "Is this Bemis one of the boys who's been bullying you all along?"

Through a sneer Duncan says, "Yeah. He's the leader of that group of shits." He slams his hand down on the handle bars. "I just want to kick his ass!"

"What did your dad say when you told him?"

"Aw, he's got his own problems. There's nothing he can do about it anyway. Why bother him with it?" Duncan pauses. "I told him I fell on the stairs, same as I did you."

"I think you should tell him the truth. He's your dad. He would want to know."

Duncan shakes his head slowly, lifts the front of the bike and turns it away from Brock. "I gotta go." He quickly pedals away.

Brock wishes he could help Duncan with the bullies. But he has no idea how?

######

Sunday on the drive to the trailer, Brock is nervous about meeting Duncan's father. Prepared for a negative encounter, he knows he can return the old bike and pick up the Raleigh if that's what the man wants. He's also sensitive that the family may have fallen on hard times and he certainly doesn't want to offend. And then there's the issue of Duncan being bullied at school and not telling his father about it.

Once inside the trailer park, Brock finds the address he was given. But the trailer is not a small, rundown unit like he envisioned. Rather, the doublewide, mobile home looks to be in mint condition. Parked beside the unit is a shiny SUV, no more than a year old. He realizes his earlier perception of Duncan's family economic status may have been off target.

Brock knocks and Duncan opens the door. "Hey, Brock. Thanks for coming." Inside the trailer, Brock finds gently used, but quite serviceable, furniture in a fastidious setting. The smell of cleaning products is further evidence of strict housekeeping standards. A 90-inch holoscreen, projecting a football game in progress, consumes the far wall of the living room that spans the double wide unit. A middle-aged man rises from the sofa as he lowers the volume on the haloscreen.

Duncan does the introductions. "Brock, this is my father. Dad, this is Brock, the guy I told you about."

Brock steps forward and extends his hand. "Good afternoon, Mr...." Brock blushes. "I'm afraid I don't know your name, sir. Duncan and I are on a first-name basis."

The man smiles, shaking Brock's hand. "It's Jamison. Matt Jamison. Welcome, Brock."

Brock's knees grow week. "Sorry, I think I need to sit down? I'm a little dizzy all of a sudden."

"Sure," Mr. Jamison says pointing to a spot on the sofa. "Can I get you a water?"

Brock eases himself onto the sofa, his hands shaking, and tries to comprehend what he's just heard. *Mr. Jamison.* The words course through his brain like powerful light shining into a tunnel, its beam disappearing into the darkness.

Mr. Jamison hands Brock a bottle of water and stands near, twisting his watch on his wrist. "Are you all right, son? You look like you've seen a ghost."

Brock drinks from the bottled water and studies the man who is not in any way familiar. He then nods. "I think so, sir. If I can sit for a minute until my head clears, I'm sure I'll be okay."

"Sure, you sit as long as you like. Duncan and I were just watching the Texans game. We couldn't get the Eagles on the local cable. I guess we'll need to become Texans fans if we're going to live here."

Brock grins at the man and Duncan. He tries to show a quick recovery. "They're not the same team since J.J.Watt retired some years back. But they're still fun to watch."

After a series of downs where the Texans fail to move the ball and punt, Mr. Jamison says, "Feeling any better, Brock?"

Still very much confused but feeling okay physically, Brock says, "Yes, sir. I'm fine now. I guess I was more nervous about meeting you than I realized. I'm good now."

"Why would you be nervous?"

Brock looks toward Duncan then back to Mr. Jamison. "I want Duncan to have the bike and I was...or am afraid you won't allow him to have it. To be sure, sir, the Raleigh is a gift. I saw the old bike Duncan was using and my bike had not been used in several years. It's a good bike and needs to be used not just hang in our garage. He's welcome to it...that is, if you approve."

"It's a nice gesture, Brock. But that's an expensive bike. You could sell it for a handsome sum rather than just give it away. Besides, as soon as we get settled into a house in a few months, we can buy Duncan a bike to get around on. He had nearly outgrown his bike at home and we really didn't have room in the car to bring it. He looks at his son. "To be honest, Duncan, I would not expect to buy you a bike of the Raleigh quality. But we can get you something nice."

Brock interrupts, "Sir, that bike was a gift to me. I could sell it but I would prefer it to belong to someone who will actually use it. It's my gift to Duncan, no strings attached."

Duncan fidgets and bites his lip while watching his father consider Brock's offer. Mr. Jamison returns his son's gaze for several seconds. Finally, a smile blooms on Mr. Jamison. "Son, what do you say to the nice man who gives you a fancy bike?"

Duncan jumps up almost hitting his head on the low ceiling of the trailer. "Yes!" he says as he pumps his fist. "Thank you, Brock! This is so cool. Thank you very much."

Brock grins at the boy. "You're most welcome."

Duncan, still smiling from ear to ear, turns to his father, "Thanks, Dad."

To Mr. Jamison, Brock says, "One stipulation I made to Duncan was that he wear a helmet any time he rides the bike. Will you enforce that rule, sir?"

"Damn right I will." He looks at Duncan. "That won't be a problem will it, son?"

"No, sir," a still grinning Duncan says.

Brock stands to leave. "Thanks for the water Mr. Jamison. But I better be going. It was good to meet you."

Mr. Jamison stands also and shakes Brock's hand. "Are you sure you're okay to drive?"

Brock nods and says he's fine.

"Thank you again for the bike. And for being so kind to Duncan. We're new here and he hasn't made many friends yet. But you give me hope knowing there are still some good people in this world."

Struggling to control his emotions, Mr. Jamison continues, "Brock, in several ways you remind me of my son, Isaac, who passed away recently. He was a good man who cared about others. You're a good man too." Tears creep down Mr. Jamison's face as he pulls Duncan to his side with a loving hug.

CHAPTER 55   Dec 9 & 10, Sunday & Monday

Trance-like, Brock stumbles to the Mustang, aware that Mr. Jamison or Duncan may be watching from a window of the trailer. In a dense mental fog he manages to start the car and drive off the property. Two blocks further he stops head-in at a closed business in a strip center and turns off the engine.

Brock lets his head fall back on the seat's headrest and stares upward at first seeing nothing, then Isaac's body in the casket in the front room of the Jamison home in Philadelphia. If that was all a dream, how can the Mr. Jamison he just met have a son named Isaac who also died in an accident in Philadelphia about the same time? And another son named Duncan? These can't be just coincidences!

He jerks his head forward and finds himself staring at a consignment shop storefront only feet from the Mustang's front bumper and with only a vague memory of how he got there. When he awoke in Pennsylvania Hospital, he feared he was hallucinating. Those same fears creep back into his mind now as images of formal dresses and women's business suits on display in the shop's windows register with him. Is this here and now real? Or, was Philadelphia real? What if neither is real?

With thoughts of the experimental drug he received and the fentanyl, Brock's panic returns. What if his mind has been altered by either of the drugs or their combination? And what if it's permanent? His hands, still on the steering wheel, are shaking.

######

When Brock arrives home, his mom asks how his meeting went with Duncan's father. He lowers himself into a chair in the family room where his dad is watching the game before he answers. His mom sits down near her son, smoothing her pants leg nervously. "What's wrong, honey? You look lost."

Trip mutes the game and with a look of genuine concern turns to his son. "Talk to us, son."

For the next several minutes Brock shares what he learned from Duncan's father, both the surname "Jamison" and his son, Isaac, who died in an accident in Philadelphia. "You might remember that in my dream of being in Philadelphia, I lived with the Jamison family including their son, Isaac, who was killed in an accident at the hospital. And that Mr. Jamison owned a general store and the Mr. Jamison in the trailer worked at a Big Jake store in Philadelphia." Brock slumps in his chair and hugs his arms to his body. "All this scares me. I'm afraid my memory or some part of my brain is screwed up. I don't know what's real and what's not."

Trip watches his son. "Brock, I don't have the answer to this Jamison thing. But I do know that there must be an explanation." He stands and moves closer to his son. "First thing tomorrow we'll get to Dr. Keller and, the psychiatrist that interviewed you. They're more likely to have some answers than we are."

######

Monday morning, after a struggle on the phone, Trip finally gets through to Dr. Keller and explains the situation. The doctor says he will contact Dr. Alstead for a meeting at 11:00 a.m.

Brock, with his parents, is across from the two doctors in the familiar conference room. He is not optimistic that he will get viable explanations for the similarities between the Jamison family he described a month ago during the panel review sessions and the family he met recently. His experience in Ben Franklin's Philadelphia has to be more than just a dream caused by the drugs and an audio feed. It was too complex, too detailed and too real to just be something his mind conjured up.

In chronological order Brock relays to the doctors what he learned from Duncan about the Jamison family. He explains their impending move to Texas and shares what Mr. Jamison said on Sunday at the trailer. At Dr. Keller's insistence, Brock tries to remember every word said both in the dojang parking lot by Duncan and in the trailer by Mr. Jamison. Dr. Alstead takes notes continuously as Brock shares the details that he contends are remarkably similar to what he reported at the post-coma reviews. Brock does clarify, however, that neither Duncan nor Mr. Jamison looks even remotely like their counterparts in his dream.

Dr. Alstead says, "Brock, remember that while you were in the coma, you were exposed to roughly twenty thousand pages of information either from or about Ben Franklin and the late eighteenth century. A few days after the second panel review, Dr. Alstead, Prof. Grant and I met to discuss steps forward. One approach was to request the Library of Congress to do a word search for the name 'Jamison' in the audio material played for you. After three weeks they got back to us with only one reference to that name, a Thomas Jamison, a plantation owner in

Virginia. 'Isaac' and 'Duncan' were probably common names in that century that could have been in the recordings. But if they do not have the 'Jamison' surname, it would not support the link we are looking for."

Brock clenches his jaw and shakes his head at his parents.

Dr. Keller continues, "As we discussed earlier, your brain was likely working in overdrive during the coma to build a reality for you consistent with what was coming through the ear buds. It may have picked the surname 'Jamison' that was found in the search then latched onto the given names from audio material. The names matching those of the people you met who moved from Pennsylvania recently could be nothing more than an extraordinary coincidence."

Brock nods once slowly. "I hear what you're saying, Dr. Alstead." The nod changes to a slow shaking of his head. "But, with no disrespect intended to your credentials or experience, I can't buy the coincidence notion. One name yes. Two names maybe. But three names, Isaac's accidental death in Pennsylvania, a sister and brother still at home and Mr. Jamison's occupations being so similar are just too much for me to accept."

Trip joins the exchange, "I agree that it would be a very unlikely coincidence. There must be a logical explanation." He clasps his hands on the table. "And please don't anyone suggest that there's a supernatural force at work here."

"I don't know, Dad. Sometimes things occur that can't be explained. What about that Franklin guy you met back before I was born? You never did figure out where he came from." Brock raises his eyebrows as he faces his dad. "There were several strange things about him, if I remember the story correctly. Like the gold coins he left you?"

Trip blushes as he shakes his head. "That was a long time ago, son, and has nothing to do with this situation." He runs his fingers through his hair as he looks toward Laura then back to the doctors. "There has to be a link of some kind that would explain the similar names and circumstances."

Dr. Keller's brow furrows as he stares at Trip, perhaps expecting a response to Brock's reference about another Franklin.

Trip folds his arms across his chest. "Let's move on."

"Very well," Dr. Keller says. "There's another aspect of Brock's experience that you should know. It concerns an entry in Sara Bache's diary." The doctor tells of the finding that Professor Grant shared and that a search of the audio material had come up negative for it. "It also came up negative for the initials FS. I ask that you keep this information in strict confidence for now since there appears to be no way to substantiate the diary entry."

Brock grins and leans forward then pounds his fists on the table gently. "FS? I knew there was more to my coma than just a made-up dream." He pauses. "And that's why Grant was pushing so hard on the details of the battery experiment I had with Dr. Franklin." He bites his lip. "I may owe the professor an apology."

CHAPTER 56   Dec 11 & 12, Tuesday & Wednesday

When not otherwise occupied, Brock recalls the details of his Philadelphia experience (he resists calling it a dream), trying to resolve the coincidence with the Jamison family in Conroe and the family he lived with in Philadelphia. He also puzzles about the "FS" entry in the Sarah Bache diary. Yet no links emerge. Each time his frustration threatens to test his sanity, he recalls the advice of Dr. Franklin about having the wisdom to accept what you cannot change and pursue what you can.

His agreement to assist Master Kim in his Taekwondo classes three days per week is a blessing in that it distracts Brock from his coincidence fixation. Additionally, he sees Duncan on occasion riding by or watching through the window of the dojang. The boy has gotten under his skin, but in a good way.

Between classes on Wednesday Brock steps outside to speak to Duncan. "Hey, guy. Wasup?"

Duncan grins at the out-of-date greeting. "Watching you guys. It don't look all that hard. You're just doing a lot of the same movements over and over."

"Well, you might be surprised at the amount of practice it takes to get good at the sport. Those 'moves' are a critical part of the training. They promote muscle memory so that the student can strike almost without thinking."

Duncan looks down. "Tell me, how long does it take to learn how to kick ass?"

Surprised by Duncan's question, Brock thinks he recognizes what's driving Duncan's interest. "Is that Bemis kid and his friends still hassling you?"

"Almost every day! They don't hit me because that would get them into trouble if somebody sees it. But they will intentionally bump into me or try to trip me as they walk by in the hall or lunch room. I just want them to leave me alone."

Brock has real compassion for his young friend and his situation. He thumbs in the direction of the dojang. "You seem interested in Taekwondo. After Friday I'll have a key to the dojang while Master Kim is out of town for a week. What say I give you a private lesson on Saturday to see how you like it? If you want to continue, I'll let you join the teen class next week since I'll be teaching it by myself."

Duncan presses his lips into a tight line as he considers the offer. "But I don't have those white pajamas everybody wears."

"Actually, the uniform is called a dobok." Brock smiles, knowing he's just hooked his target. Now to reel him in. "Don't worry about that. If you think you want to continue after Saturday, I'll make sure you get a dobok just like the other students wear."

After arranging a time to meet on Saturday and giving Duncan his phone number if anything changes, Brock goes back into the dojang to assist with the adult class. During the session he ponders Duncan's problem and how he can help besides some self-defense training. Later, on his way home he comes up with an idea. But he'll need some cooperation.

######

Thursday morning Brock calls Ranger Garcia to discuss his request to testify against the Flores brothers. It was Thanksgiving when he discussed the issue with his folks. And although he had been ninety-nine percent sure it was the right thing to do, he had procrastinated making the call. Now seemed like the right time.

When Ranger Garcia answers the phone, Brock tells him of his decision to cooperate.

"That's outstanding, Brock. The DA will be delighted. Actually, he called yesterday to ask if I'd heard back from you."

Brock hems and haws. "I've been busy with college plans, helping out at a Taekwondo dojang and some other things."

"That's okay, Brock. The thing is you got to the right decision. Thank you. Now, we need to set a schedule for you to do a deposition." The Ranger says he will contact the DA and have him set up a convenient time. "And Brock, if you are asked to actually testify, I intend to be there just to show you I'm behind you on this thing."

"Ranger Garcia, now that I've agreed to do my part with the trial, I wonder if you would do me a big favor."

CHAPTER 57   Dec 12 - 15, Wednesday-Saturday

When Brock arrives at the dark dojang Saturday morning for Duncan's private introduction to Taekwondo, the boy is waiting outside the building. He's wearing baggy pants and an old sweat shirt with a faded "Penn State" on the front.

"Are you ready, sport?" Brock says as he unlocks the door. Duncan nods, following his friend inside, rolling his bike along for safe keeping.

"Before we start, Duncan, there are a couple of housekeeping rules you need to know."

The boy squints but nods.

"First, when we are in the dojang, you refer to me as 'sir' or Nim Sinclair. You will address Master Kim as 'sir' or 'Master Kim'. Understand?"

Duncan nods again.

"Secondly, before you enter the workout area, you bow slightly to show respect. And when you leave the workout area, you turn and bow again." Brock demonstrates the proper posture before crossing the threshold and watches as Duncan executes a crude version of the bow.

With the preliminaries out of the way, Brock and Duncan sit cross-legged on the floor facing each other. Brock begins in a serious tone, "Duncan, I think you showed up today to learn how to defend yourself."

The boy nods vigorously.

Looking directly into Duncan's eyes, Brock continues, "Taekwondo can teach you that. But Taekwondo is much more. It's way of life to help achieve harmony with nature, a balanced and peaceful existence." He pauses to let his words sink in. "It will take time and commitment to make progress. Do *not* expect instant results. If you do, you *will* be disappointed and you'll probably quit. Do you understand?"

"I'm not sure, Brock, er. sir. But if you think it will help me, I want to try."

"Good." He holds up his closed hand. "There are five tenets or principles of Taekwondo. You will hear them again and again. More importantly, you must strive to live them." Brock straightens a finger from his fist as he denotes each tenet: "Courtesy, Integrity, Perseverance, Self-Control and Indomitable Spirit."

For the next several minutes Brock and Duncan discuss the meaning of each of the tenets. Where Duncan is vague on the meanings, Brock clarifies and gives examples. At last Brock's satisfied he's given Duncan an introduction to Taekwondo and to his relief the boy didn't run from the room or fall asleep, both good signs.

When they, at last, stand, Duncan groans from having remained in the same position during the lengthy introduction. Brock hops to his feet and grins. "We'll work on your flexibility as part of the training."

For the next hour Brock demonstrates and helps Duncan execute a simple Taekwondo move. The teen initially struggles to mimic his teacher as they both do the move again and again. Yet he never quits despite sweat running down his face after the first twenty minutes.

When Brock calls for a water break, he says, "Duncan, you're raw at this. But I see real potential. I also see determination." He slaps his student on the back and smiles, "And I see some sore muscles tomorrow or the next day. But that's good. Some soreness means you pushed yourself beyond what you normally do. In another word, progress."

At the end of the hour, Duncan has done enough for his first day. "Well, what's your first impression? Do you want to do more another day?"

Wiping sweat from his brow with his shirt sleeve, Duncan says, "You were right. It's not as easy as it looks. But yes, I want to come back."

"Good. You'll join the teen class Monday at 4:00 o'clock?"

Duncan fiddles with his shirt sleeves. "What did you say about using a dobuck?"

"No problem. Master Kim has some spares in the back that you can borrow until we get you your own. And, by the way, it's dobok not dobuck. Let's go find your size."

######

Monday morning, Ranger Garcia rings the buzzer at the side door of Conroe United Church of Christ. When a casually dressed, middle-age man appears, the Ranger says, "Reverend Bemis?"

"Yes. Can I help you?"

The Ranger introduces himself and flips open a small leather case, displaying his ID. "Perhaps I can help *you*, Reverend. May I come in so we can talk in private?"

The Reverend stands aside to fully open the door as the Ranger removes his hat and enters then follows the Reverend into his small office.

The two sit across from each other at a small conference table. "Reverend, I'll get right to it. It has come to my attention that your son, Roy, can be, shall we say, aggressive at times."

Reverend Bemis smooths his graying hair while his lips form a straight line. "I guess you mean he's bullying again? It must be more serious this time."

"No, sir. There's no specific incident that I'm aware of, just a general pattern of intimidation."

The Reverend fiddles with his shirt sleeve then, with sad eyes, looks up at the Ranger. "I've tried my best. But I just can't seem to get through to my son. It's like he wants to be counter to everything I believe in. I pray every day that he'll straighten out. So far my prayers haven't been answered."

The Ranger nods slowly. "Reverend, let me clarify that I am not here in any official capacity. Normally, school discipline matters are outside my purview. But I was made aware of Roy's behavior and I may be able to use my position in a positive way."

The Reverend tilts his head to the side and purses his lips.

"Let me explain." The Ranger details what he has been told about Roy and his friends and their tendency to pick on fellow students, one in particular. The Reverend listens closely, seemingly not surprised at the Ranger's claims.

"Reverend, I have a plan that may help keep Roy out of trouble, if you're willing to approve it. I certainly won't be physical with your son, but I intend to have a 'Come-to-Jesus meeting' with him if you'll pardon the expression."

The Reverend smiles broadly. "Ranger, I *love* the expression and I'm all ears."

######

Although Brock has been assuming more and more of the leadership role in the Taekwondo classes over the last two weeks, today will be the first day to fly solo. And he's a bit anxious but also pumped. Master Kim's schedule should have him at the home of his parents in South Korea by this time and not available for support.

Brock's also uneasy about this being Duncan's first day attending the teen class. He knows there is a range of skill levels among the teens he has worked with over the last two weeks. However, Duncan will definitely be the rank novice among them. He's optimistic, however, that Duncan's desire to learn will allow him to shed any giggling or snide comments that might come from the older, more experienced students.

Once the class starts, it's obvious that Duncan has a way to go to catch up even with the least skilled in the class. Yet he does not give up. In fact, his persistence is recognized by a few of the students. At one point, however, Duncan gets totally lost in his move. Brock hears a small laugh from one of the older teens.

"Class, Charyut!" Brock shouts. The class members immediately stop their movements, turn in Brock's direction and come to attention.

Brock moves in the general direction of the laugh. He stops. "Turner, Attention!"

The embarrassed teen shouts, "Yes, Nim Sinclair!"

"What are the five tenets of Taekwondo?"

"Nim Sinclair, the five tenets are Courtesy, Integrity, Perseverance, Self-Control and Indomitable Spirit."

Brock strolls among the students, making eye contact with each. When he has glared at each student, he yells, "Students! You will all now recite the five tenets together. Begin!"

In unison the students shout the core teachings of Taekwondo.

Still moving among the students he says, "You know the tenets. Now follow them today and every day." He then releases the students to continue practicing their moves.

At the end of class the students are unusually quiet as they gather their belongings and begin to leave the dojang. Duncan, despite his mistakes, receives a few nods of encouragement from among the other students. He grins in response.

As the teens disperse and the adults filter in for their 5 o'clock class, Brock pulls Duncan aside. "You did good for your first class. How did you like it? And more importantly, will you be here Wednesday."

Duncan smiles. "Those guys are a lot better than me now. But I'll catch up if I work hard." He wipes the sweat from his eyes. "And I *will* be back. Thank you, Brock. For everything."

"Glad to have you in class. See you Wednesday."

CHAPTER 58　　Dec 18, Tuesday

The Administrative Assistant at Armstrong Elementary buzzes Ranger Garcia through the security door early Tuesday afternoon and escorts him to the main office as instructed. She then excuses herself to join the remainder of the office personnel in the staff lounge for a meeting with the Principal.

Waiting in the office is a stout, black woman in a Conroe PD uniform. "You must be Ranger Garcia," she says extending her hand, grinning. "You're a lot taller than you sounded on the phone. I'm Janet Tremont, the Resource Officer for Armstrong and Rice Elementary. I split my time between the two schools."

"Good to actually meet you, Officer Tremont." He nods toward the inner office door. "Is he in there?"

"Yes, sir." The officer's lips form a tight line. "I don't know whether this will make a difference, but I salute you for trying."

"Thanks." The ranger nods toward the office. "Let's see if we can change a young man's priorities."

The Ranger opens the door labeled "Principal" and leads the officer into the room, then closes the door with just enough force to suggest that he'll decide when it's to be reopened. He turns to face the room with his bright Texas Star and his weapon clearly visible through his open sport coat. Officer Tremont moves to stand behind the principal's desk with her back to the window.

Slouched in a chair facing the desk is Roy Bemis, told to report to the Principal, but not why, and who has been waiting for the last ten minutes. At the sight of the big Ranger and the uniformed officer, he straightens slightly in the chair.

The Ranger moves slowly toward the boy, his Tony Lama's marking each stride on the tile floor. He stops at the Principal's desk and pointedly places his Stetson on the corner.

The Ranger's stern demeanor cannot be mistaken. The boy's widening eyes belie his sneer.

With one powerful hand the Ranger lifts the other chair in front of the desk and turns its back toward the tense boy. He then lowers it to the floor firmly and sits astride it with his forearms resting on its back. In a commanding, yet patient voice, he begins, "I'm Ranger Garcia of the Texas Rangers." He nods toward the officer at the window. "If you don't know this lady, she's officer Tremont."

He turns back to the boy. "Do you know why we're here today, Roy?"

The boy folds his arms across his chest and stares straight ahead, a smirk prominent on his face.

"I'll tell you why we're here. It has come to our attention that you routinely pick on some of the other students. You and your *crew* seem to take pleasure in harassing them, bumping them in the hall, shoving them on the playground or lunch room, and insulting them. Do you know what that's called, Roy?"

"Why don't you tell me?"

The fingers of Ranger Garcia's hands slip between the slats of the chair back, his crushing grip straining the frame. Quickly, he regains his internal composure and says, "It's called bullying, Roy. And from the information I have you are guilty of it."

Roy shrugs. "Whatever."

"You're admitting to being a bully then? Maybe you're even proud of it?" The Ranger straightens slightly in his chair. "Well, Officer Tremont and I are here to talk about that."

Roy slides lower in the chair, continuing to avoid eye contact with the Ranger.

When the Ranger glances at Officer Tremont, she nods ever so slightly, prompting the Ranger to pull his phone from a jacket pocket. He punches a single number and puts the phone to his ear. After a few seconds he speaks into the phone, "This is Ranger Garcia. Is he ready?" The Ranger then puts his phone on speaker and lays it on the desk in front of the defiant boy.

A voice on the phone can be heard by all three in the room. "Roy? Are you there?"

Roy's eyes blink rapidly as he leans forward, closer to the phone. "Bobby? Bobby, is that you?"

"Who else would be calling you on a Texas Ranger's phone?"

"Are you still in…" The boy looks at the Ranger beside him, whose lips tighten as he nods.

"Yes, Roy, I'm still inside." A throat being cleared is heard over the phone. "I've got four more years in here."

Tears form in Roy's eyes. "I'm sorry we haven't visited in a while. Lamesa is a really long drive and with school and Dad preaching on the weekends…Well, you know."

"It's hard, Roy. I know. It's okay though." There is a pause. "Hey, are you and Dad doin' okay?"

"Yeah, he's fine I guess and I'm good."

Bobby's voice hardens. "Okay. Listen, Roy. The Ranger tells me you've been harassing the other students. Said you've done some detention for it. What's up with that crap?"

"It's no big deal, Bobby. We were just kidding around and some nerd snitched on me. It's nothing."

"That's bullshit, Bobby! You listen to me, little brother and you listen good. Do you know why I'm in this *correction facility*? Do you?"

Roy hesitates. "Because of the robbery? And the gun?"

"Yeah, that's why I was sent here. But it was all the stupid shit I did before then that really got me the five to ten."

Roy frowns. "I don't understand, Bobby. I thought the judge—"

"The judge just did what the law says. Me, I screwed up. Do you hear me? I screwed up! After Mom died, Dad was busy taking care of you and his church while he was still grieving. I was pissed about Mom suffering all that time before she died and I took it out on anybody that looked at me wrong. When Dad got on my case, I pushed back. Eventually, he stopped trying.

"I was making some bad decisions, some really bad decisions!" There is a slight pause. "I'm not saying my problems are Dad's fault. Not at all, they're all on me. I was the one who got in trouble at school and on the street. Me and my crew, we thought we were cool. But we weren't cool; we were bullies and stupid. Now Joey's dead, Ralph's in Huntsville and I'm here. That sound cool to you, Roy?"

"No, Bobby. But why are you telling me all this?"

"I'll tell you why, Squirt. You remember how I used to punch you and hold you down just to hear you scream and cry? I did it because I could. I was bigger than you and I thought it proved I was tough. What I was, Roy was a bully. You hated the name Squirt. So, that's why I used it; it made me feel like a bad ass. But I never considered how it made you feel." The voice is choking up, "I'm sorry, Roy. I was wrong to do that to you."

Tears run down Roy's face. "It's okay, Bobby. I just want you to come home."

A deep sniff on the phone. "That's just the thing, Roy. I can't come home, not for a long time yet. What I can do is try to convince you to not to follow what I did. You're bullying other students. And you're encouraging your crew to do it." The voice becomes more urgent. "And let me tell you, the guys in your crew are not really your friends. They're just using you to make themselves feel big. Tell me, how many times have you been in detention when they're not? They're outside playing, maybe even laughing at you, while you sit inside. I know because I've been there. I didn't know all this then, but I know it now. Bullying is wrong, Roy. It's a habit that leads you where you don't want to go. Trust me; I know what I'm talking about."

Ranger Garcia looks at his watch. "Fellows, let's wrap it up."

"Okay, I gotta go, Roy. Tell Dad I'm sorry, will ya? And Roy, it's because I care about you that I'm telling you to get your act together. And do it now!"

Roy is openly crying now. "I love you, Bobby."

Ranger Garcia retrieves his phone and terminates the call. No one speaks for several long seconds. Roy wipes his eyes and sits staring at his hands, knitted in his lap. The Resource Office and the Ranger make eye contact before returning their attention to the boy.

"Well, Roy. I believe you've got a decision to make," the Ranger says.

The boy turns to look at the Ranger.

"You can continue to be a bully here at Armstrong and see where that gets you. But know that you are on the radar of the entire school staff as well as Officer Tremont. So that kind of behavior may have severe repercussions. And if you make it to middle school and continue picking on students, you might just get your ass handed to you by some of the bigger kids there."

Roy takes a deep breath and looks across the room.

The Ranger leans forward. "Or, if you really pay attention to what your brother said, concentrate on your school work and maybe get involved in a team sport, you just might survive and enjoy life."

"What team sport?"

The Resource Office steps forward. "Roy, I hear you're a soccer fan. Well, the Conroe United Youth Soccer League is registering players now for evaluations in January with practices starting in February. They play at Carl Barton, Jr. Park over on Loop 336, just a few miles from here."

"I know where it is. I'm not a kid." Roy crosses his arms.

Officer Tremont's eye brows rise. "I'm sure you do. Well, I have some applications if you're interested." She picks at a piece of lint on her sleeve. "Of course, kids have to have some soccer skills to make the teams and you'd need to be in shape too." She crosses her arms. "Maybe you wouldn't make the teams anyway."

To salvage the exchange, the Ranger says, "Don't forget the Police Activities League here in Conroe. They do a number of activities including summer camps and a fishing tournament. And you already know about the church youth basketball league. I understand you used to play and were pretty good at it until you dropped out."

The Ranger stands, then shrugs. "There are several opportunities, Roy. It's up to you to make a decision. Just remember what your brother said about decisions."

Roy places his hands on the arms of his chair, ready to push himself up. "Can I go now?"

"We're done here for now," Ranger Garcia says.

Roy stands and starts to move toward the door. The big Ranger moves to block his path. "Roy, I'm convinced you have the smarts to make good decisions. Don't prove me wrong and disappoint your dad. Or your brother. Today I'm your friend. If I meet you later in an official capacity, I may not be your friend."

Ranger Garcia steps aside. "You won't be returning to class. Your dad is outside waiting. He's got some things he wants to discuss with you."

CHAPTER 59 Dec 19 & 20, Wednesday & Thursday

At the dojang's Wednesday's teen class Duncan arrives a few minutes early. He's moving slowly and grimaces with each step. His respectful bow before he steps onto the workout floor is slow; he straightens up even slower.

A knowing Brock suppresses a smile and offers a concerned expression as he greets his newest student. "Duncan, you're moving kind of slow. Does something hurt?"

His face showing a level-five wince, the boy looks at his instructor. "Sir, everything hurts."

"Well, the best thing for that is another workout," Brock says, grinning broadly. "And knowing that it will hurt less on Friday." He pauses. "Here's where I say, 'Trust me'."

Despite his muscle soreness, Duncan shows improvement compared to his first day. It's clear he has practiced at home.

There are no further incidents of the more-experienced students dissing Duncan. Brock hopes his lecture on the tenets of Taekwondo at the last session, particularly the first tenet, courtesy, will have a permanent effect. Yet he is aware that he must not show favoritism toward Duncan in front of the other class members. Such would undermine Duncan's chance to earn his own place with his fellow students.

When the session ends and the other students have gone, Duncan steps close and lowers his voice, "Something strange happened at school with Bemis."

Brock listens closely.

"Yesterday after school, Bemis was nowhere to be seen. He had been there at lunch time and even bumped my chair when he walked behind me in the cafeteria. But after school his gang was waiting for him on the playground. But as far as I could tell, he never showed." Duncan shakes his head.

"Then today at lunch Bemis didn't sit with his gang in the cafeteria. And after school he walked right by where I was unlocking my bike even though his gang was milling around, ready to hassle me. He didn't say or do anything. He just kept walking. It was weird, you know."

Brock stifles a grin. "I wonder what's different with this Bemis guy?" He pats Duncan on the back and chuckles. "Maybe he learned you're taking Taekwondo and decided to back off."

Duncan rolls his eyes. "Yeah, right. He was probably just feeling sick today or something."

"You're right. That's probably it." Brock turns away. "Well, I need to get prepared for the next class. See you Friday."

######

Thursday morning Brock lies in bed considering his options for the day. With no classes to teach, he has no commitments. In the calm of his bed he does some mental calculations: five days to Christmas, only one gift left to buy; New Year's Eve a week later, but no party invitations; move-in at school a week later.

It occurs to Brock that he has fixated on the Jamison family coincidence less in the past few days. Maybe that's a good thing. Maybe he was taking to heart Dr. Franklin's advice about dwelling on what he couldn't change. Brock reminds himself that he did not actually hear Dr. Franklin say those words. He only experienced the comments because something in the audio feed had quoted the man. Or, the material in the audio feed prompted Brock's brain to deduce from Dr. Franklin's writings or letters that he would have had that opinion. He smiles at his ability to still recall his adventures in Philadelphia in such vivid detail. Yet all the other information from those 20,000 pages is not something he can readily recollect. What a powerful tool it would be if people could just absorb all the knowledge on a specific subject while they slept, then be able to recall it at will later when they awoke. Maybe his experience will help the development of APX207 in that area.

Despite Dr. Franklin's words of wisdom, the link between the Jamisons in his coma and Duncan's family never completely leaves him. He wonders if a direct approach to the issue would have merit.

Brock's cell phone vibrates on the night stand. The caller's number is recognizable but he's surprised to hear from Master Kim. They exchange pleasantries, with Master Kim apologizing for disturbing him. He also wants to know how Brock's classes are going. Brock assures him that all is well.

Master Kim explains that his business in Seoul is taking longer than he had anticipated. And that the Christmas holidays are complicating his transactions. He asks Brock if he would be willing to teach the classes for a second week. And in return he will offer six months' worth of classes to be used any time Brock is in the area.

Brock hesitates only seconds before agreeing to cover the classes, at the same time realizing he will probably never use up the earned class time.

When the call is terminated, Brock reclines against the headboard to consider the implications of his second week of teaching and his payment. When he reaches a decision, a faint smile comes to his face.

CHAPTER 60 Dec 23, Sunday

The Sunday before Christmas is cloudy and cold for Southeast Texas. But the weather doesn't dampen Brock's commitment to his mission. Yet what reaction he will get to his offer?

At the Jamison trailer the large SUV Brock observed on his visit two weeks earlier is missing, replaced by a small import. Briefly, Brock wonders if he is at the correct address before recognizing the Raleigh, secured to the trailer's stairs.

At the door the sound of men's voices inside stops Brock. But he's here, so he knocks.

Mr. Jamison answers the door, his face beaming. "Brock, this *is* a nice surprise. My nephew's here and I was telling him about you and all you've done for Duncan. The Texans' game is on but we're recording it for later. Come in and join us."

"I don't want to intrude. I can come back another time."

"Nonsense. Get in here!" Mr. Jamison extends his hand and gently pulls Brock inside when he accepts it.

A man is rising from the sofa, smiling as Brock crosses the threshold. He recognizes the guy but cannot remember his name or how he knows him.

"Brock, it's good to see you," the guy says as he steps forward. "How you doin? It's been a month or so since you left the hospital."

The word "hospital" spurs Brock's memory and a name bubbles up. "Miguel isn't it? Sorry, I'm terrible with names."

A big hand is thrust toward Brock. "Well, you got it right this time. You doing okay, man?"

"Yeah, I'm fine." Brock nods, confused.

Mr. Jamison says, "I don't mean to pry, Brock, but was your hospital stay something serious?"

Brock blushes, glances at Miguel then looks back at his host. "It's a long story, sir. But I'm fine now."

Mr. Jamison nods, tight-lipped.

Changing the subject, Brock turns to Miguel. "How...how do you know the Jamisons?"

Miguel snickers. "My mother is my Uncle Matt's younger sister. She moved down here after college and married my dad." Miguel playfully slaps Mr. Jamison on the back of the shoulder. "My favorite uncle here even let me live with him and his family in Philly for a summer when I was growing up."

Mr. Jamison interrupts with a broad grin. "The truth is I'm his *only* uncle and what really attracts him is my wife's cooking."

Miguel splays his hands and raises his eyebrows. "What can I say? Her cooking really is amazing."

"Brock, you just missed Edith and the kids. They left to buy some warm weather clothes and Duncan went with them to help with directions."

Brock narrows his eyes. "I'm confused. Duncan said the rest of your family was still in Philadelphia."

"They haven't moved down yet, but we wanted to be together for Christmas. They flew in yesterday and will help with the house hunting while they're here."

"I'm sorry I missed them, perhaps another time." Brock leans forward in his seat. "With Duncan not here, there's something I wanted to talk to you about." Brock looks at the paused haloscreen. "Is this a bad time?"

"No, not at all. Like I said, we're recording the game. We got all afternoon to watch it." He reaches and clicks off the haloscreen then gestures toward his nephew. "You don't mind Miguel being here do you? After all, he's family."

Brock shakes his head. "Of course not. I just wanted to get your permission on something before mentioning it to Duncan." He clears his throat. "I assume you're aware that Duncan has been participating in the teenage Taekwondo class at Master Kim's dojang this past week," Brock says.

"Aware? That's all he's talked about. When he's not eating or doing his homework, he's doing some strange arm and leg positions he calls a 'move'. Is the boy paying attention?"

"For someone just getting started, he's an excellent student." Brock nods. "Actually, that's what I wanted to talk to you about. You see, Master Kim, who owns the dojang, is in South Korea for two weeks. While he's gone, I'm teaching some of his classes including Duncan's"

Mr. Jamison nods.

"The thing is Master Kim's not paying me in cash to run the classes while he's gone. Instead, I'm earning several months' worth of class time. But I'm off to Stephen F. Austin in January and would like for Duncan to have the class time I earn."

"Oh, Brock. You've already done so much for Duncan. It wouldn't be right for him to use the class time you worked for."

"Sir, the thing is, I enjoy teaching the teen class, and the adult class I teach is the same one I would be attending anyway. I'm just glad I can help out Master Kim and pleased he trusts me with his students."

"I don't know what the classes cost. But I'd insist on paying you for what Duncan uses."

Brock shakes his head respectfully. "I'd much rather he attend the classes and show me his progress when I'm home for spring break. That'll be more than enough payment."

Mr. Jamison then rises and shakes Brock's hand. "Thank you, son. You're very generous. I so wish Edith was here to meet you. She was impressed that you gave Duncan the bike and have kind of taken him under your wing. And Duncan has talked non-stop about you to Amelia and Nathan."

Taking a deep breath, Brock sits back down. He's not surprised at the names of Mr. Jamison's wife, other son and daughter, but actually hearing them is still unnerving. "Could I have some water, sir?"

"I'll get it, Mr. J." Miguel springs to his feet and retrieves a bottle from the fridge.

Brock takes a long drink then leans forward. He then looks directly at Mr. Jamison. "Sir, I haven't been totally candid with you about my recent health...issues."

A frown forms on Mr. Jamison. "I don't understand, Brock. Are you okay?"

Brock shakes his head. "Physically, I'm fine. But..." He takes another drink of water. "Let me explain."

Mr. Jamison knits his fingers as he focuses on Brock.

"Back in October I fell and hit my head and was in a coma for three weeks." Brock walks Mr. Jamison through his experimental treatment in some detail.

Mr. Jamison leans forward in his chair and rests his forearms on his knees. "Did it work?"

Brock bites the inside of his cheek. "Well...let me finish." He sighs. "The doctors tell me that soon after the APX207 drip started and the audio began playing, the scans suggested my brain activity was similar to an elaborate dream in progress."

Brock rubs the front of his pants legs. "In the dream I woke up in Pennsylvania Hospital in Philadelphia but in the year 1787.

And for almost three weeks I lived in that time, meeting people, seeing the city as it was then, all the while trying to figure out how I got there and how to get back here. The experience was so real that when I first came out of the coma I could not believe that I hadn't actually been there. It took a while for the doctors and my parents to convince me I had been in Memorial Herman in The Woodlands the whole time. Since being released from the hospital, I've tried to get my strength back and move on with my life and have no apparent physical effects from the incident."

Miguel, his eyebrows raised, looks at Mr. Jamison. "Memorial Hermann in The Woodlands is where I work, Mr. J. I knew he was in a coma, but I didn't know anything about his treatment or his 'dream'. That's confidential information and I would not be privy to it." He shrugs and looks at Brock. "Unless the patient shares it."

Brock nods to the orderly. "Mr. Jamison, during my experience in the coma, I met a young intern named Isaac in 1787 Philadelphia."

Mr. Jamison inhales deeply and puts a hand on his chest.

"Isaac was a fine, young man who helped me even though I told him I came from a place called Texas, a place he'd never heard of, and was from the year 2029. Despite him thinking I had mental problems, he befriended me. He walked me out of the hospital and took me to his home and introduced me to his parents. There I met a Mr. Jamison who owned a general store, his wife, Edith, their teenage daughter, Amelia, and their two younger sons, Duncan and Nathan."

"Oh, my God!" Mr. Jamison exclaims.

Looking back and forth at Mr. Jamison and Miguel, Brock says, "I know all this sounds bizarre. But I assure you that all the details I'm sharing with you are documented and recorded in debriefings with several physicians and an attorney while I was still in the hospital." He looks down at his hands then back up at Mr. Jamison.

"Sir, when Duncan told me he was from Philadelphia and his father worked in retail, I just considered it an unusual coincidence. However, when I met you and you said your name was Jamison and that your son Isaac had been killed in an accident, I was afraid I was losing my mind. And to be consistent with the coincidence, I assumed your daughter would be Amelia and other son, Nathan. But hearing you say their names today sent a chill through me."

Mr. Jamison sits back in his chair, squinting. "Why are you telling me all this?"

"Sir, at my request, the hospital performed an electronic search of all the information they played into my ear buds. And there was no mention of the Jamison name in Pennsylvania. There were a few references to the name 'Isaac', since that was a common name back then. None of whom were doctors, by the way. The doctors at the hospital and I are at a loss of how my brain identified your family by name, your profession, Isaac's death, etc.

"I know it's a long shot unloading all this on you. But I'm desperate to know how you and your family came to be in my coma dream."

Mr. Jamison rubs his chin, turning to look at Miguel, as if to assure himself he has an ally if needed.

Miguel's face is slack, unreadable.

Returning his focus to Brock, Mr. Jamison says, "I don't know what to say. Up until now I thought you were an unexpected, positive influence on Duncan." He pauses. "Now I don't know what to think. My first concern is if you constitute a risk for my son. Just the mention of fentanyl raises significant alarms for me."

"I completely understand, sir." Brock details how he and his friend became exposed to the powerful drug.

Mr. Jamison shakes his head and says, "I know cannabis is legal in many states including Pennsylvania and Texas. But, Brock, you're not yet twenty-one."

Brock's eyes turn down. "Yes, sir." He then meets Mr. Jamison's stare. "I've made some poor choices in the past. Some I regret deeply."

Brock slides forward to the edge of his chair, one hand on his knee. "But, sir, I've changed since that experience. It's not like I decided to be a better person. The people I met in Philadelphia made a profound difference in my life. A very positive difference."

Mr. Jamison leans back. "Still, it's a lot to process."

Brock nods. "If I were in your shoes, I'd have reservations also. But, sir, I swear what I've just told you is the truth. And I swear I would never do anything to harm Duncan."

In the brief silence that follows, Brock stands. "Maybe I should go."

"Perhaps it's for the best. My wife and I will need some time to sort this out."

Miguel stands also, his eyes on the floor. "I'll walk you out." Brock frowns then nods at the orderly before leading him through the door.

Before Brock reaches the Mustang, Miguel says, "Hold on a minute, Brock."

Brock turns back, his voice flat. "What is it?"

The hospital orderly looks down as he toes a loose stone. He then looks up. "Ah…" He smiles weakly. "Give my uncle a little time. He'll probably come around."

Brock raises his eyebrows. "Sure. I'll just have to wait and see." He opens the car door. "Look, I've got to go. I'll see you."

As he drives away disheartened, but not totally surprised by Mr. Jamison's reaction, Brock regards Miguel's image standing outside the trailer in the rearview mirror.

CHAPTER 61   Dec 28, Friday

Brock's mood during the Christmas holiday had alternated between his excitement about attending SFA in January and his frustration with the unknowns of his coma experience. He had tried not to let the latter put a damper on his family's gift exchange and the holiday dinner. But he was sure his efforts had not been totally successful. His mom had even commented that he seemed distracted and distant.

Invitations to a couple of holiday parties from high school friends had initially sparked interest in Brock. But on the day of each event, he withdrew inside himself. He told his parents he didn't want to be peppered with questions about his accident and the coma. And, of course, Wally's death still lingered with him. He begged off from each invitation at the last minute claiming he had not fully recovered from his hospitalization.

Late afternoon Thursday the 27th, Brock answered a call from Dr. Keller who apologized for interrupting the holidays. He advised that he had some new information that would be very interesting to both Brock and his parents and asked they would come to the hospital the following morning for a short meeting.

Brock committed to nine o'clock, hoping his parents would be available to attend.

######

When the three Sinclairs enter the 4th floor conference room of the hospital on Friday, Dr. Keller is seated across the table. Brock is surprised to see Miguel seated beside the doctor and cannot imagine why he is present. The orderly, dressed in hospital scrubs, is glum-faced with heavy bags under his eyes.

Dr. Keller says, "Welcome. And thank you for coming on such short notice." He turns toward the orderly. "This is Miguel Alvarez, an orderly here at the hospital." He faces Brock. "I believe the two of you have met."

Miguel delivers a curt nod with Brock responding in kind.

"What's this about, doctor?" Trip says, his hand folded on the table.

Dr. Keller faces Trip. "Very well." He steeples his fingers as he looks across the table. "Miguel works the night shift in this wing. Yesterday morning he was waiting for me when I arrived at the hospital. Over the course of an hour he shared some very enlightening information."

The doctor leans forward. "Miguel reported that last Sunday he was at the residence of a Mr. Matthew Jamison, his uncle, to watch a football game. While there, Brock arrived and was welcomed into the home." Dr. Keller focuses on Trip and Laura. "Were you aware of your son's visit?"

Trip speaks for the couple. "Yes, Brock mentioned that he had talked with Mr. Jamison and shared his coma experience with him. But he didn't mention Miguel. Why is any of this important, doctor?"

Dr. Keller continues, "Because of the hospital confidentiality policy, Miguel was not made aware of Brock's coma experience since his position did not require him to be informed." The doctor clasps his hands. "When Brock shared the details of what he experienced during his coma with Mr. Jamison on Sunday, Miguel was surprised, as anyone would be."

Trip shrugs before the doctor can continue.

"Here's why this is important. Miguel reported to me yesterday that on two occasions he took his break during his night shift in Brock's room while the patient was in the coma." He holds up his hands to forestall an interruption. "Know that taking breaks in patient rooms is against hospital policy and Miguel's actions will be addressed in the incident review."

"Dr. Keller, I'm sure your employee's behavior is an issue, but why are we here?" Trip says.

"I am getting to that. Shortly after Brock arrived here in his coma, Matt Jamison's son, Isaac, was killed in an automobile accident in Philadelphia."

Trip frowns and looks toward his wife and then his son.

Dr. Keller continues, "Since Miguel is very close to the Jamison family, on two occasions, when the employee lounge was crowded, he sought privacy in Brock's room to call his mother about the Jamison family following Isaac's death. Miguel's mother, who lives locally, is Matt Jamison's sister and was in regular contact with the family to get updates on how the family was coping, funeral arrangements, and such. In the process of those calls, Miguel reports that he likely mentioned Matt, his wife and his children by name. Also, he remembers asking about Matt's oldest son, Seth, and his family, who also live in the Philadelphia area. Miguel says that in the course of those conversations with his mother, he could have mentioned details such as ages, professions, etc."

Dr. Keller straightens in his chair. "With Miguel's confession, I immediately convened a meeting with my colleagues involved in Brock's case to discuss and analyze these new facts." He removes his glasses. "We believe that Brock's hearing was enhanced by the APX207 and with the patient rooms and hallways being intentionally quiet at night, Brock overheard at least part of Miguel's phone conversations with his mother."

Trip frowns, "Is this for real, Doc?"

Dr. Keller nods enthusiastically. "My colleagues and I believe that Brock's mind took the names and other details from Miguel's phone conversations and ran with them to create a narrative that fit what he was hearing through the ear buds along with his prior experiences."

Brock hadn't spoken since he entered the room, just sat stone-faced, listening to the doctor. He had smiled weakly when Dr. Keller explained the Jamison connection. Now, he frowns at Miguel and opens his hands. "Why didn't you tell me about the phone calls on Sunday? This is awesome news, Miguel."

Miguel's chin drops to his chest. "I was scared to say anything. I knew I wasn't supposed to be in your room but at the time I was so upset about Isaac and pissed that I couldn't afford to go to the funeral. I had to have a quiet place to call my mom." He tears up. "And then at uncle Matt's you told about all the grief I had caused you and your folks, I didn't know what to do." Miguel shakes his head. "I'm really sorry…for everything."

Brock's soothing tone reaches across the table, "It's okay, Miguel. You didn't intend for any of this to happen. I'm just relieved to know what the connection is."

Trip turns to his son and playfully slaps him on the back. "I told you there had to be a link."

Laura joins the conversation. "Dr. Keller, is this the first incident of APX207 enhancing a patient's hearing?"

"There was a case in Canada earlier this year where the patient claimed to have heard room chatter when he awoke from a coma. But he could not recall anything specific and it's noteworthy that aural stimulation was not used on that patient." He turns to Miguel. "Actually, this discovery may be a breakthrough in trauma patient treatment."

Brock looks at both the doctor and Miguel. "Dr. Keller, is Miguel in trouble?"

Dr. Keller turns toward the orderly then back to Brock. "Miguel broke a hospital rule, twice. On the other hand, he did come forward when he became aware of the repercussions of his actions. And we did learn some important medical information." He faces Miguel again with a faint smile and a nod. "We will do a review of the incident per our policy. But I'm optimistic that he'll be treated fairly."

Lacing his fingers on the table, Dr. Keller grins. "But we still don't know how Brock learned about the accident in Ben Franklin's lab."

"You're right. I had forgotten about that," Trip says.

Brock looks at his dad. "I haven't"

######

That same afternoon Mr. Jamison calls Brock explaining that he got the number from Duncan. He says that Miguel came by Big Jake's earlier to tell him about the hospital room phone calls and the connection to Brock's coma.

Mr. Jamison claims he's relieved to hear the explanation but has other questions. He insists Brock come by the trailer Sunday afternoon about one o'clock.

Surprised by the call, yet eager to salvage his relationship with Duncan, Brock agrees.

There had been an unusual tone in Mr. Jamison's voice. Brock couldn't put his finger on what it was but it sounded like the man was holding something back. Will he get a polite, "stay away from Duncan" order? If that's the case, he'd have to live with it. Brock runs his fingers through his hair and sighs.

CHAPTER 62   Dec 28 – 30, Friday – Sunday

Teaching his Taekwondo classes is a relief for Brock, anything to take his mind off of the mixed message he got from Mr. Jamison on the phone. Driving to the dojang, Brock forces himself to concentrate on his commitment to Master Kim and his students. He expects low attendance today at both the teen and adult classes because of family holiday activities and travel. It may be a good opportunity for individual attention to the few students who do show up.

Since there were no classes on Monday, Christmas Eve, or the day after Christmas, it's been a week since Brock has seen Duncan. He wonders how much the boy knows about Brock's Sunday afternoon exchange with his father or Miguel's late-night phone calls to his mother from the hospital. Or, if he's been told anything at all. Brock decides that if Duncan raises the issue, he'll address it. Otherwise, he'll act as if nothing has transpired since last Friday's class.

When the teen class, including Duncan, assembles, the headcount is about half of normal. As anticipated, Brock is able to give extra attention to these dedicated students. And to Brock's relief, Duncan shows no indication that he is even aware that Brock was at the trailer on Sunday. Nor does he mention the six-months of free classes. Mr. Jamison must have changed his mind on accepting the offer.

######

Sunday afternoon when Brock arrives at the Jamison trailer, only the big SUV is parked outside, suggesting he is the lone visitor. At the door Brock knocks, dreading scrutiny and rejection.

Brock is surprised when an attractive, middle-age woman answers the door at the Jamison trailer. "You must be Brock. I'm Edith Jamison," she says with a surprising lilt in her voice. "Please, come in."

Brock musters a smile. "Thank you." Inside, the aroma of fresh-baked bread is tantalizing. However, the sight of Duncan between a younger boy and a vaguely familiar teenage girl on the sofa with their eyes focused on their visitor screams "inquisition." Duncan's grin is the only sign of support.

Mr. Jamison stands. "Welcome, Brock." He points to a chair that will have Brock facing the family. The man's tone is civil, not hostile, but not exactly warm either.

Brock takes the offered seat, facing Mr. Jamison but also nodding politely to the two boys and the striking, teen he assumes is Amelia, a younger version of her mother. The smaller boy, who must be Nathan, is in pre-squirm stage.

Mr. Jamison gestures toward the sofa. "This is Amelia and Nathan on the other end. You know Duncan, of course."

"Nice to meet you," Brock says to Amelia and Nathan.

Mr. Jamison clears his throat. "Thank you for coming, Brock. You should know that we," he nods toward his family, "have had multiple conversations about you, your recent hospital experiences as well as your generosity and your relationship with

Duncan. Speaking strictly for myself, I found your friendship with Duncan a bit suspicious at first. However, after your visit to explain the bike, I was convinced you were on the up and up and no threat to my son. But later learning about your coma and its cause and its impact on you caused me to question if you were a good influence or not.

"When you left on Sunday, I spoke with Miguel at length about his impression of you. He was a bit evasive but had only positive things to say. Then, when he came by the store on Thursday and explained the whole situation, I felt compassion for you as well as relief for my son's safety." Mr. Jamison allows himself a small smile.

Brock releases a breath. "Is a 'thank you' appropriate, sir?"

"Let us finish first. We've discussed your impact on our family, particularly Duncan. And we have a few questions."

Brock's eyes open wide. With hesitation, he says, "Sure."

Mrs. Jamison is the next to speak. "Brock, can you describe the Edith Jamison you encountered in your coma?"

Brock considers his response. "Well, ma'am, I only knew her as Mrs. Jamison and her appearance was consistent with the paintings of eighteenth century women I've seen except she did not generally wear the flowing gowns of the noble women. She was a wife and mother first."

Brock studies each of the family members briefly then emits a chuckle. "Only Amelia has a faint resemblance to the Amelia I met in Philadelphia. Everyone else's appearance is unfamiliar."

Brock looks directly at Mr. Jamison again. "But if you think about the circumstances of my experience, that makes sense. Miguel said he spoke with his mother about how your family was doing emotionally after…your loss. I don't imagine he talked about physical appearances. My mind must have used other inputs to assign how each person in my dream looked."

For a few seconds he focuses on the Jamison daughter, who's now blushing. "Amelia, I can't explain your familiar appearance other than to say you're much prettier than the Amelia I met during my coma."

Brock can feel his face flush but returns to Mrs. Jamison. "To respond to your question, ma'am, the woman I met was handsome but not attractive in the contemporary sense like you."

Mrs. Jamison raises her eyebrows and smiles at her husband. "I like this young man, Matthew."

Brock continues. "Mrs. Jamison had a strong figure that reflected the strenuous lifestyle of the time. Her hair was very dark with a bit of gray, always gathered on the back of her head." Brock pauses, searching his memory. "She was a kind but firm mother. Protective of her family. She respected her husband as being the 'man of the house' but was not shy about speaking her mind." He opened his hands. "Those are the images that come immediately to mind. We didn't have a lot of one-on-one conversations but she impressed me."

With a nod, Mrs. Jamison thanks Brock. Mr. Jamison does not immediately comment. He looks at his children. "Questions from anyone else?"

In a pleasing voice Amelia, "Tell us about Amelia's life."

"Amelia was a cute girl compared to the few others of her age that I saw. Shiny hair and beautiful eyes. And slim. Her smile was marred by the lack of dental work. But her personality was such that it overcame any flaw she might have. She was quiet and a good helper to her mother. Amelia desperately wanted to get more education, something which was not common for girls in the 1780's. She had a particular interest in math, an even more unlikely study for girls." Brock blushed again. "I worked as her tutor for reading and math in the evenings in the poor light of a candle or an oil lamp. She was an eager student." Brock looks at Mr. Jamison. "I probably shouldn't say this but I think Amelia and I had a crush on each other."

Amelia smiles and averts her eyes.

Mr. Jamison grins at his daughter then says, "Duncan, Nathan, questions?"

The boys both shake their heads in response.

Looking at his wife, Mr. Jamison slaps his knee with his hand. "Edith, I don't know about anybody else, but I'm starved. The smells from the kitchen suggest a beef roast with potatoes and carrots. And fresh bread?"

His wife nods to confirm his assumption.

"Brock, I trust you haven't eaten," Mr. Jamison says. "Please join us for dinner. You won't be disappointed."

Brock had braced for a negative visit to the Jamison trailer. He never expected to be invited to dinner and even though the conversation had been cordial, he felt like an intruder to this close-knit family. "I wouldn't want to impose, sir."

"Nonsense." Mr. Jamison rises and stands by Brock's chair with his hand extended toward a dining table near the kitchen.

Brock rises also. "If you insist. It does smell amazing." When Brock turns and notices that the table is already set for six, he frowns. Me staying for dinner was part of the plan all along. He grins at Mr. Jamison who returns the smile.

Mr. Jamison directs Brock to a chair beside Duncan on one side of the table across from Amelia and Nathan with Mr. and Mrs. Jamison at the ends. They all grow quiet. "Let's join hands and bow our heads in prayer."

Brock takes Duncan's hand and that of Mr. Jamison. It's a practice he's done on only one previous occasion and it was awkward then. Today, however, it's natural and feels right.

Mr. Jamison delivers a brief blessing asking God to bless his family and to provide them patience as they start new lives in Texas. He thanks Him in particular for bringing Brock into their lives. And he asks for guidance for Brock as he pursues his education and for understanding as he continues his recovery. Lastly, a request for a blessing of the food, lovingly prepared. The family then says "Amen" in unison.

The somber atmosphere quickly evaporates, replaced with a feeling of joy and anticipation as the serving dishes are passed and light conversation begins. As expected, the food is scrumptious. Miguel had been correct that Mrs. Jamison had marvelous skills in the kitchen.

During the meal the conversation returns not to Brock's coma experience but rather to an eclectic suite of topics, including house hunting in the area, Brock's pursuit of a teaching degree at SFA, Houston weather and, of course, the upcoming NFL playoffs.

As the meal, including dessert, winds down, Brock finds himself stuffed. He's also content. And the word "blessed" comes to mind. Not only does he have loving and supportive parents, he also has another family that has welcomed him. He has his health and classes start in little more than a week. His life has taken a turn for the better.

At three o'clock Mrs. Jamison announces that the movie they want to see starts in fifteen minutes. The boys scramble from their chairs as their mother begins to clear the table. Amelia jumps up to help with the kitchen duties but expresses less enthusiasm for the film than her siblings. Mr. Jamison begs off, claiming he has a long day tomorrow and will watch some football. When asked to join the movie crew, Brock politely declines saying that after such a huge, delicious meal, he would probably just fall asleep.

Minutes later, after pleasant good-bye's, Mrs. Jamison and all the three siblings rush off to their movie outing.

Mr. Jamison plops down in the only recliner among the rented furniture in the trailer. "Sit, Brock. We should talk."

CHAPTER 63   Dec 30, Sunday

Brock takes a deep breath, rubs his full belly and takes the seat he used upon arrival. Despite his lethargy from the meal, Brock's mind is on guard after hearing "We should talk."

"You have a wonderful family, sir. It's a pleasure getting to meet them all." Brock moves out on a limb. "Maybe someday I'll get to meet Seth, Margaret, Lucas and little Christopher."

Mr. Jamison sits up straighter. "You know of them also?" He smirks and rolls his eyes. "Of course you do."

Brock nods affirmatively and grins. "Seth was a big help in getting me out of a jam with Benjamin Rush."

"It only makes sense that Miguel would have mentioned them at some point in his phone conversations with my sister." Mr. Jamison emits a deep, gratifying sigh. "Yes, you would like Seth. He's a fine attorney."

Mr. Jamison leans forward. "Brock, there's something I've wanted to ask you in private." His tone becomes serious. "How did Isaac die in your dream?"

Brock stalls, staring down at the floor. "Sir, I remind you that everything I experienced in my coma was a storyline produced in my head with the influence of the APX207 and the audio that was played into my ears. Why and how things were put together by my brain is way beyond my understanding."

"I know. It's just that your description of Amelia was so accurate that I'm curious to hear a little about Isaac even though you never met him."

Brock clears his throat. "Isaac was an intern at Pennsylvania Hospital in Philly. He often studied at the hospital in the evenings with the other interns. One evening not long after I had been in the city, I was with the Jamison family at their home reading when a boy came to the door saying Isaac had been hurt at the hospital. Mr. Jamison and I ran to the hospital and learned that Isaac had been attacked by a mental patient he was attempting to calm. The patient had used a wooden stool in his room and beaten Isaac with it." Brock pauses to compose himself.

"He had multiple head injuries and was gone by the time we arrived. Mr. Jamison was clearly upset at Dr. Rush for allowing his deranged patients to be in a hospital intended for sick people.

"Later, I was impressed at the way Mr. Jamison was able to compartmentalize his grief and set about the process of organizing a funeral. He maintained his focus on the many tasks all the way through the wake and the funeral that followed. I could tell that inside his heart was breaking, but he was a model of composure." Brock sniffs.

"There was a large crowd at the funeral with everyone expressing what a good man Isaac had been and what a loss it was for the community. I heard several times that he had already become a good doctor. Interestingly, not once did I hear a whisper about an issue with Isaac's eyesight, something Mr. Jamison shared with me later that evening."

Tears flow down Mr. Jamison's face. He makes no attempt to wipe them away and shows no embarrassment from his grief being on full display in front of the young man he only recently met. In time he gets his emotions in control.

"Thank you for sharing that with me, Brock. It does seem like my Isaac in many ways."

"As you said, I never actually met him but I'll always feel like I did."

Brock pauses and clears his throat. Looking directly into Mr. Jamison's eyes, Brock says, "Because of Isaac's positive influence on me, I'd like to respect his memory by picking up part of his "big brother" role with Duncan. And Nathan too, if he'll accept me. I know that Seth is actually their big brother, but he's back in Philly with his own family and his career. Even though I'll be away at school a lot, I'd like to spend time with the boys when I'm back home. Take them places like Isaac would have. Maybe teach them to be Texans." He laughs then turns serious. "It would mean a lot to me, sir."

Mr. Jamison is silent for a long time, leaving Brock feeling he may have stepped outside a boundary. Finally, Mr. Jamison nods. "I believe Isaac would approve."

Tears collect in Brock's eyes. "Sir, that's exactly what Mr. Jamison said after the funeral when he offered to let me sleep in Isaac's bed. He said, 'I believe Isaac would approve.'"

Mr. Jamison's lips form a straight line as a faraway look comes to his eyes. "But it's true. Isaac had a special relationship with his younger brothers, especially Duncan. They looked up to him and he, in turn, spent whatever time he had with them. I'm sure he'd be happy for you to step in. Thank you."

"Mr. Jamison?"

"Brock, please call me 'Matt', my other friends do."

Brock grins. "Okay, sir...Matt." He starts again. "I've spoken of Isaac's impact on me during my coma experience. But you should know that there were other men who influenced me during that time."

"Such as who?" Mr. Jamison wrinkles his brow.

"Dr. Franklin, for one, was a thread of hope in trying to understand how I got to his time and to Philadelphia. He was understandably reluctant to help at first. Later, he seemed to accept me and tried to provide some solutions and some guidance." Brock leans forward.

"If you consider the thousands of pages of audio information they fed me, much of it related to Dr. Franklin, it's easy to see why he was prominent in my coma episode. History says he was a man of wisdom and a sharp, analytical thinker. It only makes sense that my mind would use that information to depict him as a critical figure in my dream."

Brock takes a deep breath and continues. "The other man who had a very positive impact on me was Mr. Jamison. He was a hard-working, family man and husband. He practiced his faith and made it a part of his family's life. Despite not believing my wild tales of Texas and the twenty-first century, he provided me food and shelter. He even gave me a job where I tested his patience with my lack of experience. Knowing how desperate I was to get Dr. Franklin's help, he facilitated my meetings with the man. In time he grew to trust me. He and Seth saved me from excessive bleedings by Dr. Rush and then tried to figure a way to get me somewhere safe. I can say without hesitation that my experience in Philadelphia was bearable in large part due to the kindness of Mr. Jamison."

Brock gestures toward his host. "In fact, when I came out of my coma and was confused as to my surroundings, I looked for Mr. Jamison to reassure me."

Mr. Jamison rears back slightly in his chair. "I don't understand. The only input you had about me and my family was from Miguel's one-sided phone conversations. Is that not true?"

Brock nods. "I can't imagine there was any other source. But what I believe happened is that the respect and concern Miguel has for you and your family were evident in the questions he asked and the comments he made on the phone. And the tone in his voice must have been so caring that my receptive mind recognized those nuances and created the unforgettable personalities I encountered."

"I don't know what to say, Brock. I've always tried to do what's right but…well, I'm just a guy with my share of faults."

Brock chuckles. "I'm sure we all have our faults, sir. But you and I have met for only a couple of hours in total. And in that brief time and through your counterpart in my coma experience, I believe you are a man to be trusted. And a man I respect."

Mr. Jamison rises from his chair, as does Brock, each extending their right hands. They then clasp hands firmly. "Brock, no one will ever replace my son, Isaac. But through you sharing your extraordinary experience, you have helped mend the hole in my heart." His voice quivers. "And your friendship with Duncan and your generosity to him have been a true blessing. You are always welcome in our home." His watering eyes scan the trailer. "Wherever it is."

Brock's eyes glisten also. "Thank you, sir."

CHAPTER 64   Mar 8, Friday

As Brock hurries home from Nacogdoches Friday afternoon for spring break, he reflects on the past two months at Stephen F. Austin. Even though it's only a two-hour drive to The Woodlands, he had not made the trip home since starting school, preferring to immerse himself in his course work and campus life. Technically a first-year, secondary education student, Brock is actually in his second year of college with only fleeting homesickness symptoms.

The freshman classes in communication, western civilization, U.S. history and political science are all interesting, unlike the constant grind of the engineering course work he endured at UT. His credits from his science and math courses at UT *did* transfer, thus avoiding him taking similar courses in his first semester at SFA. So far, the decision to major in secondary education at a smaller school has been a choice he doesn't regret.

Brock had FaceTimed with Duncan on a couple of occasions since he left for college, but he still looks forward to seeing his young friend and hearing how he's doing at school and with his Taekwondo training. In a single phone conversation in late

February with Master Kim at the dojang, the instructor reported only that Duncan had attended all his sessions and was "punctual." The lack of details about Duncan's progress from his instructor had concerned Brock. To gauge Duncan's development himself, he had asked Mister Kim for permission to observe the teen class on Friday. He's eager to see if the boy is at least, showing commitment to the training.

Watching from his Mustang as the teens gather for their regular Friday class, Brock's concerned that Duncan may not show up. But, just prior to four o'clock Duncan streaks up on the Raleigh and locks it outside the entrance to the dojang. Duncan's wearing what looks like a clean, pressed dobock as he hurries into the dojang.

Rather than disrupting the class after it starts, Brock enters the dojang to greet Master Kim and, more importantly, Duncan. Master Kim and Brock greet each other with a firm handshake and an exchange of pleasantries. Master Kim makes Brock promise to stay after the class so they can talk for a few minutes.

Duncan is on the mats stretching when he spots Brock talking with Master Kim. He jumps to his feet and takes a quick step toward Brock but stops then stands at attention. When Brock walks over, Duncan flawlessly executes the traditional bow to his former instructor. Brock returns the salute then extends his hand to his young friend.

"How you doin', fellow?" Brock says, smiling broadly. He notices with a bit of disappointment that Duncan's belt is white with a gold stripe. He had expected to see a gold belt, the next higher level, instead.

Duncan nods and returns the smile. "I'm doing okay. You?"

"I'm good." He hears Master Kim give the command for the class to begin. "You focus on the class. We'll talk after."

When the class begins their routines, Brock watches Duncan closely. His form is sharp, his movements precise and his execution much better than his belt would suggest. For a new student Duncan appears to be all that an instructor could want. Although he respects Master Kim's experience and judgement, he wonders if Duncan is being slighted for some reason. Brock clenches and releases his jaw repeatedly in frustration as the class winds down.

Before Master Kim releases his students, he disappears into the office. He returns and brings the class to attention. Fighting a smile, he approaches Duncan. "During your tests last Friday, you surpassed the Gold Belt requirements and achieved a Green Stripe for your new Gold Belt." He presented the new belt to the smiling boy and shook his hand. "Congratulations!"

Spontaneous applause erupts from the class, even from the more advanced belt holders who had snickered at Duncan's limited ability when he first started. Duncan beams and bows politely to instructor. "Thank you, Master Kim."

With the class dismissed and the back slapping by the other students over, Duncan stands astride his bike when Brock approaches. His shoulders are back, his posture erect as he fingers the new Green Stripe on the Gold Belt.

"Sorry to hold you up, guy. But I promised to speak with Master Kim after the class." Brock grinned. "That old conniver kept the Green Stripe a secret from you so I could be here when he presented it. I told him on the phone a while back that I'd stop by in early March to visit." He raises his hand for a high-five that Duncan slaps, smiling.

"Man, I'm so proud of you. For someone who's been training for only three months, you're amazing. A normal person just starting out would take at least six months to get to the level you're at. You either work extra hard or you're a natural."

Duncan blushes. "Thanks." He leans slightly toward Brock as if his next statement is confidential. "How long have you got before you have to go back to college?"

"I've got about ten days. You out of school any next week?"

Duncan frowns and shakes his head. "No, we get some days off around Easter but none now."

Thinking fast, Brock says, "Okay. I know you have Taekwondo after school Monday, Wednesday and Friday. How about if I pick you up after school on Tuesday and we can hang out? Maybe get dinner somewhere?"

Duncan's eyes sparkle. "That'd be great. I'll need to clear it with Dad, but I don't see a problem."

"Okay, you get on home." Brock pauses. "By the way, are you and your dad in your new place yet?"

"Yeah, we moved out of the trailer last month. But Mom, Amelia and Nate won't be here until school is out."

"Well, if you and your dad are still doing your own cooking, maybe I can take you both to dinner."

Duncan lowers his chin and frowns.

"What's wrong, Dude?"

"I was hoping it could be just you and me. Talk about Taekwondo and stuff."

Pulling in his lips and nodding, Brock says, "I get that. Maybe you and I can meet after school one day just to hang out."

The smile returns to Duncan's face. "Awesome."

"Where *is* your new place?"

Duncan points north of the strip center. "It takes me about fifteen minutes to get home from here on the side streets."

"Okay. Look, Duncan, you get on home and talk to your dad about going to dinner one night next week. I'll call him Sunday to see what might fit his schedule."

Duncan mounts the bike. "Brock, thanks for coming to class today. You being here meant a lot." He starts to roll. "See ya."

######

That evening when Trip arrives home from work, he hugs his son almost as intensely as his mother had done when Brock first arrived. Later, as Brock and his parents enjoy his mom's cooking, Brock is animated as he provides updates on dorm life at SFA, his roommate, his passion for his courses and his part-time teaching job at a dojang in Nacogdoches. His enthusiasm for life is obvious to Trip and Laura, both smiling at their son's happiness.

Risking a cloud over the homecoming, Trip says, "How did the deposition go yesterday?"

Brock smiles broadly. "Well, about that. The day before the prosecutor was to drive up to school to do the recording, Ranger Garcia called to say that the Flores brothers had made a deal to plead guilty to the lesser charge of manslaughter in return for their cooperation in identifying their sources of illegal weed and the fentanyl. Consequently, a deposition won't be necessary."

"Will you have to appear in court?" Trip asks.

Brock shakes his head, smiling. "No. The penalty phase hearing will be held in a few months but since they pleaded guilty they don't need me at all."

"Are you saying you're done with anything related to Wally's...passing?" Laura says softly. "And that there's no risk to you or us from the drug ring members?"

Brock nods. "As far as I know, that's all behind us."

After chewing another bite of his mother's roasted chicken, Brock says, "I mentioned Ranger Garcia a minute ago. Well, you'll remember back before Christmas I asked him if he could maybe do something about a bully at Duncan's school."

His parents nod in unison.

"I never did know exactly what happened, but apparently the kid got the message and changed his attitude soon after."

Brock continues. "When the Ranger called me the other day to tell me about the cancelled deposition, he told me that the bully's older brother, who's in Lamesa State Prison, had been instrumental in turning his little brother around. Anyway the experience apparently impacted the older brother too. Garcia said he had followed up and learned that the brother had become a model prisoner, was teaching Bible study and may even get his sentence reduced for good behavior."

Trip and Laura smile at each other.

"You need to realize that you had a hand in that," his father says. "We're proud of you, son."

"You know, I'm impressed with the way Ranger Garcia conducted himself from the very first day I met him even though he scared the bejeebers out of me then. I might even look into law enforcement someday." He faces his dad. "Can you picture me as a Texas Ranger?" He laughs.

Trip hides a grin. "Son, your potential is unlimited. If you set your mind to being a Ranger, I have no doubt you'll succeed."

After pushing his plate forward, Trip rests his elbows on the table and nests one hand within the other, facing Brock. "Son, while you were lying in that hospital bed for what seemed like eternity, I had a lot of time to think." He struggles to control his emotions. "In a lot of ways I've failed you as a father. And—"

"Dad, you did *not* fail me! We—"

"Let me finish, son. Many times I guess I treated you like an employee, telling you what to do and what not do, making decisions for you, thinking I knew best." Tears form in Trip's eyes. "Well, I should have listened to you. Listened to what you wanted to do with your life. I'm sorry, son. I love you and I promise to do better going forward."

Both Trip and Brock stand and hug. "Dad, I love you too. I know we didn't always agree on some things. But I always knew I could count on you in a crisis. And in truth, your guidance saved me from a lot of bad decisions." Brock smiles at both of his parents. "But obviously, not all of them."

CHAPTER 65   Mar 10, Sunday

Making good on his commitment to Duncan, early Sunday afternoon Brock calls Mr. Jamison to invite him and his son to dinner during the upcoming week.

Before Brock can even mention the dinner, Mr. Jamison insists that Brock come over to watch the NBA game between Philadelphia and Houston. "We've got snacks and I promised Duncan we'd order a pizza later. You coming over would be icing on the cake." He pauses. "Just to be clear, there is no cake."

Brock laughs then accepts the invitation. He gets the address and agrees to be there before tipoff.

When Brock arrives at the large, relatively new house in a subdivision in the southwest corner of Conroe, he laments that he will not get to see the rest of the family. He would like to at least say "hi" to all of them. Mrs. Jamison had been so gracious and pleasant during the family dinner they shared at their trailer. And Amelia...well, she had made a lasting impression.

Mr. Jamison answers the door and welcomes Brock with a vigorous handshake and a friendly grasp of the shoulder. "Come in, Brock. It's good to see you. How's college treating you?"

"Really good, Mr. Jamison. Thank you."

"It's Matt, remember?"

"Yes, sir." He hands two packages to his host. "I read somewhere that Pennsylvania is pretzel country. I bought two kinds since I don't know anything about pretzels."

Mr. Jamison examines the bags. "Unique Splits! I didn't expect to find these down here. This is great, Brock. You didn't need to bring anything, but Duncan and I love these."

Duncan rushes into the room. "Hey, Brock. You're here to watch the game?" He stops short and displays a false frown, folding his arms emphatically across his chest. "So, I guess you're a Rockets fan?"

Brock strikes a cowboy pose with his thumbs in his belt. In his best John Wayne impression he says, "Well, I was brought up in these here parts, Pilgrim. So, I gotta support the home team."

Mr. Jamison chuckles and joins the exchange, "We're long-time Sixers fans, but we don't always get their games on local broadcasts. I've signed up for SpaceX's StarLink TCS but we're not scheduled for installation until April. Until then, we'll watch the Rockets when we can't get the Sixers." He glances at the haloscreen. "This game today should be intense with both teams leading their divisions."

Mr. Jamison looks at his watch. "We've got half hour before the game starts. Let's go sit on the patio; it's such a beautiful day. Back home they're still shoveling snow."

As Brock turns to follow Mr. Jamison toward the patio, he says, "This place is certainly a step up in space from the trailer...Matt. I'm sure you're anxious to get the rest of the family moved in."

"Yeah, Duncan and I like the extra room. Then again, it's pretty Spartan until our furniture gets here." He sighs then smiles. "After Memorial Day Edith, Amelia and Nathan will move down. But they'll be here for a visit during Easter break before that."

As they step onto the patio, Mr. Jamison spreads his arms wide to embrace the warmth of the sun. "Isn't this weather glorious?"

Brock smiles at the man's enthusiasm. "It *is* a beautiful time of year." He clears his throat. "But let's talk again in July or August and see how you feel about the 'glorious' weather."

His smile disappearing, Mr. Jamison says. "The daffodils started coming up in February and all the trees have budded out and some are green already. That's unheard of by us northerners." He frowns. "A neighbor says this is the earliest she can remember things blooming. Global warming is really here."

Once seated at a weathered picnic table left by the previous property owners, Mr. Jamison asks Brock many of the same questions his parents had posed. Brock senses close attention to his responses particularly about the Stephen F. Austin campus and student life.

Mr. Jamison says, "You know, Amelia will graduate from high school this spring and is looking at a math degree somewhere. She's been scouting schools here in Texas, including SFA. What's your opinion of the school so far?"

Brock rubs the edge of the rough table top and avoids Mr. Jamison's eyes before he responds. "I attended the University of Texas in Austin my freshman year. That's a great school but it's huge and I didn't do very well in my engineering studies." He brightens and finally meets Mr. Jamison's stare. "I've only been at SFA for a couple of months, but I think it's an outstanding school and I'm really enjoying my Education major. If Amelia wants a medium-sized campus, and if they have the math degree she wants, it would certainly be worth checking out." Brock blushes. "What other schools is she looking at?"

Mr. Jamison grins ever so slightly. "Well, I'm only on the perimeter of the search, but I know she's applied to several schools in the state and has several acceptances so far. She says some schools are too big, others are inside big cities." He pauses. "Would you mind if she called to pump you for details about SFA & Nacogdoches?"

"Sure, no problem. You've got my number to pass along. Have her call anytime."

Mr. Jamison rises. "It's warmer out here than I expected. How about a cold beer, Brock?"

Brock's initial reaction is to accept but sees Duncan shooting glances in his direction. "You go ahead. I think I'll just have some water."

"Water coming up. Duncan, how about you?"

The preteen looks toward Brock. "I'll have some water too, Dad." He starts to get up. "You want some help?"

"No, I got this. Keep our guest company. I'll be right back."

Duncan is telling Brock about the test he took to earn his new Taekwondo belt when Mr. Jamison returns with three tumblers of water. "The ice water sounded good so I decided to join you."

Brock wants Duncan more involved in the conversation. "Matt, are you aware that the young fellow next to you is a Taekwondo natural?" Brock glances at Duncan, who's grinning broadly now.

Mr. Jamison laughs. "Well, I don't know squat about Taekwondo but I do know he practices all the time at home and hasn't missed a session." He reaches to squeeze his son's shoulder. "I'm proud of Duncan. Isaac's passing was hard for all of us but especially difficult on Duncan. They were very close. Having Duncan committed to something that teaches discipline and exercise at this point in his life is a positive thing. Isaac would be pleased." He nods to Brock. "Thank you for getting him involved in the sport. When the sessions you gifted him run out, he'll sign up for more." He looks at his son, "assuming he's still interested."

Duncan rolls his eyes. "Daaad, I'll be interested! I want to get a *black belt* like Brock."

Brock grins at his young friend. "Excellent goal, Duncan. And I'm sure you can get there with your potential." He raises his eyebrows. "As long as you stay committed."

"I'm going to stick with it. I actually enjoy going to the classes. The older guys sometimes tease me for being so gung ho. But I just ignore 'em."

"That reminds me," Brock says. "What ever happened to that bully at your school? You said he walked away from his gang a while back."

Duncan's eyes grow large. "You mean Roy Bemis?"

"Yeah, that's the name. Is he still at your school?"

Duncan talks fast. "Did you see that kid who was on my right during class on Friday?"

Brock visualizes the class. "The one with the orange, spiky hair?"

Duncan nods.

"Yeah, I saw him. So?"

"That was Bemis! He went out for a soccer team over at Carl Barton Park but I heard he didn't do so well in the try-outs. Anyway, he showed up at the dojang one day and has been coming ever since."

"And he's a bully?" Mr. Jamison shifts on the bench. "Does he behave himself at Taekwondo?"

Duncan turns toward his father. "It's fine, Dad. Besides, Master Kim wouldn't tolerate bullying or anything like that." He faces Brock. "I wouldn't say that Bemis and I are buds, but we get along okay. He's starting to get the moves, he just needs more practice. And at school I don't see him with his old gang anymore at all."

Brock smiles at the news of the bully's transformation; Ranger Garcia's involvement must have made a significant difference. He makes a mental note to call the Ranger to give him this detail and to thank him again.

Mr. Jamison changes the subject. "We've been busy since Christmas, house hunting, closing on it and getting moved. But February 20th was Isaac's birthday and I've thought about him a lot." There's a catch in his throat as he continues. "Anyway, I remembered something you told me when you and I discussed your dream back at the trailer. It was the afternoon you met Edith and the kids and they had left for their movie after dinner."

Duncan's voice is flat when he interrupts, "Dad, I've got a math test tomorrow. I better go study now if we're going to watch the game later."

"Sure, son. We'll be inside in a bit." He sees the look on his son's face. "You okay?"

Duncan nods as he slowly gets to his feet.

Brock catches Duncan's eye before he turns. "We'll talk more later, maybe at half time."

When the patio door slides closed behind Duncan, Mr. Jamison says, "Isaac being gone still upsets him at times. I'm sorry I mentioned his brother with Duncan sitting here."

Brock nods to Mr. Jamison but doesn't know what to say. After a pause, he says, "Sir, what specifically did I say that afternoon that came to mind recently?"

"Well, you claimed that the Isaac in your coma had failing eyesight. Right?"

Brock nods. "Yes, sir. Mr. Jamison told me about it on the night of Isaac's funeral. He said Isaac had kept his failing eyesight a secret so it wouldn't ruin his standing as an intern." He shakes his head. "Remember, sir, it's just a detail my mind conjured up. There were a lot of details that seemed to come out of nowhere."

"Well, the truth is my Isaac *did* have a progressive eye disease that was affecting his vision. He was being treated privately to slow the effects but currently there is no cure. Isaac kept his condition secret from everyone; he only told Edith and me since he knew we would see the insurance claims. But nobody at his hospital knew. Certainly, my sister and Miguel didn't know." His stare at Brock intensifies. "So, how could you have learned about it?"

Brock shakes his head. "I have no idea. Are you sure your sister didn't know about Isaac's eye problem?"

"Absolutely! Isaac made me and his mom swear not to tell her because, although I love her dearly, my sister would blab it all over Texas and Pennsylvania. That's just how she is."

Brock shakes his head slightly and pauses. "My dad says that often what we call coincidences have viable explanations. And he *was* right about a link to your family in my coma. I wonder if there is an explanation for Isaac's real eye problem and what I reported in my dream."

Mr. Jamison knits his fingers above the table. "You know, I guess that one could be a true coincidence."

"You may be right." Brock pauses then smiles to himself. "There's another, unexplained issue from my coma experience. I'm not supposed to talk about it but I trust you sir and feel you deserve to hear about it."

Brock explains about the 10/31/1787, entry in Sally Bache's rarely-seen diary where she recorded that "FS" was hurt in Dr. Franklin's lab. And that's the day I woke up from my coma.

"There was no reference to the diary in the audio material they played for me during my coma." He raises his brows. "My full name is Franklin Brock Sinclair and technically my initials would be "FS." No one has yet come up with an explanation how my experience could contain those details either."

Mr. Jamison's eyes widen. "That's kind of spooky."

Brock nods then thinks a moment before shaking his head very slowly. "I don't know, but I wonder if there are forces at work that we don't understand." He looks down then back at his host. "When I noticed Duncan and that old, rusted bike first outside the dojang and then again at the library where my mom said he'd been coming after school for a few weeks, something clicked inside me.

"The Jamisons had helped me and trusted me when I needed it during my dream. Subconsciously, I probably wanted to help somebody in return. But what was it that drove me to choose Duncan rather than the hundreds of other people I might have offered to help? But because I *did* ask Duncan, a total stranger, if I could help him with the bike, I eventually learned about your family's link to my coma. That's something I probably would never have known otherwise.

"I respect my father's opinion that situations are often called coincidences when, in fact, they have legitimate explanations. But I believe the path that led me to learn of my connection to your family is too extraordinary to be labeled a coincidence. Was it a force of the universe or a divine hand that guided me to help Duncan?" He shakes his head. "I wish I knew."

Mr. Jamison smiles from across the table. "I can't answer that either, son. But, as the saying goes, 'The Lord moves in mysterious ways.'"

"That's something from the Bible?"

Mr. Jamison grins. "Actually, it's not. I used to think it was until I recently took a short test online and learned it comes from the first line of a hymn written by an English poet in the eighteenth century."

Brock's eyes widen. "*Eighteenth* century?" He shakes his head.

Grinning, Mr. Jamison says, "It was a poem first then became a hymn."

Brock's smile fades. "My folks are good people whom I love dearly. But church wasn't a big part of my upbringing. I guess you could call us 'Holiday Christians'; we attended church generally on Easter and Christmas.

"Your family, on the other hand, has a strong faith as, of course, did the Jamison family I lived with in my coma. I wonder if all this time I've been missing out on something...maybe something important."

"Everyone has their own faith journey. Maybe this is the start of yours. If my family helped in a small way, I'm pleased."

Brock struggles to hold his emotions in check. "Over the last few months I've realized how grateful I am that my dream, although difficult and scary at times, was an overall positive experience. I cringe when I think how my coma experience could have gone and how I might have been affected if I had overheard conversations about violence, greed or hatred. But thanks to Miguel I heard some sad news but only positive things about the Jamison family."

Looking down at the table, Brock says, "I'm thankful to the Mr. Jamison and Isaac I met in my coma for their kindness and trust. Because of their influence, I became a better person then and, I believe, a better person now."

Brock raises his head and looks squarely at Mr. Jamison. In a clear, confident voice he says, "Actually, sir, I have you and your sons to thank for that."

THE END

AUTHOR'S NOTES

In Part I of "Time Tested" Brock used the word "fan" in his discussions with Dr. Franklin and the latter appeared to understand the meaning. However, "fan" (likely a shortened form of fanatic) made an early appearance in the late 17th century only to disappear for two centuries, resurfacing in the late 19th century (Merriam-Webster). But since there was a slight chance Dr. Franklin, a well-read individual, had come across the word, I let him understand the meaning.

In Chapter 36 Brock used the word "scalawag" (meaning rascal or rogue) in conversation with Miguel. I let him pick up the word during his time in Philadelphia in Part I. Actually, the word didn't come into use until 1808 but it's a cool word and I figured 1787 was close enough.

Throughout the story, the sport and discipline of Taekwondo was spelled as shown. The Internet shows various spellings, i.e. Tae Kwon Do, Taekwon-Do, etc. But I went with the World Taekwondo Federation (WTF) spelling of the word.

Part I was written in past tense and Part II was written in present tense to help separate Brock's historical experience with his present-day life. Did you even notice?

"Time Tested" occurs a generation after "Coins on Franklin's Grave", a novel about Brock's parents before he was born. Their extraordinary experiences profoundly influenced their lives and carried over into their son's. "Coins on Franklin's Grave" is also available from Amazon.

ACKNOWLEDGEMENTS

"Time Tested," in its current form, would not have been possible without the help from many.

The Saturday Scribblers writing group critiqued chapters over many months. Their input and guidance is always beneficial and only improves my work. Specific members to acknowledge are: Clem Page, Pat & Marilyn Klimcho, Henry Youndt, Frank Mulligan, Mike Shiffman and The Berks County Genealogical Society for the use of their meeting space.

Beta Readers are critical to point out flaws in the final drafts. Their time to read the manuscript and provide input is greatly appreciated. Thanks to: Connie Killian, Dixie Warmkessel, Gail Royster, Jack McGuire, Linda Dawe and Mary Jo Morris.

Technical Advisors help keep the details accurate but don't stop me from straying for the benefit of the story. Thanks go to:

Kathy Herman for her critical eye on medical procedures and hospital protocol in the story,

Robert Nase for helping me understand the nomenclature pharmaceutical companies use for drugs in trial and

Charles Chauca, owner of Next Level Martial Arts in Eastern Pennsylvania, for his input to my understanding of Taekwondo terminology and practices.

Website, Facebook and photography credits and sincere thanks go to April and Tony Stuck for sharing their time and expertise.

SAM MORRIS – AUTHOR

Sam was raised in the mountains of Virginia along I-64 and actually worked a summer after high school on construction of this part of the Interstate Highway System. After graduating from the University of Tennessee with a degree in chemical engineering, he moved to Texas seeking fortune and fame. Well, at least to find work to pay off college debts.

A short career in the oil well industry developing drilling fluids did not offer the opportunities he craved. A move to the manufacture of chemicals in the Houston area kicked off a 34-year career making chlorine, caustic soda, PVC (compound and pellets) at ten locations in five states and Canada.

In retirement in southeast Pennsylvania, Sam focused on his life-long interest in exercise, sampling various beers, home projects and some travel. Then he decided to give writing a try. With no training in writing fiction, he read books, searched the Internet, took courses, and joined writing groups in search of the basics. The result was "Coins on Franklin's Grave" in 2015, an immediate hit with at least a dozen people at his church.

"Time Tested" was a struggle with the amount of historic research and the ever-present goal of "getting it right." If you enjoyed "Time Tested," you are encouraged to submit a review at Amazon. However, if you weren't enamored with the story, perhaps you shouldn't bother. Either way, thanks for reading.

Visit Sam's website at sammorriswrites.com for more and for contact information.